THE [illegible]

BY THE SAME AUTHOR

Unsafe Deposit 2016

Rickie Raven's Dilemma 2020

THE FALSE WILLS

J.E. KELLENBERGER

Matador
Unit E2 Airfield Business Park,
Harrison Road, Market Harborough,
Leicestershire. LE16 7UL
Tel: 0116 2792299
Email: books@troubador.co.uk
Web: www.troubador.co.uk/matador
Twitter: @matadorbooks

ISBN 978 1803131 764

British Library Cataloguing in Publication Data.
A catalogue record for this book is available from the British Library.

Printed and bound by CPI Group (UK) Ltd, Croydon, CR0 4YY
Typeset in 11.5pt Bembo by Troubador Publishing Ltd, Leicester, UK

Matador is an imprint of Troubador Publishing Ltd

MIX
Paper from responsible sources
FSC® C013604

To

Rene and Kelly

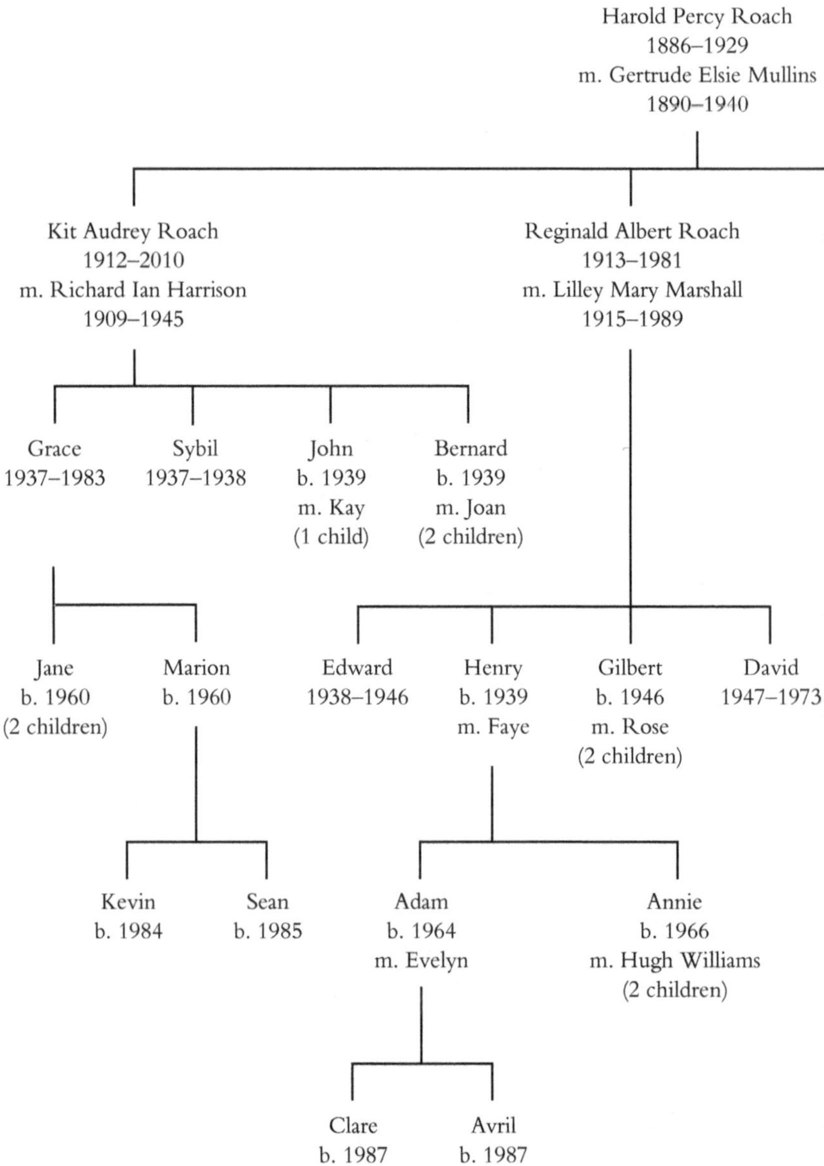
Harold Percy Roach
1886–1929
m. Gertrude Elsie Mullins
1890–1940
Kit Audrey Roach
1912–2010
m. Richard Ian Harrison
1909–1945
Reginald Albert Roach
1913–1981
m. Lilley Mary Marshall
1915–1989
Grace
1937–1983
Sybil
1937–1938
John
b. 1939
m. Kay
(1 child)
Bernard
b. 1939
m. Joan
(2 children)
Jane
b. 1960
(2 children)
Marion
b. 1960
Edward
1938–1946
Henry
b. 1939
m. Faye
Gilbert
b. 1946
m. Rose
(2 children)
David
1947–1973
Kevin
b. 1984
Sean
b. 1985
Adam
b. 1964
m. Evelyn
Annie
b. 1966
m. Hugh Williams
(2 children)
Clare
b. 1987
Avril
b. 1987

Peter Arnold Roach
1914–1988
m. Thelma Anne Carter
1915–2000

Two other brothers
(5 children)

Frank
1936–1941

Simon
b. 1938
m. Margaret

Clare Roach
1963–1986
m. Paul Irwin
1962–1986

Georgina Kit Irwin
b. 1980

James
1980–1989

PROLOGUE

The letter was lying face up on the doormat when Kit arrived home from work. She stared at it for a moment before picking it up. The quality of the stationery gave it an air of substance and authority. The postmark was Berwick-upon-Tweed which Kit thought was near the Scottish border. She wasn't used to letters; emails and texts were now her norm. She would open it later after a refreshing shower and a bite to eat. She slipped a frozen pizza into the oven and headed for the bathroom. Her partner, Martin, was away on business and no *proper* cooking with its time-consuming preparation and clearing up afterwards was required. Later that evening, wrapped in a silky dressing-gown and fully relaxed with her feet up on the sofa, she opened the envelope and read its contents.

The next day, following instructions, she telephoned the office number on the letterhead of Newman, Wilson & Saddler. The letter was specific. She must ring between ten and twelve noon on a landline and not use a mobile. And she must ask to speak to Mr. Newman. From her small office just off the visual optics laboratory where the undergraduates did their experiments, on the third floor of the university building in central London, she obtained an outside line and punched the numbers for the location in Northumberland.

'Good morning, Miss Irwin,' said a sedate-sounding voice eventually over a rather crackly line. 'I hope you can hear me well enough. I'm Thomas Newman, the person who sent you the letter and the joint-executor with you of the last will and testament of your distant relative, the late Kit Audrey Harrison.'

'I don't know anybody with that name or have any reason to believe that your client is related to me,' answered Kit truthfully, after a moment's hesitation. 'Are you sure you have the right person?'

'I am perfectly sure, Miss Irwin, as my client kept me fully apprised of your whereabouts and personal details.'

'But I don't know anybody with that name or anyone who lives in the Northumberland region,' protested Kit repeating herself. 'Is this some joke or a case of mistaken identity?'

'Neither,' replied the solicitor in an even voice. 'I hope I can convince you that you are truly the person I seek when I tell you that the deceased told me that you had had a minor operation on the tip of your left thumb just before your sixth birthday which left a tiny scar.'

'Oh. Gosh,' murmured Kit, looking intently at the white scar line, now almost invisible, extending downwards from her thumb's tip almost to the joint. 'That's true,' she said finally into the mouthpiece.

'In law, Miss Irwin,' said Mr. Newman unhurriedly,

allowing Kit a few milliseconds to recognise the new situation, 'if you have been named an executor of a will but you are unwilling to act, then you can refuse the role and renounce as executor. I very much hope that you will not do this as it is in your interest, and to your advantage, to act as your late relative had planned. Under the terms of the will, I am not permitted to offer any further information before a face-to-face meeting in my office. Will you come? Your expenses will be covered including hotel accommodation. Trains run regularly from King's Cross direct to Berwick and usually take just under four hours.'

'I'm working full-time,' replied Kit, somewhat irritated that she was not in charge of the conversation. 'It's term time at the university. I can't just down tools and come even if I decide to co-operate.'

'There is no rush. You may leave it several weeks. Just let me know your travel plans in advance and I will book overnight accommodation. My office is within walking distance of the station. Please bring your birth certificate and passport, and in the interim, refrain from discussing this matter with anyone else including your partner. I shall look forward to meeting you in due course. Goodbye.'

Chapter 1

THE LETTER

She thought she'd have plenty of time on the long train journey to consider the strange turn of events that were leading her to the northernmost tip of England, but the East Coast main line train sped through the countryside and whooshed through the stations at a breathless rate. Before long they were in the flatlands of Cambridgeshire and passing through the South Yorkshire station of Doncaster. The train was not full and after purchasing some sandwiches and coffee from the catering car she sat back and contemplated her life in general.

It was now more than three weeks since she had received the letter. Following Mr. Newman's advice she had arranged a meeting with him after the end of the summer term and when she had marked and dealt with the examinations and results including the inevitable queries that arose therefrom. She had planned to accompany Martin on one of his lecture tours on the continent – he was in pharmaceutical research and development working in a university laboratory sponsored by a global company specialising in tropical remedies – but found a spare couple of days to journey north. They had first met as undergraduates at Oxford. She was reading physics and he, chemistry, but their paths crossed in shared lectures and practical work in a few subjects like laser light. They shared a similar sense of humour and soon became an item easy in one another's company. They kept in contact after graduating and when Kit took up her post in London, with Martin working in Reading, it seemed logical to get on the property ladder by combining their financial resources. They had cohabitated now for more than five years in a happy and full relationship but one without any goals or planned future pathway. She sighed. She shouldn't ask for more. She had no right to do so. She had so much already: her dream job in the subject she had adored ever since her primary school teacher had told her that the constant movement of those tiny dust particles caught in a shaft of light was named Brownian Motion. She'd read her first beginner's guide to physics book even before she started secondary education. And she enjoyed teaching and sharing her knowledge and enthusiasm for the subject. University life as a don was good. A regular pay cheque and the prospect of advancement. And home life was good too. Martin was a kind and considerate companion. He loved his field hockey – something she didn't, but forced herself to go and watch from the touchline with feigned pleasure on many cold and wet Saturday afternoons – and had recently taken on the onerous task of executive officer in one of his sport's governing bodies. They shared a brilliant social life with her university formal dinners and his executive functions. She sighed again. In her heart she sensed that something was missing in their relationship.

Before she knew it, after a brief halt at Newcastle-upon-Tyne, the view from the window was of the spectacular north-east coastline with the normally menacingly grey and choppy North Sea shimmering placidly in the midday sun. She hastened to prepare herself for the interview ahead. She must be patient and polite and listen to what the solicitor had to say even though she felt sure that the trip was a wild goose chase. Sadly, she had few relatives left since the death of her parents many years before in a road traffic accident and the merciful demise some years later of her brother who had been the sole survivor of the head-on collision with a lorry. His injuries had been life-changing and he'd been in a care home for the remainder of his short life until a chest infection finally brought him peace. For her, relatives were thin on the ground and it was highly unlikely that Mr. Newman's client had any filial connection with her.

The train pulled into the island platform at Berwick station on time; the number of its carriages extending exactly the entire length of the long platform. While serving the two capitals of London and Edinburgh with a frequent fast service, the station also served as a hub for cross country trains to Glasgow in the north-west and Leeds and Manchester in the south-west.

As her arrival time was just after noon, Mr. Newman Sr had asked his son, Mr. Newman Jr, to meet Miss Irwin at the station and escort her to her hotel where she could check-in and have something to eat before the appointment in his office at two o'clock. Mr. Newman Jr had a photograph of his father's client and quickly spotted her exiting through the automatic ticket barrier. In the flesh she looked taller, shapelier and more vibrant than the picture of the person in his hand. With just above shoulder-length blonde curly hair and an old-fashioned hour glass figure she cut a striking picture. She wore trendy spectacles in a deep bronze frame which accentuated her skin tone. If he hadn't spent a life time – well, thirty-five years to be precise – of restrained behaviour towards his father's clients, he would have laughed out loud at her shoes with stilettos so high and tapering to such a minuscule tip that the wearing of them would only be possible in a metropolitan area. He wondered if the overnight bag she was pulling contained clothes of a more suitable style for the wilds of his home county than the formal attire she was wearing.

'Miss Irwin,' he called out, moving towards her. 'I have got the right person, haven't I?'

'Yes,' she stuttered in response, surprised to have been singled out.

'Mr. Newman asked me to see you safely to your hotel and to point out his office which we shall pass on the way there. Let me take your case.'

'Oh. Thank you.' She was metaphorically stumped for words and didn't know what else to add.

'I hope your journey was trouble free,' he continued. 'You must have left home early to catch the eight-thirty from King's Cross.'

'Very early. The first train from Reading, then the tube to King's Cross.'

The offices of Newman, Wilson & Saddler were modern and swanky. The same young man who met her at the station opened the door to Mr. Newman's room. It was large and airy and the solicitor stood up immediately to greet his co-executor. But he was not as she imagined him to be in her mind's eye from the telephone conversation they had had: a bygone example of yesteryear in a pinstripe suit, white shirt and old school tie, with a rotund midriff and short grey hair brushed carefully to show an arrow-straight side parting. Instead, he was tall and slim and wearing a tweedy jacket over a checked shirt with dark grey chinos. His snowy white hair was thick and cut short to a number five setting on the hair clippers which made it look spiky and tactile.

'Good morning, Miss Irwin. It is a pleasure to meet you,' he said smiling, in the quiet but authoritative voice she remembered from their phone call. 'Please come in and take a seat.'

'Thank you, Mr. Newman.'

'I trust the hotel arrangements are satisfactory. It is a small but comfortable lodging. In modern parlance I believe they are known as *bijou* hotels.'

'It is very nice,' she replied. For the second time in a day, meaningful words failed to flow. She was out of her depth in a world she knew little about and her normal patter, or auto-babble as her students sometimes called it, had dried up like a former river bed under a relentless sun.

Mr. Newman Sr, although in sync with modern times – something he couldn't fail to be with three grandchildren and a wife fifteen years younger than himself – still retained a secretary as he didn't care much for twenty-first century gadgets with keyboards and the like. Emily had been with him for more than thirty years and he suspected that she now knew as much about the law as he did. In addition, she had the knack of running his diary so competently that both parties, solicitor and client, were always satisfied with the arrangements she made. Without being bidden, she placed the tray of tea and biscuits on a corner of his desk and closed the door quietly behind her. Kit sat calmly in the client chair masking the inward nervousness she actually felt. It was time for business. At his request she pushed over the documents she had been clutching in her hand.

'Thank you, Miss Irwin,' he said formally, after having compared them with photocopies of both documents that he had obtained from other sources. 'They are just as I reckoned.' He then ummed and ahhed for a few seconds over an awkward little matter that he felt the need to address forthwith. 'May I address you less formally by the first name by which you prefer to be known? That is, Kit. Or, even more helpfully as you will shortly learn, by the moniker Young Kit?' Miss Irwin, or Young Kit as she was now to be known, nodded her head imperceptibly with no idea where all this was leading. 'You see, Young Kit,' he said smiling kindly at her, 'the deceased, who I intend to call Old Kit from now on, will play a major part in your future and tagging on something as simple as "Young" or "Old" will help avoid unwanted mix ups.' Young Kit didn't see it at all but she said nothing and waited patiently for further explanation. Her brain was beginning to overcome her nerves. Mr. Newman Sr opened the box folder sitting on his desk top and withdrew a large, sealed white envelope addressed in a flowery handwriting to Georgina Kit Irwin. 'The deceased, Old Kit,' he continued, 'left instructions to hand this letter to you at our first meeting before embarking on a detailed account of her will. She wished you to open it in my presence but to read it on your own.' He handed her a paper knife and she duly slit the end and removed its contents. 'I shall follow her instructions and leave you alone in my office for as long as it will take to read it through twice. I am also instructed to tell you that I have read a copy of that letter two hours ago. Old Kit was insistent that the copy she left addressed to me should only be read when your arrival in my office was imminent, although I can add that the deceased had already made known its contents to me verbally. When you have had sufficient time to digest its implications, would you please press this button to alert my secretary that you are ready for the reading of the will.' With that he closed his office door quietly behind him and Young Kit was alone. The same flowery but neat handwriting, in a black ink, covered many sheets of a high-quality vellum paper and as Kit settled down to read it, all thoughts of mistaken identity were abandoned.

Dear Kit,

I can just imagine your surprise at being asked to travel north from your base in the Greater London area at the behest of a deceased person whose name, apart from Kit, means nothing to you and to whom you therefore feel you owe no allegiance. Should you believe that we have never met, then you would be mistaken although the chances of you recollecting our one and only meeting would be infinitesimal as at the time you were just a few weeks short of your sixth birthday and I was already seventy-four. But we are related as you are my great grandniece and Mr. Newman Sr, the son of one of my very dear friends, will show you an ancestry chart so that you may trace for yourself the pathway that indelibly links us, one to the other. Or, you can think of our relationship in different terms as your great, great grandparents were my parents. Or, as another permutation, my great grandchildren are your first cousins twice removed. Whichever way you throw the dice they will come up showing our linkage.

But back to our only living encounter. What was it about you that made such a deep impression in my mind? With my direct family of two daughters and two sons, six grandchildren and thirteen great grandchildren numbering twenty-three in total and my indirect family of four brothers, eight nieces and nephews, fifteen grandnieces and nephews and twenty-four great grandnieces and nephews totalling fifty-one, what was it that was so unforgettable about you? At a family gathering to celebrate my seventy-fifth birthday when almost the entire family were present, how did I remember you from amongst almost sixty-five invitees including youngsters and babies some of whom, like you, I had never met? I singled you out at that gathering because your great grandfather Peter, my second eldest and favourite brother, was also godfather to my daughter Sybil who sadly died in childhood. It was just an additional tie I had with you that I didn't have with the others. At any family gathering large or small I always made a point of searching out and chatting with Peter's offspring through his children Simon and Frank and getting down the line as far as you via your mother Clare. On meeting, I addressed you as Georgina. You had been christened Georgina Kit. In a very forthright way, with fists on your hips and a look of affront on your face, you told me unequivocally that your name was Kit not Georgina. Your mother and I laughed and you went off in search of more congenial company, but not before I had recognised in you the same sort of fierce independence that was also part of my personality. The road traffic accident that so cruelly robbed you of your parents and twin brother not many weeks after our encounter was my galvanising force for following your progress in life over the ensuing decades. Not for one moment did I fear that the dramatic events of that day would overcome your temperament. I had seen the inner strength in your eyes and knew you would prevail against such harsh odds. And your achievements to date have not dented my confidence in you. Your grandparents provided you with a safe and caring environment, although of course they could never match in any way the love of your parents. And you were happy growing up there and socialising regularly with your cousins and uncles and aunts. Very soon you were taking your A-levels and departing for university. I was thrilled to learn that you would be reading Physics because like you, I too am, or was, a scientist at heart. I was already in my ninetieth year by the time you graduated and your grandparents so proudly showed me your graduation photograph. You looked so thrilled holding up your Master degree certificate. After that they kept me au courant with your working life and I silently applauded your decision to become a university lecturer. After several years in halls of residence and the like, you formally took leave of your grandparents' home and started living with your boyfriend, at first in rented accommodation, and now in a home of your own using the money bequeathed you by your parents for the deposit on what I am told is a stylish end of terrace house within walking distance of Reading railway station. Which brings me to the present day as far as your life is concerned.

But you will be asking yourself about my background. You still know very little about me and doubtless will be eager to learn more. I was born in 1912, the eldest and only female child of five siblings. My parents were working class and seemed to work from morn to night to provide the five of us with whatever they could. Treats were rare but there was always plenty of food on the table. My father worked in a tailoring shop as a cutter. It was a specialised job and he had worked his way up from general cleaning boy. Some Sundays, I would accompany him to the shop if he was particularly busy. We lived in a village outside Berwick and Father either cycled the three miles into town or walked in inclement weather. Even in those days Berwick was the region's big town and many of the skilled trades had shops in the high street. It wasn't long after the end of the first World War and men's suits were becoming increasingly popular amongst the growing middle classes swelled by those who had survived service in the trenches and who had vowed never to return to menial chores. They set up on their own and soon realised that wearing a suit of clothes could be good for business. So, life in the shop was usually hectic for Father. It was there, with him, that he taught me the self-discipline required for a successful working life. He was always trying to improve his methods. Quantity, he said, was important but not at the expense of quality, and between us we honed his methods with a few simple changes to his routine that had an impact on his productivity. And it was there also, in the shop's basement cutting room that I whispered to him that I wanted to be a scientist when I grew up. I thought he would laugh but he didn't. It was 1921 and women from my background didn't go to university. And of those from the posher classes who did go, few studied science subjects. At what would have been considerable expense for my parents, my father paid for a monthly one-on-one tutoring lesson over several years in Latin, Greek and algebra, subjects not usually taught in schools attended by the working classes but knowledge of which was a prerequisite for entry to university. My brother, Peter, kind and generous as was his nature, was supportive but it fuelled in my other brothers a lifetime of resentment. That the eldest in that epoch had special treatment was not uncommon in most households as long as that child was not female. The male siblings were not amused and when my father died unexpectedly, their joint clamour for redress of the perceived wrong done to them knew no bounds. I was now approaching seventeen and my only friend in the family was my fifteen-year-old brother Peter. It was 1929 and girls of my age were out earning money to supplement the family's income. Peter himself had left school the previous year and had been working full-time as a junior apprentice carpenter. It was at this pivotal moment in my life that a Good Samaritan stepped forward. While attending full-time the only higher education school in our neck of the woods – I was the only girl in the class – I had been working on Saturdays and during school holidays in the tailoring shop. The owner, a man of a similar age to my father, had expanded over the years and opened two other shops. He had also established a programme for training apprentices; boys who would have no other alternative than to go down the mines. His motives were entirely altruistic; he was convinced that the correct strategy for the future lay in teaching them all aspects of tailoring so that one day, if they chose, they could become master tailors. He wanted someone to manage his three apprentices and asked me to devise a plan of action to teach them everything. I agreed and set about it in a scientific way that ensured that the boys learned each job – understanding fabric and how it was made, how it draped, cutting, sewing and fitting – and attained a satisfactory standard before moving on to the next discipline. I devised charts and graphs and log sheets to record their activity and progress. They were just three poor boys saved from the pits but under Mr. Harrison's benevolent wing they reached a level of attainment and self-belief that they could not have done without him. Soon I was to move away to the ancient city of Edinburgh for my university studies in the natural sciences; a combination of the physical, earth and life sciences that we today recognise more commonly as physics, biology, chemistry and astronomy. It had been a choice between Newcastle in the south and Edinburgh in the north, both being equidistant from Berwick but both offering no hope of daily travel home. As Mr. Harrison knew a fellow master tailor in Edinburgh who could arrange decent and safe accommodation for me during term time, the choice was made, and on a quid pro quo basis for my continued unpaid work with the apprentices during university holidays, he paid my lodging fees. It was an exhilarating time but there would soon be a hefty penalty to pay. My mother became increasingly poorly. She had been a quiet but robust woman living a calm life with a good husband. But with the stress of coping alone her mental state suffered and under the constant haranguing of my eldest brother, Reginald, she turned against me. According to him, my father had become besotted with me and neglected his first-born son. It was all my fault that he had been deprived of his birthright, and together with my two youngest and feeble-minded brothers, he waged a campaign against me which caused a rift in the family which has endured until the present day. Loyal Peter was caught in the crossfire because by that time, having lived away from home and worked for money, I wasn't prepared to suffer the petty jealousies of three whining siblings unprepared to get off their backsides and go out in the world to help themselves. Peter looked on with mixed feelings. He didn't take sides but remained my trusted friend.

After university – it was now 1932 and women's suffrage had been extended in line with men to include the under thirty age group thanks to the protestations of the suffragettes – and having failed to find a position locally in which my knowledge of science could be used, I moved to Manchester and started work in a laboratory exploring the possible uses of synthetic fabric. It was already a big deal in the United States where scientists were predicting a rosy future for man-made fibres which they predicted would soon outclass their natural counterparts such as cotton and wool. I was content working there as a junior lab technician having the opportunity to use my understanding of chemistry and physics on a daily basis and the chance to read published scientific papers on the subject. But life changed all too soon when my mother passed away and I felt obliged, family feud notwithstanding, to return to my childhood home whilst my younger brothers were still living there. When Mr. Harrison learned of my return he offered me the job of managing his ever-expanding tailoring empire – now with a shop in each of the five biggest towns in Northumberland and two in Newcastle – which I did on the understanding that once the futures of my younger brothers were settled, I would again seek work in a big city where what I had learned at university could be put to good use. But, again, life intervened and by the time I was twenty-five I was married to his son and expecting my first child.

Mr. Paul Harrison's son, my husband Richard, wasn't a bad man, but over the course of the early years I often questioned why I had agreed to marry him for he was a man without a passion to pursue any particular pathway in life. He had no goals and therefore no drive and while he was mostly gentle and considerate towards me and the children, there was no spark to weld us together. Life with him was comfortable to a degree of boredom. It was with his father that I shared the bond of attainment, striving to better ourselves and reach a higher standard of living for our respective families. It had been a marriage of convenience. I had no place to go, no family apart from Peter to consider, no money with which to set out to start a new life in the metropolis and no easy access to a worthwhile job in science. Richard was easy going. We got along well together. We cared for one another, although I recognised that on my part, my caring didn't constitute love. Family life with him was ordered and harmonious and I held his father, my mentor since my own father's death and who I secretly adored, in great respect.

Young Kit paused and set down on the desk with trembling hands the third sheet of Old Kit's letter. She cupped her head in her palms and ran her long, slim fingers through the soft, curly hair around her neck. There were uncanny parallels to be drawn here between Old Kit's early life and her own. It was food for serious thought and several minutes passed before she started on the fourth page of her distant relative's letter.

The years might have rolled by languidly in that vein, continued the letter, and be lost in the ether of time had not two life-changing events occurred in 1937: at the age of 53, Paul Harrison died suddenly of a massive heart attack and later that same year, a communication from my erstwhile employers in Manchester notified me that a small experiment that I had devised, tested and written up in time-honoured scientific format as a helpful adjunct to their work in artificial yarn evaluation, had been incorporated in a recently published paper for one of the main scientific journals of the day with my name added as a contributor. Whilst the former hit home hard with the loss to the local community, and to me in particular, of a man of high moral standing, it was the latter that would have the greatest impact on my life. You see the small experiment I had devised, almost crude in its conception, showed that the composition of polymers could be engineered in textiles in much the same way as in other chemical products and this idea lead ultimately to the production by the American chemical giant DuPont of the first commercially viable synthetic fibre, dubbed Nylon. Based on its comfort, ease, strength and elasticity, it was, I knew instinctively, a product that my late father-in-law would have been in the vanguard of tailoring to embrace in his shops.

Young Kit caught her breath. Nylon was iconic. Every science student in modern times knew it had been invented in 1938 and that it had ushered in a textile revolution for consumers and the military alike. *But it would be the former,* Old Kit continued, *that would be the first to rear its head.*

On the death of his father, apart from several smallish bequests including a rather generous one to me, my husband Richard, an only child, inherited his entire estate. Paul had often hinted to me in cryptic sentences that I would have been the natural leader of the business had it not been a partnership of Harrison & Son and that he feared his son's talents might not be best suited to a commercial enterprise. He was right and he realised that I shared his view. In conversations well before his untimely death at a relatively young age, his veiled thoughts about the future of the business in the hands of his son, made me determined when he died to stash away for a rainy day the legacy he would be leaving me. And it wasn't long before the goodwill was challenged as attitudes and commercial common sense floundered. Richard wasn't a bad man, indeed far from it, but he wasn't a leader and couldn't cope with the pressures of command. Moreover, my continuing management of the day-to-day tasks and the concomitant decisions to be made, a position I believe is called CEO in modern day parlance, irked him. He was the titular head of our family of five – one of our twins having died in infancy – and our commercial family of three dozen employees and various business associates and felt the need to justify his position by interfering in even smooth-running minor matters. It was as they say, a recipe for disaster.

By the time the second world started in September 1939, we had already lost several of our loyal and hard-working senior staff who had grown fed up with his unnecessary meddling. The first wave of conscription then deprived us of our younger members leaving a body of older, less physically able and female employees. It should have been a moment for radical re-organisation to make the most of who and what we had and to assess and act on any likely wartime demands but my prompting in these areas fell completely on deaf ears resulting in nothing being done to mitigate the looming cash flow crisis while we sat on our hands. Richard grew miserable and tense and returned home one day with the news that he had joined up. At thirty-one, his conscription papers were metaphorically in the post, but he pre-empted their arrival as a way out of the mess he had created. He would have been a good conscript. He would have taken orders and done what he was told and got on well with his fellow non-commissioned soldiers. He wouldn't have been as fit to fight as those just turning twenty nor as aggressive as some of the characters from difficult family backgrounds but he would have given of his best and been an emollient figure within his company of men. He saw action in several theatres of war serving in the ordnance corps. He never returned. The communication from the Ministry of War announcing his death in early March 1945 gave no indication of the circumstances and it was not until after hostilities ceased when some of his colleagues contacted me that I learnt that he had simply succumbed to the bitter cold weather during the Battle of the Bulge campaign. I was gratified to learn from them that he had been popular amongst his comrades, a fact that was confirmed by the letter I received several months after the war's end from his former commanding officer. It closed a chapter on my life with him in a positive way knowing that his true personality had shone through in the harshest of circumstances, war.

They were all encouraged by the powers that be to make a simple will before departing our shores for action in foreign climes. Richard's will when he left England for the first and only time in his life was simple in the extreme as I was named his sole benefactor. However, borne maybe of the regular letters I wrote containing news in the main about the activities of our growing children, Grace, John and Bernard who by 1944 were aged seven, five and five respectively, he wrote a more complex will in early 1944 in which he left the business in its entirety to John and Bernard in equal shares on their maturity at age twenty-one. I was made, effectively, the caretaker until they attained adulthood. But this will did not come to light until one day in 1953 when I received a visitor from Richard's former regiment. The will had been found in an Army Records Office when his regiment amalgamated with another and any remaining stored physical records were shifted to a new, larger location. It had been misfiled, the visitor said shrugging his shoulders as if that was the way of the world, and he was now delivering my husband's last will and testament nine years late with no real apology.

Kit paused again as the story of Old Kit's life took another twist. Her hands were no longer trembling but her heart was racing as the tale slowly unwound. Her mouth was dry and her slim lips felt sticky. She pressed the button on the telephone's base station and asked for another cup of tea which Mr. Newman's secretary brought promptly and without comment. She sipped the hot tea gratefully and sat for some time staring into space as the story tumbled around in her mind. Mr. Newman's office, in the swanky building on the main thoroughfare, was swanky in a toned-down sort of way. The room was large and airy and looked uncluttered despite the large wooden pieces with which it was furnished. Notwithstanding their unfashionable dark brown appearance, they had classic lines that allowed them to sit comfortably in a décor of any era. Young Kit picked up the next sheet of the saga and continued reading.

It wasn't so much a body blow to learn that the business wasn't mine to direct but more a profound worry that it wouldn't be safe in the twins' hands. Grace, poor darling, was a sweet girl but was neither physically nor mentally strong. Perhaps her development had been affected by the loss of her identical twin sister when Sybil died eleven months after birth as the direct result of a dog bite. From birth, the boys were rumbustious attention seekers without any apparent care for their sister's wellbeing. They had each other and it appeared that no one else merited their concern. In just seven years' time in 1960 they would attain adulthood and the tailoring empire built by Paul and his staff's hard work over almost four decades and based on altruistic principles would be theirs. I loved my boys but I didn't like them. And I feared for the future.

Kit wondered for a moment why Old Kit had disclosed the existence of the new will. Had she considered keeping it secret? Destroying it in the fire maybe or locking it away in a bank safe? But her questions were soon answered.

I considered throwing it away, pretending that I had never received it, and lying on oath if need be that it didn't exist, or legally challenging its right to be enforced. The house and grounds, grand by most people's standards was a source of particular concern as I had had to mortgage it after the war to rescue the business from the financially disastrous three years of Richard's tenure of leadership and the ensuing war years when we lost so many of our valuable staff. The business made good progress after the tricky procedure of turning the partnership into a private limited company – how I first met and availed myself of the legal services of Mr. Newman Sr – amalgamating firstly with a three-branch group in Sunderland of classic men's outfitters who were also stockists of school uniforms, and later, joining forces with an eleven-branch firm with high street shops serving the Greater Manchester and Leeds areas. Their products were generally off-the-peg, a trend that was becoming increasingly popular amongst the middle classes. Thus, we became a group of outfitters of both ready-to-wear and bespoke tailoring and the firm, Northern Tailoring Limited, thrived. Ergo, my director's fees and annual share of the profits could provide adequately for the children's education and upbringing whilst allowing me to repay some of the capital of the mortgage on our house. Which brings me neatly, on this financial note, to the unexpected income stream related to the other momentous event for me in 1937; the ripple effect caused by my simple chemical experiment.

The laboratory in Manchester where I worked for two years as a postgraduate technician was funded by the textile industry. It was 1932 and women with science degrees were tolerated rather than cherished. My time there was interesting and I was well treated but little was expected of me intellectually other than to do as I was instructed by senior male colleagues. But as in all aspects of life, there are occasions when you miss the glaringly obvious. You're so intent on a particular course of action that you fail to discern what is directly under your nose; the simple solution to a problem with which you are wrestling. The prosaic, the uncomplicated, the down-to-earth answer. It just eludes you because you weren't looking in that direction. It was just such a scenario that led me to devise and complete a small experiment that I knew would yield far more reliable results than the experiment I had been instructed to carry out, and crucially, one which would act as a pointer to the right path for future development. I wrote it up in the rigorous format demanded of scientific experiments in those times and submitted it to my boss in lieu of what I had been asked to do. At first it led to consternation that a junior assistant had spotted a flaw, but the professor in overall charge – a man who was keen not to let the Americans who were also working to produce synthetic yarn take all the glory – saw its value immediately both as a piece of scientific work and as a bargaining chip. It was a highly competitive industry but he knew that the sharing of knowledge in advance of the official publication in a hallowed scientific journal would ensure that the source of the shared information was acknowledged in print. And as nylon became one of the most famous discoveries of the age, fame and fortune followed in one guise or another. The use of nylon took off as licenced manufacturers geared up for the start of the second world war. Crude as it was by today's standards, its strength and flexibility made it ideal for the paraphernalia of war. From parachutes to mosquito netting, shoe laces to flak jackets, hammocks to aircraft fuel tanks, nylon thread's versatility knew no bounds. It earned the moniker "the fibre that won the war" and deserved it. I was a civilian bringing up young children on my own and working full-time in Northern Tailoring Limited. It was not until the late forties that my association with the product became known. It was then that I received invitations from universities to make speeches, give lectures and lend my name to all manner of events. You see, the know-how to make nylon had been "intellectual property" and when this was made available to the wider world, it came at a price. While the main contributors each received a king's ransom, my pay out was far smaller but still sizeable. It was money that I invested in a company gearing up to supply cloth to the high street clothing industry of a mixed blend of artificial and natural fibres. And I was co-opted onto the committee of the tailors' trade association and invited to join the board of one of the numerous bodies representing the textile industry. It was a frenetic period as the original synthetic polymer that we had all come to know as nylon was modified by countless manufacturers across the globe and begat a whole range of "improved yarns" with their own brand names – Bri-Nylon, Dacron, Terylene, Crimplene, Tricel – which they claimed improved comfort and drape.

But lingering in the background of my mind were unsettling thoughts, and as a consequence I decided to make the most of my position while it lasted. When the twins came of age in 1960 they reshaped the company's management structure. With a nod to the two minority shareholders from the amalgamations in the early thirties who kept their places, and holding over seventy percent of the share capital between them, they had carte blanche to do as they wished. I was demoted from the board to the role of general manager, or as I came to regard it "general factotum". It marked the prelude to difficult times both family and business-wise and is the direct result of today's distressing situation which I trust you will take on the challenge of resolving. Mr. Newman Sr will go into great detail about the legal and financial side while I now undertake to make you au fait with the family matters that led to this deep and frightful rift which has left my great grandchildren at each other's throats.

But Young Kit had had enough for the moment at least. The letter from her great grandaunt had been a rollercoaster thus far and she needed thinking time before embarking on the final pages. She looked at her watch. She had been so engrossed in the letter, written as if Old Kit was within touching distance and speaking to her intimately, that she had not noticed how time had flown. She made her excuses promising to return early the following morning and headed back to the hotel for a relaxing bath and early dinner before launching herself into the story's finale. But the evening didn't pan out as she had expected. Mr. Newman Jr, the young man who had met her at the station and escorted her to the hotel and who she had later learnt was the solicitor's son, found her in the hotel restaurant eating dinner.

'I hope I'm not disturbing you,' said Edmund courteously, 'but my father was keen for you to have the ancestry tree before your meeting tomorrow so that you could more easily see your position in the genealogy of the family and locate the various persons to whom you have just been introduced by Old Kit.'

'Thank you,' she replied, 'that will be very helpful as my head is in a spin and I am fast losing track of where I fit in.' He smiled. She had a nice manner and he liked the blonde curls bobbing on her shoulders.

'May I join you for a moment? I'm Edmund.'

'Please do. It's lonely eating alone in this vast room. I thought about looking for a fast-food outlet but they don't serve any decent wine.' She signalled the waiter to bring another glass and they both sat back for a moment savouring the taste of the pinot noir. Eventually, he handed over the chart. 'Goodness,' Kit exclaimed loudly, 'it's more complicated than a flow diagram showing the half-life decay of nuclear particles.'

'Not when you start at the top and work your way down slowly,' he assured her. 'Look, here is Old Kit,' he continued, pointing with a biro tip at the topmost but one rank of names. And here you are, right at the bottom. You could draw a diagonal line to take you right up to her.'

'A bit like snakes and ladders,' she replied giggling.

'Something tells me that you are not taking this totally seriously,' he chuckled. 'If that's the case, why not let me show you the sights. It's a lovely evening and up here close to the Scottish border it won't be dark for at least another two hours. I can show you the castle and we can walk the ramparts. Then we can go down onto one of the wonderful wide-open beaches and dip our toes in the North Sea. It would be much more fun than spending the evening in your room doing the homework my father set you.'

'I don't think my high heels can manage the ramparts but my bare feet will love the sea.'

The final pages told of the family's downward spiral into distrust, jealousy and turmoil. Kit read them early the following morning before her meeting with Mr. Newman Sr. It was still not clear why she had been summoned to sort out an internecine feud although she did now accept that she was related to the deceased and some of the names on the ancestry tree did ring vague bells. She hoped the will would provide the answer and it mostly did, although in a large part it was Mr. Newman Sr who filled in all the gaps. She rang Martin. He was now back from his business trip. She brought him up to speed with her visit to Berwick. She intended to catch the afternoon train back to London she told him but it was possible that her great grandaunt's complicated affairs might delay her return by a further day. There was an exchange of affectionate remarks before they hung up. She smiled wistfully. She had made no mention of her evening with Edmund, nor how she was somehow going to find time to nip to the shops to buy a pair of flat walking shoes so that she could walk the castle ramparts with him this evening. Mr. Newman Jr was interesting, she thought.

Thomas Newman stretched out his arm across the desk to shake his co-executor's hand. She was still in formal attire he noted but was wearing a trouser suit today. She looked relaxed and replied to his question that she had indeed slept well and enjoyed a hearty breakfast, and that she had, of course, finished reading Old Kit's astonishingly long letter.

'Did you find the ancestry tree useful?' he asked.

'I did,' she replied. 'It was kind of you to get Mr. Newman Jr to deliver it.'

'On that point,' stated Mr. Newman Sr unambiguously, 'it would be helpful if you address my son and me informally as Edmund and Thomas. My father, Frederick, was the original Mr. Newman in the practice. When I commenced here as a young man in the early seventies, working titles were strictly formal. My father became Mr. Newman Sr and I was addressed as Mr. Newman Jr. Later, when my father retired and my own son joined, we shifted the suffixes down a generation. It was done out of respect for Frederick who we now both look upon as Mr. Newman Grandfather.' Kit smiled. 'But these terms have always proved confusing for our clients and when the twenty-first century heralded in a relaxed attitude, we embraced it. Now we keep formal titles for correspondence and legal documents only.'

'I will, if you will call me Kit and drop the "young" prefix. I am thirty after all. And by the way, what happened about the funeral? I suppose it has taken place but I seem to have missed any mention of it.'

'I was about to say,' responded Thomas in a kindly manner, 'that it took place on the same day as I sent you the letter. It was held in accordance with Old Kit's instructions: a short service with the least possible delay at St. Margaret's church which is within walking distance of the care home, followed by a formal luncheon at a manor house turned restaurant on the outskirts of town. Old Kit used to walk to the church on Sunday mornings alone with just her walking stick until the last couple of years when someone from the home would take her there and pick her up. Likewise, the restaurant. It was a favourite of hers over many decades.'

'And who attended?'

'We numbered fifteen. All local mourners: two care assistants from the home, the manager of Carter & Roach who Old Kit had known for many years, her general practitioner, the daughter of her closest female friend now deceased, an odd-job man who had looked after the fabric of her house when she owned it, two gardeners who had tended the extensive grounds full-time, her brother Peter's very aged best friend and his wife, the hairdresser who visited the home weekly, and my wife, son, Emily and myself.'

'Nobody else? Not even my grandparents?'

'Nobody else was invited. I was honouring her stated wish. She had already accounted for your grandparents with a letter that was duly posted by Emily on the very morning of her death. As her brother, Peter's younger son, Simon and his wife Margaret who looked after you for most of your life before you reached adulthood, would have been the very people she would have wanted to be present. But now approaching their mid-seventies and neither in robust health, she felt that a long, unplanned trip from Cornwall to Berwick might be too demanding.'

'It probably would have been,' agreed Kit, 'I visit them whenever I can and stay a few nights so that I can do any odd jobs they need doing but can't manage themselves. They are becoming increasingly doddery.' Thomas nodded and Kit continued. 'But a person of Old Kit's mettle is surely worthy of more.'

'She was cremated and her ashes scattered over a chosen flowerbed in her former grounds, with the consent of the current owner. And I have instructions to arrange a remembrance service in Newcastle-upon-Tyne cathedral. Old Kit had put a lot of irons into the fire during her lifetime and a wide range of people from all different backgrounds will wish to attend her remembrance service. At Newcastle, there will be the alternative of travel by plane if their journey is long.'

'I agree.'

'Very good then,' replied Thomas, 'and we can now move on to the reading of the will. I shall ask my secretary and Edmund to sit in as witnesses. My client has stipulated that they should be present but no one else.'

It was a simple will with only two bequests but its very simplicity masked a myriad of questions. Kit would receive the sum of one thousand pounds plus any reasonable expenses incurred in discharging her duties as co-executor. Any remaining monies would form the residue of the estate which would be gifted to the care home in which she had spent the last few years of her life. That was it apart from the codicil, written in the same vein and in the first person as the deceased's letter to Kit, which Thomas opened and set about reading out loud.

Marion and Jane, the next generation of twins amongst my direct descendants, were illegitimate. Born out of wedlock certainly, but more importantly, born as a result of the rape of my only surviving daughter, poor sweet Grace.

There seemed to be an inaudible sigh and pause written into the text before Thomas continued.

Dear gentle Grace who could be spun a yarn by anyone as she did not have the intellectual wherewithal to distinguish between fact and fiction. I spent many unprofitable years trying to find the low-level life who took advantage of her for his carnal pleasure. It was then that I encountered Mr. Newman, junior as his suffix was in those days while his father Frederick was a partner in the firm and he just learning the ropes as a newly-qualified solicitor. It was 1961. I was forty-nine then and Thomas a mere twenty-one, so we have known one another for almost half a century. It was Thomas who found an "investigator" for hire but despite his best efforts and my deep pockets, the perpetrator remained undiscovered. It has remained a sore point throughout the rest of my life and was particularly nagging after Grace's death in 1977 at the age of forty of cause or causes unknown, according to the autopsy. That she died of natural causes I can accept without demur but her unsolved ravishment will haunt me to the day I die as I had my suspicions at the time but never aired them.

The twin girls were seventeen when their mother died. Even to me, their grandmother, they seemed a churlish pair. Charmless and moody was how most people described them and it was hard not to disagree. I had supported them financially all their lives and rarely received a thank you in return, but after Grace's death I made it clear that the money tap was about to be turned off. This sparked a series of recriminations based mainly on the mistaken belief that my financial resources were limitless. It was indeed true that I had become a wealthy woman through my own endeavours and in spite of my late husband's will which had effectively disinherited me, but the twins had failed to factor in such worthy sentiments as love and respect and the glimmer from time to time of gratitude. Apart from family gatherings which I steadfastly organised every five years or so in a forlorn attempt to temporarily paper over the cracks, I saw them rarely after their twenty-fifth birthdays when I gave each a final gift of five thousand pounds. And it was an outcome that could be fairly said to have suited both parties.

My other grandchildren: Thomas, Neil and Lucy, were in many respects distanced from me since their parents had removed me from the board of Northern Tailoring Limited around the time of their births. That Northern Tailoring went into a slow but inexorable death spiral under their leadership was never a source of "I told you so" but rather an agonising terminal illness that I was forced to watch from outside the ropes. John and Bernard were never going to admit to their failings and rather than ask for my advice as to how to save the firm, they just let it grind down to a point where a canny and wealthy Lancastrian from Rochdale seized the opportunity to buy them out at a knockdown price. The boys moved into pig farming, selling their family homes in Berwick and sinking their joint proceeds into one hundred and thirty acres of land in North Yorkshire. Still as thick as thieves, the two families shared the modest farmhouse and nothing was said about the downsizing of accommodation and lifestyle. I had hoped for some empathy between the pigs and the boys that would spur success but eventually news filtered out that they were making as much mess of farming as the pigs were making in the paddocks. And it wasn't long before the begging letters started to arrive. Their credit cards were "maxed out" and they turned to me to clear the debts. I didn't expect words of love or kindness or even gratitude but I was incensed by their implication that it was my responsibility to bail them out. From that point my unconditional love was no longer on offer and I wiped my hands of them and the grandchildren. In moments of reflection, I wondered how Richard and I could have spawned two such unpleasant children but as the years passed any residual guilt I felt in leaving them to climb out of their own holes faded. My only contact with them became the organised gatherings I arranged periodically when it was my custom to provide a sit-down meal with wrapped presents for the children and cheques for the adults. Attendance was predictably high as was the cost of putting on the get-together but I felt the personal need to maintain the family framework so that younger generations might understand who they were and from whence they came. In the course of time my five grandchildren produced eleven offspring most of whom were just names to me as indeed I was to them; an old woman whose relevance to them amounted to near zero. They were, of course, not privy to the squabbling and contretemps between parents and grandparents as to who should inherit my estate. That they were all acting like vultures ready to pounce and pick at my still warm carcass at the very first opportunity was obvious and endeared them to me even less. I took the decision then that not a penny piece of my wealth would find its way into any of their pockets.

My dear brother Peter, just two years my junior, was my lone family friend and the only one I trusted. He was quiet and unassuming and always there if I needed comfort or help. He didn't really enjoy carpentry and after completing his apprenticeship, he started working in a corner shop and married the owner's daughter, Thelma, before going off to war as a cook. On demob, his father-in-law offered him a partnership and they opened a shop in a good position in the high street as Carter & Roach, Grocers.

Thomas Newman looked up from the codicil lying flat on his desk.

'Peter was your great grandfather and their original shop in the high street is still there under the same name although it is now a purveyor of outdoor clothing with the tourist rambling fraternity very much in mind.'

'Is it possible,' Kit blurted out, being reminded that she wanted to buy some suitable shoes, 'that we take a break from this reading? It does seem endless and I am becoming more and more confused.'

'Certainly,' replied Thomas. 'We can reconvene at midday if that suits and I will lay on some sandwiches so that we can work throughout the afternoon. I know it's a lot to take in but we are almost at the point where Old Kit reveals the essence of your task.' He had never dealt with such a lengthy codicil as this. He had advised Old Kit to keep it as succinct as possible lest it meandered to a point of boring verbosity. But she had been adamant that Young Kit needed to know as much as possible about the characters in her wider family if she was to fulfil Old Kit's aim of bringing justice and accord to the latest generation of children: her great grandchildren and great grandnieces and nephews. Thomas sighed. Despite the age difference – almost thirty years – Old Kit had been one of his best friends. It had started as a client-solicitor relationship and developed into an enduring camaraderie. And when physical frailty dictated, it was the Newmans who had arranged the care home and who were her regular visitors and supportive companions. Thomas sighed again. He would miss her.

Young Kit's shopping trip did not go unnoticed. Emily saw her leave, and by leaning out of a half-opened window on the first floor followed her passage down the high street to Messrs. Carter & Roach, outdoor wear specialists. And Edmund saw her return about an hour later with a broad smile on her face. He guessed she had bought several items and dropped them off at her hotel before returning for another gruelling session with his father. He grinned. He was looking forward to showing her the ramparts that evening and afterwards would take her out to dinner.

Emily said Kit had a longstanding partner – Emily always knew everything that was going on, she made the cogs synchronise in the law practice – but Edmund was not put off. He was thirty-five and had been looking for a soulmate for some time. He had explained to his parents – who were anxious for him to get married and produce the next Mr. Newman – that he just hadn't found the right person yet, but when he met her, he would know.

It took a further hour for Thomas to complete the reading of the codicil which had turned into a monologue of Old Kit's thoughts. She had firstly concentrated on her eldest brother, Reginald, and the animosity that had grown between them, originally due to their father's overt love and nurturing of his only daughter, and later to Reginald's jealousy and disgust that as eldest son, his position had been undermined by a woman. Reginald never recovered psychologically from this perceived wrong done to him which was later inflamed by his sister's success in the business world. Reginald had become a union man. He was powerful in his own right representing workers in Northumbria where coal mining had been a way of life for generations of men. He, himself, had started in the pits, followed by two of his younger brothers, David and Nathan, who waited on his every word. But Reginald was always destined for a position in which he could cause trouble and he found it in the union where his aggressive stance at every opportunity that came this way whipped up the expectations, often unreasonably, of the men at the coal face. He attended union conferences and meetings with pit owners and was elected to represent the north-east on the National Executive Committee of the Labour

Party. He grew wealthy in his own right cashing in on the perks and salaries afforded to union representatives, and distancing himself from his flock who continued their daily grind in dangerous and dirty conditions which his posturing had failed to improve materially.

But success was not sufficient to blunt his rancour for his sister, and privy as he was to labour party thinking, he lobbied pugnaciously for additional workers' rights and punitive taxation for captains of industry. That the textile industry was the usual butt of his invective was in the main due to his sister's position as a director of one of the country's major cloth producing companies. A swipe at her was his perpetual goal. He invested heavily in private education for his son, Henry. Subsidised by his union, it was just one of the many perks a top-ranking union man could expect in those days. And Reginald ensured that his son mixed with and knew all the right people for future ascent up the political ladder, leaving the hoi polloi to fend for themselves. The feud with his sister would be ongoing until Reginald tasted sufficient triumph to assuage his resentment, and that, he vowed to himself, would never happen. Under the watchful eye of his father, after university Henry made rapid progress in his chosen career of politics. He wasn't a firebrand like his father but he had a quiet ruthlessness that could transcend acceptable behaviour, making him unpopular with his peers. He wasn't a man with whom it was wise to mess and as a result he failed to rise above junior ministerial rank. He left politics after a damaging affair with a married woman, a liberal member of parliament with whom he had shared an office when he was first elected to Westminster. Reginald was furious and many said that the massive stroke he had a short time later, was a direct result of Henry's philandering. Reginald died after several months in a vegetative state in a nursing home in Berwick. It was 1981 and the mining community of the northeast was about to be decimated by the new conservative government, and damaged goods or not, he was welcomed back into the union fold. It was from this platform that he got his teeth well and truly stuck into his Aunt Kit's affairs. She had always been prudent in her dealings with the inland revenue choosing to use an accountant to ensure that she submitted the correct and accurate information each year, and accordingly, Henry found little dirt to dig up to embarrass her. He was certain that she held offshore accounts in years when they could be held legally but was unable to prove that they had been closed when Treasury tinkering brought in legislation to regulate their use. So, Henry's main thrust to unsettle his aunt lay in her business connections and here he found rich pickings as trawling his way slavishly through reams of paper and microfiche he discovered some commercial indiscretions and cover-ups. It was not long before questions were being raised in the press about the use of slave labour in south-east Asia in the manufacture of various products by a certain company of which Old Kit was a non-executive director. And he found evidence too that the financial director of that same company had been involved in a scandal which was hushed up lest it adversely affected the share price. He was quietly replaced on the board. But it was a manufacturing fault in the production of parachutes that gave Henry his best chance to damage his aunt's good repute. Henry had found a newspaper article from the early nineteen-seventies reporting on the unexplained death of seven young recruits to the parachute regiment. Further research including covert meetings with former paratroopers suggested that problems with the static line – a fixed cord attached inside military planes to open parachutes automatically – may have been the cause. Insider information from a company employee pointed to the likelihood of a batch of faulty yarn being the culprit and for a further bribe information was obtained showing the company's awareness of its culpability. It didn't come forward of its own accord to accept liability, but Henry knew the right people to exert the sustained pressure required to obtain a settlement out of court. The whole episode had a lasting impact on the trading position of the company and severely dented Old Kit's standing. For Henry, imbued as he had been since childhood by his father with a loathing for his aunt, it was a moment of sheer satisfaction. He had cut away her moral high ground and impaired her finances. The family acrimony could have ended there but in victory Henry was not magnanimous and the ill will between his late father and his aunt was passed down to the next generation: Old Kit's grandnieces and nephews. Thomas laid the codicil face down on his old-fashioned blotter.

'Is that it?' asked Kit expectantly.

'Not quite,' replied Thomas, 'but my instruction at this point is to read the real will before continuing to a conclusion with the codicil.' Kit raised her eyebrows but said nothing. There was disappointment written on her pale face. 'It's a very short will, basic almost,' ventured Thomas, 'it really won't take long to read.'

'But you've already read the will,' said Kit looking very confused. 'Your secretary and Edmund came in to witness its reading.'

'That's true. But it was not the final will. It was a ruse. It was for appearance-sake only. The dispersal of her remaining assets will be reported as per that will, and her family will not challenge it as it would have reinforced their belief that there was nothing worthwhile for them to inherit.'

'I'm mega confused now.'

'It was a false will designed to put the bloodhounds off the scent. The real will, written the day after the false one, is enclosed in the codicil. It truly is the last will and testament.'

'Can you do that legally?' asked Kit.

'Certainly, it is completely legal. And you can attach as many codicils as you wish as long as they have been correctly witnessed.'

'It would have been simpler to just rewrite it. A completely new will and tear up the old,' said Kit, 'but if her intent was playing cloak and dagger games then I suppose that the codicil was a way of masking the true will.'

'Just so. Old Kit employed devious ways when it suited her.'

'But don't the beneficiaries need to be present?' queried Kit, as Thomas prepared to open the sealed envelope. 'Like Old Kit's great grandchildren and.....,' she trailed off.

'No, they don't. But I shall ask Emily to come in to witness the actual reading.' When Emily was seated, he opened the envelope and withdrew the single folded sheet of paper. Thomas read out some standard blurb about it representing her last will and testament and renouncing all previous ones, and of Old Kit being of sound mind when she signed the document. Then he dropped the bombshell. 'After official and legal expenses are paid,' Thomas said, 'and any outstanding debts cleared, the residue of the estate is left to Georgina Kit Irwin. There are no other beneficiaries.'

'What?' questioned Kit. 'Me?'

'Yes. You are the sole beneficiary,' confirmed Thomas.

'Why me?'

'That question will be answered in the remaining passages of the codicil. You are the only person to receive a bequest in this will,' repeated Thomas, flourishing the sheet of paper in the air. 'That concludes the reading of the will,' he announced, 'thank you Emily for your presence.' Thomas removed his reading spectacles and looked Young Kit directly in the eye. 'The codicil now cuts to the chase. It will answer your questions but it will raise more queries than it answers.'

'A warning?'

'No, not exactly. Just an indication that the path ahead will not be a speedy motorway but rather a country lane with constant twists and turns.'

'But why chose me to sort out whatever it is that Old Kit wants sorting out before she feels she can rest in peace?'

'Because you are the only person in her extended family who she deems trustworthy.'

'But it would seem,' replied Kit evenly, 'that as the only beneficiary, I now have a vested interest.'

'When I complete the reading of the codicil you will appreciate that this simple will, although absolutely legal, is in fact another false will as Old Kit wishes you to sort out and distribute her assets according to your own judgement of who in her family, if any, is worthy of receiving anything. And I don't think you will be able to complete that task before the start of the next university term.'

'I'm beginning to accept that everything related to Old Kit grinds slowly. The undergraduates are due back the first week of October but I need to be back at work by mid-September at the latest. And then there's Martin, my partner. I'm not sure how he would feel about my spending the next nine weeks of my time worrying about this,' she said, pointing at the will lying innocently on the desk top. 'We are due off on holiday for ten days in late August and then I'm accompanying Martin on one of his hockey jamborees.' As an afterthought she added, 'we both live busy lives.'

'I understand your possible dilemma.' Thomas shifted in his chair leaning back, folding his arms across his chest and resting his chin on a fisted hand. He was contemplating something and said finally, 'I am familiar with the contents of the codicil. I think I can summarise it concisely and relay Old Kit's message to you more meaningfully than her written word. Would that be acceptable?'

'Yes, it would. Quicker and clearer would be great.'

Thomas started by explaining that a short time before Old Kit chose to move into a care home – a home of high standards where her accommodation was effectively a small flat with a balcony – Thomas had, on her behalf, sold her substantial house with three acres of cultivated grounds. With those proceeds he had negotiated the purchase of a "share" in the care home which would allow Old Kit to remain there until her death without further payment and regardless of how many years that might be. It had been a large chunk of money and Thomas had pointed out that an early death would not be cost effective. Old Kit had laughed and enjoyed the joke but had been insistent that she wished to appear as having shed all her worldly assets. She made some large gifts to charities and set up bursaries at various educational establishments. Her name was also linked publicly with funding sundry good causes in Northumbria including promoting the ecology of the region. She had been very generous. It had been a choreographed plan Thomas had told Young Kit when she had enquired the reason for the big giveaway. She had wanted there to be no doubt in any of her descendants' minds that she had not a penny piece to leave them in her will when she died. That way, Thomas had said, Old Kit hoped that the monies in her offshore accounts would go under their radar and there would be no squabbles about unfair inheritance and no contesting of the will, nothing to provoke further discord amongst her wider family.

'But when they learn that I have inherited every remaining penny,' said Kit, with an anxious frown, 'they will be baying for my blood if they are as mercenary as my great grandaunt portrays.'

'But when they contact me, I shall tell them the truth,' replied Thomas.

'And that is?

‘Exactly what I have already told you, and more importantly, exactly what she had already told them. You see, Kit, I have no actual evidence of any offshore accounts. Throughout our long association as solicitor and client she was always honest with me. And I with her. Our business dealings ran smoothly because we could rely on one another.’ He paused to choose his next words. ‘There was an overlap between our professional relationship and our friendship. There was no clear demarcation line separating the two associations, and, over time, I just became aware that she salted money away for a rainy day in a place secure from her family. No details were ever mentioned. And it was not part of my brief to investigate the veracity of her list of assets.’ He paused again before resuming. ‘And you mustn’t forget that she made it clear to everyone that she had turned philanthropist and given away all her assets save those small amounts required to sustain her on a daily basis until her death. So, you can dismiss any anxiety in that department. What is left is for our joint expenses and is ring fenced. There is nothing more left in the pot unless you discover these putative accounts.’

‘So, I could step back, do nothing and walk away. And that would be an end to the matter.’ Thomas looked a little exasperated but said nothing. He just nodded his head. It was the stance he feared she might take. He had warned Old Kit of the possibility that her great grandniece might just walk away, unprepared to invest time and effort on a chase into a cul-de-sac. But Old Kit had been adamant that would not happen. She had seen the glint in Young Kit’s eyes all those years before and had no qualms that she wouldn’t take up the challenge.

'I won't, of course,' said Kit in due course, 'walk away, that is. It's not in my nature. But you still haven't told me what she wants me to do with any assets I discover.'

'The point of her rainy-day nest eggs,' started Thomas, 'was the laudable desire to help those of her descendants who merited help. Through no fault of their own she knew that some were experiencing physical hardship and others had been instilled over their formative years with ill feeling towards her. She had thirty-six living descendants of your generation: eleven great grandchildren and twenty-five great grandnieces or nephews and they are the essence of your task because, in a nutshell, she wants you to find the money, if it exists, and to distribute it amongst the other thirty-five in accordance with their needs and their worthiness as you judge fit.' He added, 'despite the family feuds and her previously sworn position, blood is proving thicker than water.'

'But how can I judge who is worthy and who is not?' Kit demanded not unreasonably.

'The very reason she chose you was because you don't really know any of them save your grandparents who brought you up and a couple of first cousins. You wouldn't even know the majority of them by sight, hence you have no preconceived ideas about any of them and no family prejudices to cloud your judgement. Yours would be a judgement based on integrity.'

The evening was calm; not a breath of wind. Edmund had met her in the hotel's lobby and they had walked the short distance to the castle which was within a stone's throw of the railway station. He had wondered what she would turn up wearing. New flat shoes, of course, but what else suitable for walking the ramparts before going out to dinner. She wore trousers in the olive green so popular with outdoor enthusiasts. They were new he noted but she had not yet sussed out the idea of loading all the pockets with essential knick-knacks to avoid hefting around her heavy handbag. But she looked good, he thought. The informal clothing with a bright blue T-shirt suited her figure and enhanced her complexion. She was quiet at first and he wondered if it was a result of his father boring her intensely with Old Kit's stuff.

'The castle was founded in the twelfth century,' he explained. 'It changed ownership several times over the following centuries as conflicts raged between the English and Scottish forces.' She looked lost in her thoughts but he continued light-heartedly with the tourist guide patter. 'The ramparts date back to the sixteenth century and we can walk a complete circuit around the castle although care is required as some sections are steep and have unguarded drops.' She still seemed distracted but he pressed on. 'The castle's Great Hall was demolished in modern times to make way for the railway station, and the whole complex is now administered by English Heritage.' At a high point they stopped to admire the view across the river Tweed.

'I thought I would take you abroad for dinner,' he announced, when they had completed their circuit and taken in the best views. The surprise remark broke her almost melancholic mood and she arched her blonde eyebrows enquiringly. 'To Scotland,' he answered, pointing northwards, 'It's two and a half miles in that direction and there's a pub just over the border which serves knockout haggis. It's pub grub as you have never known it.'

The Cross Keys pub, which almost straddled the border but was, by a few feet, entirely in Scotland, was doing good trade when they arrived mid-evening. The atmosphere was laid back and lively. Diners were seated mostly outside under an impressively-sized awning but when a small table became available indoors, they settled for that and ordered the haggis dish of the day. It was a time to discover more about one another although Edmund knew far more about her than she did about him.

'Are you returning home tomorrow?' he asked as a starter.

'Yes. I'm catching the noon train and hope to be back in Reading by early evening.'

'Will your partner, Martin, pick you up at the station?' he asked cheekily, 'now that you have more clothes to take home.' He winked and added, 'flat shoes look comfy.'

'They are,' she said completely unfazed, 'but I prefer the stilettos for protection from predatory men.'

'Okay, truce,' he said, holding up his palms in mock surrender. 'I forgot that you have years of experience getting undergraduates to toe the line. But tell me about Martin. What's so special about him that takes you out of circulation from humble predators like me?'

'You're pumping me for info when I know next to nothing about you,' she replied evasively. 'Tell me about yourself instead.'

'Right. Born and bred in Berwick. Read law at Durham University. Always destined to take over in the practice after my father's forthcoming retirement. Love the landscape in this part of the world and go rambling whenever I can. Wouldn't want to live anywhere else. Don't enjoy the big cities except for visits and big occasions. Have been looking for a wife for ages but haven't found her yet. Running out of time as I'm thirty-five now and my mother is worried that I'll remain a bachelor. Aspirations in local politics, but haven't told the parents yet. Will that do?'

'It will do for now.'

'Does that mean,' he said hopefully, 'that I'm in with a chance?'

'No, it doesn't,' Kit replied a little too coyly to slam the door shut on that subject, 'it just means that that will do for now as I can see that the waitress is bringing our plates of haggis.'

After their meal, washed down with a strong ale and a tot of whisky – apparently the only drinks to do proper justice to the famous offal – it was Edmund's turn to pry.

'Tell me about Martin. He must be special to you to have lived with him for so long.'

'I met Martin at university; at a lecture about lasers. We were both just nineteen. He had joined the field hockey club and signed up, inadvertently it appeared, for Scottish country dancing. When our paths first crossed in the lecture hall, he invited me to join him in the country dancing society. From the start we got on well together. No real arguments, no histrionics, just the occasional exchange of sharp words. Mostly we were just happy-go-lucky. When I had the time, I would go and watch his matches against other universities or local sides. He was good; their best player by far. Dancing is my thing but not really his, however, in one another's company we both enjoyed it. We were soon regarded as a pair and nothing has changed since then. We are still a pair.'

'A married pair?' probed Edmund.

'Er…,' she hesitated before finally saying, 'not yet. But a happy pair.'

They said their goodbyes and shook hands in the hotel's lobby. After her final appointment the following morning with his father, he would help her to the station with her extra luggage and wave goodbye on the platform as the London-bound train departed at noon. But he would extract a kiss before she left, leaving her in no doubt that Martin was not her only suitor.

Newcastle had come and gone before Kit got her brain back into gear. Edmund had kissed her tenderly, and despite herself, she had returned it willingly. She waved from the window as the engine speed increased from walking pace to a run. She was feeling flushed and once clear of the platform, a look in her hand mirror showed the tell-tale signs of a deep blush. It was a further complication in an evolving scenario in which she was not in control. But for the moment she needed to refocus on her teaching and research. And Martin.

Whilst Martin was cooking the evening meal Kit told him about her trip up north. They had bought a small semi-detached on the outskirts of Reading, but with local knowledge of alleyways linking streets and a short traverse across some rough ground belonging to the council, it was within walking distance of the main line station. Recently, they had paid a local contractor to convert the galley kitchen into a modern kitchen-diner and as Martin prepped the vegetables he listened as Kit's story unfolded.

'So, you *are* distantly related to this deceased lady,' Martin said, wiping the chopping board with a damp cloth. 'And you *have* inherited her entire estate.'

'Yes, both are true, but neither reflects the real story,' Kit explained. 'One has to dig deep to appreciate the actual situation.'

'Will you go ahead and do what she wants?' inquired Martin, as ever posing his questions in the kind of straightforward language she liked. As ever, he was frank and dependable.

'I said I would, but the long journey home gave me time to reflect. What do I know about high finance? What skills have I got to uncover offshore funds? I wouldn't know where to start. And who am I to sit in judgement on the morals of all my first cousins twice removed?'

'From what you've told me, it seems that the old lady wanted you to use your scientific expertise to find the solution,' Martin said. He removed his apron, turned on the hob, and sat down next to Kit. 'It's nice to have you home again,' he added.

'And I'm glad to be home,' she replied, putting her arms around his neck, all thoughts of dinner shelved for a while.

It was an earnest woman who approached the conundrum early the following morning. Martin, tall and lanky, with extra-large feet, fitted himself into their only armchair and prepared to listen. Kit was in methodical mode. She set out in rigorous order the happenings of the last few days and went into detail about Old Kit's life and times. She showed Martin the family tree that the Newmans – senior and junior – had drawn up and gave him as much information as she could remember about the characters in the family tree. He raised some pertinent questions that she hadn't considered as she recounted the story. Normally calm and in control, she felt agitated and was glad to share her anxiety with him. All too soon he was off to work, leaving her, she now realised, to make one of the biggest decisions of her life.

Her mobile bleeped. She swiped the screen and opened a text message. It was from Edmund. He hoped she had got home safely and was wondering if she had already started number crunching Old Kit's challenge. Could he help? He had addresses and telephone numbers of some of the family members. And she should be aware that the contents of the will would soon be in the public domain. She swore. She hadn't thought of that. Old Kit was a person well known in various circles and if the local rags put the information in print it might stir up trouble. She thanked Edmund for his message and signed off without committing herself to any course of action in relation to his questions.

Logging on to her university website, she attempted to deal with any pending correspondence. It was hard going as her mind was not fully on the task at hand. Nor could she concentrate on lecture preparation for the new academic year, now less than nine weeks away. She always tried to update her lectures for the freshers so that her delivery of the same information didn't become stale. A few bright ideas came to her but she didn't seem to have the fortitude to follow them through. Eventually, frustrated with herself, she logged off and spent the rest of the morning in a desultory attempt at housework. It took until the late afternoon for Kit to realise that studying the A3 sheet on which the family tree had been painstakingly drawn was the unavoidable and inevitable solution to her malaise. Its flow from top to bottom covered five generations whereas its flow across the page was of the same cohort. She traced carefully all the family members Old Kit had mentioned in her long letter and highlighted their names. Then those that Thomas had read out from the codicil. She was slowly becoming familiar with some while others remained completely unknown. In number, including spouses, the names totalled an astonishing seventy-nine. It was head-spinning stuff.

The call from Edmund came later that same afternoon. He would be down in London the following day and would like to meet her for lunch. He didn't state the reason for his trip and she didn't ask there being, somehow, a tacit agreement over the airwaves not to ask. She pressed the terminate call sign and wondered about the "physics" of such a situation. It wasn't possible. There were no laws of physics that covered vibes.

They met in a sandwich bar in the concourse of King's Cross station. He had wanted to meet her outside the university but she was wary of being spotted on the off chance by a colleague or a member of the support staff. Seeing him waiting for her outside the café's entrance made her nervous with anticipation. She wondered what his trip was all about and soon learnt the reasons.

'It's a lovely, balmy day,' he commenced, 'and after our snack it would be nice to take a stroll in Hyde Park.'

'Is that why you've journeyed down?'

'No. Not the primary reason, but it's a good enough reason in its own right. Seeing you, that is,' he replied brazenly.

'So, what's the main reason?'

'I've cobbled together a list of all the names on the ancestry chart. I've verified their dates of birth, and where possible I've included a contact number and postal address. Also, I've checked the electoral rolls to establish who are property owners.'

'Is that relevant?' interjected Kit.

'Maybe not directly, but it gives a measure of that person's prosperity.'

'And you think that should be taken into account if or when I make a judgement about division of the spoils?'

'It might be helpful,' Edmund replied, 'but it's your call. And there's another thing. My father, through his many decades practising law in the region, soaked up a great deal of information about the legal rectitude of the local populace. He told me the names of a few miscreants appearing on Old Kit's tree. And with a bit more ferreting, I can tell you the names of those on the chart with criminal records.'

'Oh!' responded Kit in alarm. 'I don't like the sound of that.'

They banished all shop talk for their walk in Hyde Park. After a short taxi ride, they alighted at Marble Arch and entered the royal park at Speaker's Corner. Edmund would have liked to have walked down to the Serpentine to see the Princess Diana memorial but he had noticed that Kit was back in high heels. Instead, they took a short, circuitous route and stopped at a bench affording a fine view of the rose garden and other floral displays. They were silent for several minutes, just enjoying the views and the fine early August weather and watching the world go slowly by.

'I mustn't be too long,' said Kit eventually, looking at her watch, although she had no really pressing work planned for the afternoon. She wasn't sure why she said it as she was enjoying sitting there next to Edmund.

'I hope you're not prevaricating about your task as joint-executor,' he said turning to face her. 'You said something earlier about if or when.'

'It's an option,' she replied somewhat diffidently.

'No, it's not,' said Edmund earnestly. 'It's not an option at all if you think through the logic. Old Kit was relying on you to distribute her money to her descendants in accordance with their need and merit. She picked you above everyone else because she thought she could trust you to take on the responsibility of doing it in a totally unbiased way. She didn't leave all her estate to you because she wanted you to have it. Not at all.'

'Is the lecture over?' said Kit when Edmund fell silent.

'No, it's not. It's a moral obligation that you cannot shirk. And as co-executor, you'd be letting my father down too.'

'My life with Martin and my university work was ideal until this business came along,' she said, wafting a hand in a gesture of discontent.

'Not *that* ideal,' replied Edmund sharply.

'What do you mean by that?' Kit asked, although she feared she already knew the answer.

'Just that …,' replied Edmund softening his tone, 'just that, to me, you seem a little lonely.'

'Well, I'm not.'

'Fine.' He checked his watch. 'I'd better start back for the terminus. My train leaves in half an hour and I have some legal papers to deal with on the journey home.' He picked up his satchel and they made their way back to Marble Arch where, after a brief kiss, he dived down into the underground system to take him to King's Cross and she crossed over busy Park Lane heading for her office near the Embankment. She didn't rush back. She walked slowly and thoughtfully. It had been a sobering moment when Edmund had suggested that her life was not as ideal as she had professed it to be. He was right, of course, but what made him think that? What had been the giveaway? She shook her head. In all the years she had known Martin, the subject of marriage had never arisen. Not a single time to her recollection. Surely that was odd. And although more and more couples were living together without feeling the need to marry, they did start families. But starting a family had never been on the agenda either. Kit remembered Alice crying "curiouser and curiouser" in one of her favourite children's books, Alice in Wonderland. And, indeed, it was curious that a relative stranger such as Edmund could spot the shortcoming in her long-term relationship with Martin.

Over dinner that evening, Martin had news of his own to relate. He was to be seconded for a period of up to six months to a project involving joint co-operation between his firm's R & D department and a European team made up of scientists from different disciplines and pharmaceutical boffins from three other European Union countries. Martin's company was in the throes of developing a new medication with great potential to control water-borne parasites normally found only in certain tropical climes. The project was about to undergo stringent trials and needed the expertise of impartial outsiders.

'A disease like bilharzia?' asked Kit.

'Yes, sort of. A genetic mutation over time in response to the successful drug developed to combat it. Tinkering with its current formulation will no longer suffice. A radical rethink was necessary and we came up with what we believe can eradicate similar conditions entirely.'

'Very important then.'

'Not just important for those living in south-eastern Europe and the Middle East, but also for our company. A lot of resources have been poured into the new drug's development. We can't afford to fail.'

'Will you be away much of the time?' asked Kit, starting to clear the dining table.

'More than now, certainly. But not for long periods. Hurry up with that,' he said, indicating the dirty dishes she was about to load into the dishwasher, 'the live televised golf in Texas is about to start.' Kit didn't care for golf. She didn't care for football, cricket or rugby either. They were all Martin's favourite sports to watch. She didn't even care for field hockey – his sporting passion – although she would never dream of saying so. And hockey was, she had to admit, the source of frequent enjoyable social functions now that Martin was one of the big guns running the national organisation.

'Will you miss me?' she asked, joining him on the sofa.

'I sure will,' he replied, giving her thigh a gentle squeeze but looking steadfastly at the screen. 'Will *you* miss me?'

'I guess so, but it might depend on whether or not I decide to take on the role mapped out for me by the old lady.'

'Is that the old lady of Threadneedle Street or just *any* old lady?' he asked jokingly, 'because if it's any old lady then I advise you to stand well clear and let her do her own dirty work.'

'From the grave?'

'Women can do wonders from the grave. Boadicea is still driving her chariot over Westminster Bridge despite her untimely death in 61AD.'

Chapter 2

THE MEMORIAL

Kit's lack of contact was causing Thomas and Edmund real concern. Was she going to fulfil the expectations of the deceased? Or, was this effectively closure? They had not heard from her since Edmund's day trip to London some two weeks prior. She had told him then that she would be in touch, but so far, no news. Should the practice consider that aspect of the case as closed leaving just the memorial service to organise?

'We have to know,' said Thomas to his son.

'Agreed,' replied Edmund. 'She had mentioned going away on holiday sometime in August with her partner. Maybe she has chosen to be "incommunicado" for the period.'

'I think you should try contacting her again,' said Thomas, 'we have arrangements to make for the memorial service.'

'Who will give the eulogy?'

'Young Kit is the obvious choice even though she didn't know the old lady. I could write it and she could deliver it.'

'I think you should do it,' replied his son. 'You were her good friend.'

★ ★ ★

They had motored down to the south of France for their last holiday together in the immediate future, dictated by Martin's impending secondment for at least six months or possibly more. As Edmund had correctly guessed, they had agreed that their mobiles should be switched off for the duration of the journey with its overnight stop in Tours and once in their rented apartment in Sète, a working fishing town on the Mediterranean, they should answer emails to their business addresses only. It was an arrangement that suited both but for their own private reasons.

The town, formerly a sleepy fishing village near the Spanish border, had small trawlers tied up by thick, gnarly ropes with ingenious knots to large, stout metal rings set into the harbour wall. Birds perched on railings overseeing their unloading as they returned from their daily fishing trips in the hope of pinching the odd, stray titbit of nourishment from the boat's deck. Outdoor cafés lined the harbour wall; it was a popular spot with both the mainly French tourists and the locals after a day's toil. There were beach areas on either side of the harbour but visitors were generally types who used it as a base for exploring the coastline and surrounding countryside. They hired bikes and after a good night's sleep were ready the following morning to explore.

For a couple engaged for so long in a co-habiting partnership they were strangely uneasy in each other's presence. Kit knew her reasons for this unease – Edmund mostly, and the small matter of her great grandaunt's affairs – but she sensed that Martin too was struggling with something that he hadn't told her about. He just wasn't his normal self. He seemed easily distracted. There was nothing that she could really put her finger on directly but her intuition warned her that this was not his normal mien.

Their first day was spent pleasurably on a leisurely cycle ride to visit the Château de Villeroy. A circular route anti-clockwise around the Ėtang de Thau was their choice the following day stopping off frequently at wooden benches around the grand pond to admire the scenery and eat freshly baked baguettes. By their last full day, they judged their leg muscles sufficiently toned for the challenge of a seventy kilometres round trip to Montpellier to stroll in the Old Town dating back to the twelfth century and do some shopping in the designer outlets. It was France after all, Kit reminded herself, and there was an absolute need to purchase something chic to wear.

Kit had checked her university email address each day for work related messages and responded accordingly to the sort of minor queries that always arose before the start of the new academic year. Nothing had been untoward until she opened a message referenced Andorra. "Trust you will have time to check out Andorra for Old Kit's offshore funds whilst you're enjoying your vacation in the south of France" the message started and continued "it's within easy driving distance of the Med and the banks there are super secretive, Edmund". When Martin had inquired the reason for catching her breath and the minor expletive that followed, Kit had mumbled that one of the second-year students was causing trouble and she would have a lot to sort out when she got back to her office.

Both were quiet on their homeward passage north to the channel tunnel; anticipation of the lifestyle changes that their new circumstances would impose on their lives and filter through to affect their relationship being uppermost in their thoughts. Kit had asked him if he was looking forward to working abroad for a long period, and would he miss being away from home for several consecutive months. She told him she would miss him being about the house; who would mow the lawn for example and where would she find such a good dancing partner for his hockey dinner dances? He had smiled and with a flat hand had bounced her blonde curls on her shoulder. Yes, he would miss her too but he was looking forward to the new challenges ahead. And the period of secondment would soon be over and they would be back to normal. But Kit doubted that. He was different, and it wasn't just the beat to which his big feet in their chunky sandals were tapping. However, she was soon back to wondering how Edmund had found her business email address. It should only have been available to students and staff. What skulduggery had he employed to obtain it? She didn't really care; she had been longing to hear from him.

Her mind made up, Kit phoned Thomas from her office. She would continue as Martin's partner, and to the unobservant, their relationship would still appear hunky-dory, but she would follow her brain which was pleading with her to look for new horizons. There was little that she could remember about her own mother save a short phrase her mother employed whenever Kit was grizzling about some perceived pre-school injustice. When one door closes her mother had told her solemnly, another will open.

'Thomas,' she said boldly into the mouthpiece when the line was connected, 'I have decided to fulfil my obligation in respect of Old Kit.'

'I'm glad you took your time to think through the whole venture,' he replied warmly. 'Your great grandaunt's motives in her last few years were entirely altruistic. I hope you will find the pot of gold and be able to share it amongst the deserving. I cannot help you on that score but Edmund can.' It was exactly what Kit wanted to hear.

'Have you arranged the date of the memorial service?' she asked. 'I will give over my free time to do the best I can but my priority will always be my work. That comes first.'

Permission had been granted to hold the memorial service in the cathedral church of St. Nicholas. Thomas knew the right people to ask for such a privilege not normally available to local worshippers. Many mourners, he had explained, from different walks of life would wish to attend to pay their last respects to a woman of outstanding ability and well known for her philanthropy, and although their anticipated numbers would be dwarfed by the sheer size of the building, there was nowhere else suitable in the vicinity that would afford sufficient space for a large gathering and also have the necessary travel links for attendees from long distances.

Kit travelled up to the north-east again by train, but this time she was accompanied by Martin. The chosen date had been convenient for both falling as it did before the start of term and before Martin's imminent departure to his new base in Vienna. Kit wondered, although never voiced her inner thought, if it would be their last hurrah together. She had been in contact with Edmund several times since the holiday in France and speculated how the first meeting between the two men might pan out. She didn't know if Martin had sensed, or even cared, that he might have a rival.

She had declined to give the eulogy but had accepted that as joint-executor, after the ceremony she should stand with Thomas to thank the invitees for their presence there. It would also be, Thomas quite rightly pointed out, an opportunity for him to introduce her to any members of Old Kit's family he recognised. Afterwards, lavish refreshments would be available for all in a marquee set up in the cathedral grounds. Thomas had asked Edmund to track down as many of Old Kit's great grandchildren as possible and introduce them to Kit whilst the meal was in swing and Kit had done her homework to familiarise herself with the ancestry tree. As climax to the proceedings there would be a short speech by the chairman of the board of one of the companies on which Old Kit had served as a non-executive director, outlining the deceased's contribution to the textile industry. Guests would then make their farewells and Thomas warned her that it would be at this point that any festering acrimony they felt towards Kit's role as joint-executor, would surface.

It turned out to be a foul day in more ways than one. The early September weather, settled and balmy for the first few days, spat cold, chilling rain whipped up by a gusty north-easterly blowing off the North Sea. It wasn't how Kit had remembered it from her visit earlier that summer when strolling along the beach barefoot in Berwick with Edmund on a calm and warm summer evening. It had been ideal then but was showing its teeth now. Kit shivered in her formal thin ensemble of navy matching jacket and skirt teamed with a pale green blouse. Her wardrobe hadn't included attire suitable for a memorial service on such a grand stage and she had had to go shopping to find something befitting the occasion. She felt ill at ease in such clothes and Martin looked equally uncomfortable. He had regained his natural ever friendly manner and Kit was beginning to wonder if she had misinterpreted his previous body language.

Following instructions, they had waited for Thomas and his family in the hotel lobby where they had stayed the night; the earliest morning train arriving too late for the planned proceedings of the day. Introductions of his wife and daughter to Kit and Martin, and of Martin to the various members of the Newman family had been by formal handshake tempered by first names and friendly smiles. While Thomas and Kit found a quiet corner to run through the day's schedule, Thomas's wife ensured that the Newmans, together with Emily and Martin, enjoyed a friendly get together over their coffees and Danish pastries. Edmund took the opportunity to give Martin a visual once-over; the tall friendly man with supersized feet seemed oblivious to his inspection but deep, down Martin was as much aware of Edmund as he was of him.

The mourners filed into the cavernous knave, some dressed in bright colours, others preferring more sombre tones. They spanned all ages: from those assisted by a younger family member as they shuffled along with the aid of a walking stick, to the very young who skipped down the knave holding a parent's hand. The music was uplifting and bright and piped throughout the knave; toes tapped and bodies swayed to the beat as they waited for the service to commence. A church official directed family members to the reserved seating on the left-hand side of the aisle. By the time the service commenced both sides of the passageway were almost full. Kit and Martin had already taken their seats midway down the left side of the knave. As the clock ticked round to eleven o'clock Thomas and his wife were the last to take their seats in the front pew on the right. As they sat for a few moments whilst the music's refrain drew to a natural close, Thomas whispered in his wife's ear that the chance of a good lunch always brought in the hordes.

Members of the congregation sat respectfully silent throughout the service, but once passed the greeting and handshake duo of Thomas and Kit and out from under the building's stone portico there was a mad dash for the refreshment marquee, where as was the deceased's custom at family gatherings, champagne was served. It was at this stage in the day's proceedings that Kit had a missive pressed into her hand that would change the nature of the task she had committed to undertake on her relative's behalf. Stuffed into her handbag for reading when seated, she had failed to note the person who delivered it. A quick glance at the words scrawled on the outside of the envelope would have told her instantly that the contents inside would not make for happy reading. "Rich bitch" were two words likely to cause a bitter taste in her mouth. But for the moment, standing around in the entrance of the enormous marquee juggling a half-full long-stemmed flute, her handbag and an order of service whilst a master of ceremonies did his best to get over two hundred guests seated in double-quick time, proved an effective distraction. It was here that Edmund introduced Kit to three of her first cousins twice removed: Samuel, Anthony and Lee. The three brothers, aged nineteen, twenty and twenty-one respectively, had little to say for themselves and Kit's normally fluid conversation soon ran dry. She was grateful when they sidled off in search of a champagne refill. Edmund muttered in her ear that they weren't all like that, some were considerably worse. Kit giggled and Edmund chuckled and a knowing nod passed between them which was not lost on Martin.

They shared a round table of nine: Martin on Kit's right, Kevin and his new wife immediately on her left and next to them Kevin's younger brother Sean. Together with their mother Marion and her latest boyfriend and two descendants of workers with whom Old Kit had worked at Northern Tailoring Limited, they comprised a young group. The food was delicious and Kit began to appreciate why the call to a family gathering should be so compelling, even to the disaffected. Marion was a twin. She was the daughter of Old Kit's dear Grace who had died in the early nineteen-eighties. There was constant reference to the family tree – the chart itself becoming dog-eared with the endless folding and unfolding – and Kit showed Marion their respective positions amongst the branches. Marion didn't appear particularly interested and made no comment when Kit – for want of some friendly banter – told her that she too was a twin. Even between mother and sons few words were exchanged. There was no obvious warmth amongst them but also no obvious hostility. When asked by Martin what they all did for a living, Marion replied "not a lot, can't do much on benefits". It wasn't until the toastmaster requested the great grandchildren to be upstanding to drink to each other's good health that Kit felt brave enough to ask Marion to point out which one was her twin; she appeared equally dowdy and Kit had no expectation of lively conversation with her.

With some relief, Kit, with a lecturer's ability to project her voice across the table, was able to engage in interesting chat with the two descendants from the tailoring business. Both were men in their late thirties, and they had engaging stories and anecdotes to tell passed down by their forebears. Edmund came over, and crouched low between Kit and Martin, said quietly to pay attention to the next group taking a toast as it would be the great grandnieces and nephews, Kit's set. Apparently, they were all present bar two. Thirty-one of them plus Kit. A motley lot, according to Edmund. Martin winced at his words and Kit looked self-conscious. She hoped they weren't all like Marion's charmless pair but when they did all eventually rise to take the toast, it was evident that they covered not only the socio-economic spectrum but that there were some very bright personalities amongst them.

Kit took a quiet moment to open the envelope still in her handbag. She was shocked to read the two-word address on the outside but hid both it and her own reaction to it from Martin. Daring to read its contents, she tore open the envelope and unfolded the single sheet of paper. The communication was typed and from its layout she guessed it had been written by a well-educated person as the grammar and spelling were streets ahead of the prose submitted by her own undergraduate students. And the message bore the hallmarks of a devious mind. It told her that their luggage, an overnight bag each, left in the hotel's storeroom when they had checked out earlier that morning, and which were to be collected on their way to the station to catch the late afternoon fast service back to London, would not be "available" to them until the following evening at the earliest. She swore quietly and when asked by Martin what was up, Kit told him that as he was off to Vienna the following morning, he would have to return home alone that afternoon without his holdall and that she would travel back as soon as she had sorted out an issue with their luggage.

'But what problem is there with our luggage?' asked Martin perplexed. 'We left it at the hotel.'

'I don't know,' she replied, 'but read this letter and you will see that someone is playing silly buggers with us.'

'It's not an amusing joke,' said Martin gruffly, after reading the letter, 'if indeed it is a joke,' adding as he waved his hand discreetly at the people sitting around the table, 'and I shall not be sorry to say goodbye to this lot. I'm glad they're not my relatives.'

At that moment Edmund came over to their table with the news that the hotel had telephoned to inform him of missing luggage for room forty-six; the locked storeroom door had been forced and closed-circuit television footage showed a figure departing via the staff entrance with two overnight-style bags. 'Welcome to Geordie land,' said Edmund sarcastically, after he had read the letter Kit had shown him. 'Someone wants to ensure that you remember your visit to Newcastle. The hotel has already informed the police of the theft but the letter suggests that the holdalls will be returned to you in the fullness of time. What will you do?'

'Martin's travelling home on the late afternoon train as per our plans, but I shall stay another night or two in the hope that the bags will appear miraculously by my bedroom door.'

'Good decision,' said Edmund, although it was clear from Martin's expression that he thought otherwise. 'I haven't a scintilla of doubt that rightful ownership will be resumed,' he added. Kit pushed her spectacles up her nose and got stuck into some more monosyllabic chat with Marion. She wasn't going to be beaten by some annoying juvenile prank.

There was a buzz of social interaction in the time gap between the tables being cleared and the final speech and goodbyes. Guests stretched their legs and appeared to mingle contentedly with those nearby, thoroughly sated by the splendid repast. Some made bee lines to folks they recognised on other tables and had animated conversations. But nobody slipped away quietly as Old Kit's habit of presenting a departing gift to her guests was well known. Waiting staff with silver trays piled high with rectangular shallow boxes handed a gift box to each diner with a small red disc stuck on the back of their chair, marking each as a non-relative. Inside, and to a general murmur of pleasure, they found a handmade glazed porcelain plaque in a chunky design of a wildflower of Northumbria for the women and the diagrammatic representation of a native tree for the men. The stamp on the back indicated that it had been made by a pottery local to Berwick. Martin found the plaque surprisingly weighty when he removed it from the box. Its irregular lumpiness was tactile and the design appealing. He made the comment to Kit that royal funerals couldn't boast more detailed planning than her great grandaunt's swansong. And it was true, thought Kit, that the entire proceedings must have been planned several years before her demise. Another toast followed before the same waiting staff returned, each clutching a bundle of mint-green envelopes on which was printed the name of a relative in bold, black capitals. They promised much but delivered little. As one envelope after the other was torn open and the premium bond gift token removed, hopes of fat pay outs were finally extinguished. The five-pound token, the minimum sum that could be purchased around the time of the millennium, was attached by a paperclip to a small card bearing the pithy remark in the deceased's own handwriting that she hoped the gift would bring them good luck in the monthly draws but if it didn't then there was always hard work and honest endeavour to fall back on. It was a message that went down like a lead balloon, snuffing out all hope and causing a buzz of sharp and disgruntled words. Kit appeared to be the only relative to see the funny side. Unable to conceal her amusement, her spectacles slid down her nose and her curls bounced vigorously as she giggled uncontrollably. She was beginning to warm to her great grandaunt.

Looking around the vast interior of the marquee, Kit could see a group of guests forming a huddle around Thomas who was only visible because of his height. She could hear raised voices and see gesticulations and some of the fingers raised in anger were pointing at her. She shivered and prepared herself for the inevitable onslaught. They would come to her, but she would pre-empt their angry arrival at her table by going to them. It was the perfect time to say goodbye to Martin with a full-bloodied kiss and wish him a safe journey to Vienna. He would be in touch tomorrow, he said, as Kit pulled herself up to her full height of five feet six inches and strode over to confront the melee. She had met some of her late great grandaunt's waifs and strays, she was now about to meet the actively aggrieved.

John and Bernard, the loathsome twins, as she had heard Edmund once refer to them, now in their early seventies were badgering Thomas with loud and unpleasant remarks. He was remaining calm under pressure and replying to their discordant arguments, verging on abusive, with differing but cogent points of view. Alas, the twins were too het up to listen as Thomas repeated for the umpteenth time that their mother had made it clear some years previous, and on a number of following occasions, to all her direct and indirect descendants that she would give away all her wealth to good causes when she entered the care home where she intended to live out the remainder of her life. Indeed, she had even sent copies to her two living children and five grandchildren, of the paragraph in her will in which she had made her intentions clear that there would be no bequests to them. There was no money in the pot, Kit heard Thomas repeat to the macho dunderheads, simulating pulling out the linings of his trouser pockets to show nothing there. But they would have none of it. Spotting her arrival in the group they refocussed their attention on her.

'So, you're the other joint-executor,' sneered John, usually the leader of the pair, 'not even a direct descendant and I'll bet you're getting something.'

'Then you would lose your money,' Kit replied crisply.

'Although there was a codicil,' interjected Thomas swiftly and looking sternly at John, 'in which your mother left the military medal your father won at the battle of El Alamein to his regiment, the fountain pen that she used when working in the laboratory in Manchester to Kit and her physics degree certificate she gained at Edinburgh University to me for display in my office. So, if you deem these cherished items to be "something" then you are right, but if your "something" means money then you are wrong.' But this explanation only fuelled further resentment and the twins went off to convene with their own children and grandchildren.

Adam stood quietly in the wings of the agitated group observing and listening intently to the claims of injustice they made to Thomas. He was the grandson of Old Kit's eldest brother Reginald and was a chip off both his block and that of his father, Henry. Civilised and sanitised by private education and an upbringing in urban Berkshire, he had learnt how to handle himself smartly in all situations. Backed up by his father, he was fond of flexing his muscles on all manner of matters, some exceedingly trivial, as a way of keeping his name at the forefront of his constituents' minds, especially near election time. He was the member of parliament for a safe London seat but acted as if he was intimate with the north-east, its peoples and its needs although he had never lived there and seldom set foot in Northumbria. His presence alone was sufficient to alert Edmund to the possibility of a potentially awkward encounter and Edmund took place next to Thomas in a show of support. Like his father, he was almost six feet tall, but unlike Martin his physique was robust rather than gangly. When away from his professional work it was obvious by his glowing tanned cheeks that he was an outdoors person. But he had a quick brain which his ageing father would appreciate right now and it was Edmund who stepped in and replied when Adam, in the half-ingratiating half-supercilious manner he often adopted when speaking to people he regarded as his underlings, started questioning the veracity of the will. For a career politician without a profession to fall back on if he lost his seat, Adam had learnt to be a smart operator. That sharpness together with informed knowledge he always seemed to be able to obtain on no matter what subject, thanks to his father's contacts, made him a dangerous adversary. And Edmund knew that it was a question not to be taken lightly as his father's role as joint-executor of Old Kit's will was fraught with the complication that Thomas was acting not just as his client's legal adviser but as her best friend. Edmund had reminded his father on several occasions recently of the warnings he himself had received from his father of the dangers of mixing business with pleasure. When Adam asked for a copy of the will to be sent to him, it was clear that the late Kit Audrey Harrison's complicated affairs would not die with her. Her hope and plan for an orderly exit from the world of the living was not going to happen. Edmund bit his lip and wondered how it would all pan out.

It was the manager who greeted Kit when she finally arrived back at the hotel, exhausted by the events and emotion of the day. Full of apologies for the missing luggage which he said had now been found, he assured her that her extra, unscheduled night with them would be on complimentary terms. Sometime during the day a note had been left for her and it was, together with the couple's cases, now in her room. And it wasn't long before Edmund rang.

'Are you okay?' he asked.

'Sort of,' Kit replied. 'Well, I was sort of okay until I got back to the hotel to find our luggage had been returned and a note left in my room about its mysterious disappearance.'

'What did it say?'

'I'll read it.' Pushing her specs up her nose, she read, "This is what you can expect if you illegally withhold our legacies".

'Cryptic. Any signature?'

'None,' replied Kit, 'nothing at all to identify the originator.'

There was silence at the other end while Edmund was thinking. 'Let's go for a stroll in the city this evening,' he said. 'I'll pick you up in an hour's time.'

'No flat shoes?' enquired Edmund when they met later.

'No flat shoes,' confirmed Kit. 'It was meant to be an overnight trip only.'

'Well, I'm glad you're staying for a second night,' he replied warmly. 'We'll stroll along the paved banks of the Tyne and find some good views to enjoy.'

'That man, Adam.'

'Your first cousin once removed,' interrupted Edmund.

'Yes. Him,' she said reflectively. 'He seems quietly dangerous.'

'He is. He's a stirrer. No profession of his own so he's made a life of sticking his nose into other people's affairs.'

'But I suppose he would argue that his grandaunt's affairs are also his, and that he is only trying to protect his less nimble-minded relatives from corrupt officialdom.'

'Probably. Although he's the type that usually causes more harm than good. He may possess in-depth knowledge of the subject but he fails to understand it in context.'

They walked on in silence, Edmund pointing out various landmarks for he knew Newcastle well; as a student solicitor he had attended the law courts there regularly. They stopped to purchase coffees from an outdoor bar and continued ambling along the river bank. The late evening was just beginning to turn cool. The clear skies afforded sharp views across the Tyne. There was still activity on the river to engage their attention. They sat on a bench to watch the human traffic crossing a foot bridge. A frisson of the chilling air made Kit tremble momentarily and Edmund took the opportunity to put his arm around her shoulders. She did not demur.

Edmund was waiting in his father's office when Thomas arrived the following morning. 'I'm concerned, Father, about the properness of your position in Old Kit's affairs,' he started without preamble, 'I do not want you to cross the legitimate bounds of impartiality. I do not want you to be accused of illegal conduct after a lifetime of observing the Law Society rules.'

'And you think I have crossed that line?'

'No,' replied his son slowly, 'but if eldest brother Reginald's tribe are set on uncovering every detail of his sister's estate, then I fear that you will be portrayed as untrustworthy.'

'The false will. Is that what's worrying you?'

'I suppose so. Yes.'

'But that's just a moniker we've given it, or I should say more accurately, that Old Kit gave it. It was just an ordinary will and was superseded by another,' replied Thomas patiently. 'It was the desire of our client to make it clear to her descendants well in advance of her death that there would be nothing in the pot for them to inherit. She made it crystal clear to them by sending photocopies showing that none of them would receive bequests.'

'I know that, Father,' resumed Edmund, 'but you have kept from them the knowledge that the so-called false will existed, and the fact that it *did* materially change the situation of bequests. And by not doing so they will believe you have something to hide.'

Thomas sat down at his desk. His son had pushed on a sore point. There was no denying that in following the instructions of his client and best friend, his actions could be regarded as "irregular" at best. 'I have agonised a great deal over this situation,' he said, as his son pulled up a chair opposite him. 'To satisfy the law and to satisfy my dear client both at the same time has presented me with a real conundrum.'

'I know, Father. I don't doubt your motives for one second. But, unfortunately, others might.' His father was looking drawn; yesterday's memorial service, even with the help of Emily's organisational skills, had drained him. His upright bearing and sartorial elegance normally disguised his age, but not this morning. He's in his seventies and should be retired by now, was what Edmund thought. He's doing what his best friend asked him to do without sufficient regard to his own wellbeing. Edmund made a mental note to tell his mother that his father needed some pampering. 'Now that a copy of the will has been requested by that odious man, Henry,' said Edmund, 'we must make it clear to all the descendants that Old Kit left a final will and in it, Georgina Kit Irwin was named as sole beneficiary. You must then add something to the effect that after death expenses have been paid, you estimate that the residue sum of money will be well below four figures.'

'I rather think you are right,' responded Thomas. 'I've come to that conclusion myself. Old Kit's hope that when her family realised that there were no gold coins left in the pot, they would accept the situation without further ado and just get on with their lives, is not going to happen. They're snarling around her embers already led by Adam who won't give up until he's caused trouble. He's a typical career politician: promises much but delivers little.'

'True, and someone whose activities we need to follow closely,' replied Edmund. 'Am I right in believing that apart from the date, obviously, and the naming of Young Kit as a joint-executor, the only difference between the two wills is the naming of Young Kit as the sole beneficiary of the residue rather than it going to the care home?'

'That's correct. And none of her descendants were named as benefactors in either will apart from her.'

'And the joint-executors in the first will were yourself and the manager of Martin's bank who she had known for many years.'

'Again, that's correct. But Mr. King had made it known that when he retired, he would be moving to the south. On the surface this explains the change of joint-exec, but I'm pretty sure that Old Kit had in mind all along to make her great grandniece an executor.'

'So, on the surface, the only possible bone of contention appears to be the recipient of the residue which amount we know is very small indeed. Correct?'

'Correct,' confirmed Thomas. 'It's the codicil which encloses the final will which is the problem. What's written there in black and white speaks for itself. But it's what is *not* written that is the real source of my difficulty.'

'Your belief that the deceased had offshore funds and that the codicil charged your co-executor with finding them and distributing the monies to her great grand-descendants on a needs and merit basis.'

'Despite nothing being written down in it about possible offshore funds, it's a huge moral issue for me.'

'I know, Father,' replied his son. 'I know, and it's for that reason that I feel you should stand down and let me handle any affairs outstanding in order to finalise this estate.'

'Renounce in favour of you?'

'Yes. That is exactly what I think you should do,' said Edmund seriously. 'You are just too wrapped up in doing the decent thing and you may miss seeing the pitfalls ahead.'

'If you are going to renounce you normally have to do so immediately, but it is possible to start and then stop before reaching probate if something unexpected arises to change the executor's ability to see it through to a conclusion.'

'Exactly,' said Edmund. 'We could apply to the High Court to pass over the intermeddling executor's rights to someone else. Me.'

'It would be a burden off my shoulders,' admitted Thomas without further persuasion. 'I would be grateful, and your mother would be too. She wants me to retire as soon as possible.'

'A phased handover would be ideal if your partners agree.'

'I always wanted you to become a third-generation partner despite the trend of modern times to appear uninterested in any form of longevity. But I had hoped that by the time you took over from me you would have lined up your own son or daughter to follow you.'

'I'm working on that, Father. Don't give up hope yet.'

They met for a very late breakfast in her hotel. She was looking relieved that the formalities of the previous day were over. And was there just a hint in her demeanour of relief too that Martin had returned home and she was alone with her thoughts?

'That was a splendid eulogy your father gave yesterday,' she said, buttering her toast. 'It was a positive account of her life delivered with some welcomed humour.'

'He put a lot of effort into that,' replied Edmund. 'My mother said she'd found him practising it in front of a mirror on several occasions. What did you think of "the family"?'

'Well,' started Kit, but then ran out of words.

The waiter was hovering by their table. He wanted to know if they would be long as the restaurant would soon be serving luncheon. If they could please finish their coffees in the lobby then he could get on with his work.

'And I must check-out,' said Kit, looking at her watch. 'It's almost noon. I've stayed the night free of charge due to the mix up with our luggage. I don't want to incur charges for overstaying my freebie.'

'But where are you going?'

'Back to London, of course. I should have gone back yesterday with Martin. I only stayed on to recover our luggage.'

'But how can you complete the task the deceased left you when you are in London and your joint-executor is up here? And I have news for you on that score which we need to discuss. Also, my father has a small trinket to hand over to you; left to you by Old Kit.'

'Where is your father?' she asked.

'I drove my parents back last night. Saw Thomas in the office early this morning and then drove back to Newcastle to see you now.'

'Oh. You have been busy.'

'Why don't you come up to Berwick and stay a few nights. We have a lot to chew over. And it requires attention sooner rather than later. You're in the university vacation so there should be some wriggle room to spend a few days up here. You could stay with me.'

'That would go down like a lead balloon with Martin,' replied Kit, shaking her head in disbelief at the suggestion.

'Okay, if that's not acceptable,' he said, 'then I could find you a suitable hotel for a few nights. And anyhow, monies are ring-fenced in the will to cover executor-expenses so you wouldn't be out of pocket.'

'Well, I suppose I could consider doing that but I haven't got much with me in the way of clothes.'

'Another visit to Carter & Roach maybe?' he said with a broadening grin and arched left eyebrow.

'Fine. Let's do it,' said Kit decisively, in the gung-ho manner in which her undergraduates often spoke. She couldn't tell him, but a few days in Berwick in the company of Mr. Newman Jr was a prospect that excited her.

'Let's get a move on then,' said Edmund, 'and as we drive north, I can explain why I am now your co-executor.'

The journey time was just under an hour as they sped north up the A1 at a steady seventy miles per hour in light traffic, deep in conversation. She had met as many distant relatives as she could the previous day, she told Edmund, and used the same system she used at university to grade her students. A simple conversion of the emoji pictographs of thumbs up and thumbs down pointing to different clock positions to show the level of "brilliant" or "useless" she considered the work submitted by each of her students to be. Of course, she told him, in regard to her relatives, it was "like" or "dislike". And the small circle she drew in red ballpoint on the ancestry tree next to each relative's name indicated her instantaneous dislike for many she had met, with just a few earning a promising like. A slash stroke bisecting the circle with a dot on one of its ends indicated whether the number should be counted clockwise or anticlockwise. What appeared as an unfavourable two clockwise was a far more promising four read from the other way around. Edmund had wondered how she had given zeros to Marion and her twin boys on whose table she had sat, and Kit had responded that no slash left the circle looking like a big zero.

Established once again in the bijou hotel on the high street, Kit's first port of call was the outdoor wear specialists just down the road from her lodgings. There she recognised the manager as a guest at her great grandaunt's memorial bash. Pleasantries exchanged, and in the knowledge that she didn't have to cover her hotel expenses, Kit chose with care a few items that were casual without being overwhelmingly outdoorsy. Smart casual was what she was after and following a quick change and a satisfactory reflection in the hotel mirror she was soon on her way to the offices of Newman, Wilson & Saddler where her appointment this time was with Edmund in his own office.'

'Nice top,' said Edmund approvingly as she strode into his room. 'You couldn't get one of those in London. Emily knows every item they've got on the shop floor and she's probably tried on every one of them in her size.'

'They've got good merchandise for this neck of the woods,' admitted Kit.

'Praise indeed for my wonderful county,' replied Edmund jokingly, 'and in the fullness of time, I hope to have the occasion to show you its jewels. But for now, it's down to business.'

Kit pulled her chair closer to his desk and adjusted her spectacles. There would have to be some plain speaking. Her teaching job came first and her executorship second. There was no leeway for negotiation. But she was forestalled by Edmund holding up his hands in mock surrender.

'I accept that you have an important full-time job to which you wish to give your more or less undivided attention. But as I explained to you on the drive back to Berwick, as your co-executor now, I'm in a position to take on the lion's share of the investigation. I've inhabited a very different working world to you. While you may not feel confident of how to go about the search for offshore accounts, I do. I know the ropes and if I get stuck, I know who to contact. We do all manner of litigation here: civil and criminal. And I know how to go about the dark art of probing.'

'I don't doubt that at all, Edmund,' replied Kit. 'But it is not just the treasure hunt that worries me, it is also the worry that if any money is found, I'm the person charged with its distribution. That would need the skills of an experienced social worker.'

'But you must have developed man management skills in your job. Surely more than you credit yourself with,' said Edmund. 'And your ability to assess personalities is probably just as sharp as that of any case worker.'

'Yes. But this scenario is very different.'

'It is only different in one respect,' retorted Edmund immediately. 'In your university work you assess your candidate and then award a mark whereas in our scenario you award them money. Both can be life changing.'

'And both can result in unhappy punters.'

'Vengeful even,' said Edmund thoughtfully. 'Every job has a down side. And then there would be the question of inheritance tax if we found some undeclared money.'

'That would be a further complication,' remarked Kit.

'Yes. But not insurmountable. The amount payable would be a tidy sum. Offshore funds usually come in millions, not in hundreds,' he added perceptively. Kit said nothing. Edmund seized the moment and summed up. Kit would base herself at home in Reading but travel up to Berwick as and when necessary and to fit in around her teaching work. He would attend to winding up Old Kit's estate and achieving probate. Meanwhile, Thomas, he told her, would be winding down his workload and taking retirement as soon as practicable. As a new partner, and by far the youngest, Edmund would be expected to increase his caseload. However, the practice would be taking on a work experience law graduate for a year who would be assigned to helping all three partners with some of their basic tasks.

'So,' pronounced Edmund, 'my future will be busy but I shall still have enough energy to contribute to our joint project.'

'Which is?'

'Working together to resolve the exciting challenge created for us by your distant relative. And I've already got some thoughts about getting to know the relatives. Getting passed the superficial acquaintance stuff and drilling down into their real persona.'

'Well, if we work together and make decisions together, then that would be helpful. But what about the copy of the will that Adam was intent on receiving?'

'That has been a sticky area morally,' confessed Edmund, 'but it is now resolved. I've had a full discussion with my father and I'm clear in my head that his unfaltering friendship with the deceased over many decades and what she has set out to achieve in this convoluted manner are legally sound. You see, the penultimate will and the actual last will, in legal terms, are so simple and basic, that there is nothing in either that could be challenged.'

'You haven't mentioned the codicil.'

'I haven't mentioned it for a reason,' said Edmund. 'It is not a will. It is not even a codicil to the last will and testament. It is simply a wrapper.'

'But your father called it a codicil,' Kit stated firmly. 'When he read it to me, he definitely called it a codicil.'

'A codicil is an official alteration to a will. It is not a will in itself. It is a way of changing a will without rewriting it. The statement Thomas read to you – the one in which the last will was enclosed – was simply another letter to you from Old Kit. It has no legal status. It was merely a further annotation of her thoughts.'

'What she thought, what she wanted me to do. So, anyone asking for a copy of the will,' continued Kit, 'will not be entitled to receive that information.'

'Exactly. That we know she has asked you to "distribute" any remaining funds after the death expenses have been paid amongst her great grandchildren on merit, will not be relayed to them. It will remain confidential known only to Thomas, Emily and us.'

'And Emily is trustworthy?'

'Absolutely. I'm not a betting man but if I was, I'd stake my life on it.'

Kit liked that. She wasn't a betting person either. The science never stacked up in the punters' favour. Mr. Newman Jr was becoming increasingly attractive. And it was becoming obvious that he had a genuine passion to fulfil a promise that she supposed was made by his father to his dear, late friend. Yes, passion. That was what Martin never appeared to have for anything. He was enthusiastic for his field hockey, that was true. He also loved his work, but for neither could his feelings be described as passionate. That was it, Kit thought suddenly. Something had clicked. The revelation that passion was the missing ingredient in their relationship. It came as a relief to know that there was a reason why she would never find lasting contentment with Martin. She must move on as surely as Martin should do the same.

'Are you alright?' asked Edmund looking at her with concern.

'Sorry. Someone just walked over my grave.' She paused and drew a deep breath. 'I'm okay now and I'm finally ready to co-operate fully in this quest.'

'I'm so glad,' said Edmund. 'We should start by looking at Reginald's tribe as that's the likely source of any major troublemaking. And I must give you this before I forget,' he continued, handing over a small, slim box. 'It's the trinket that Old Kit bequeathed to you.' Kit removed the lid to reveal an old fountain pen with a mulberry-coloured marble-effect casing showing wear and tear but with a nib in seemingly workable condition.

Chapter 3

REGINALD'S TRIBE

Kit had useful connections. The staff of the university IT department, when not teaching in the light and airy student laboratories, beavered away at their own research projects in the bowels of the noble, stone building near the Thames embankment. The staff there always knew when Kit was on her way; the clickety-clack of her stilettos on the stone floor sounding a warning of her impending arrival. This particular morning was quid pro quo time. As payback for her help in explaining the detailed physics of matrices – a government-funded project that the head of department together with two postgraduates in scientific apps for mobiles were working on – she was hoping for some help in converting the ancestry tree into a chart that could be viewed on her own mobile. There was a chorus of oohs and aahs when she described what she wanted. The head of department scratched his head and the epiglottis of one of the postgraduates rose and fell like a conductor's baton with his unsuppressed mirth. As nobody said a word, Kit reminded them in the nicest possible way that without her help with matrices, they wouldn't have had the knowledge to be able to manipulate their computer graphics of three-dimensional models and project them onto a two-dimensional screen. After a short period of reflection, she was invited to sit down and explain the sketches she had made.

The other postgrad – a hyper mature student who had put fifteen years running a chain of book shops behind her for more creative and satisfying work – was quick to suggest that the methodology of producing what Kit wanted could be copied from one of the many ancestry websites that had sprung up online in recent times. How they presented the skeleton of the chart would be a reliable starting point upon which they could append all the add-ons Kit required. With the warning that her mobile package would need a large data transfer allowance, Kit could store her data in the cloud and download it in measured chunks as she tapped on each relative's name to reveal their history. It was an ace idea according to Kit and with sincere thanks she left them to bring it live.

It was quiet at home in Reading without Martin, but she didn't miss him. Her mobile pinged most days with a text from him, but generally it was regarding an inconsequential matter. She wondered if he was feeling obliged to contact her, to pretend that they were still a pair even if his emotions told him otherwise. She reminded herself that the property was partly his. True, he hadn't contributed to the deposit, but he had paid half the monthly mortgage repayments and the lion's share of the utility bills. At some stage they would have to manoeuvre crab-like around the delicate task of division of the spoils. He would be a gentleman and she a lady and no acrimony would be involved.

Her thoughts switched back to the task in hand: getting the data Edmund had collected about the relatives onto the cyberspace cloud. It was a tedious business. Names, dates, spouses, addresses, post codes, education, debts, some medical history, benefit claims, employment history and criminal convictions. Edmund had dredged up an enormous amount of detail. It would have taken hours to enter the data for just a dozen or so relatives but for seventy-six it was proving a formidable task. As she typed in the information on her laptop, she was able to put a face to several of the names. Now the likes and dislikes ratings that she had diligently marked on her crumpled paper family tree could be added into each individual's computer folder under the heading "Opinions" to swell the information Edmund had collected which would sit under the heading "Known facts". Any reader would find the particulars she had entered for Marion and her twins, Kevin and Sean, depressing; their lives led apparently without any direction save that of maximising their benefits claim. Where, Kit wondered for the umpteenth time, were the genes for hard work, ambition and self-help that their deceased grandmother and great grandmother must have handed down, to be found? There must have been a smidgen of gene tissue that was transferred into one of them. Maybe there was a good reason for their collective attitude to life. She must look into it and she mustn't condemn the twins as hopeless cases.

When she had entered all the information she had onto the cloud – a Herculean task in its own right – and worked through a few gremlins in the app software with the postgrad, she left a message on Edmund's voicemail that she had completed the data transfer.

'Hi, Kit,' Edmund said cheerily an hour or so later. 'Glad you've got the data into the right pigeon holes. I guess we ought to consider it together and plan our next move. Can you come up for a couple of nights? You could stay with my parents if my spare bedroom is a step too compromising for you.'

'It would be more logical,' Kit replied calmly, having worked through in advance her reply to this inevitable question, 'if we were both under the same roof.'

'Exactly my thought,' replied Edmund, punching the air as silently as he could. 'I'll meet you at the station.'

Edmund's flat, as he referred to it, was far grander than the image in Kit's mind of a bachelor dwelling. On the outskirts of town, it enjoyed rural views across adjoining farmland while still retaining easy access to suburban living. However, it was as far removed from the metropolitan commuter belt Kit knew and rather liked, as was possible. In a pub nearby they got down to business. After lengthy discussion over a snack lunch, there was a meeting of minds that although the lives of Old Kit's twin sons, John and Bernard, undoubtedly merited probing, and the further exploring of the rape of her daughter Grace – when loading the family data onto her app, Kit had been struck by the number of twins in the wider family and wondered whether or not the original investigator employed by her great grandaunt had tried to trace the culprit via the special genetics of twins – was also worthy of more consideration, it was her late brother Reginald's branch of the family that should receive their close scrutiny first.

'But first, I do have something to tell you about Old Kit's fountain pen,' said Kit, sipping her tonic water.

'It's yours now.'

'I suppose so, but as I have never owned one or used one, it is hard to think of it as my own. They were not really my generation type of gadget.' Kit removed the pen from its slim box. 'But strangely, since receiving it,' she continued, 'I've noticed that several of my senior colleagues use fountain pens. They seem to almost make a ritual of filling the pen from an ink bottle. Whether it's to do with status I don't know, but I felt I ought to at least give mine a go.'

'I think Old Kit would be glad that you did.'

'Well, as I guessed the innards could do with a good clean, I looked on YouTube to find out what to do. Clean, tepid water was the answer. Several flushes through something called the converter and out through the nib should be sufficient to get rid of any dried, clogged up ink particles from yesteryear. So, I unscrewed the casing and removed the converter. According to the video instructions it is then a matter of gently squeezing the bladder inside the converter through a large gap in the converter wall. But when I did this, I could feel something stiff within the rubber. I didn't know whether it was just natural ageing of the rubber or whether there was actually something in the bladder. I inspected it under a magnifier at work. The bladder was loose and with a pair of forceps I was able to pull it out of its housing in the converter. I slit it lengthwise with a scalpel and this fell out,' she said, holding up a tight roll of discoloured paper about two centimetres long.

'You've unfurled it?'

'Yes.'

'What does it say?'

'See for yourself,' said Kit, handing the scrap of paper to Edmund.

'Guernsey 270038.'

'Is it a telephone number?'

'We can check. Or, maybe it's a bank account number. Guernsey is, after all, offshore.' He got out his mobile and started tapping. 'The area code for Guernsey is 1481,' he reported. 'If it is a telephone number then we might have expected her to write the number rather than the island name.'

'Not necessarily,' retorted Kit. 'This was all planned some years before her death. She might have been fearful that the code would be changed, and opted for the island name as a better alternative.'

'That's logical,' agreed Edmund, 'but somehow I don't think it's a telephone number, although I'll try.' He entered the number after the area code and waited. 'No normal ringing tone. Number unobtainable,' he said after a short wait.

'Seems you may be correct. But I suppose there are a plethora of banks in the Channel Islands offering clients these dubious accounts.'

'Without a doubt. We'll have to plan our approach carefully. Better sleep on it,' he said absentmindedly.

‘Oh,’ blurted Kit awkwardly, but made no further comment.

If Reginald had been alive, Edmund and Kit would have thought twice before approaching him, such was Reggie’s reputation for causing aggravation. That his quarrelsome nature left most outsiders feeling battered and bruised following even the briefest of encounters was one thing, but ultimately, it was the high level of excitable chemicals flowing through his blood vessels causing his aggressive behaviour during most of his waking hours that led to a massive coronary and death at the age of sixty-eight. He had never recovered any sense of proportion or poise after his sister and older sibling Kit, had been favoured with their father’s time and attention, unjustly so in Reggie’s narrow-minded opinion. That he made it almost to his eighth decade was, some muttered, a miracle such was the level of venom coursing through his being.

The only person truly comfortable with Reggie was his wife, Lilley Mary; their marriage over almost half a century proving surprisingly resilient. She was the only woman to gain his respect, possibly because she chose never to argue with him. She was his only oasis of calm and the only person with whom he could drop his guard and be himself, because inside, Reggie was a hurting soul. It was her deft handling of her husband without his awareness of any manipulation that sowed the seed of getting his own back on his sister by channelling their wherewithal into the education of the odious Henry, following the death of their first-born in bizarre circumstances on the day the nation celebrated the end of the second world war in Europe. Hit on the head when the drum major's flying mace was caught in a swirling wind, the seven-year-old sustained a fractured cranium and died shortly after of complications from the accident. For Reggie, it was history repeating itself with another hammer blow to the first-born male. But for Lilley's dogged temperament of que sera sera, Reggie might have cracked. She persuaded him that Henry was a far better prospect for achieving his revenge, quick-witted and cunning even at the age of six, Henry would develop into the epitome of selfishness. And when his brother Gilbert was born in 1946, the then seven-year-old Henry had someone on whom to practise the dark art of one-upmanship.

'Although Reginald had no police convictions, he was charged several times with incitement,' said Edmund, 'but all charges failed because he claimed that the incitement he caused, was not illegal. Incitement is only illegal if harm is intended, in which case it's called an "inchoate offence". Or used to be until recent changes were made to common law.'

'I was wondering about that,' replied Kit. 'I didn't really understand it in the stuff you sent me about him.' They were sitting at the wooden table in Edmund's galley kitchen. There was not much room to swing a cat but Kit imagined that it would be very cosy in the long, dark winter months. 'I didn't meet Gilbert at the memorial service,' she added, consulting her bespoke mobile app. 'What's he like?'

'Quiet. Still waters run deep,' said Edmund. 'It was state schooling for him whilst his elder brother enjoyed all the trappings of the private sector.'

'An unknown quantity then. Covering his true feelings.'

'Without a doubt,' responded Edmund, nodding. 'One to watch; might be harbouring a score to settle with his brother. He's sixty-six and worked his entire life as a clerical officer in the civil service until he retired recently.'

'Two sons and five grandchildren,' commented Kit, scrolling through his biopic on her mobile. 'Not much footprint to work on.'

'Unlike his inestimable brother,' declared Edmund, 'whose life we must micro-examine after a long walk and some more pub grub. Got your flat shoes?'

Kit had left her holdall in the bedroom. The room wasn't large but was tidy and perfectly adequate as second bedrooms go and someone had been to the trouble of putting some stylish bedding on its double bed. According to Edmund, the lady who did his cleaning had been sent out to purchase some bed linen in a woman's taste. Thoughts whirred in Kit's mind that there had been some serious pre-planning in her stay there, and the later discovery that there was only one bedroom – unsurprising since the apartment, or cottage, or maisonette, or whatever he wanted to call it – in the small dwelling reinforced her belief that there was no going back. As her last exchange of texts with Martin could best be described as cordial; two old chums touching base with one another without any particular reason and whose messages could have concluded with "kind regards", she felt no guilt whatsoever. No, there was no going back now, and anyhow, I'm thirty thought Kit. So, the natural progression, when it came later that evening, of being bodily lifted by Edmund and gently set down on the new Egyptian cotton bedding came as a welcomed finale to the day.

Somewhat disoriented on waking the following morning, but with the blurred recollection of a soft kiss on the cheek and some verbal information about a meeting place in town, before she drifted back to sleep, Kit found written instructions to meet Edmund at Harding's Designs in the high street at one o'clock sharp.

'You will marry me, won't you,' asked Edmund, before pushing open the door to the jeweller's shop. 'I'd look a complete fool trying to buy you an engagement ring if you turned me down.'

'You know I will,' she replied softly.

'It was meant to be,' Edmund said emphatically. 'As the Arabs would say, it is writ.'

* * *

Most noteworthy on cursory inspection, amongst Reginald's direct descendants were his second son and first-born grandson. That Henry and Adam respectively had the highest profiles and made the loudest noises may easily have masked to the casual observer the bright light of his daughter-in-law, Rose. Married to Gilbert, Reggie's youngest living child, she was the tribe's only intellectual rising through the state school system without the need of any extra-curricular coaching or the disappointment of failed examinations to study economics at a provincial university. A quiet, unassuming woman echoing the reserved manners of her parents, she rose steadily in the civil service to occupy a position of influence in the

Treasury. Recently retired after a working life interrupted by just two breaks of maternity leave, she decamped from the suburbs with Gilbert to the coast to enjoy an even quieter lifestyle leaving their daughter and son to pursue their own careers and make their own decisions.

Kit knew quite a lot about Henry from the potted history in her great grandaunt's introductory letter to the family. That there was unfair bias of opinion on both sides, was highly likely and despite Kit's intention to remain "neutral", she couldn't help taking an instant dislike to both Henry and Adam. She kept asking herself what they did for a living, what contribution they made to society, what piece of concrete achievement she could point to, and always came up with the same answer. Nothing.

Following Henry's demand, a copy of the final will had been sent to each descendant, direct or indirect, Edmund had told her, and they could now expect their nit-picking to commence.

Another layer of sophistication had been added at grandson level. From the blunt, rough and ready father Reginald, to the privately educated but supercilious Henry, a veneer of the manners of old-world money was now part of Adam's identity.

'The will is simple, Dad,' he said, after reading his father's copy. 'I received one myself so I guess a copy has been posted to every descendant.'

'Too simple by far for that cunning woman,' Henry replied, his upper lid curling upwards unattractively. 'There's some dirt to dig up, of that, I'm sure. I don't believe in her Wonder Woman image.'

'Money?'

'Stashed away in some tax-free haven. She was never the type to give away all her worldly goods long before her death. Secretive bitch,' he added with feeling. 'Clever, mind you.'

'Well, whatever is hidden away, if anything, will now go to Georgina Kit Irwin,' Adam declared. 'No one else gets a mention, not even her grandchildren and great grandchildren.'

'Then there's no time to waste. We must start poking into her affairs,' said his father. 'Reggie would have said "another fat cow to disembowel".' They laughed. Grandfather Reggie had always been direct.

'Turks and Caicos? Or, Andorra, or the Channel Islands? Or, backstop, Switzerland?'

'Any of those,' replied Henry. 'Union people usually favour the Channel Islands. So, Jersey and Guernsey should be our starting points. I'll start with a few general enquiries through my contacts there.'

'The search for secret accounts is our only viable avenue for success,' Adam said, summing up their position. 'We'd get laughed out of court if we contested the will and claimed someone else was more entitled to the inheritance. After all, one hundred percent of nothing is nothing.'

'If there is anything to find, we'll find it,' replied his father firmly. 'I haven't spent a lifetime cosseting acquaintances without purpose. I've done them favours over the years. Now they can repay me.'

Grandson Adam's background had gravitated from the coal pits of his grandfather's Northumbria, via the style of gentleman country farmer in the semi-rural living of his father's home county of Berkshire, to the gentrified area of Angel, Islington on the fringes of north London. A self-styled adviser to the arts and sports sectors, in addition to his main occupation as a twice re-elected member of parliament for a safe seat in the metropolis, he and his nuclear family of wife and two daughters, had moved with propitious timing into a street of solid, well-proportioned Georgian terrace houses with period features and black iron railings and whose residents were drawn from the intelligentsia. With next door neighbours in the film industry and an owner of a premiership rugby club two doors away, his place in society as an upstanding, staunch mid-forties good egg was cemented. He was a man who seemed to have everything. Unfortunately, one of the things he had was a gambling habit. Thus far he had kept it in check, and the other, a tiny brown mole peeking through a displaced lock of hair near his right ear. While the former, mounting debts from poker playing sessions in a private room of a discreet casino within walking distance of the Palace of Westminster were, he told himself in a version of self-denial, completely under his control and as it pleased him to restrict, the latter was neither obvious from the mirror nor painful in an alerting way, and was only discernible to his barber.

Henry's general enquiries produced some promising results which he was quick to share with Adam and would have been even quicker to relate had he known about his son's gambling debt.

'It transpires,' said Henry into the mouthpiece of the landline phone – a precaution they always took when discussing sensitive matters – that a bank in St. Peter Port might have some really interesting information relating to confidential accounts they administer.'

'Go on.'

'The initial enquiries were just that. Initial,' continued Henry. 'To initiate in-depth enquiries would require a percentage of payment up front.'

'Any amount mentioned?'

'Not so far.'

'Can you trust your source?'

'Absolutely. Not because the man in question is a saint. Just because he owes me. And even then, he doesn't come completely free of charge.'

'Before any sort of payment, I think we should try to establish that the info on offer relates to the person we are researching.'

'I do agree,' replied Henry, in his oily voice. 'I'll set in motion some more precise follow up questions.'

'Can you come to Arsenal's first home game of the new season next Saturday? I've got some freebie tickets. We could discuss our options then if your man comes up with more info,' Adam asked. He hoped his father could. He was very attached to him.

'Good idea. We will be able to chat as much as we wish whilst you are showing the flag to your local constituents and seen to be keeping au fait with sporting affairs.'

* * *

The facilities at Bisham Abbey, the seat of the England Women's Hockey Association, were first class. Indeed, the complex was considered one of the best in the world for field hockey. Clare Roach had been angling for some time to get an invitation to join one of the training squads. Such an invitation, while not guaranteeing or even suggesting the likelihood of a formal contract, gave the invitee a taste of elite sport and the opportunity to showcase their skills.

In addition to her own efforts, strings had been pulled by her father to secure a place on the weekend training course for young players showing exceptional promise in the women's premier division. At twenty-three, Clare was neither young in the sense that the governing body was looking for seventeen and eighteen-year-olds whose raw skills could be refined to turn them into elite athletes, nor could she command a regular place in the women's premier division, usually a pre-requisite for receiving an invite. Her appearances were mainly in the women's conferences, southern division, one step down from the premier games although on occasions when injuries intervened, she had had the chance to represent her club in the higher echelon. It would be another little something to add to her curriculum vitae and the astute Clare wasn't going to miss that opportunity. Moreover, Clare's inherited aptitude and flair for logging in her brain any detail that she might conceivably find useful in a subsequent circumstance, told her that there would be all manner of acquaintances to make hobnobbing worthwhile with both management and elite players. Like her grandfather Henry, she was an exponent of name dropping and unapologetic of its use.

After the welcoming brunch, the main Saturday session of assessment of physical fitness and skills testing began. Clare was fit and skilful and in most other surroundings would have fared well, but judged against the class of player who received their invitation on merit alone, she was found wanting. It was not until the last period of the afternoon – short ten-minute bursts of team play with everyone given the opportunity to race up and down the pitch to show off their wares – that Clare's mental composure and experience weighed in with some telling passes and deft switching of play across the pitch to unsettle her opponents. Not unhappy with her overall performance and sufficiently realistic to appreciate that further invitations would not come her way, she set about rubbing shoulders with as many influential people as possible.

The evening get-together, casual as planned, with food and drink befitting older teenagers, rewarded those who stuck around with a glass of white wine and an adult conversation. Whilst the youngsters drifted off to their bedrooms for some serious mobile phone usage or into games rooms for ping pong and table football, Clare carefully cultivated the organisers. She was a good talker and in the right situation, a good listener too and knew how to work an audience without being perceived as ingratiating. Discussion and general chitchat covered all manner of topics and when someone mentioned moving upstairs to the bar for some decent wine, Clare was included. It was here that she started spreading her own brand of charisma amongst the association's top people. She would leave them not only with an impression of allure and guile, but with the knowledge that her father chaired the main parliamentary committee responsible for sport. And with the Olympic Games due to be hosted in London in two years' time, Clare would not easily be forgotten.

Indeed, the following morning, after some exhaustive physical training routines, goal shooting and five-aside plays, Clare found herself, if not the centre of attention, then certainly as a person of note. She was introduced to various other personnel who were attending on the Sunday only, including an executive officer of the men's governing body. He was a tall, lanky man who played in the first team for Reading, a hockey club with a long history of producing fine players. He said that he was working mostly abroad currently, but as he lived relatively nearby, had found time to come to Bisham this particular morning to support the women's game. As he seemed an affable fellow and wasn't wearing a wedding ring, Clare made a play for him and was rewarded with a dinner date in London.

Over dinner a few days later in a stylish trattoria in The City, Clare admitted to Martin that she had not been surprised to learn on leaving Bisham that she was not quite at the level they required for consideration at international representation.

'You looked pretty effective on the pitch to me,' said Martin gallantly, 'but they have to take age into account too and are only really interested in teenagers.'

'Over the hill at twenty-three,' Clare replied coquettishly. 'Who would have guessed it?'

'A nicely youthful twenty-three,' added Martin, again gallantly, 'if I may be so bold as to say so. When is your next birthday?'

'Next month.'

'Ah. Then you will become twenty-four whilst I am still thirty.'

'Is that important?'

'Yes. I won't need to feel like a dinosaur at only six years older when I mention the type of music I like,' he said, his big feet tapping out some unknown rhythm on the floor.

There had been some simple starter questions to break the ice, but Clare's next question led to a more profound subject. 'Like dancing, do you?' she enquired with amusement, gazing at the brown shoes and black socks jigging about under the table.

'So-so,' Martin replied, holding up a wagging hand. 'It's really my partner who .....,' he trailed off, leaving Clare to finish the sentence. 'Your partner who enjoys dancing.'

'It was my *former* partner who enjoyed dancing,' corrected Martin, regaining his aplomb. 'We split recently.' Clare said nothing in reply but looked at him steadfastly until he added, 'we were together for a long time and old habits die hard.'

'And now you're at a loose end.'

'No. Now I'm back in circulation and enjoying your company,' he said somewhat defiantly. It was hockey talk after that: what role he played on the board of the men's governing body, how much he had enjoyed his three appearances in an England shirt in minor internationals, his favourite position on the pitch at right inner, her hockey escapades with her twin sister and revelations about the power her father wielded in the political sporting arena.

'What do you do, Clare?' he asked over coffee once the table had been cleared.

'I work for my father as his private secretary.'

'Is that the term PPS?'

'No. Ministers have Parliamentary Private Secretaries and are MPs themselves. Dad's not a minister. He's an influential backbencher who chairs one of the select committees.'

'I guess it's a job that keeps you on your toes.'

'No room for mistakes,' agreed Clare, 'and when parliament is in session, I'm super busy.'

'But as you're only twenty-three going on twenty-four, you can't have been doing it for long.'

'I finished at Cambridge in June just over a year ago and went to work in my father's constituency the following morning.'

'No gap year?'

'No. Unlike my twin sister who swanned off to Brazil for six months to do something "educational" for the folk living along the banks of the Amazon, I got stuck into politics in double quick time. But that suited me as I read politics, psychology and economics at university.'

'I love my job too,' said Martin, 'it must be depressing to go to work every day in a dead-end job or one that gives you no satisfaction.'

'What do you do exactly?' asked Clare, pumping Martin without him realising it.

'I'm in pharmaceuticals. I'm attached to a government laboratory. We're exploring new remedies for tropical water-borne disease. I'm actually on a six-month secondment in Vienna working with European colleagues to get a new preparation through its final trials. It's exciting as the existing medicine is fast losing its efficacy.'

'Yes, I can understand that. And Vienna. What a great place for a secondment.'

'Have you been there?'

'Not to Vienna itself, but to Austria for skiing.'

'Then you must let me show you the sights, if you can wangle a long weekend away.'

'If that's possible,' replied Clare, knowing full well that she would make it possible, but using the politician's age-old trick of not committing herself. There was an exchange of mobile numbers and private email addresses plus a full-on kiss before she stepped into the taxi and was gone.

Martin took the tube to St. Pancreas and ran across the concourse to catch the last fast train of the day to Reading. With a journey time of forty minutes, he should have had adequate thinking time to decide how to handle the situation at home. Kit was there, and it was her home as much as it was his. She was now engaged to the bloke in Berwick and Martin had no desire to hang around as a cuckold. Whilst on secondment he could delay renting a flat near his work. Unless there were definite reasons for returning to England, he could while away his time in Vienna quite easily. There would be an honourable sharing of the house proceeds if they chose to sell, which he presumed they would. Of that he was certain. The real problem was the same one as usual. The same one that had stopped him proposing to Kit on countless occasions and discussing babies and families and the like. All due to the timeworn problem of his family's ignominious background that he dared not tell her about.

As the train pulled into Reading station, suddenly overcome, he cupped his face in his hands while a flow of tears cascaded down his cheeks just as if a light switch had been turned from off to on. He hadn't cried uncontrollably since childhood, in fact he couldn't remember the last time he had shed tears, but he was now going "home" to a house which was no longer his home and in which the woman he loved was engaged to another man.

The train terminated at Reading. He was still sitting in his seat oblivious to his surroundings and but for the guard walking through the train to inspect each carriage, he would have still been riveted to his seat as the train shunted into the sidings. 'Saved you having to find an excuse to tell the missus why you were out all night,' said the guard cheerily with a wink, but his remark fell flat on deaf ears.

His watch showed eleven-forty-five and his plane departed in the morning at seven-thirty. He would sit on the sofa bed in the living room sorting out his most essential belongings and take as much with him as possible. He would not be returning to their erstwhile home. The pit in his stomach would ease with time and he would make new friendships to replace old. He had already greased the wheels with his evening out with Clare. She wasn't really his type, but needs must. He had to look forward not back, and he would try to get some sleep on the plane so that he was fit for work when he arrived in Vienna.

It was not only Martin who felt dispirited that night, Kit too was in melancholic mood. Martin had announced his departure for good the previous day. They had agreed to wait a couple of months before deciding on what to do with the house; they would share the bills until then. Kit pulled at one of her curls absentmindedly while wondering how it had all come to this. It was a bittersweet moment. Her happiness at being engaged to Edmund was tinged with nostalgia for the many happy years spent with Martin. Tomorrow she would feel like a bad landlord turfing out a decent tenant with no good reason other than increased profit. She sighed. It was the end of an era.

Ostensibly, Clare shared few traits with her twin sister, Avril, except their hair colour. They were both full-on redheads. However, where Clare was of average height, Avril grew to be three inches taller and had a far more powerful and rangy physique. When dressed up in her goalkeeper's safety clobber, she cut a formidable presence guarding the first-team goal. Her sporting ability was actually well beyond that of Clare's but unlike her sister, she didn't hanker after international recognition for the sake of impressing others. She played hard to win just like her sibling, but found more reward by regarding Saturday and Sunday afternoons as an enjoyable package of physical exertion and social interaction with her teammates.

And there were real, hidden differences between the twins. Notwithstanding their mental sharpness and cunning natures, Avril was less concerned about image than Clare. Image was everything for Clare whereas Avril's attitude was more rounded. It explained in large part why Clare was daddy's girl and why Avril was more in tune with her grandfather, Henry. Henry was first generation white-collar worker but when the mask or the accent slipped from time to time as it inevitably did, it revealed his working-class origins. Avril preferred this small slice of honesty to her father's unremitting pretension to be from "old money".

She had moved out of the imposing house in Islington a year ago to join as an internee a local radio station serving the East Midlands. After successful completion of the period, she was taken on as a trainee announcer where her computer knowhow and dogged persistence flourished. Mixing with workmates and the general public from all walks of life quickly broadened her horizons and sharpened her interpersonal skills. She was seldom short of a local story of interest such were her guileful ways and within months she was filling in for main presenters during holiday times. A permanent "spot" became available on the mid-afternoon show as a new feature to boost listening numbers was introduced. Avril persuaded her boss that she could develop the niche into a short questions and answers sessions on the subject of today's tech aimed at the older generation who still did not feel sufficiently competent to embrace the internet. She would act as their computer guru and run through their queries slowly and in an as simplified manner as possible. Under the patronage of her boss, the computer guru spot became a hit.

The fire in Avril's belly had been fuelled for some time by an increasing dislike of her twin's lack of principles. To her, Clare seemed shallow and superficial and without any core values. Plastic. Fake. That's how she summed up her sister. And always on the make for something better. It had been the final, tiny trigger movement to spur Avril to leave the family home as soon as she had been granted paid employment by the broadcaster. No more snide remarks to endure about Avril's lack of boyfriends, or the flat shoes she wore, or suffer Clare's general imperiousness. Avril would make a name for herself in the media, and by her own devices, would outshine her older twin. She knew she'd never grow rich in radio – only the top presenters earned high salaries even in television – but whereas Clare scowled at the memorial service when she opened the envelope and found a five-pound voucher for a premium bond, Avril had laughed out loud at the humour of the situation and been impressed at just how her late great relative was still manipulating the emotions of so many of her descendants from the graveyard.

The round trip from Peterborough, where she now lived, to Newcastle for the memorial service was just over four hundred miles. She had only met Old Kit at the legendary get-togethers she funded periodically and even then, the age disparity acted as a natural barrier to anything verging on a close relationship. But as one of life's loners, and that's what Avril guessed she was, she had enjoyed touching base with relatives, distant or otherwise, thus reinforcing the knowledge that she was still part of a human tribe. And for her first clan meeting as an adult at age twenty-three, it proved a fascinating experience.

Way over the legal alcohol limit when she drove herself home at a speed not too sedate nor too fast to arouse the suspicions of the traffic police – she didn't wish to become a news item on her own radio station – she chuckled to herself at the scope of first cousins twice removed to which she belonged. The range in age was small, maybe fifteen years at the most, but the span of personalities was immense. She didn't have a family tree but she was struck by the number of twins present. And the Queen Bee, the one chosen to be an executor, was a twin herself it transpired. Perhaps the subject could form the basis, she pondered, of another guru spot on a morning broadcast: asking her listeners how many twins were in their genealogy chart. It could enthuse her listeners, both young and old, to phone in with histories about their own pairs, and fact, Avril was beginning to learn, was so often stranger than fiction. Fraternal twins. Yes, it was a subject worthy of investigation and although the Queen Bee was part of a pair, Avril seemed to recall that there had been, a long time ago, some drama surrounding her parents. Her short chat with Kit as Clare and Avril exited the cathedral at the memorial service had been, understandably, stilted. Avril's impression of Kit was of a generally calm and serious person who felt uncomfortable in the limelight of that particular day. They had exchanged the usual platitudes but gone no further. As the sisters made their way across to the refreshment marquee, Avril relived Clare's gratuitous swipe at both her and Kit. It was something about the bespectacled Queen Bee, Clare's choice of words, an older woman– although by only seven years – at least managing to wear high heels. It was a damning remark so very typical of her sister.

At the offices of Newman, Wilson and Saddler, an electronic request popped up on Emily's monitor requesting a list of Old Kit's great grandchildren and great grandnieces and nephews. It was from one of them, namely, Avril Roach. After consulting with Edmund, Emily duly replied. To have declined the request might have appeared surly and thus they decided to send a copy of the ancestry tree as it provided full names and dates of birth and would, they hoped, obviate the need for any further correspondence. Avril Roach would then be in a position, Edmund had declared, to follow up on any of her family members under her own steam. Emily had pursed her lips and when Edmund had enquired why, she had reminded him that Avril was one of Reggie's tribe.

Avril printed off the family tree attachment in the office she shared with all the other junior staff: two of them. The radio station served the easternmost fringes of The Midlands together with parts of Lincolnshire, Leicestershire and the northernmost tip of Bedfordshire, with a mixture of talk shows, news and light music. Avril sat back for a few moments marvelling at the level of detail recorded on the tree and mentally assessing the length of time it must have taken to assemble it. With her highlighter pen she was soon daubing the chart with yellow bands across the names of siblings with the same date of birth. Eight sets. Three sets of twins amongst Old Kit's direct descendants alone. Surely that would be statistically significant, thought Avril. Counting the offspring from the chart generated by Old Kit's parents until the present day, out of a grand total of seventy-seven blood relatives, sixteen were twins. Just over twenty percent. Avril made a mental note to contact a statistics boffin to discuss the theory of probability and she knew just the person. Aunt Annie.

Aunt Annie had a blemish-free record with the law until she and husband Hugh moved to the north-east and got entangled with a small-time drug dealer. Reared in rural Berkshire with her brother Adam, she had been endowed with all the benefits that their father Henry could wangle out of his high position in the union and the acquaintances he had made during his period in the House of Commons. Educated privately, she had been a star pupil with an IQ that permitted membership to Mensa. Henry's plan for his daughter – he was not a misogynist unlike many of his union comrades – was to pay for an education equal to that of his only son Adam and direct her along the path to becoming an actuary in the insurance world as her forte was all matters mathematical. It was a top-rated profession with real status and Henry, as ever, loved status.

But Aunt Annie got bored and on a weekend trip home – despite a mega salary she had chosen to live in a small, modest flat in Hornchurch on the fringes of the East End and journey into her office by tube – to her childhood home in rural Berkshire, she told Henry that she was going to chuck in her job. Henry was furious. It wasn't so much about the money he had poured into her education with the promise of some future payback, although that in itself was infuriating, it was about his loss of bragging rights. My daughter, the *former* actuary, had little or no boasting value. When he inquired in a caustic tongue what she intended to do instead and learned that Annie's idea was to live on a small holding deep in the countryside somewhere and be self-sufficient with various farmyard animals, he almost blew his top. He was incandescent for several hours. When she approached him later, he agreed, as his last and final monetary gift, to partially fund the purchase of a small holding in Glamorganshire. She was a plain girl in many ways with no desire for the fripperies of life and had saved most of her salary during the short time she was earning top dollar. She would, she assured her father, live off the land with the animals she would be able to purchase with her savings. Her preference for a back-to-nature existence living in a small, near derelict cottage miles from a town and with few neighbours was beyond Henry's understanding. But she was plain and she was dowdy and it was only her brilliant brain that Henry really valued.

Annie embraced the new lifestyle fully. All outdoor shoes deemed superfluous to needs were discarded in favour of two pairs of Wellington boots: one pair of ankle height, the other up to her knees with a deep tread and a little tab to adjust for a snug fit around the calf. She bought chickens and pigs and some DIY tools and materials and set about constructing a chicken run safe from foxes. She produced a blueprint for a pigsty based on an A-frame and recycled bits of timber and metal that she found on her land or had been discarded in skips or dumped on verges along the windy lanes in her vicinity.

From time to time she made contact with her neighbours, either a chat across a boundary wire fence or when she had to collect one of her animals that had gone walkabout across one of their fields, but her only regular visitor was the postie, a local man named Hugh. He would drive his Royal Mail van as fast as he could up her muddy access road and do a handbrake turn in front of her sitting room window leaving the flying mud to harden and dry on the window panes unless Annie remembered to wipe them in time. About the same age, they would regularly pass the time of day. He was thin and scrawny with hollow cheeks and passed on gossip about her neighbours but was well versed in the care of animals, seemed to know all about the cultivation of potatoes, and showed her how to set up her runner bean supports with coppiced poles. It was not long before he was going into the cottage for a cup of tea and a biscuit and as one thing led to another, she was soon in the position of having to break the news to Hugh and her father that she was pregnant. Hugh grinned inanely with delight but for Henry it was the last straw. She wasn't on the telephone and broadband had not yet penetrated to her locale, thus the news about his forthcoming grandchild arrived by post. Disgusted, he tore up the letter and chucked it into his wood burner without a further thought.

Until the arrival of their second child, another boy, twelve months after the first, they led a Bohemian life free of conventional rules and practices and without care for personal appearance or the opinion of others. Apart from Hugh's modest postman salary, they lived in voluntary poverty and embraced frugality. They were happy in their own way and might have continued their life of simple living had not a busybody from the child welfare section of the local authority intervened. Doubts were cast on their ability to provide their offspring with the safe and secure environment demanded by law. This situation was exacerbated when Hugh was made redundant due to changed procedures at the Royal Mail. Annie knew better than to turn to her father or brother for assistance. With a heavy heart, she contemplated the prospect of a return to work in the insurance industry. But fate intervened in the form of an article in The Sunday Times – their sole weekly luxury as Annie's intellect thrived on the broadsheet page full of mathematical and cryptic puzzles – outlining the shortages of bus drivers in rural settings. From a pub telephone, Annie obtained further information by contacting a number printed in the article and a week later they read in the literature they received back, contact numbers of bus companies in desperate need of drivers. Umbrian, a bus company providing regional services as far north as Berwick-upon-Tweed, west as far as Carlisle in Cumbria and south as far as Scarborough in North Yorkshire were short of long-distance drivers. Another trip to the pub telephone elicited the information that a standard driving licence without any penalty points or convictions was all that was required as all successful applicants would attend a course to earn their Drivers Certificate of Professional Confidence including hours spent out on the road under the tutelage of a qualified instructor.

Annie had never lived north of the Thames although she had been almost within sight of its northern bank during her upbringing in Berkshire. However, she had made the journey up to Northumbria with her parents and brother on at least a couple of occasions for Old Kit's not-to-be-missed jamborees. She remembered the countryside as rugged and wild. It appealed to her and with Hugh's agreement they set in motion the family's relocation to the north-east. Based in Newcastle, Annie and Hugh would join the bus company as long-distance drivers when qualified. They would criss-cross the moors and national parks, skirt around the fells and hill ranges, to serve the communities in the small towns and villages spreadeagled over the vast area between the North Sea and the North Atlantic. Bus travel in these parts was popular and in great demand from residents and visitors alike. The extensive network of local and long-distance routes was practically self-funding without subsidy from the local authority. It was a system still operating with the sort of passenger numbers redolent of the omnibus' heyday in the early twentieth century before the widespread use of private vehicles. Bus drivers were addressed by their first name and passengers greeted with friendly asides. Annie and Hugh loved it.

They job shared for the first year while sorting out childcare, working one week on and one week off. From rented accommodation in Newcastle, they found an affordable low-cost home in a hamlet beyond the city suburbs served by one of their own bus routes. Hugh did some overnight stops in Scarborough while Annie regularly drove the day round-trip from Newcastle to Carlisle. Money was tight but they seemed content. Nevertheless, the search for spare cash was a constant concern. Annie turned her enjoyment of the puzzle page in their Sunday paper into the more serious business of winning prizes. And once she disciplined herself to submit the answers on time and in the format dictated, she was soon winning prizes: vouchers, reference books, writing equipment and most valuable of all, cheques. It became her cottage industry and her passion. Hugh too, stepped up to the mark to further augment their finances, but unfortunately his route to earning more cash had unwelcome consequences.

In a pub in Scarborough, overnighting on one of his long trips from base, he got talking, unwittingly, to a small-time crook. Asked about his job, Hugh was happy to divulge what he did, where he went and when he went there. Following his rota, Hugh was back in the same pub a fortnight later where the small-time crook sought him out with a proposition. Was he interested in making a few bob on the side? Yes, of course he was. Could he deliver once a month a few small packets on his bus runs out into the countryside? Yes, of course he could, provided that they were on his route. And could he do it discreetly? Hugh tapped the side of his nose in reply because he'd seen it done on the television. They agreed to meet two weeks later when Hugh was next back in Scarborough.

'See,' said the small-time crook, a hapless bloke not much older than Hugh, 'the job is part of a click-and-collect purchase by customers on the internet. Only they don't have much in the way of useful internet in those villages on your bus route. Very dodgy connections most of the time. That's where I come in.'

'How?' asked Hugh enthusiastically and without a trace of disbelief.

'My clients have regular orders,' he stated. 'I do their ordering on my laptop. See?' Hugh nodded but didn't "see". 'I collect their orders,' he continued, 'but need a reliable person to distribute them.'

'Why don't you give their delivery addresses on the order?' asked Hugh sensibly, 'then the purchase would be sent to them automatically.'

'Ah,' replied the small-time crook, 'some of them don't want the packets to arrive in the post. Don't want the missus to find out. That sort of thing. Like to do it all private like.'

'Like sex toys?' asked the innocent Hugh.

'Yeah. A bit like that. See, I put what they've ordered in a plain brown envelope and they go and collect it when it suits them at the village shop.'

'Or a spicy magazine,' Hugh suggested, his mind still working on what one partner wished the other partner not to know.

'Yeah. Right. All manner of things, I imagine, but I don't know what they are. I just put each internet purchase in a simple wrapper and write the drop off point on it. It's simple. You can't go wrong.'

'And what's in it for me?'

'Every month you do your run here at least once. Correct?' Hugh nodded. 'I give you the packages for delivery and on your return journey to Newcastle you drop them off. Yes?' Hugh nodded again. 'For every successful "run" you get some cash in hand the following month.'

'Payment in arrears.'

'Yes, spot on.'

'And what exactly do I get? Spell it out,' said Hugh, biting his upper lip.

'You get a nice crisp fiver for every delivery you make provided that you do every one on the list that I give you. Miss one out and you get nowt. Do I make myself clear?' demanded the small-time crook.

'Yep. But how many deliveries would I make on each return journey?' asked Hugh, very reasonably.

'Usually, fifteen. So, that makes seventy-five pounds once a month. Easy money.' But Hugh didn't look too sure. His bus had to keep to a fairly tight schedule. There would be hell to pay, he knew, from the passengers and company alike if he started arriving late at each bus stop. 'Trying to think of good excuses to go into the village shop?' asked the small-time crook, reading Hugh's mind. 'Toilet is the obvious one. But you won't be able to use that excuse fifteen times,' he added with a snarly laugh. Hugh still didn't look convinced; he was unworldly but not simple. 'Tell you what,' continued his prospective employer, 'I'll make it a hundred. Can't say fairer than that.' And the deal was clinched. On his return journey, Hugh drove speedily along certain stretches to discover where he could gain a little time and noted the position of each village shop vis-a-vis to how far away it was from the bus stop.

Hugh was well aware that several of his colleagues pulled fast ones with company rules and regulations; some even bragging about how much they made on the side. Still, linking up with this bloke in Scarborough would be a step into something he didn't fully understand. He didn't want to lose his job because he loved it. Out on the open road every workday with the wonderful views. Nobody to boss him about. Getting to know the first names of his regular passengers and the cheery waves goodbye when they got off at their stops and he drove off. It wasn't a job to jeopardise. But it didn't pay well and they needed the money to look after their growing family.

Four weeks later, the small-time crook handed him a crumpled supermarket carrier containing the purportedly internet purchases. Fifteen brown envelopes, some square, others rectangular, and one or two padded, but all small. In his overnight accommodation, Hugh sorted them into route sequence. Each envelope bore the name of the village and the recipient's initials. All Hugh had to do was to hand each one to the shop assistant. Nothing more. What happened after that was none of this business, although he gathered that purchasers went into the shop to collect their individual packages on payment of five pounds to the shop as a sort of delivery charge. It would have been a winning formula had the contents of each packet been a real internet purchase, but unfortunately for Hugh, each envelope contained the wrong type of recreational substance. Marijuana.

The system worked perfectly for a few months; Hugh's driving prowess getting him to all the bus stops as per the timetable yet affording a few minutes at the relevant village shops to make his deliveries. Annie never questioned the five twenty-pound notes that he was able to toss into the piggy bank every month. It represented the allowance the company paid to crew doing overnight circuits for accommodation and meals. Hugh told her that he dossed down in the flat of a friend of a mate instead of staying at an hotel. He didn't pay a bean to the friend of his mate but in lieu of payment Hugh arranged for some "free" travel on the bus. It was a method of payment for dodgy services rendered that was endemic amongst the bus crews and of which Annie was well aware. It wasn't until a particular passenger got off at the same stop as Hugh and followed him innocently into the village shop that the days of the nice little earner became numbered.

Whilst waiting to be served, the passenger observed the handing over of a brown envelope to the shop assistant. The passenger, a former policeman in South Yorkshire, now retired and living in a pretty cottage in the village with his wife and two, slightly older maiden sisters, learned from the short conversation between them, that the bus driver's name was Hugh and that the shop assistant would see him again next month. It sparked an interest as the retired copper was now a peripatetic agent of the bus company – a job he took on to get away from his three women at home – to ensure that standards were kept high and corruption low. One month later, he arranged to be in the shop when the same driver was completing his homeward run to base and noted another envelope being passed across the counter to the assistant. The ex-copper hung around and from just outside the shop's entrance door, he heard most of the assistant's telephone call to someone he assumed was the rightful recipient. Shoppers came and went in a slow but steady stream. Eventually an exchange of envelope and banknote took place and the ex-copper, ready with a plan, managed to bump into the departing middle-aged woman outside the shop loosening her grip on the envelope so that it fell to the ground. He was quick to pick it up and return it to her with a fulsome apology for his clumsiness. The apparently innocuous stumble allowed the bus agent to clearly see two initials written on the envelope and to feel its contents with his fingertips. Something soft and powdery he believed, and something of a contraband nature he felt sure. Following up, as was his habit after so many years in law enforcement, incriminating evidence was collected in the shape of photographs and the reaction of a sniffer dog which made prosecution inevitable.

The drivers' union representative arranged a solicitor to support Hugh but Annie was unimpressed by his competence and attitude. Invitations to Old Kit's gatherings always arrived via a legal practice in Berwick and it was to Newman, Wilson and Saddler that she turned for the proper defence of her husband. There were mitigating circumstances and one way or another she would ensure that they were taken into account. It was 1995 and Mr. Thomas Newman took charge of the case aided and abetted by his young law student son, Edmund, whenever he was on one of his interminable university vacations. Thomas knew that Annie was one of Old Kit's relatives and supposed that she had contacted him because of the family link. He vacillated over whether or not to tell her immediately, but as she was one of Reggie's tribe, decided against doing so until an opportune moment arrived as he doubted that Old Kit would have paid for the legal services that Hugh required such was the enduring enmity between her and her late brother. But Annie wouldn't have accepted a handout anyhow. After having been cut off by her father and brother, she had sworn never to ask for financial help from anyone. She agreed fees with Mr. Newman and they would take out a loan, if necessary, to square the bill. In due course, Hugh was charged in the County Court with distributing illegal substances. He had originally wanted to plead guilty to the distribution and not guilty to the illegal substances but agreed to plead guilty to the entire charge when Mr. Newman advised him that ignorance of the facts was no defence in a court of law. Extenuating factors – the judge genuinely believed that Hugh had no idea what it was that he was distributing – and no previous convictions or recorded involvement with drugs resulted in a community service order of sixty hours. And it was Edmund who came to Hugh's rescue by cheekily suggesting to his employer that they would be far better served by treating Hugh's misdemeanour not by sacking but by making an example of him to his colleagues. He would be clocking up three hours every Sunday for the next twenty weeks picking up rubbish strewn on verges of arterial roads in the Newcastle neighbourhood as his court sentence. On his other day off, Edmund suggested to the bus company's regional manager that as Hugh had been a heretofore good employee and the company was always struggling to recruit and retain sufficient drivers, Hugh should be asked to mirror his time working off his community order by giving him some menial job to do such as sweeping the floors of the bus terminus building. The idea was not dismissed out of hand, indeed it found favour with Human Resources who were relieved not to be losing a competent driver over an issue that had caused no real harm to the company itself. When they offered Hugh the choice of the sack or repainting the iron railings surrounding the terminus, Hugh accepted the painting job without equivocation.

Edmund's solution came as a relief to Annie. She was the mainstay of their family unit but she couldn't have managed without Hugh's contribution. He was a devoted father and friendly husband if a somewhat gullible adult. However, it was a seminal moment for Annie. A realisation that the success or failure of their family relied on her and she could look to no one else for comfort. With a silent prayer to her gods and to Newman, Wilson & Saddler for extricating her partner from a sticky position, she resolved to re-engage fully with life.

Annie was already making a name for herself in the world of cryptic newspaper puzzles under the snappy pseudonym of "Ann of a thousand painted railings", a reference, and reminder of exactly what could happen, to both Ann Boleyn who kept her head for just one thousand days as Henry VIII's consort and to Hugh's black paint-encrusted fingernails during his mammoth single-handed task over twenty consecutive weeks with the iron railings. She had received a number of enquiries, fed through to her by the newspaper, about her availability to join various teams engaged in higher mathematics. That the world revolved around the use of algorithms was now a fact of life, but there were still comparatively few people with the brainpower that could grapple with such complexities.

It was now several years since she had left the world of intellectual employment and buried herself in the Welsh countryside as a back-to-nature disciple. She had cast aside normal conventions in the belief that a life based on finer principles would bring greater philosophical rewards. When all it brought were calloused hands, straggly hair and muddy boots, she had married Hugh and set up her family in a quasi-version of simple living in the rolling countryside of Northumbria doing unchallenging jobs requiring no more than basic social interaction. Despite her outstanding mental capacity, she had failed to factor in such prosaic ingredients as intellectual starvation, personal development and ambition. It was only when one of her sons started showing signs of intelligence way above the average for his age that she decided a return to conventional living was the best way forward.

Annie had always been a plain girl, nondescript in fact. She would never have been picked out by a witness in a police identity parade. But she was now plainer than ever and had grown stout and careless about her dishevelled appearance. She had been invited to attend an interview in London for some kind of work involving pure and applied mathematics – the notoriety being a result of her prize-winning performances with the Sunday puzzles. She scrubbed up well for her trip down south and with renewed confidence due to a restyled hairdo and a suit of clothes fitting the occasion – courtesy of a credit card – she pushed open the main door of a featureless building in Whitehall and took the lift to the fifth floor as directed. The elderly man standing there to greet her when the doors opened led Annie along a corridor into a square, austerely-furnished room with a large window overlooking a grand courtyard. He motioned to Annie to take a seat by the desk while he, himself, settled back into an equally uncomfortable looking upright chair. He placed the buff file that he had been holding on the desk and opened its cover.

'Please state your full name and date of birth,' he instructed. When Annie complied, he asked for further information about her parents' names, dates of birth and current addresses. Annie again complied but was becoming annoyed by the one-way demands.

'I'm here to find out about a possible job,' she said flatly, 'not to be grilled about places and dates of birth.'

'Just so, Mrs. Williams,' he replied calmly, removing his reading spectacles, 'but establishing your bona fides is a preliminary necessity.' Annie looked sullen but said nothing. He slipped a sheet of paper out of the file and pushed it across to Annie together with a pencil and ballpoint. He then opened a desk drawer and took out a stopwatch. 'Please complete the puzzle,' he continued, 'you will be assessed on both accuracy and time taken.' He pressed the start button and left Annie to decide whether or not she wished to take up the cudgel and follow his instructions.

'This Sudoku is impossible,' she said, after less than two minutes.

'You can't complete it. Is that correct?'

'Nobody can complete it because it is flawed,' retorted Annie, 'it is designed to be unsolvable.' He made no comment but noted the stopwatch time of how long she had taken to recognise the puzzle's impossible intention. She had been quick, he thought, but how would she cope with the department's killer Sudoku which he next slid across to her. A series of further puzzles followed: cryptic crosswords, encoded sentences to be decoded, diagrams of flowing water to be adjusted with the minimum intervention possible to divert the inundation along an alternate pathway, number games, mathematical equations to be solved, IQ tests of Mensa standard, and stories of one hundred words in length to be made up and told orally from a single given word all within a three-minute timespan. By the end of the twelfth mini test Annie was looking tense but no longer sullen. She was in her element and smiled broadly across the desk at her interrogator.

'Would you like a cup of tea, Mrs. Williams?' he inquired, with genuine warmth in his voice for the first time.

Annie only learned the name of the elderly man when the refreshments were served. A young woman with a silver tray poured the Indian tea from a pot with a long, thin spout and handed each China tea cup sitting in its dainty saucer to the room's two occupants. On departing, she asked Mr. Atwell if there was anything else he required, but his slight shake of the head indicated none. One further test remained. Annie was required to complete a one-hundred-and-fifty-piece jigsaw puzzle without any discernible outline. The trick was to ignore the picture and concentrate solely on interlocking shapes. It was the final test and shortly after completion the same young woman who had served the tea returned to guide Annie out of the building, or as Annie guessed, to ensure that she left without having the chance to poke her nose into their affairs.

'Who is he, this Mr. Atwell? Who is he?' demanded Annie, as they descended in the lift.

'*Mister* Atwell is actually Emeritus Professor Atwell of Imperial College, London. He is a cryptologist.' At the main entrance, she handed Annie a travel warrant, and assured her that they would be in touch. Annie crossed the wide thoroughfare and lingered a while surveying the building in which she had just spent the last two hours. She had been given no overt hint of the nature of any job on offer, but she was excited with anticipation. Annie dived down into the underground and was followed by a colleague of the young woman who served the tea.

One week later, in a larger but equally sparsely furnished room in the same building in Whitehall, four men and a woman sat at one end of a long conference table. The chair, a woman in her late fifties with flecked salt and pepper hair and sagging jowls, opened the meeting about Annie Williams with a short report from a junior colleague who had trailed Annie back to her home just outside Newcastle. The report concluded that Annie Williams was, in fact, exactly who she claimed to be, and that there was no evidence to suggest that Annie was acting on anyone else's behalf.

Mr. Atwell was then invited to report on the subject's mental capacity. His report was short because, he explained, the subject had negotiated the various tests without any apparent difficulty and had completed them in a timely manner. There was no doubt in his mind, he further stated, that her IQ as calculated by an organisation such as Mensa, would place her amongst the top one percent of the population. On mental power alone she was indeed gifted, but like others of her ilk it would be the boredom factor that determined her suitability.

There was a shuffling of papers by the man opposite him. Equally aged, he pulled a sheet from his file and with a quivering hand read out an assessment about Annie's brief working life as an actuary. Attributes for the job, he reminded his colleague opposite him, also included mundane qualities such as self-discipline and determination to see a project through to its conclusion. Annie had grown bored, he reported, with the repetitive nature of commerce, and swanned off to a version of a rural ideal without regard for her employer. It was not balanced behaviour, he stated, but by the nature of their brainpower most tend to be mavericks. The chair nodded with the wisdom of thirty years in the civil service and nearly as many raising a family of two excitable daughters.

On a nod from the chair, a younger man, mid-forties, gave an account of Annie's family background. Attention around the table was heightened as they were all aware that this could be crucial as well as insightful. The younger man, noticeable amongst the conferring five by his full head of dark brown hair, appeared to start with her grandparents, Reginald and Lilley, but moved furtively sideways to really begin with her grandaunt, Kit Audrey Harrison. No eyebrows were raised and facial expressions remained inscrutable but deep down in all but the younger man was a weariness with a person who they regarded had turned philanthropist at the tax payers' expense. It was a concise résumé of her life to date. In her mid-eighties, she was still enjoying the glory of her association with nylon and living off the profits generated by the private limited companies with which she had been associated during her working life. With a clearing of his throat, the younger man reminded his colleagues that Kit Audrey had had a clandestine relationship over a number of years with their department and information regarding her participation in events had still to be treated as classified. With an instruction from the chair to move on without further ado, the younger man continued on less sensitive ground mentioning briefly the longstanding feud between Annie's grandfather, Reginald, and grandaunt before covering her father and brother in greater detail. But in truth there was little more to add about the late Reginald Roach. A man without subtlety or charm, or the ability to mask his feelings. Apart from various failed charges of incitement of his union members, he had no criminal record and it appeared from his collated tax returns and other official documents that he had spent his every last penny on the private education of his son, Henry. He was what he was, warts and all concluded the younger man and received four concurring nods.

Henry bore little resemblance to his father. He was a man without roots. Several eyebrows around the table arched at this pronouncement as the dangers of rootlessness were well known. He was self-serving owing allegiance to neither his father's northern background nor to his home counties living. He was a man with guile and subterfuge, and was only interested in what was best for himself and his son, Adam. He had money, that was for sure, although there was no hint that he had obtained it by treasonable means. He had just wrung every penny he could out of the union funds and together with some nods and winks from various *associates*, he had placed bets and bought shares at opportune times. He had an offshore account in both Jersey and Guernsey with balances sufficient to fund a comfortable lifestyle and support his son, Adam, whenever required. He knew people in high places but these were no more than cultivated acquaintanceships and he was well past his days of sexual dalliances. He represented no real threat; he was just a paper tiger.

His son Adam, Annie's brother, was the character to watch according to the younger man. A career politician with no other obvious source of income save handouts from his besotted father. With a string of debts and a grandiose way of living to support, he was open to bribes from vested interests for lobbying their cause, and, more importantly, from foreign sources who wished to interfere with the nation's democratic procedures. As yet, the younger man reported, no security barriers had been breached, but it was, in his opinion, just a matter of time before Adam Roach stepped into territory beyond his pay scale. With the file closed, the chair thanked the younger man for his diligent report and opened the meeting to general discussion.

'It is,' said the man representing Foreign Office interests, and who looked and sounded as if he was even older than Mr. Atwell, 'the threat from eastern European countries, in particular those sandwiched geographically between northern Italy and Greece, that we believe are poising themselves to de-stabilise our bureaucracy by the spread of misinformation.'

'It is true,' said the man from the Intelligence Bureau, 'that since many of these countries joined the European Union and the close scrutiny of their nationals entering the United Kingdom ceased, they have formed gangs to harry and discredit anyone in their path as they go about spreading spurious information in their quest for power and riches.'

'Treating our system as just a soft underbelly ready to be exploited at their will,' added the chair with feeling. 'After all the centuries it has taken to build up the freedoms and trusts that we rightly value,' she went on, 'it makes my blood boil to see our democratic principles attacked by malicious persons from overseas who we have no ability to deport.'

'Indeed,' replied the Intelligence Bureau representative calmly, somewhat taken aback by the chair's outburst. 'But this time we do have a plan to rid ourselves of some of these ill-intentioned people.'

'Snuff them out?' asked Mr. Atwell expectantly.

'No, Sir. Not directly. Not us. But if we can penetrate their hierarchy then we can allow them to be snuffed out by others.'

'Set them up for a fatal fall,' said the chair.

'Yes, Dame Barbara, exactly that. This particular group, code name Albino, is targeting our banking system, in particular our previously reliable interfaces with the banking systems of other western European countries. Legitimate transfers of both institutional and private funds between countries is now insecure, and verging on high-risk. It is hampering our normal trading patterns by preventing the transfer of large amounts by computer alone. A raft of checks including face-to-face meetings has had to be introduced to combat some serious losses already sustained.'

'And you want someone with Annie Williams's abilities to put a spanner in this gang's works. But how could she do this?' asked the chair, who much preferred to be addressed by her position on the committee rather than by her name and title.

'Well,' he started confidently, 'you will all be aware that the banking system uses the standard method of asymmetric key algorithms for encryption, more simply known as Public-key Cryptography. Every Tom, Dick and Harry making purchases on the internet uses, usually unbeknown to them, this very same system. It keeps everyone safe in most cases. However, this eastern European gang has been able to gain access to the Public-key which allows them to alter the plaintext after they have used the key to decrypt the message. They can then divert payment to an institution of their choice.' He drew breath; he had everyone's attention. 'Well,' he repeated, 'in order to overcome this local difficulty, the banking industry has had to introduce a new layer of security for international transfers of over five million euros within Europe. The international banking language in Europe is English. It is a language full of subtle nuances which can easily trip up non-native speakers. Or, to turn it on its head, nuances which only native speakers can appreciate. This extra layer is designed to identify when a breach of security might be about to take place.' His audience looked expectant. Clearly, they wanted to know how. 'Well,' he repeated for the third time, 'this new protocol asks questions which require plain language answers before one can proceed to the next step.'

'What sort of questions?' inquired the chair.

'Questions such as "Are the fees you charge for your services just Hobson's choice?". Or, another question such as "Is there wiggle room in your formal charges?".

'I see,' said Mr. Atwell, the semi-retired cryptologist. 'Give them the opportunity to hang themselves.'

'Yes, but more importantly, give them the space for someone else to hang them.'

'But I still don't see where Annie Williams, or someone with similar talents fits in,' interrupted the chair.

'In the first instance,' the Intelligence Department representative replied, 'this layer puts a hold on the process and gives us a chance to identify whether the Public-key holder is genuine. If we believe them to be bona fide then we allow the transfer to continue. If not, we have the chance to halt the process and identify the culprit.'

'Why bother to identify them? Isn't just preventing the fraud sufficient?' asked the fourth man who had not until this moment spoken.

'Not if we want to rid our country of these criminal gangs. We can't deport them legally if we identify and arrest them because of European Union laws. But as you know, Commissioner, there is as much internecine activity amongst criminal gangs as there is against honest, law-abiding citizens and institutions. Each gang is protective of its own patch, and a bit like animals in the wild, they are constantly marking out their territory. Any incursion into their area is treated summarily. If we can identify the gang involved, we can through our intelligence network, alert a rival gang that someone else is poaching from them.'

'Then we can leave, shall we say, disposal to them,' said the chair flatly. 'The dark art of ditching our enemies without soiling our own hands.' There was a murmur of agreement around the table. It was an art they all knew well. Exposing your prey to other carnivores.

'The real gem of the extra layer with the cryptic question,' added the agent, 'is that we can vary the complexity of the question.'

'And in so doing,' butted in Mr. Atwell, 'you can determine if you are dealing with the same person each time.'

'Yes. A sort of signature of the person answering the question. The same way that your instinct tells you that an email purportedly from a friend, is not what it appears to be. The choice and style of words and greetings used not in the manner of that particular chum. He paused briefly. 'You see, this particular gang must be receiving some insider information. Their attempts to defraud are not random. They seem to know when big money is involved. Someone is feeding them information. Just preventing the fraud from happening is not our only goal. Catching the informant is of equal importance.'

'Do the fraudulent attempts concentrate on a particular commercial sector or government department?' asked the Commissioner.

'Yes, Sir,' replied the Intelligence agent. It wasn't a deferential "Sir", simply an expedient since the committee did not favour the use of real names. He kicked himself for his previous clumsy error in referring to the chair as Dame Barbara. He had seen her thin lips tighten and almost disappear into her mouth with disapproval. He knew the same mistake would be regarded as unpardonable. 'This gang always seems to know when payments relating to EU subsidies are being made.'

'Someone in the EU parliament maybe involved,' said the Foreign Office official. 'Sitting on one of their financial sub-committees perhaps.'

'I fear we could waste a great deal of time in speculation and still be none the wiser,' suggested the chair. 'It is time to move on and decide if Annie Williams née Roach is going to be useful to us.' She turned to the cryptologist.

'On mental dexterity alone,' said Mr. Atwell, taking his cue, 'she is eminently suitable. But we would have to work hard at retaining her interest. Boredom sets in easily in these ultra-high IQ people.'

'And if I have understood everyone else correctly,' said the chair summarising, 'she has no direct links with organised crime and she is in need of financial resources.' They all concurred although the man from Intelligence re-affirmed the need to closely monitor Annie's brother, Adam.

'So,' stated the chair matter-of-factly, 'we can make use of her as a temporary operative.'

Annie received the news of her apparent success by letter. It came with some stipulations which would cause domestic upheaval. The family were to relocate to rented accommodation in Berwick – where broadband access and reliability had recently been upgraded – and from where Hugh's job on local bus routes only would now be based. The department had earmarked a playgroup for their children which would provide the necessary stimulation for a possibly gifted child. And Annie's cover for her cryptology would be part-time work in her former profession. She recognised the news for what it was. The government department, or whoever they represented, were going to use her for some nefarious reason. Strings had been pulled and there was no reason why, Annie figured, she should not take advantage and return the compliment.

Chapter 4

TWINS

When she googled "Twins", Kit used several refining words to narrow down her search: genes, probability, fraternal, Mendelian inheritance and age. Despite the engagement ring on her finger, she still felt a loneliness at home in Reading and her thoughts turned to Martin. Was he experiencing the same withdrawal symptoms too? Both had moved on, but the memories could not be easily erased. She felt melancholic. To pass the evening in a more upbeat mood, she settled down on the sofa with her laptop and while a twenty-four hours news programme was running in the background, she tried to understand Mendel's law of inheritance. The simple examples quoted were at the same time both easy to understand and fun. Eye colour, height, earlobe attachment, handedness. The path of inheritance of these traits were all clearly shown in amusing diagrams with stick men and women in bright blue and red. But after the introductory paragraphs of the website's explanation of how things worked – chosen as a source of previously reliable information – she soon became confused. Inheritance was proving to be a far more complicated discipline than she had imagined. But with eight sets of twins in her wider family, she was not going to give up. Who had raped Grace? She guessed that Old Kit had known but had had to reluctantly let the matter rest as her hired investigator had found no proof. But science was what Kit did, and Kit was determined to test twenty-first century science to see if she could find the answer. While Edmund concentrated on the search for bank accounts, she would drill down into who had fathered Marion and Jane.

In a seat of scientific learning there was always someone to turn to for advice. And when they reached the limits of their own knowledge, they knew who to contact for more. Thus, by a path of stepping stones she ended up conversing over the internet with a professor of genetics in Austin, Texas, whose speciality was twins. Kit had already grasped the simple facts – the chances of having fraternal twins is more than two and a half times greater for women whose mothers or sisters had had fraternal twins themselves, and this increased chance was due to a gene that promotes hyper-ovulation – but the professor was able to enlighten her further. Apart from impregnation, the effect of the male sperm in the process of producing twins was negligible. It was a blow as Kit had, what she now realised was, a naïve hope of tracing the rapist from the ancestry tree, and that now seemed unlikely. However, with so many twins in her extended family, the professor was willing to take a critical look at Kit's family tree to see if there were any other factors that could influence the progeny. After she had emailed a copy to him, she sat back and considered at length her next move.

She drew the bare bones of the ancestry chart onto paper; the crumpled one that Edmund's father had given her not so many weeks ago, but which now seemed like a lifetime away, was fussy with too much detail. Something simpler, highlighting the position of twins in the overall picture, might prove more revealing. And it was, in a roundabout way. Having looked on YouTube and been impressed by the horizontal charts, she had drawn her simplified flow chart across the page. She traced a finger across the paper, lingering on all the boxes she had coloured with red outlines to indicate each twin. But, on first inspection, nothing pinged in her brain. Nothing stood out. She shrugged her shoulders with exasperation and retraced the lineage backwards. It was when she got back to Old Kit herself that young Kit spotted something.

Only one person in the entire family displayed in the diagram had more than one set of twins. And it was Old Kit. True, it might have been for socio-economic reasons that once having had twins a couple would be fearful of two more mouths to feed should they have another pregnancy. It was the availability of improved and more convenient birth control measures that allowed the younger members to tailor their family to a manageable size. Such advanced methods of contraception wouldn't have been available to Old Kit during her child-bearing years. There was also the question of the so called "twin gene" being passed down the generations. As the professor in Texas had indicated, this gene didn't actually exist. It was just a tendency for some women to hyper-ovulate. And it was this tendency that could be passed down the female line, mostly. But, according to the chart, this leaning must have been passed to them by the marriage of their father – the direct descendant – to a woman who carried this pre-disposition. It was just speculation, of course, but Kit realised that to prove it she would have to look at the family trees – if they existed – of female spouses who "joined" the family by marriage. Another time-consuming hurdle, thought Kit, unless she could find someone to do it for her. But there was one woman's background she needed to investigate herself. Gertrude Elsie Mullins. Old Kit's mother. Gertrude had produced a girl and four boys, but no twins. And yet her only girl, Old Kit, had delivered two sets of twins and no singletons. In the opinion of the professor, male transmission of the twin-scenario was rare and unproven, and he had also debunked the "skipping a generation" theory. So, from where did Old Kit acquire this trait if not from her mother? It would have to come from her mother's sister, if indeed her mother had a sister. She didn't know anything about the family of Old Kit's mother. It crossed her mind that she could probably pay to have the Mullins tree researched professionally as there were lots of genealogical firms advertising their services on the internet. But if, say, Gertrude Mullins had no sisters then it was an apparent dead end and the only logical conclusion that could be drawn was that Gertrude was not Old Kit's birth mother.

She was half asleep, hunched over her laptop when Edmund rang. The chirruping noise of the ringtone took some time to register. 'Hallo,' she said sleepily.

'Are you in bed or still up at eleven o'clock burning the midnight oil?' asked Edmund cautiously. 'Sorry if I've disturbed you, fiancée.' She smiled. She liked being called fiancée. 'I was hoping you could come up this weekend,' he went on. 'It would make it a full weekend if you could catch the four o'clock service on Friday afternoon and leave on the early morning train on Monday.'

'Probably, but I'll have to consult my work diary. Off hand, I can't think of any reason why not. I'd love to come. It's a bit lonely down here.'

'And I'm a bit lonely without you,' he replied softly, sensing her spirits needed a boost.

'I've got something to discuss with you about the family twins.'

'Good. And I've made a little headway with the offshore accounts. We'll have a lot to talk about,' he replied. 'I'll meet you at the station on Friday. Don't forget to bring your flat shoes.'

* * *

The barber's shop was just next to one of the entrances to Angel, Islington tube station. Adam felt in need of a new, more modern haircut and fancied a pampered shave too. Luigi was Italian and had worked there with his cousin for many years. The salon was small but cheerful with its black and white diamond-shaped floor tiles and large illuminated mirrors. The classic barbershop chairs, as seen in the movies, swivelled and reclined, and were upholstered in soft red leather. Luigi's grandson, when not at school, was in charge of sweeping the floor and producing hot towels for the close shaves. It was busy as usual and Adam waited his turn in the cramped waiting area next to the door. He was due in the House for a select committee meeting later that morning and would need time to walk the short distance home to change into formal attire before travelling to Westminster. His watch showed he had sufficient time and he relaxed and enjoyed the prospect of the expensive indulgence.

It was the current version, with shorter back and sides and longer crown, of the classic crew cut that had been around for decades, that he chose to have and Luigi nodded knowingly when Adam asked for the trendy look. With a full head of light brown hair, the new style would enhance his still youthful face. With a display of scissor skills and a deft touch with the cut-throat razor, Luigi soon had Adam looking well groomed. But with no parting and short hair there were no locks to cover and conceal the brown blob growing on Adam's scalp just above the hairline behind his right ear. Luigi had seen it and considered what to do about it for a few minutes whilst finishing off the haircut and brushing away the loose hair from Adam's shoulders. The two-tone brown mole with an odd shape didn't look friendly. He was about to mention it to his client when Adam jumped up out of the chair, stuck a large tip into Luigi's palm and was off. Luigi shrugged his shoulders in a display of Italian indifference and welcomed his next client into the comfy chair.

The special select committee assembled at eleven o'clock that same morning in a room off the committee corridor, in the heart of the Palace of Westminster. Adam was not its chair. He took his place around the U-shaped table from where all members of the committee had a full view of the person to be grilled. The interviewee was defending a position taken by his well-known company regarding the use of tax payers' money in a third-world country. There had been condemnation in the press that these funds were being used inappropriately. He faced intense questioning from the committee members who were not in the mood to accept puerile excuses.

Seated next to Adam on his right-hand side was a member representing a constituency in the west Midlands who was also a practising doctor. The back of Adam's right ear had been in her line of sight during the two-hour hearing. She tapped him on his shoulder before they left the desk to warn him that there was a mole in his hairline that in her opinion looked suspicious and that he should have it checked by his own general practitioner forthwith. Adam thanked her for the advice but dismissed any urgency. It would be examined in the fullness of time when he next had cause to consult his doctor. Several weeks passed before he took seriously his wife's moans about blood on the pillowcase and by then his fate was sealed.

* * *

Breakfast on Saturday morning was late and unhurried. Edmund had banned all shop talk until after their outing along the Scottish border; a circular trail on a smooth but undulating surface through established woods and farmland before the homeward run along the banks of the Tweed. It was late autumn and despite a murky sky, the landscape was still stunning and other ramblers aplenty were out enjoying the freedom of the countryside. With lightweight backpacks – Edmund had purchased two small ones in the high street shop, a "his" and "hers", with padded shoulder straps and elasticated outer pockets – they made fast progress along the winding route. Kit felt "naked" without her handbag but had grasped the principle of loading her important stuff into the capacious pockets of her cargo trousers. She was also wearing proper walking boots. She had slipped out of her office one lunchtime and taken the tube to the West End, emerging at Piccadilly Circus where a well-known outdoor clothing store had been selling boots and shoes for more than a century. Waterproof, supple and padded at all the possible blister points, she had taken ages to get the laces tied symmetrically for a snug fit. Kit was glad she now looked the part and fitted in; she looked like all the other walkers they met along the way and didn't stick out like a sore thumb. It was a satisfying feeling.

Almost inevitably as they made their way back along the river, conversation turned to matters in hand. It was Edmund who broke his own ban by telling Kit he had discovered, through his intermediaries, that a bank in St. Peter Port, the island's capital, held a series of accounts bearing Old Kit's full name. He stopped suddenly in his tracks. 'Of course,' he said in earnest looking at her intently, 'these might belong to another Kit Audrey Harrison but somehow I don't think so.'

'I don't think so either.'

'Well,' carried on Edmund, 'it seems that further investigation is required to discover if they belong to *our* Kit Audrey Harrison.'

'How?'

'Maybe they hold details like date of birth, a secret number, or some password.'

'Or a passport photo of her.'

'Yes, that's a decent bet,' said Edmund. 'I wonder what happened to her personal effects like debit cards and passport. I must ask my father. We'll be seeing him tonight as he has invited us to dinner.'

'And if you do establish that the account holder is our client, then what next?'

'I'm not sure at the moment,' replied Edmund. 'We might need the services of a hacker to crack the nut.'

'The *illegal* services of a hacker, I presume,' said Kit with distaste. 'Wouldn't a simple visit in person with all the right documentation showing that she is dead and that we are the joint executors be more fruitful?'

'Possibly.'

'Even probably,' suggested Kit.

'Yes, I concede,' Edmund laughed. 'It might be the better option although definitely not covert. Anyhow, what about your news of the twins?'

'Now that's very interesting, very interesting indeed.'

'Are you going to tell me?' he asked, looping an arm under her shoulder and swinging her bodily, backpack and all, into her arms. 'Or have I got to wheedle it out of you.'

Edmund's mother was tall and slender and very youthful in relation to his father, but all Kit really noted were the sleek, black high heel shoes she was wearing. Looking down at her own flatties, Kit felt like a country bumpkin in comparison and with a semi-scowl to her fiancé, at whose insistence she had travelled north without her beloved stilettos, she recorded her feelings unequivocally.

The Newmans lived life quietly in an elegant retreat off the main road out of Berwick. A paddock adjoined their expansive garden and was where Edmund's mother spent much of her time schooling ponies and young riders for dressage events. They had both missed Edmund when he left home for a more independent life, and his mother had channelled her energies into equestrian pastimes. This evening they would be joined by Emily from the practice. His mother and Emily were of a similar age and were best friends and when her husband had recently mostly retired, Emily had done much the same.

It was a relaxing and happy evening with good food and wine. Wide-ranging topics were discussed and the world put to right. The subject of the wedding, a certainty for discourse, was raised. Where it would be held was not in question as Kit had no close family except her aged grandparents in Cornwall and no real ties with anywhere except her house in Reading and work in London. About the date, both Edmund and Kit were somewhat enigmatic. Soon, was the best his mother could obtain from Edmund and she left it there on the understanding that she would need time to get out the invitations, etcetera and that her only son and prospective daughter-in-law would be having a traditional wedding come what may. No objections were raised; with full working schedules both were pleased to leave the organisation to a trusted "project manager".

It was only whilst the women were in the kitchen marvelling at his mother's latest cooking gadget for cutting vegetables in a spiral shape that Edmund was able to have a quick word with his father about Old Kit's personal belongings. He knew better than to mention the matter in front of the others; discretion was needed.

'Did Old Kit have a passport, Father?' he asked quietly when they were alone.

'Yes. She travelled widely for many years. But she stopped going abroad when she went into the care home. Said she had had her fill of all the silly palaver at airports.'

'What happened to it?'

'I don't know. It would have expired at some stage during her stay in the care home. She was there for her last ten years. It wouldn't have been any use to her. What became of it I don't know. She certainly didn't give it to me.'

'I suppose I could ask at the home whether they disposed of it or not. And her debit and credit cards too.'

'Those I can tell you about. On her death the home gave them to me and I disposed of them in the normal way with a pair of scissors.'

'But no passport,' said Edmund.

'No passport,' confirmed his father.

They sat up late that evening, sprawled on Edmund's sofa which took up most of the space in the small living-room. He told her about the missing passport and they chewed over the possibilities of what might have happened to it. The most likely scenario was that she destroyed it herself after deciding that she would no longer need it for journeys abroad but it was possible that, somehow, it had fallen into the hands of a person who did not wish her well. And as both Edmund and Kit were learning, there were many of them who felt that way. In any event they didn't have it and accepted that they wouldn't be able to present themselves at the Guernsey bank with cast iron credentials.

Kit gave a résumé of her researches about twins and told Edmund of the possibility that Old Kit might not have been who she seemed to be. She might have been a foundling adopted by the Roaches or the illegitimate daughter of Harold Roach who his wife brought up as her own.

'That's an intriguing possibility,' said Edmund, 'because it would mean that her four brothers were not actually that. They were not blood relatives at all.'

'And then you could extrapolate and conjecture that the animosity Reginald held for his sister was based on more than Reggie's annoyance as the first-born son, not being given pride of place in his parents' affection.'

'It's food for thought,' mused Edmund. 'But there *are* twins in the families of their four sons and you are one of them, my darling.'

'True. Obviously,' agreed Kit, 'but down the line, female spouses and sisters thereof, could have introduced the so-called twin gene. No, it's Old Kit herself who is the key here. She had two sets of twins without apparently having the twin gene passed on to her by Gertrude Roach.'

'So, who did pass it on?'

'Solve that and we might find the answer or just open up a can of wriggling worms.'

'Shall we leave that topic for later?' Edmund asked, his amorous intentions perfectly plain.

Kit was beginning to value the time she spent in the train journeying up and down the spine of England. She had learnt to relax into the rhythm of the clickety-clack as the wheels ran over the points and the whooshing noise as the train sped through stations where it wasn't scheduled to stop. It was a tempo unique to the east coast line where rolling stock and line infrastructure were almost outdated in comparison to the sanitised silence of the modern continental railways. She was warm and comfortable in her seat and drifted off with thoughts of the lovely weekend she had had with Edmund in the bosom of his family and in his own beautiful part of England.

The loud discordant station announcement at Newcastle finally woke her from her reverie and she was soon wide awake with all the commotion of the joining passengers walking through the carriage seeking a suitable seat for the remaining three hours of the journey to London. Amid whistles and waves from the platform, the train settled back into its previous pace and before long, the guard's voice over the loudspeaker announced the breakfast service was now open in the catering carriage farther down the train. She closed her eyes for a few moments longer and thought about twins: in general, and in particular. What would it have been like if her twin brother had not been killed? Would he have been her best friend? Would she have always shared her thoughts with him? Sadly, she would never know, but it seemed highly likely that there would have been an indelible bond between them. Maybe even the same sort of inseparable bond that Old Kit had written about in length in her original letter that was shared between John and Bernard, her second pair of twins; a bond so close as to effectively exclude all others.

Edmund had nicknamed them the "loathsome twins" although from Kit's first encounter with them at the memorial service, she had mentally labelled them the "angry brothers". Whichever sobriquet was used, she thought, they were aptly named. With jutting chins and stabbing fingers, their stentorian voices and lack of personal hygiene, they would be on few people's guest list. And it wasn't hard to understand how Northern Tailoring Limited had nosedived under their management. Crowded around Thomas Newman in the refreshment marquee, and egged on by members of Reggie's tribe, they had only one thing in mind. Money. Or, to be more precise, Old Kit's money. They hadn't made a success of pig farming according to Old Kit's letter, and she wondered what they were doing now. They were seventy-one but could have been mistaken for being five years older. They had two sons and a daughter between them and seven grandchildren but none were twins. They were hostile towards Old Kit, that was for sure, but was most of it bluster? Probably. It seemed unlikely that they had the expertise and application required to delve into their late mother's finances – except maybe as the whipping boys of someone more artful – but, awful as it was to contemplate, they might have been involved in the suspected rape of their sister, Grace. It was a disgusting thought that disturbed Kit but one that would have to be probed since there was a distinct facial likeness between them and their nieces, Marion and Jane, which might not have been transmitted down two generations entirely by Old Kit herself. And there was no denying either, from what she had seen and noted sitting around the same table as Marion and her offspring at the memorial service, that they had no business acumen whatsoever and seemed prepared to live their lives on handouts. Or, more correctly, spend their lives demanding handouts to which they were not fully entitled. It was a sad state of affairs concluded Kit, learning how some strands of society lived.

That left just two sets of twins for consideration, if she omitted herself and her late brother. Old Kit's third and fourth born brothers, David and Nathan respectively, had sired five children between them, all singletons. But amongst their grandchildren who numbered eleven, were a set of twins each. Not much was known about these brothers – she consulted her mobile app and found that Edmund had struggled to unearth any useful information save that they both lived in Newcastle – or indeed about their rapidly expanding families – twenty-three great grandchildren to date. It appeared that they kept very much under the radar, but with so many mouths to feed and bodies to clothe, it was hardly surprising. Kit sighed; a sigh of exasperation. She couldn't dismiss any of them from involvement in the feud against Old Kit, but as family members go, these low-profile persons would have to be put on the back burner whilst she concentrated on the more likely troublemakers.

* * *

When the limits of their managerial skills were exposed in 1981 and they were forced to sell their controlling interest in Northern Tailoring Limited at a bargain basement price, John and Bernard's financial circumstances took a big hit and they were forced to acknowledge their inadequacies in the business world. Downsizing and unskilled work became the only viable options available to the unemployable forty-two-years old twins. With the sale of both their heavily-mortgaged homes, they would have sufficient to set up a combined household with some cash leftover for investment in a start-up venture.

They scanned the windows of estate agents in the high street for suitable accommodation and spotted a working farm with over a hundred acres of land in North Yorkshire that was up for auction following the death of its owner. It would be a forced sale since none of the owner's children wished to take on the gruelling daily work of farming in the high pastures and on the moorland. The twins, still lacking the self-discipline to cut their cloth to match the reality of their position, bid beyond the bounds of their limited resources, and paid over the odds. The farmhouse was in decent condition and sufficiently spacious to house both families but the barns and other outbuildings were in need of repair and modernisation. It had been a working farm before the farmer's death with his flock of hardy sheep grazing the lush high pastures in summer and roaming loose, out on the moorland in wintertime, a business model which had stood the test of time for any owner willing to be out in all weathers. But John and Bernard didn't have sufficient funds to buy the flock; it was sold and the proceeds became part of the deceased's estate. With money tight, the only affordable animals were a small drove of pigs.

It made amusing chatter in the pubs nearby. A standing joke amongst the pub's farming fraternity regulars who were bewildered by the choice of animal when the very essence of the farm had always been the rearing of hardy sheep. "What do you do with one hundred and thirty acres of prime grazing land in God's own country?" had the inevitable riposte of "nothing" accompanied by raucous laughter. New punchlines were invented every evening such was the astonishment of the locals at the newcomers' lack of understanding of the terrain they had purchased. Pint pots were raised and toasts were made to halfwits and the like, and there was brass-necked speculation as to when the farm would be up for sale again. John and Bernard were the centre of attention whenever they walked the three long miles to their nearest hostelry, often in the dark. They had no spare money for petrol, but surprisingly often, they were to be found sitting glumly at a small table in the public bar engrossed in one another's company to the exclusion of their audience. Scruffy and unkempt, no onlooker was prepared to venture forward with a welcoming salutation or piece of friendly advice.

The pigs, all fifteen of them, brought endless delight to their young children until they tired of the grunting, the flying mud, the mucking out and the constant feeding of the Gloucester Old Spots, a breed native to England. With salvaged wood from around the farm buildings, John and Bernard constructed some rudimentary pig styes to give them cover from the weather, but left the real care of their animals to their beleaguered wives. It was typical behaviour of the twins: sit back, do nothing, see what happens. And it wasn't long before the wives brought to their attention a blotchy skin rash on one of the swine. A discussion between John and Bernard – John always led and Bernard always followed – ensued. Should they call in a veterinary or wait to see what transpired? It was a question that would only ever have one answer, and as usual they dithered and nothing was done. Had it not been for the wife of the landlord of The Woolpack Inn where they imbibed their daily pint, they might have lost their entire stock. She had taken pity on them. She didn't as a rule work in the bar but helped out when needed. She had heard all manner of derogatory remarks made by the regulars and felt sorry for the twins who simply didn't fit in. They were neither old nor frail but they seemed troubled and the landlord's wife sensed an underlying sadness. She wanted to help them. On a flimsy pretext she arranged to stop by their farm one afternoon and was surprised to discover that they were both married with children. For all the world they had appeared in her eyes as confirmed bachelors. The twins were nowhere to the seen, but unlike their husbands the wives appeared willing to talk. They were anxious about the welfare of one of the pigs and showed her the sow with the skin condition which had by now spread across most of its back. The publican's wife was not from farming stock, but over the years running the pub she had become familiar with the day-to-day exigencies of raising livestock from the general conversation to be heard circulating in the bar most evenings and advised calling in the vet immediately. Apparently, the wives had already urged the pair to consider contacting the vet, but that was as far as it had gone and they were dubious that their husbands would take any action. From what the wives hinted, it appeared that the twins' lives had always been plagued by chronic indecision which prevented them acting in a timely manner to the problems that arose in life, and the older they grew the more marked this ambivalence became.

She had a quiet word with one of the pub's regulars when he arrived that evening. His wife was the local vet and she asked that his wife make a visit to Moor Farm as they had a poorly sow, and from what she had learned on her visit there earlier in the day, the brothers were unlikely to seek the professional advice that the sick animal deserved. The vet's visit the following day did not go well. She was a woman and the twins made it known to her in no uncertain terms that they would have no truck with being told what to do by some toffee-nosed superior woman. Her visit was unsolicited and they could manage perfectly well without her poking her nose into their affairs and they would thank her to be on her way immediately. But the vet stood her ground and insisted on examining the poorly sow before she would leave. She had been in practice for many years and had seen it all before and no amount of finger pointing and coarse language from the twins would shift her.

It was the wives who finally broke the impasse by guiding the sickly animal from its shelter into the vet's view. And before the brothers could react, she vaulted the galvanised iron gate and her rubber boots squelched across the paddock to the pig. It was Swine Pox, she announced, after running a finger over some lesions with black scabs and pointing out to the wives some newly-forming lesions which would develop black scabs when they ruptured spilling the fluid inside them. It wasn't serious she added with a reassuring smile but the sow would need antibiotics to treat the secondary bacterial infection and the pigpen should be disinfected. She had a course of tablets in her car that could be administered in the sow's feed to make it feel more comfortable. The wives looked dubious. Beyond earshot of the twins, they warned the vet that unless she handed the tablets to them surreptitiously, the boys would block accepting them. It wouldn't be a malicious act, one of the wives said to mitigate the twins' behaviour, but simply because they could never make up their minds. They get bees in their bonnet, she added, and get stuck about what to do.

The vet's visit set in train a course of events which could not have been predicted. A few days later, whilst the twins were glumly ensconced in the bar, the publican's wife knocked on the farmhouse door, ostensibly to enquire how the sickly pig was progressing. The wives were not unwelcoming and although she was not invited in, they were willing to listen to her news. At the auction when the twins bought the farm and its acreage, they had outbid a young, local shepherd who was hoping to secure his first farm. The twins, through their ignorance of farming matters, had paid over the odds and the shepherd had reluctantly withdrawn from the bidding process once his maximum was passed. But he had heard on the grapevine of the goings-on at Moor Farm and would still be prepared to buy it at his original maximum bid. It would be a way out, she suggested, without loss of face should the twins agree and they would have capital to buy accommodation in the suburbs where they were more suited and familiar with the lifestyle. It was an exit strategy with much to recommend it. The wives looked relieved. The deep worry lines on their faces eased as they thought of all the potential benefits: jobs, for them and the twins, easy access to the schools and shops, near to neighbours for help and support, and no more mud right outside their front door. It was a heavenly thought but would remain only a dream unless they could find a way which would suggest that the twins themselves had come up with the idea. A neat plan came to the publican's wife and the wives agreed to the subterfuge.

The twins announced a few days later, that is, John with Bernard at his side, that they had found a buyer for the farm who would also be willing to take on the pigs. Furthermore, two adjoining terrace houses in a terrace of twelve in a suburb of Gateshead had become available for purchase, and the proceeds of the farm would be sufficient to cover the costs of the relocation including legal fees. Work in Gateshead was available through the job centre, John had added, and the children would be entitled to places in local schools. It wasn't quite back to their roots in Berwick but Gateshead was definitely part of their cherished north-east. The wives nodded sagely when told, muttered their approval of the plan and did not inquire how this turn of events had come about. Away from the brothers they were cock-a-hoop that the smart ploy put into action by the landlord's wife had worked so smoothly. Evidently, they correctly construed, someone behind the scenes had greased the wheels of the master plan and it was unlikely to have been the young shepherd. Just who was delving into the affairs of the Harrison twins was not their business. They were just happy to have the prospect of full-time jobs and be able to earn some money of their own.

The uprooting of the Harrison twins had not been due to the interception of divine providence but to a lingering filial loyalty. It was 1982 and their mother, Old Kit, had not yet given up on them. She mused that at forty-three years of age they still had time to mend their ways and find salvation. And, for the final time she vowed, she put aside her hurt at the injustices of the past, to give them one last opportunity.

She owned property in Gateshead in both suburban and semi-industrialised settings; it was part of a large portfolio of housing stock in the north-east that she had prudently purchased over the years as her trusty pension fund. She owned three houses in a particular terrace which were currently on short-term rental as student accommodation. All three would shortly become unoccupied when the student holidays commenced. When she was alerted to the twins' plight by one of the regulars at The Woolpack Inn – a former colleague at Northern Tailoring Limited who had recognised them as the Harrison twins – she gave notice to the college that she would not be renting them out again. Redecorated and with new floor coverings, two of the modest houses would serve as a sound base for a realistic new start in life. Old Kit had no doubt that the wives, given half a chance, would wholeheartedly embrace the opportunity of paid work but was far less sanguine about the twins. With jobs in construction in a region shifting from old industries to new, they had every chance of steady work for years to come. Moreover, it would be work they would be directed to do; physical work without the requirement on their part for decision making. The boys didn't know, thought Old Kit, but it really was their last chance saloon.

The occupants of the parade of terrace houses – a nineteen-seventies take on the old, interwar back-to-back slums so common in the industrialised areas of the north-east – were in constant flux. Apart from the second-year students living term-time in three of the houses, the remainder were rented out to construction companies for some of their skilled workforce whose numbers rose and fell depending on the building schedule. It was the same all over the locale as the city dragged itself out of the hardships of the past and modernised to share in the affluence of the prevailing times. Workers with trades came and stayed in short sessions as they plied their particular skills, and left on completion freeing up the accommodation for new arrivals. The constant toing and froing in the street were like the endless turning of a merry-go-round. It was a street, similar to so many in the vicinity, where anonymity was almost guaranteed.

The Harrisons settled into the adjoining houses of number seventeen and nineteen. The properties were small and basic, but clean, newly-decorated and had some built-in labour-saving devices in the kitchens which were a joy to the wives. They found jobs in catering and as soon as their three children were happy and could be trusted with a latch-door key, together, they took over a fast-food stall on a massive new town centre construction site. Opening six days a week from eight to four they served hot-dogs and drinks and fully participated in the cheeky banter with their customers. They loved every minute of it. But whilst they flourished the twins stagnated. It was a constant bone of contention with the staff at the job centre that they dismissed every job on offer out of hand if they could not work together. After many months of encouragement, effort, facilitation and endeavour to find them jobs side by side, the wrangling over this one issue with the twins took a toll on the job centre staff who finally gave in, marked them as unemployable and put them on benefits.

The brothers, still young and vigorous by most people's standards, settled into their new life in the terrace without contrition. Still easily provoked into episodes of vehement protestation for no apparent good reason, they sat side by side for long periods by the window in John's front room, barely speaking, acting as voyeurs of the action taking place on the street outside and in the terrace opposite. And as they trudged out daily for a pub lunch like two old men, they would whisper between themselves that the person who had just passed them by, was the new occupant of number three or wherever. Number five's latest tenant, together with a young wife and toddler, wore a uniform to go to work. It was black. The embroidery on the shirt and the stencil in bold, yellow lettering on the jacket's back warned that he was a security guard.

Chapter 5

MARTIN'S TALE

Martin was just two years old when his parents moved to Gateshead for work. They were Londoners seeking a fresh start away from the capital where things had gone awry. His father had been in and out of different jobs in the metropolis since leaving the army in his early thirties despite the skills as a vehicle mechanic that his spell in the military had taught him. He could be a hothead and didn't respond well to criticism. His first job, post-army, was as a garage mechanic. He was a reliable employee for almost three years until one day he finally lost his temper with one of the supervisors and invited him to "do it himself if he knew so fucking much". The argument between the two men became heated and came to an explosive head when he gripped the lapels of the senior technician very tightly and banged his head against a wall. The incident was hushed up by the workshop manager on the proviso that Martin's father left their employ forthwith. In return, no formal charge of assault would be made and his clean record with the police would remain intact.

The supervisor's protestations at the lenient way in which he considered the incident to have been resolved drew scant sympathy from the manager who pointed out to him in unequivocal terms that he had lost one of his best mechanics because of the supervisor's constantly carping attitude towards nearly all of his mechanics.

Over the next few years, he drifted from one employ to another, never settling. He was a single man without responsibilities. But his outlook changed when the young woman he had been flirting with for some months became pregnant. He might have walked away had he not realised that he actually cared for her. They set up in a rented flat, she gave birth to a boy, Martin, and he knuckled down to his job in the security industry. Pay was low, London accommodation rents were high, and when his company offered him a twelve-month contract at a facility in Gateshead in a more senior role, the family moved north and settled in to house number five in the terrace.

They found adaptation to life in the north-east challenging. Marked out because of their southern accents, they found it difficult to integrate into the culture of the region. Where outdoor cafes and eateries and the hustle and bustle that went hand in glove with it were ten-a-penny in the metropolis, they were still in short supply in the Gateshead area. And he stood out amongst the crowd as he made this way to and from work in the black uniform with hi-vis waterproof jacket. He'd been a corporal in the army and his employers deemed the experience learned there would make him a suitable candidate to be a shift supervisor of the stores warehouse – one of the first buildings on site to be erected to house the huge range of construction tools and materials required – for the new town centre. It was a job to which he applied himself with rigour but one in which he wasn't truly comfortable. On commencement of his shift every workday, there would be a verbal and written handover from the previous shift supervisor detailing any problems or issues that had arisen during that period. It was, effectively, a rubber stamp document which had to be accepted on trust as there was no way in which the incoming supervisor could possibly check that the actual stock tallied with the computer listings. And with a squad of just three guards to patrol the premises inside and out, his job required confidence in his colleagues. But there didn't exist the sort of comradeship that he had experienced in army life and he soon discovered that giving orders in civvy street was often met with insolence and derision or a leave of sickness, and orders were usually disobeyed on principle. A different tack was required which tested his patience. His frustration boiled over sometimes. He needed more guards than three to do the job properly and the ones he had were incompetent skivers. In those days it was still endemic in the culture to challenge authority at every level or to go crying to the union representative with claims of victimisation at the merest hint of your boss's dissatisfaction with your work.

He knew too well from his service life how things could so easily go missing; the falling off the back of a lorry syndrome. Concerned that he might be the fall guy if a spot check revealed missing stock, he took to stealthily checking the presence of a few of the stored items on each of his shifts to match the numbers with the computer stock held. It was truly a thankless task and he should have realised that nobody was going to be pleased if he uncovered even widespread pilfering. It had been factored in to the project costs at the outset under the eponymous heading "displacements". But he couldn't stop himself and when he found evidence that a group of the security guards themselves, including a shift supervisor and a computer operator, were into large scale stealing he went berserk. His fiery, unbridled aggression, so necessary in many military scenarios, was to be his undoing. He didn't even wait for his next shift. He barged into the compound, sought out the supervising guard and accused him of bigtime theft. A heated argument ensued which developed into a brawl when the other guards overheard what was going on. It was four against one and somebody was going to get badly hurt. He slipped the old army knife down his forearm into a firm grip in his hand and wielded it threateningly. It was a pivotal moment for two of the guards who retreated to a safe distance with their hands aloft; they wanted no further part in the unfolding action. With the tip of the pointed blade glinting menacingly he thrust it into the chest of the deceitful supervisor. The first attack didn't penetrate the rib cage but the second did. The man collapsed and lay prostrate on the rough concrete floor but the attacks didn't stop until the frenzy passed.

It was the start of a nightmare for Martin, although at just three years of age it would be several years before he would understand its full implications. The conviction of his father for murder and the life sentence handed out by the judge who found no extenuating circumstances for consideration of early release despite the man in the dock having no previous convictions and a good record with his current employer. It was the deranged act of multiple stabbings that swayed his lordship to order, additionally, a mental health check. The trial in the high court was covered in minute detail by the media and spawned a cult following of those seeking justice for whistle blowers. For a period of several months, it became a cause célèbre but when the psychiatrists reported Martin's father to be of sound mind but with uncontrollable aggressive tendencies, his cult following faded away.

By the time the case had come to court, Martin and his mother had been in and out of a variety of rental accommodation. The Harrison twins had watched them leave house number five in the terrace shortly after Martin's father had been charged and bail refused; the company needed the small dwelling for another of their contract workers. Tightly clasping his mother's hand, John and Bernard waved at the toddler as he walked past their front room window and Martin waved back. During the next weeks they moved from pillar to post in a succession of downward steps until the local authority finally took over responsibility for housing them.

Martin's mother was not a slut – she had reciprocated the genuine affection held by her partner and was prepared for a lasting relationship – but as a young woman faced with the negative press, lack of income and a young child to support, she was overwhelmed and crushed by the enormity of her situation. She couldn't cope. The local authority stepped in with a care order to safeguard the young child when she took up with some unseemly characters. Thus, Martin was separated from his mother and initially spent many months in a children's home before being fostered in the community by various families and contact with his mother was, during this period, spasmodic.

He was too young to read and worry about what was written in the newspaper column inches, especially in the tabloids, much of it sensationalising the grubby story. But as the months and years passed and he grew into an older boy he became aware that wherever he went, his background was the source of critical attention. Words were used in the playground and in whichever home he was living at the time that were hurtful and upsetting. He needed his mother for comfort, but she herself was in poor spirits and unable to provide the encouragement he needed. At their occasional meetings arranged by his child safeguarding officer, Martin realised that his poor mother was still too traumatised by past events in her life to be able to provide a stable home for them to live together as a family.

By his early teens, he was back living in a children's home in north London as no foster family could be found to provide a home for the now turbulent teenager. His heart had sunk to its lowest point as he grappled with loneliness and puberty. A kindly teacher at his comprehensive recognised his plight and was prepared to give up some of her valuable spare time to help. It would be a Good Samaritan turn that Martin would never forget; someone offering practical advice without making snide remarks about his background or looking down on him from a moral high ground. She wasn't even his class teacher but in her quiet, non-judgemental manner he had felt able to open up to her in a flood of heartfelt words. She sat patiently for over an hour as the words tumbled out about his anxieties: his mother who had been sectioned, his father who was now in the seventh year of his sentence in prison, his feelings of being forsaken, and worst of all in Martin's eyes, his shame.

She was a science teacher but also a charity worker, and invited Martin to join her at the busy food bank where she spent her Sunday mornings putting together carriers of basic food stuffs for those in need. They always welcomed young people who could do some heavy lifting; stacking cans of baked beans and the like onto shelves so that they were easily accessible to be put into food parcels. It would be a way, she had said, for him to realise that he was not alone in the world; their "customers" too were struggling with their own particular circumstances and demons. And if his mother couldn't provide a home for him, then perhaps when he was older, he could provide a home for her out of his earnings. She had added that his life wasn't defined by what people thought of him but by what he thought of himself. They were simple words but ones that Martin took to heart. Self-help could start, she had continued with an engaging smile, if he so wished, with some general science tutoring at her house. It would be distracting in their cramped living room she warned with two toddlers of her own, a husband with a loud voice and a hamster spinning in his wheel but in her opinion, Martin could do well in science if he tried and he smiled back.

He was accepted for a place at university to study chemistry when just eighteen. Study and weekend work had been part of his daily agenda since unburdening himself to the teacher. He still felt intense shame about his background but he had learned how to manage his feelings. He spent his weekend earnings on periodic trips to visit his mother who was living in supervised accommodation in Bristol. Every month he would take the early morning train to the West Country and armed with a small present he would sit with her for hours: talking or reading or just gazing at this small lady who meant so much to him. She was still young and appeared lucid but there was a harrowing look in her eyes which could not be disguised and any requests by him to take her for an outing into town were always denied. They parted each time with tears in their eyes; an expression of the depth of the bond still existing between them. And on each sad return journey, he swore he would always care for her.

Fresher's week was a period of optimistic promise. The Great Hall, where all the student clubs and groups made their pitches for new members, was abuzz with gauche nineteen-year-olds who were away from parental guidance for the first time in their lives. Stalls, decorated with bunting and banners proclaiming the nature of their club: artistic, sporting, political, intellectual, religious – if you didn't find what you sought you were advised to start it yourself – were laid out with information sheets and joining lists. Martin struggled to the front of several crowded tables. He had little recollection of how he was enrolled for Scottish country dancing; a second-year student in charge of the stall flashed her white teeth at him and said she would find him a tall partner.

As he extricated himself from the scrum of freshers, he felt a tug on his elbow. 'We need you over there,' said a young man with a posh accent, pointing to the rowing club placard. 'Long levers, you see. Just what is needed.'

'Long levers?' repeated Martin quizzically.

'Yes. Knee to toe and elbow to wrist. Long levers. Good for rowing.'

'Oh,' stammered Martin, 'I've never rowed a boat.'

'We'll teach you. See, you're the same height as me. Just a bit gangly. Some sessions in the gym will soon fill you out.'

'I don't know,' replied Martin evasively, concerned that all the other rowers might have posh accents too. Having just been signed up for country dancing, he didn't intend to register for anything else, but as he left the Great Hall, he stopped at the field hockey stand. An older man, possibly a coach, was tidying his paperwork in preparation for shutting up shop. They exchanged smiles.

'All fixed up with several clubs?' asked the coach cordially.

'Only the one. Country dancing.'

'You need more than that, lad. University is about learning and recreation. All work and no play is not a good mix.'

'I don't think I can afford some of them,' Martin blurted out. 'I've only got my grant. I don't want to get an evening job as I intend to study then.'

'I understand,' said the coach. 'But to come to university and spend all your spare time studying would be a crime.' He looked the new student up and down. He looked younger than most. 'How old are you, lad?'

'Eighteen.'

'What course are you doing?'

'Chemistry. Four-year Master's course.'

'There's no expense with field hockey. A pair of boots, shin pads and a stick, is all you need. I can find you some shin pads and a stick. Don't think I've got anything in the way of boots your size though,' said the coach looking down at Martin's large feet. 'You're not really the right shape and size for hockey. Best to be medium height with a sturdy build. But you could come and try. Mixed bunch of students learn to play hockey with us. Mostly beginners. Not many schools play field hockey these days,' the coach added, sighing with regret. 'Come along, lad. In four years, I can turn any novice into a decent player so long as there is the will and enthusiasm to play.'

The comprehensive school, and life in foster or care homes, hadn't afforded Martin many opportunities for recreation, and sport in particular had been limited to the odd football knockabout in the playground or in the streets. The coach was true to his word and sorted out some second-hand kit, but there was no way around the shoe situation and Martin had to buy some cheap boots.

Despite his initial reservations, Martin enjoyed the training sessions and the Saturday match afternoons. He was hopeless at first but was quick to learn new skills once he developed a feel for the game. He had never really understood why sport provoked such deep passion and entrenched views. The level of joy and disappointment that some stalwart fans felt when their team won or lost was incomprehensible to him. That a vast number of fans would never miss a single team fixture even for a family birth, marriage or death was even more bizarre. But by the summer term, he was beginning to understand the importance of the link with their team. Somehow, they belonged. And it was that sense of belonging that inspired their loyalty and gave them pleasure. Martin too was beginning to feel he belonged. He was only picked occasionally for the second team when they were short of players, but he would watch from the side lines and cheer them on.

In slow steps, his sense of belonging grew. He began to feel part of university life and steadily loosened the grip on his hitherto rigid guard. Nobody knew his background and nobody seemed to care. And he had a variety of evasive answers ready to get him over most personal questions and a tale to tell, if needed, about his upbringing. And now that he was an adult, he was free of care homes forever. His welfare officer had wished him well when they said their final goodbyes and told him that she had arranged with the university that Martin could stay on in a hall of residence during university vacations. He had been no trouble to her and she hoped he would do well in life.

Over time, his hockey skills improved and he became a regular member of the second team. The women used a pitch alongside the men's and socialising after their games became the norm. It was here that he met his first girlfriend, a young woman who had been playing field hockey for several years. She taught him the essential moves some of which were not strictly about hockey. And Saturday evenings with his growing gang of friends became a highlight of the week as they wined, dined and partied until the small hours as young students do. With a growing reputation as a moderate and affable guy and whose hockey skills were now worthy of a first team place, and with two years more of studies to complete, he was proposed and seconded for the position of vice-captain to be followed in his final year as captain. The coach had a wry smile; rags to riches in twenty-four months.

It was late 2000, and as Martin commenced his third year, he had every expectation of good times ahead. He had excelled at his studies so far. He had a network of student friends, and he was now the person behind the hockey stall at fresher's week signing up newcomers. But life was about to take a twist that would change his new world order; the death in prison of his father. It came as a shock; a bolt from the blue. And it took some time to register that his past could never be tucked away in a closed drawer and forgotten. It would always be part of his psyche; part of the tapestry of his living.

He didn't have access to a private television and he wasn't viewing the one in the students' common room when the death of an infamous killer was announced on the morning news. It was only in the pub that evening with some mates whilst watching a premiership match on their widescreen, that he saw the news clip that was broadcast during the halftime interval. David Oakeshott, the frenzied stabber, as he had been dubbed previously by the tabloids, had taken his own life while serving his sentence for murder in one of Her Majesty's prisons. He had been due to be transferred the following day to a secure mental health institution to serve out the remainder of his sentence; a short period of only nine months. He was forty-nine and had developed diabetes. Martin fell silent and stared at the screen long after the clip had finished. The match restarted and his mates became very vocal again with every shot on target or missed passes. Martin drained his glass and excused himself on the grounds of a headache, an excuse that received several ribald comments. He made his way back to his hall with a descending gloom in his heart. He had escaped the shackles of his background, or so it seemed, only to be cruelly awakened to reality. He could never leave his past behind.

On waking the following morning, Martin had no recollection of getting back to his room. He had been on automatic pilot since learning the news of his father's death. He had sat down on his bed bereft of feeling except for a cold chill throughout his body. He hunkered down under the covers for warmth and cupped his hands over his face to console himself, something he had practised regularly in the children's homes when he felt in need of support.

There was extensive coverage of the murderer's death in the following day's Telegraph, which he forced himself to buy. It chronicled the whole sorry story from beginning to end. David Oakeshott's life was laid bare for all to read; it was a cradle to grave job leaving no miniscule fact unturned. Moreover, the paper rehashed the extraordinary rise from just a handful of whistle blowers seeking moderation of sentence for David to a nationwide craze involving thousands of do-gooders thumping their drums for legislative changes to be made to criminal sentencing. But the real damage as far as Martin was concerned was a subsidiary article headed "Where is he now?". And Martin was in no doubt that the "he" in the title was a reference to him, the then three-year old toddler son of David.

The reporter had dredged up a photograph from the archives of Martin holding his mother's hand as they disconsolately walked up the road to house number five in the terrace on their way back from completing some official task to do with the death. Martin held the newspaper in both hands. He was shaking with anger. Faced with the image of his young mother, his fingers clenched uncontrollably and crumpled and gouged the newsprint into tatters. It was too much to bear, but the copy printed alongside the image of mother and son was potentially far more damaging. According to the journalist, Martin would now be a youthful twenty-year old. With brown hair and a possible Geordie accent, he'd lived most of his early days in care. The reporter had traced most of his early life as far as his first year in secondary education. The trail had petered out after that. The care system in Martin's opinion wasn't renown for accuracy or good record-keeping. And he had been moved from pillar to post all over the country as foster parents and places in children's homes became available or dried up. It had been a tortuous path but one that, he realised, might afford some level of protection from nosey parkers. And he gained a little confidence when he looked closely at the spelling of the surname. His name was Oakeshott with an "e" and ending with a double "t". But the name in print was "Oakshot". A simple error, probably a typo, but one which would afford some protection against the inevitable computer search. He thought back to his days in care and the number of times over the years his name had been mangled by child care services; attention to detail had not been their forte. He remembered bitterly how much it had hurt that they couldn't even get that right. His only truly personal possession, his name. He'd had to answer to anything he was called or labelled in his passage from toddler to late teenager and it was only when he obtained his birth certificate from Somerset House that he established beyond doubt his full name and it wasn't Oakeshott, it was Oakeshill. His mother wasn't married, she must just have assumed her partner's name.

It had been a big story for the journalist, but not big enough it seemed to have done sufficient due diligence to check the toddler's birth certificate. Or maybe it was just a careless oversight on the part of the correspondent; easy to mistake Oakeshill for Oakeshott or to "see" what you expect to see. For Martin too, learning his true surname was a momentous moment. He tried to run through in his mind the implications of the uncanny coincidence; two parents with similar surnames. Should he contact the relevant authorities to change his name to Oakeshill or would he draw unnecessary attention to himself in so doing? Or should he just keep his head down and hope for the best? Over the last two years he had established a foundation for his life. He revelled in the chemistry Masters course and would have hated to leave midway through, he enjoyed the field hockey, in which he was beginning to excel despite his height, and his social life which was set fair. In the event, he spent a couple of quiet weeks and when he though the dust had settled, he resumed his life as before. So long as nobody ferreted around in his personal affairs, Martin felt safe. And he absolutely mustn't knowingly fraternize with anyone from the media. But, in the event, that's exactly what he did.

He was in his third year when he first met Kit at a lecture about laser light: its properties and its wide-ranging uses in the various life sciences. It was a shared lecture with undergraduates from different disciplines: physics, biology, chemistry, astronomy and medicine. He had taken his seat well in advance, neither near the front nor near the back of the auditorium. A young woman with high heels and curly blonde hair entered the lecture theatre a couple of minutes late and dithered about where to sit. She incurred the opprobrium of the lecturer for her late arrival and was told in no uncertain terms to take her place as quickly and quietly as possible. She took the first seat available which was next to Martin. He turned to smile at her but she looked steadfastly to the front as if she would incur a second rebuke if for just one instance, she dared to look away from the lectern centre stage.

'I'm sorry if I disturbed you,' she said, as they prepared to file out of the row at the end of the lecture.

'You didn't disturb me at all,' replied Martin. 'He was rather harsh on you.'

'I shouldn't have been late,' she sighed. 'It was my own fault.'

'What course are you doing?' asked Martin.

'Physics. Batchelor degree. And you?'

'Chemistry, Masters. My name is Martin,' he replied, 'and yours?'

'I'm Kit. A very simple name. I didn't realise that lasers impinged so much on chemistry.'

'They certainly do, and in so many diverse ways. Maybe we could meet up and I could explain more fully. He did rattle through his lecture. I got lost in some parts.' It wasn't the slickest of chat up lines known to man, but it was effective and a few days later they met in the library and in very hushed tones discussed the importance of laser light. They adjourned to a nearby fast-food outlet when the discussion became very technical and the pangs of hunger momentarily overcame their desire to appreciate how a monochromatic light source with intense power and pinpoint accuracy could impinge so dramatically on all the life sciences.

'What do you hope to do with your degree when you graduate?' inquired Kit.

'Chemical engineering, probably. Working in industry. Or, maybe some form of research. And you?'

'I know what I want to do. I want to teach. I'll have to do a one-year conversion course after my degree. I'd like to become a university lecturer so that I can do research in the long vacations.'

'Keep up to date.'

'Yes, exactly that,' Kit said smiling. Martin relaxed to the warmth of her smile. 'What do you do when you're not studying?' she asked.

'I'm studying most of the time,' he replied seriously. 'Only got my grant and have to eke out the money carefully because I don't want to get an evening job. I want to pass my exams first time and get a good degree so that I can get a well-paid job.' He realised that in that one reply, he had told her more about himself that he had mentioned to anyone of his university chums thus far.

'But when you're not studying what do you do?' Kit persisted.

'I play hockey and I Scottish country dance.'

'You look far too tall to bend down sufficiently quickly for hockey, and your large feet could crush any toes they come in contact with,' she said cheekily, pointing at his pair of size thirteens.

'Yes, I know. I've already lost several partners in the Gay Gordons. They want danger money to partner me. Would you like to be my next victim?' It was a daring move by Martin, who never having had a steady girlfriend before he arrived at university, had learned some cheesy chat up lines in double quick time.

'I love dancing,' said Kit. 'I joined the ballroom dancing society in my first year but I didn't really enjoy it. It was rather stuffy for my taste; a bit too prim for me. I like to let my hair down.'

'Then why not come and join me in an Eightsome reel or a faster tempo jig which is guaranteed to get your pulse racing.'

By the end of Kit's second year and Martin's third, they were an item. They loved the dancing and Kit became the society's organiser. They never missed a session. The progression from acquaintanceship to chums to lovers was swift. But always in the back of Martin's mind was the necessity not to drop his guard. An awkward moment could be just around any corner, followed by the denouement of his family background. And on that score, there was an uncanny and unspoken meeting of minds. Kit had never asked him about his family and it was a subject that he never raised with anyone less they should enquire about his own. It was rather surreal that the bedrock of a young person, their close family, should never get a mention. He wondered if Kit too had some skeletons in her cupboard.

Chapter 6

EVENTS

When he left the Reading house for good, it was with a heavy heart but with no antagonism. Both were determined that they would part on good terms albeit sad. They had sat down together and gone through the prosaic practicalities of their estrangement, most of which centred on the property. Martin had packed his bags and arranged storage for his stuff he deemed superfluous to needs while living in Vienna. Kit had arranged to become an on-call house tutor for the coming academic year which entitled her to live in a student hall during term time. With her personal possessions bundled into two large suitcases, she too had left Reading, and probably for good.

The house would be rented out furnished on a twelve-month contract. Martin would receive all the rent after the managing agent took his fees. It would reimburse him for all the contributions, usually the lion's share, he had paid towards the utility bills and council tax whilst living there. If saved, as Kit knew they would be, the rental monies would make a sizeable chunk towards a deposit on another property especially as his living expenses whilst on secondment in Vienna would be negligible and there would be tax breaks too associated with being out of the country for long periods. At the end of the fixed term contract the house would be sold and the proceeds would be Kit's alone. Kit would have no further need for a residence so far south as she would be living with Edmund. They shook hands in agreement and Martin departed for Vienna and Kit, after waving a fond farewell to her little house, took the train to the West Country to visit her frail grandparents and do for them whatever a grateful granddaughter could do. They would be thrilled to see her and despite their ill health, they would want to know all the nuts and bolts about the new life on which she was embarking.

When not working, the beautiful city of Vienna had a great deal to offer a person with time on their hands. Martin had never been on holiday abroad, indeed, he had never truly experienced what most people regard as a "holiday", home or away. The closest he had really come to the phenomenon were his day trips to Bristol to visit his mother. He would miss his regular trips there; he didn't really know the state of her mind but hoped fervently that she wouldn't pine for him. His first overseas outing had been to Paris on company business. Then there had been the mini-break in Amsterdam on a hockey jamboree, followed by another work-related trip to Paris. So now with time on his hands to explore Vienna, he followed the tourist routes to see the sights starting with a hop-on, hop-off city bus tour. Then there was the guided tour around Schönbrunn Palace and its magnificent gardens, an evening at the Vienna State Opera House and the prospect in a few weeks' time of the popular Christmas market at the Rathaus. So, when the email arrived from Clare telling him that she was free the coming weekend to join him, Martin, surprised at the speed at which she had taken up his casual invitation, knew what sights to show her. But it was with certain misgivings that he met Clare in the city centre at Vienna Mitte station where the fast train from the airport brought her less than thirty minutes after her plane had landed.

'Nice to see you again so soon,' said Martin rather clumsily as he lent forward to kiss her on the cheek.

'Oh, I think we can do better than that,' replied Clare planting a full-on kiss on his lips and setting the tone for what she expected of the weekend. Martin winced. He could forget any cultural tours to Schönbrunn Palace and the Rathaus, she had only one thing in mind. He had chatted her up on the rebound from Kit and was now regretting it. By late afternoon she was finally ready to leave his apartment having preened herself for an unconscionable time in front of the bathroom mirror while Martin was left to kick his heels, metaphorically, in frustration.

After enjoying sachertorte – a type of chocolate cake which is one of the most famous Viennese culinary specialities – at an outdoor café in the main shopping area, they strolled down one of the lively streets in the old town with its pleasing mixture of eateries, bars, sophisticated and elegant retail therapy outlets interspersed with craft shops. Time passed quickly as they wandered in and out of the stores and boutiques examining the goods on offer. Clare had a decent smattering of German and conversed freely with the shopkeepers. Martin tagged along pleased that time was passing and that he would be back at work the day after next.

The restaurant Martin had chosen had been recommended by one of his work colleagues. With a varied menu of international dishes including some traditional German fare – the inevitable bratwurst and schnitzel – it had a reputation for good, tasty food. Neither grand nor swanky from the outside, Clare hovered on the threshold as if the selected dinner venue was below her normal acceptable standard. Martin had been there once before and assured her that a warm welcome awaited them, but from her stony grimace he could tell that she wasn't convinced.

'As promised, the ambience here is very cordial,' pronounced Martin, when they were seated.

'It's called "gemütlich" in German,' corrected Clare, her mood thawing somewhat with a glass of red wine. 'Agreeably pleasant. Relations are cordial, rooms are gemütlich.'

Despite the tetchy start to the evening, Clare proved good company over their leisurely dinner, the more so when both were persuaded that their choice of a fine-dining version of bratwurst for the main course could only be fully appreciated if taken with a small stein of Viennese lager. The deep, copper-coloured beer was served in a traditionally decorated stoneware mug with hinged lid that held half a litre. And it was true that the toasted flavours of malt were the perfect complement to the all-meat sausage. With a higher than usual alcohol content, it could also have a powerful effect on inhibitions for those who had not yet encountered its charms. With a sorbet to cleanse the palette, thoughts of dessert were dismissed in favour of sampling the house herbal liqueur. Martin was not a big drinker and sipped the smooth, sticky wine slowly, whereas Clare, used to the parliamentary life involving numerous functions with free booze, drained her glass rapidly. A touch more loquacious than her normal self, she spotted the chance to pry. 'Tell me about yourself, Martin,' she started. 'You've told me all about your work – what you do, where you do it, who you work with, how long you've been doing it, what you hope to achieve – but you haven't told me much about *you*.'

'Work and field hockey take up most of my life,' said Martin slowly, alarmed at the turn of subject and wary that he was about to be put under the magnifying glass.

'But what about you,' she repeated, leaning across the table and pressing a pointed finger into his shoulder. 'Tell me about you.'

'Nothing much to tell. Nothing interesting anyhow,' replied Martin as casually as he could. 'My background is boringly unremarkable.'

'If I didn't know better, I'd think you were stonewalling,' she said. 'For instance, what about your previous partner?' she continued. 'What was she like?'

'I think it's time we left. It's going home time.' He put up the shutter and prayed she would take the hint. Clare yawned. She was tired and she wasn't going to get anything more out of him tonight.

The drug trials for the new formulation were at a critical point. The incoming data was reaching an exponential point on the graph and required careful logging by the junior assistants. There was much discussion across the conference table by the leading players involved, a small group of German, Austrian and British scientists. Martin was there as an observer. It was his company's work that had led to the reformulation and he was present to ensure that the trials were performed and carried out in accordance with the standards laid down. But Martin's mind was elsewhere. Normally controlled and focussed on his work, he was not on the ball today. Clare's bad temper at the airport when he had seen her off had rattled him and, moreover, he had to admit that there was truth in her angry reproach. She'd accused him of giving her the come on only to follow it up with the big heave-ho. She'd wasted her weekend and she wasn't going to forget the insult easily. She had stomped off in high dudgeon and left Martin feeling guilty. He wasn't used to being accused of mistreatment. It had usually been the other way around when he was in care. He accepted that his experience of relationships was extremely limited. He harked back to his happy, sedate days with Kit, both emotionally reserved, their relationship had run along smoothly without tempestuous highs and lows. He scratched his head and brought his focus back on track just in time to answer an important question posed by the chairman about the preparedness of the new drug's supply line.

It took Martin a few days to take stock of Clare's calamitous visit. For the umpteenth time he berated himself for his naivety. She was six years or so younger than him but she was worldly-wise. She had ensnared him and he had been too gullible, or perhaps just too upset at the break up with Kit, to notice. Clare wasn't even his type. He didn't like her attention-seeking style and all the one-upmanship remarks she kept dropping into conversation about her role in politics. Quiet, steady people you could rely on were his type. Boring even. He resolved that for the moment, or possibly for quite some time to come, he would need to concentrate solely on his work and not get mixed up with anyone else. He would miss most of his regular weekend hockey games and the after-game socialising that was part of it but he still had his official hockey duties to fulfil as distraction, and if he organised committee meetings carefully then he might be able to play in the odd game or two. Trips home would be limited to a handful of weekends as he no longer had a place of his own to stay, and staying away, Martin acknowledged, was the best thing for him right now. But when Martin attended an official hockey function in his capacity as senior executive officer, matters didn't quite pan out as Martin had envisaged.

He had engineered a playing spot in the second team's midday match against one of the big London clubs. The hockey association's AGM and annual prize-giving would take place later that evening in the facilities of a country club in Buckinghamshire. It was a big event in the association's calendar. He had been worrying about what best to say when the inescapable question was asked about Kit's whereabouts. She had been at his side for so long that her absence would not go unnoticed. Should he take the coward's way out and concoct a story to explain away her non-appearance? Or, should he just square up to the situation, be brave, and tell the truth no matter how much it hurt? As chance would have it, the inevitable enquiry came from an unexpected source.

'Hallo,' said a voice from slightly behind him. 'You're Martin, I believe.'

'Er, yes,' said Martin turning quickly to see who was speaking to him. 'I *am* Martin.' The speaker was a plain-looking young woman in an understated evening dress but one which highlighted her athletic physique. 'I'm sorry, but I don't recall us meeting before.'

'We haven't met as such,' she agreed, 'but we did both attend the same memorial service fairly recently.'

'Oh. Do you mean the one in Newcastle?'

'Exactly. You were with a lady who I presumed was your partner. I exchanged nods and smiles with her on exiting the cathedral. And later, in the marquee, I saw you both sitting together at one of the tables.'

'Right,' said Martin, a little stumped for what next to say and worried about where this was all leading.

'I believe your partner, Kit, is a twin. Is that correct?'

'Kit and I,' he replied, looking down and shuffling his feet, 'are no longer together. She is engaged to be married to someone else. But you are correct, she is a twin.'

'Sorry,' said Avril awkwardly, 'if I am stirring up a sensitive subject. You see, I too am a twin, and I was interested in the history of the deceased's lineage because of the number of twins in her wider family.' She paused for thought before continuing. 'The solicitor in charge kindly sent me a genealogy chart of the family on my request.'

'Why did you ask for one?' Martin asked frowning.

'I work for a radio station in the Midlands, mostly doing the research work for the main presenters. But I have my own spots mid-morning and mid-afternoon when I tackle a subject and invite listeners to call in and air their views.' She had a rich, mellifluous voice and Martin imagined that it would be pleasing to her listeners' ears. 'And my latest afternoon spot is about the occurrence of twins in families.'

'Why the subject of twins?'

'Because many of our daytime listeners engage more fully with mundane topics. They get fed up with the usual diet of politics and sport, religion and highbrow culture. They want to know about more prosaic matters. Something closer to home with which they can identify. And as I am a twin too, it seemed a good subject to select.' Her manner was quiet and unpretentious and Martin listened attentively. She reminded him of someone but he couldn't tell who. She drifted off as other guests came over to speak to the association's leader, but he would see her again when he presented the annual prizes after the banquet and it would be only then that he would realise with whom she was a twin. When called forward to accept her prize as the year's outstanding woman goalkeeper of the southern division, Avril Roach stepped forward briskly to accept the trophy from Martin. It took a few moments for the penny to drop with him that Avril shared the same surname as Clare. They were twins, and yes, there was a facial resemblance, not marked, but indelibly present. And it was an uncomfortable thought as he tossed and turned in his hotel bed that night that the girls may have swapped notes about him. Oh, how he longed for the steady, stable years with Kit. Life in a well-worn routine and with someone with whom he had the feeling of belonging.

It was a leisurely breakfast for Martin next morning. Late to bed and without much sleep, he had presented himself in the breakfast room after the eight o'clock rush. He had until the midday checkout to enjoy the country club's facilities before heading to the airport for an early evening flight back to Vienna. He was working his way through a full English when a late straggler interrupted his gastronomic feast; a couple from the Salisbury area, about to start their journey home, waved an acknowledgement of thanks as they left the breakfast room while the straggler stood opposite. Martin indicated to her to take a seat.

'Good morning, Avril,' he said formally. 'I hope you slept well.'

'Very well indeed. It's my day off so I try to sleep in late on Sunday mornings. I'm at work by seven all the other mornings of the week.' She smiled. 'I just wanted to thank you for a splendid evening.'

'You did well. A trophy to have and to hold for a year. I'm sorry I didn't get to see you play in real time but reports from your club were praiseworthy indeed.'

'Thanks,' said Avril simply. 'I also stopped by to give you the radio station's business card.' Martin looked quizzical. 'I thought you might be interested in the phone-in spots.'

'I'm working abroad at the moment on a six-month secondment,' explained Martin, 'but when I'm back permanently I could tune in. Was there a special topic you wanted me to hear?'

'There will be one coming up soon,' Avril said shyly, 'about bereavement and separation. I don't know exactly when. We don't have set lengths of time for subjects to last. How long an individual topic lasts is dependent on the number of listeners ringing in with their views.' She smiled nervously. 'I just thought,' she went on cautiously, 'that you might find some solace in their stories. Local people responding to their local radio show usually put forward practical and sensible views and say it how it is. It's not like nationwide broadcasting when the ringers-in are far more interested in being on countrywide radio rather than in putting forward cogent opinions.'

'Thank you, Avril.' It was all Martin could think of to say. She wasn't pushy like her sister and although she didn't radiate the attractive allure of Clare, she was in Martin's eyes, by far the nicer twin.

* * *

Kit rolled back the years when she awoke under her grandparent's roof in Cornwall. It was a treat she had sampled far too seldom in the past few years; her regular but occasional visits of three or four days slotted into the sort of hectic schedule that young people always had. In more recent years the timing of these trips had become increasingly dictated by the couple's failing health. Accompanied by Martin from time to time, she would attend to any jobs about the house or garden that they were no longer fit to undertake. And there would be shopping trips to stock up the larder with an able-bodied granddaughter by their side to do the heavy lifting.

This trip, possibly the last for some time, would be special. They would want to know all about her engagement to Edmund, the split up with Martin, the sale of the house in Reading, and Kit's proposed permanent departure to Northumbria. They had frequently discussed matters over the phone during the previous weeks but there was never any real substitute for face-to-face meetings when nuances of body language could be neither disguised nor ignored. She would unwind in their wholehearted attention and they would read her like a book.

Notwithstanding the direct train service from London Paddington to St. Austell and the short taxi drive to Carlyon Bay, it had felt like a gruelling journey. The train sped through the picturesque countryside until it reached Plymouth and then seemed to meander in second gear to her destination. She was tired when she arrived and understood why the couple would have been physically incapable of making the long trek up to Newcastle for the memorial service. They were only in their mid-seventies but her grandfather had longstanding heart issues and her grandma was plagued with arthritic pain. They led quiet lives but were happy in their own way tootling around the bay and watching, often from the cliffs, the activity on the wide, sandy beach. It was Daphne du Maurier country and the area had much to recommend it.

They were all agog to hear her news and see the engagement ring. Kit had taken photos on her mobile of Edmund and his family and brought with her the latest gizmo just released onto the tech market: the tablet. Making use of the town's wi-fi network, she set up the tablet, downloaded the photos and showed them how to operate the new gadget. Her grandmother was quick to learn and was soon scrolling through dozens of pictures from the cathedral and refreshment marquee and pointing out faces she knew from the past.

The dining table was set in a corner of the living room that gave a distant view of the sea. It was a good place to linger over their mid-morning coffees and to delve deeper into private thoughts. 'I thought you were happy with Martin,' said her grandma.

'We were surprised when you told us that you were going to marry Edmund,' added her grandfather.

'What brought that about? What prompted you to have a change of mind?' her grandma continued. 'You both seemed so well suited.'

'We were well suited, that's true,' replied Kit. 'But we were going nowhere. We'd been together about eight years, and lived under the same roof for almost five.' Kit took a few deep breaths. 'But our relationship had stagnated. It was treading water. We'd never discussed marriage or starting a family. I'd never even met his parents.'

'And you're worried that at the age of thirty, time is running out to enjoy such things,' said her grandma perceptively.

'Quite.'

'It is odd, I agree,' her grandfather chipped in, 'that you know nothing about his family background, but when you are as old as I am, you will realise that thirty is still amazingly young.' He patted her shoulder to reinforce his words.

'When I met Edmund, I began to take stock of the situation. See it as it was. See it as my friends see it.'

'I understand,' her grandma said, 'but happiness and friendship are surely more important that the opinions of your friends, albeit they were well intentioned.'

'Yes, I know, Grandma. I've wrestled with that point of view.'

'And Edmund offered you more?'

'We were thrown together by circumstance. I didn't actively go looking for someone else. It just occurred naturally.'

'And you're glad about Edmund but tinged with sadness about Martin,' her grandma summed up correctly. 'Then you must go forward without regrets. The past is the past. It will always be there, but it *is* the past. Concentrate on the present.'

Two days of focussing her energies on her grandparents' jobs and chores, running messages and making deliveries, cleaning and reorganising, mending and fixing, consigning to the bin or to the charity shop, and Kit felt she had made a worthwhile contribution to their well-being. Her grandmother's words had also had a chance to sink in. At teatime on the afternoon before her departure she was ready to pose questions about past family affairs. 'In the old days,' Kit started, addressing both grandparents, 'were there any rumours running in the family about, shall we say, spiteful or odd behaviour?' It was a question that elicited raised eyebrows followed by head shakes combined with tutting noises.

'If you delve back far enough, every family has its scandals to hide,' her grandfather said eventually, 'and ours is no different.'

'Is it grandfather Roach's forebears that interest you?' enquired her grandma. 'Not my side of the family.'

'Yes. Now that I am her co-executor, it is really anything unusual or unexplained about Kit Audrey Harrison née Roach that interests me.'

'I thought we might get back to her. My exceptional aunt.'

'But is she really your aunt?' asked Kit in earnest. 'That's what I'm trying to establish.' Her grandparents looked momentarily stunned. 'Have you any reason to believe that great grandfather Peter and Old Kit were not blood brother and sister?' Kit continued, 'that they did not have the same mother or even share the same father?'

'Why do you ask?' said her grandmother.

'Because there is something very strange about the family tree.' Kit had been clutching two sheets of paper on which she had drawn the ancestry tree in as clear and simple a manner as she could. For ease of understanding, and in large capitals, it incorporated only the major players, Old Kit herself, her favourite brother Peter, and troublesome Reginald. She set the pages side by side on the table top and angled them in front of her grandparents. With reading spectacles adjusted, they familiarised themselves with the individuals.

'What do you find strange?' asked her grandmother eventually.

'Twins, Grandma. Old Kit had two sets of twins.'

'Yes. We know,' replied her grandfather on both their behalf. 'It may be unusual but why is it strange?'

'Because Gertrude, supposedly her mother, and wife of Harold, had no twins herself and therefore could not pass down the line any tendency for multiple births. And according to my research, Gertrude did not have a sister either who could have done the same.'

'So, your conclusion is what?' questioned her grandfather.

'Purely on a scientific basis, there can only be one conclusion. Old Kit was not Gertrude's child but she may have been Harold's.' The grandparents exchanged glances but said nothing. 'Do you know anything that might explain this quandary?' asked Kit hopefully.

'Well,' they said in almost perfect unison. 'There were rumours,' her grandmother went on alone, 'but Grandpa should tell you because after all, it's his family line.' But it was clear from his mien that her grandfather was reluctant to mentally rummage around in the past. He wasn't well and the emotional strain of recounting tittle-tattle could easily upset the delicate balance of his heart condition. 'I can only say,' he said, 'that Reginald believed that Old Kit was an outsider. That she did not belong. And my father Peter, your great grandfather, told me that I was always to treat her well because she had had a difficult start to life.' Kit could see that he would have liked to leave the matter there, but he gamely continued. 'Apparently, she seemed to share no physical characteristics with her siblings or supposed parents and there was uncertainty about her birth certificate.'

'In what way?'

'By Peter's account, one day when Reginald was in one of his strops about being the overlooked eldest male sibling, he and his other two younger brothers forced open the wooden bureau in which their parents kept official documents. It had a lockable drawer but they found a way to open it without causing damage. It was the late 1920s and documentation, although produced on a typewriting machine, was sparse and almost rudimentary in comparison to today's standards. Every household in those days had some ordinary place where they kept such things: a lockable tin box pushed under the bed, or a small drawer in a chest of drawers, or the back of a wardrobe, sometimes even a stout box on the mantelpiece. But Reggie found no birth certificate for his sister.' Her grandfather drew breath and brushed a lock of white hair from his forehead. 'Reggie would have been about fifteen at the time and too young, and frankly too callow to know how to drill down to get to the facts related to that discovery. To him it was a black or white issue. No birth certificate, therefore no sister. And from that day forward he set his mind to treat her as an intruder.'

'Why didn't he investigate further when he was older and more worldly-wise?' asked Kit.

'He may have. I don't know. But a search at Somerset House would only be successful if you were sure of the mother's name and the correct date of birth of the person you are researching. And how was he going to get that?'

'I suppose he could have asked,' Kit said rather naively.

'Not Reggie. Reggie wasn't a man to do asking.'

'He was an unpleasant person,' added her grandmother with feeling. 'Five minutes in his company was enough for a lifetime.' On a nod from her husband, she continued. 'And there is something else about Old Kit as you call her, something unexplained,' she ventured cautiously, 'something most of the family don't appear to know, probably because the only genuine and enduring friendship she had amongst her large family was with her brother Peter. They would have shared personal thoughts and confidential matters between them right up until Peter's death in 1988, some twenty-odd years before her own.'

'Go on,' urged Kit as her grandmother's voice trailed off.

'Peter would have kept safe any secrets his sister told him, but inevitably things slip out in unguarded moments between husband and wife. After Peter's death, his widow, your great grandmother, lived a further twelve years. She became increasingly confused in her later years. We visited her regularly and listened patiently as she rambled on; her short-term memory was poor but she seemed to remember things from the distant past with comparative ease. A recurring ramble was about Old Kit and a Whitehall department. Exactly what it was about we couldn't understand but we took it that as some point in her career Old Kit worked for them.'

'Did she say which department?'

'No, but we both had the distinct impression,' her grandmother replied, looking directly at her husband as if for confirmation, 'that it was something clandestine.'

'Like MI5?'

'We don't know. But it certainly wasn't the Ministry of Works and Pensions!'

Back in her room in the hall of residence, and with fingers crossed, she sent an email to her grandparents to check that they could manage operating the new tablet without her by their side. Shortly, she received a cheery message back with an attached photo of the beach scene that morning showing that the copious notes her grandmother had had the foresight to make, were working well. The tablet would never be a substitute for their telephone chats but it brought a whole new range of possibilities for the three of them to enjoy together while physically apart. And a further cyber message from Cornwall, received hot on the heels of the first but this time from her grandmother alone and with a sense of secrecy since she implied that it would have been "difficult" to mention it in front of her husband but which she felt Kit should know, told of a newspaper article in the early 1960s citing a homosexual incident in a public lavatory somewhere in the London area in times when such activities were illegal. The short article, almost hidden in the middle pages was headed in small capitals "IMPORTUNING" and speculated that the man involved had connections with political bodies. Apparently, her grandfather had come across the article, cut it out and saved it, and she herself had found it many years later when they were turning out their writing bureau. She had asked him to whom it referred and what interest he had in the matter and he had responded that it referred to a shameful incident involving a prominent family member who had brought his kinsfolk into disrepute and he had declined to elaborate further. The article stated that for legal reasons the name of the suspected offender had been withheld. Her grandmother had added that she didn't know the publication date but the newspaper was almost certainly the Daily Gazette as it was the only paper they bought regularly.

"Importuning" thought Kit to herself, weighing the word carefully. It's not a word we use these days. It's a word from yesteryear which reflected the morals of those times. She did a google search and discovered that the first piece of legislation partially decriminalising homosexuality was passed in 1967. She fired back a message to her grandmother congratulating her on having learnt so quickly how to master the basics of the tablet and requesting her to take a picture of the newspaper clipping with the camera feature and send it to her as an attachment. Kit sighed with exasperation. She was turning up more questions than answers the deeper she dug. But if she could discover the approximate date of the article then she could request the newspaper to let her have any follow up articles they may have published. Moreover, if she knew the date when this unlawful action was committed then she might be able to make a considered guess at the name of the perpetrator. She scrolled through the ancestry tree on her mobile looking at dates of birth and working out people's ages in the period between the war and the passing of the new legislation. And then she thought of Edmund and the access he had as a solicitor to past court proceedings and various police and government files. Provide him with a date and he would be able to do the rest, she thought, but right now, born 1913 and mostly in his forties during the period in question, it was Reggie who was looking the prime suspect.

It was term time and Edmund, rushed off his feet as the new partner, the third Newman in succession in the firm of Newman, Wilson and Saddler, had to carefully time his calls to Kit in London to coincide with her non-teaching time and with his own clients. They had set up a ping pong system when the mobile of each either buzzed or vibrated according to whether they were able to answer the phone at that particular moment. One buzz and one vibration were a no-goer. A buzz from each was the required signal.

'Hallo, fiancée. Good to talk. And I've got some news.'

'So have I,' Kit replied, hooking a blonde curl behind her left ear. 'You go first.'

'Well, it's about the note that was stuffed into your hand at the memorial service.'

'The Rich Bitch note?'

'Yes, that one.' He grinned broadly at his end of the line at the very idea that she had notes stuffed into her hand on a regular basis. 'I kept it,' said Edmund, 'and now I've been able to pinpoint the source.'

'But it was typewritten apart from the "Rich Bitch" handwritten capitals scrawled on the envelope.'

'I know,' Edmund said a little too smugly, rather enjoying stringing her along. 'You said at the time that the wording of the note was the work of a well-educated mind.'

'That's right.'

'So, I turned my attention to the stationery on which it was sent: cheap white envelope which I dismissed as non-identifiable, but expensive, quality paper which by virtue of a careless error, led me to recognise it as being Houses of Parliament notepaper.'

'Whoa.'

'Whoa, indeed.'

'What gave it away?'

'The A4 sheet of paper was no longer A4 size. It had had its top cut off, the portion where the Crowned Portcullis in green is printed.'

'Go on, spill it all out. I can hear the smug tone in your voice and you're not going to be satisfied until you've totally impressed me with your sleuthing powers. What was the careless error made?'

'Can you see the shape of a portcullis in your mind's eye; the vertical and horizontal bars in the form of a strong gate? It was a rhetorical question needing no more than a murmured reply on her part. 'The bottom of each vertical, at ground level that is, is shaped like an arrowhead,' he continued. 'The sheet of paper will have been beheaded on a guillotine, and if you've ever used one of those machines then you will know how difficult it is to line it up despite the straight edges and various markings along one side of the instrument to act as guide.'

'And,' said Kit, guessing what was coming next but too wise to steal his thunder.

'And,' Edmund replied, 'a slither of the emblem was missed and obviously wasn't spotted. The green arrowheads were still there.'

'And you knew instantly what they represented,' said Kit giggling.

'No. Not instantly. Don't be daft and stop laughing, this is serious stuff.' He paused for gravitas. 'Not so much these days with increasing email correspondence, but rewind ten years or so and lots of official legal documents we dealt with then had a portcullis hallmark. So, I wrote to my member of parliament about some trivial affair, and hey presto, got a letter back on headed notepaper.'

'And you matched the paper and arrowheads.'

'Exactly that.'

'And we both know,' said Kit slowly and deliberately, 'someone in the family who has access to Houses of Parliament notepaper.'

'Not just one member of the wider family,' interrupted Edmund with the coup de grâce, 'but two. One of Adam Roach's twins, Clare, works for him as a private secretary.'

'Really?'

'Check the family tree app on your mobile, fiancée. The background stuff is all there.'

'But it was such a juvenile hoax pinching our luggage for a few hours.' Her voice trailed off as she realised that the "our" in "our luggage" referred to her and Martin. And it was not lost on Edmund who gave her time to recover. 'Would you really expect well-educated people to do such a childish prank?'

'Up here in Northumbria,' replied Edmund, 'we still mostly believe that there's nowt so queer as folk. It wasn't the nature of the prank; it was the message that it sent and the disruption that it caused. It was making a statement of intent.'

'And I suppose just who put it into my hand is immaterial. A shiny two-pound coin would have bought any kid's co-operation.'

'What's your news from Cornwall?' Edmund asked, moving the conversation on. 'I'm glad you found your grandparents in good spirits even though physically frail.'

'Yes, they're good people, and yes, I have things to report although you may find them as confusing as I do.'

'Go ahead. I'm all ears.'

'There's something and nothing. All a bit nebulous I'm afraid.' But Kit never got any farther than that as Edmund whispered into his mobile a hurried goodbye and an instruction to put it all in an email as his next client entered his room.

Newman, Wilson & Saddler had had an influx of corporate clients in the short time since Edmund had become a partner. According to one of the partners, business in the twenty-first century was evolving and the practice should evolve too. As Edmund at only thirty-five was by far the youngest, he was deemed by Messrs. Wilson & Saddler to be the right man for the corporate work as his young face would inspire confidence in his technological skills and knowledge of contemporary workday trends. Edmund was somewhat reluctant to specialise in corporate law as he enjoyed being involved in the wide variety of legal work that the practice offered its clients, but he could see the sense in his partners' suggestion.

He opened Kit's email immediately after his client had left. She had tabulated what her grandfather had told her which he found helpful. She was right. It was all hearsay or speculation – even the "missing" birth certificate story – until he got to item number six: importuning. He knew exactly what that meant as his grandfather, the original Mr. Newman, had played a small role in a high-profile case back in the 1950s when the morals and laws of the era dictated quiet prosecutions followed swiftly by wholesale sweepings of resultant debris under the carpet. But whispers inevitably surfaced and occasionally an editor could be persuaded to publish a few censored facts for his readership's titillation. According to Edmund's internet search, copies of the Daily Gazette didn't roll off the printers until 1949 when it was formed by the merger of two large and long-established regional dailies giving them nationwide coverage. The new publication had a more liberal and devil-may-care attitude towards such matters realising that the Victorian rules were outdated and that the public were ready to embrace alternative standards.

Edmund wasn't to know, but his route to discovering the name of the person generating the article – Kit had forwarded on to him the photo of the clipping her grandmother had taken – would be a great deal more straightforward than Kit's. After a few days' wait, his enquiry to the editor's office yielded the actual date of publication and attached a copy of the only follow-up report. The unnamed man in the original article remained unnamed but his age and county of residence were divulged, and it was all Edmund needed to identify him with a reasonable degree of certainty. He traced the pathway on the genealogy chart and his finger stopped when it reached the same year of birth. It would have been the end of the road for Kit, but for Edmund as a solicitor practising criminal law there was still the National Archive to search to confirm the man's name. The case proceedings filled in all the missing gaps in the story of Reggie's youngest son. He had been arrested for "an act of gross indecency" in a public space in November 1972 and sentenced to six months imprisonment when he refused probation with severe strings attached. In March 1973, with less than two full months to serve, he committed suicide in his cell. He was twenty-six years of age.

When Edmund rang Kit late that evening, it was in a serious and troubled tone. 'What could have pushed him to suicide?' he asked Kit. 'He'd almost completed his sentence. Sure, he would have had a police record for the remainder of his life but he would have been free and very few people would have had any inkling of what had happened. He could have put it all behind him.'

'Maybe he didn't see it that way,' replied Kit. 'He was still young and inexperienced in life. Maybe he was goaded by fellow inmates and it just became all too much. Or, maybe he was afraid of what his family would do when he got out.'

'I don't suppose Reggie would have been pleased; not first-born son this time but another let down with a son.'

'His aspirations dashed again,' agreed Kim. 'From what we know of Reggie's personality, it's quite likely that he would have disowned him.'

'He would have been fifty-nine when his son took his life.'

'Is that relevant?'

'Probably not, but Reggie would have been near the height of his workplace powers at that age and wouldn't have welcomed a link with homosexuality. He would have lost face with his union members. Working down the pits in those days was no place for airing alternative views.'

'You are probably right,' summed up Kit, 'he might have taken his own life for fear of his own father. But we shall never know for certain. So, what does that leave us with?'

'Just another reason why Reggie's tribe hated Old Kit.'

'And would use to justify doing anything to get hold of her money.'

'Yet it wasn't her fault. The sexual proclivity of the youngest son of her eldest brother was nothing to do with her. They just couldn't bear the thought of her looking down from the moral high ground. Changing the subject,' continued Edmund, 'can you come up for the weekend? My mother's badgering me to set a date for the wedding.'

It was Friday. In general, Kit was never scheduled to lecture or supervise student laboratory work on Fridays. Instead, she reserved the day for one-to-one tutorials in her office with any student who was falling behind in their work or in difficulty understanding the ground covered by a previous lecture. By midday she had already seen three of her students and ironed out some of their problems with a particularly difficult concept regarding the passage of light through various materials. And she was now free to concentrate on other matters, and over a sandwich and coffee at her desk, she re-read the latest article in a prominent physics journal that had implications for her own research into toroidal surfaces. She realised that the information in the scientific paper, by a Canadian physicist, would allow her to attempt a laboratory experiment by a method that should produce more reliable results. Kit adjusted her spectacles, and for the millionth time in her career in science, marvelled at the centuries' old system for the sharing of scientific knowledge which allowed anyone in the world, no matter who, where or when, to use that knowledge to help them with their own research. Her chest swelled with pride that every time one of her research papers was accepted for publication, she too became part of that benevolent system.

With time pressing, she scooped up some work papers from her desk for further consideration on the train journey, grabbed her holdall and departed for the station. The train was crowded and she had not reserved a seat. She stood for over an hour as the train hurtled through several stations, her luggage between her feet and a hand on a waist-height rail to steady herself. At the first stopping station she moved quickly to secure a seat as daily commuters to London, allowing themselves an early Friday afternoon exit from the office, got off. She hoisted her holdall into the overhead rack and swung her briefcase onto her knees. She had not shut it properly and the lid flew open spilling her papers over the carriage floor. The young man seated next to her helped gather them up. He showed no interest in the serious looking literature until he picked up the copy of Field Hockey Quarterly. In spite of her stilettoes he enquired if she played. She was bewildered as to why he had asked the question until she came across the magazine while sorting her papers back into their original neat pile. It wasn't hers. One of the students must have left it on her desk at the morning tutorial and Kit, in her haste to get to King's Cross on time, had obviously swept it into her briefcase in error.

Kit idly thumbed through the magazine before starting on more weighty reading. Martin had subscribed to it; she remembered the distinctive lettering of the title. She wasn't sure what her motives were for doing so but if she had been honest with herself, she wouldn't have been surprised to come across a photograph of Martin as he was the current chief of the hockey association. The photo depicted him presenting a cup to a young woman at the annual award ceremony. Kit felt her heart skip a beat; it was like former happy times revisited but with melancholy. It had been a mistake to look through the periodical but Kit knew she couldn't help herself. Martin was looking well and smiling broadly at the young woman in the picture, and there was something about her that looked familiar. She couldn't place her but was sure they'd met before.

Amid all the talk of wedding plans – the date now scheduled for next Easter's university vacation when the work demands on Kit would be at their minimum – Edmund's focus remained fully on resolving all the loose ends of Old Kit's will, of which there were many and some looking decidedly intractable. Ideally, he wanted it done and dusted before his marriage so that he could concentrate on building a family life. He was a little fearful that if it dragged on without a timely end in sight then their joint executorship would become a burden. If that happened, he realised, the life and times of Old Kit would reach out to ensnare him too.

'We must go to Guernsey poste-haste,' he said, as Kit lay on the sofa with her feet in his lap. 'The time for procrastination is long past. We must go together.'

'Why?'

'Because we are joint-executors and one without the other would carry little weight.'

'Even if I gave you a signed document to permit you to act on my behalf?'

'That would just be another reason for the bank to decline to see me. We must go there as soon as practicable and with as much documentation as we can muster.'

'Do you want me to give you some dates when I might be free?'

'I'm afraid it doesn't work like that. You can't just ring up and book an appointment as if you were going to the hairdresser,' Edmund said, bouncing a couple of Kit's curls on her shoulder. 'They are far too sniffy for that.'

'Then how do we get to see them?' asked Kit not unreasonably.

'Via an intermediary who will set it up.'

'One of your mysterious contacts?'

'Not really. A solicitor who lives and works on Guernsey and who will be known to the bank. One of my financial contacts has used him in the past and recommended his services. And his services don't come cheap. I've asked for a meeting on a Friday as that appears to be our best day of the week workwise. We may be given short notice and have to make flight arrangements at the last minute so please be prepared.'

'I presume flights go from London.'

'Yes. London Gatwick. Or, we could get a flight from Southampton. Either will do.' Edmund crossed his arms and gazed out of the window as the rain hammered down on the cottage's roof. 'I was hoping we could go out for an invigorating ramble but it seems we will have to wait until it brightens up.' And in reply to Kit's unspoken question, Edmund said, 'my housekeeper doesn't come at weekends.'

The photograph of Martin in the magazine had been burning a hole in Kit's focus on her great grandaunt's affairs. She had torn out the page, folded it neatly, and put it in a zipped compartment in her handbag. His smiling face and the unknown woman to whom she could not presently put a name, were absorbing her thoughts. Where had she seen that woman before? Or, more pointedly, why on earth had she saved an image of Martin when she was enjoying spending the weekend with her husband-to-be? There could be no easy answer to the second question, she knew, as it was wrapped up in her emotions to do with clinging on or letting go, but the solution to the first came with unexpected speed later that day. A mid-afternoon walk after the heavy rain front had swept through the north-east region followed by an early pub supper in front of the roaring fire in the saloon bar, was the perfect place to relax with a glass of wine. Edmund withdrew a bulky packet from his coat pocket. 'I thought this would be the right atmosphere to clock the mug shots from the memorial service.'

'The what?'

'The photos the professional photographer took at Old Kit's memorial service.'

'She arranged for them to be taken?' asked Kit in astonishment.

'Actually, no. My father did. He felt that there should be a record of everyone who attended the service and banquet just in case someone claimed to have been overlooked, either unintentionally or expressly.'

'I see. That makes good sense really when you consider the nature of the members of her family.'

'A rum lot, that's for sure.'

'And some good ones too,' said Kit, thinking about her grandparents.

'Yes, some good ones too.' Edmund gently lifted her left hand and kissed it tenderly. 'Martin is in some of the pictures. Will that upset you?' Kit thought about it for a while and then said no, although she was kidding neither of them. 'We've got the set taken as the guests left the cathedral,' Edmund went on, 'with you and my father as the greeting committee so you figure in all of those but the pictures taken in the marquee are probably better for identifying people as the photographer had more time to get full face shots and they tended to be sitting at tables with others of their immediate family.'

'Should I write their names on the reverse?' asked Kit, getting out the ancient fountain pen.

'Yes, that's a good idea and it would be very appropriate to mark Old Kit's pics with her bequest to you. I'll go and get refills for us, wine that is, not fountain pen ink,' added Edmund with an exaggerated cartoon-like wink.

Kit was so busy writing the names Edmund called out as he recognised each guest that she missed the photo of the young woman in the hockey magazine receiving the prize from Martin. It was only when they grouped immediate family members together that she spotted that Avril, and her twin Clare, shared a certain look if not resemblance.

'This twin,' said Edmund, pointing to Avril in the photo taken where she was sitting around the table with her sister, parents and grandfather, is the woman who requested the family tree as she is doing a piece on local radio about fraternal twins.'

'What slant is she exploring?'

'She didn't say when she contacted the office, but I guess you could ask the radio station for some background info. Radio East Midlands it's called.'

'I could do that. She might have sussed out something that I haven't. No need to invent the wheel twice,' said Kit resignedly. 'I have to be realistic. I can't do everything myself and I'm getting bogged down in tracing Old Kit's possible parentage. I'm spending time going nowhere fast.'

'If you're convinced that confirmation of Old Kit's parentage is vital,' said Edmund, 'then would you consider asking Emily to help you? She would be the ideal person as she knew Old Kit from her visits to the office to see my grandfather, and then later, my father. She was an ace secretary, and has time on her hands now that she's retired. Father always said that she knew more about pretty much everything legal than any of us.'

'That's a great idea. I'll ask her when we see her tomorrow evening at dinner. I'll be able to relax and think about the wedding plans. I must sort out my wedding dress. And I positively won't be wearing flat shoes.'

'Just one thing, please,' said Edmund smiling at the reference to flat shoes, 'when you talk to Emily about the lie of the land as you see it…'

'That I'm questioning Old Kit's parentage?' Kit interrupted.

'Yes, that. Please do so out of earshot of my father. I don't want him to have his thoughts about her sullied by speculation. They were true friends for so many years and it would hurt him if you suddenly started postulating theories, sordid or otherwise, about her conception. Whatever you uncover between you, please keep it to yourselves. For now, anyhow.'

Edmund's words proved a timely reminder to Kit not to trample on past happy memories and relationships and render them null and void in her quest for the truth. And she was glad when Emily, from the outset, shared Edmund's wish to tackle the paperchase sympathetically. And it would be a question of finding the right pieces of paper to guide them to the true facts. Over the years working as Thomas Newman's secretary – or personal assistant as secretaries styled themselves in the twenty-first century – Emily had been tasked on several occasions to substantiate clients' identities. She knew the ropes about how to access the parish register and she had the time to search exhaustively. And if her birth had been in a neighbouring parish, she would trace her there.

Genealogy had never been Emily's hobby but she had always enjoyed proving for her boss that clients really were who they professed to be. In her early years in the practice when Mr. Newman grandfather had been Mr. Newman Sr and Mr. Newman Sr, recently retired, had been Mr. Newman Jr and payroll was the only useful task performed by computers of gigantic physical size, all the information had to be obtained by letter or telephone requests for searches of various registers, card files or the occasional microfiche. There were no databases available to the man in the street for a quick google search. Time would stand still while letters were posted, searches made, and replies mailed back to the requester. Some registers in those early days, parish and church mostly, had been available for personal perusal and Emily remembered the requirement to wear white cotton gloves to avoid damaging the fragile pages. The longhand in which they were written in stylish calligraphy was often difficult to read but brought a sense of the era in which each entry was recorded.

With her normal disciplined approach, Emily set about trying to prove the parentage of Old Kit. Her starting point would normally have been to collect and check as many official family documents as possible and listen to ancestral stories, but in this case, where discretion didn't allow such luxuries, the marriage certificate of Harold and Gertrude would have to suffice. She would work backwards and forwards methodically checking the records and lists: birth, adoption, cemetery, baptism and christening, coroners, civil and criminal, until she found evidence that confirmed or denied Young Kit's theories. After having checked according to the documentation available to her that the couple gave rise to four legitimate sons, all of whom were christened in their local church, that there was no evidence of an adoption of a daughter, and that Gertrude's only sibling was a brother, Emily decided to make two reasoned assumptions: that Old Kit's date of birth was indeed as it was claimed to be otherwise how else could she have obtained a passport, and that she was not born in the same parish in which Gertrude and Harold lived – probably a neighbouring one – as gossip would have circulated and thrived in the sort of small communities that existed before the first world war in that part of sparsely-populated Northumbria. There, little could happen without one's neighbour knowing and it was a certainty that knowledge of a scandal would have filtered down the generations as sure as night follows day. As it turned out, they were presumptions that led Emily in the right direction although it would take perseverance to winkle out all the pieces of the true story.

When Emily was confident that the facts she had uncovered were correct, she contacted Kit. Privacy was not easy in the halls of residence and Kit's office in the university buildings saw a constant flow of students and colleagues throughout the day, and the time of year did not lend itself to outdoor communication on a mobile. She had the impression that Emily was the bearer of some hard facts and that notes should be taken. Kit stole into a caretaker's storeroom, pulled up a chair to the bench, turned on the angle-poise lamp and adjusted it so that its rays spilled only onto the bench surface, and dialled Emily. 'I'm guessing you have something illuminating to report,' said Kit enjoying the little pun when Emily answered.

'Exactly that,' replied Emily. 'It has been painstaking work but I think I have all the pieces of the jigsaw now.'

‘Is Old Kit Gertrude’s daughter?’ asked Kit, getting down to brass tacks straightaway.

‘No. She isn’t. And what’s more, she isn’t Harold’s daughter either.’

‘Oh,’ cried Kit, half expecting that to be the case but still a little stunned that it actually was.

‘But she was related to Harold. She was his niece.’

‘Oh,’ cried Kit again. ‘I wasn’t expecting that.’

‘Harold had three sisters. The youngest became pregnant in her mid-teens. At the time, the family lived in a village outside Coldstream across the border in Scotland. As the crow flies,’ continued Emily, ‘it’s about fourteen miles from Berwick. The drive would take about thirty minutes in today’s money. But in those days, the late 1890s, it would have seemed a world away. And it being in Scotland, because Coldstream just like Berwick almost straddles the border, there was little interaction between communities.’

‘So, what happened?’

‘Well, there’s a lot of guess work from here on in, based of course on some official papers – police notes, census returns, burials, that sort of thing – which guide you in a certain direction and which lead you to a believable story.’

‘Do you believe it?’

‘Yes, I do. It may not be accurate in every detail, but I feel sure that the essence of the story is correct.’

‘Then go ahead please,’ instructed Kit, glad that she had somewhere quiet to sit down without any distractions.’

‘The family,’ said Emily, who quickly corrected herself, ‘the parents that is, dreaded the disgrace of being tarred with an illegitimate birth. They lived in a community where adherence to godly principles was an unwritten law. Before word could spread, they sent her off to Berwick with her brother Harold. He would find work there and support her during her confinement. They would live as a couple and once the child was born, give it up to an adoption agency or leave it at a police station. Harold and his sister would then return to their family home.'

'I presume that's mostly your conjecture.'

'Yes, that's true. Not much hard fact to support that part of the story.'

'Go on, I shouldn't have interrupted your flow.'

'Harold found work in the town doing menial jobs and supported them for the few months before the birth. He was employed sweeping floors and doing handyman jobs in a small tailoring establishment in the main shopping street.' Emily paused. 'If you remember, there are references to this job in Old Kit's long letter to you.'

'Yes, I do recall that.'

'The next part of the story is woven around the record of a death and burial in a church record in Berwick.'

'In the area where Harold and his sister were living?'

'Presumably, yes. The dead person is female and sixteen years of age. Her name is Alice Roach.'

'His sister,' said Kit, sucking in a deep breath.

'I don't think there is much doubt about that,' replied Emily, 'the odds are that she died in childbirth.'

'And the child, need I ask?'

'She survived and is your great grandaunt, Kit Audrey Harrison, née Roach.'

There was silence on the line for some moments while this information spread out into Kit's grey cells. 'How do you work that out?' she asked.

'There was no mention in the same church record of the death or burial of a new-born on the same day as Harold's sister. And I checked the record for several days after that date and concluded that she had survived. If Harold had left her somewhere to become a foundling: on a doorstep or in a church pew, there would have been some report in a local news sheet or a written announcement on a noticeboard, but I found no evidence to support that.'

'So, what's your best guess as to what Harold did with the baby, his niece?'

'Yes, that's important for us to remember. The baby was his niece. He was only young himself; he would have acted instinctively.'

'And the instinctive action would have been to keep her.'

'Almost to guard her, I'm guessing,' Emily remarked thoughtfully, 'especially if you cast your mind back to Old Kit's infamous letter in which she described Harold as a good man. It's what a good man would have done when put on the spot.'

'Yes, I agree. It is a plausible action but how did it go from there?'

'This is pure speculation, but my guess is that he returned to Coldstream with the baby girl who was instantly rejected by her grandparents. They might not even have grieved over the death of their daughter either,' said Emily, 'it's hard to believe in today's terms but she had crossed religious bounds and made herself an outcast. Poor people had little in those days in terms of material goods and life prospects so their pride was all important to them.'

'Pride comes before a fall,' remarked Kit, the words of the proverb escaping her lips unintentionally.

'We can't judge them by our values. They lived in entirely different circumstances to us. By the way, the sister who died was a twin.'

'Oh. That's where Old Kit got the "twin gene",' said Kit, 'at last, a scientific explanation for her ability to produce twin progeny.'

'And there's more reliable "evidence" to come about what happened next,' said Emily. She paused. There was the noise of some shuffling of paper at her end and then she resumed. 'Harold returned to Berwick with the baby. In the circumstances, he couldn't have stayed at Coldstream and he had liked his job in the tailoring shop in the few months he had worked there. He had got on well with the owner and although his education was elementary – he could read and write and do basic arithmetic – he had proved to be a good and reliable worker willing and able to learn new skills. He asked for his job back and the owner agreed and told him about a girl who would look after the baby while he was at work. Within weeks Harold had married the girl, a marriage of no great love but one of great convenience for both parties.'

'How do you know all this?' pressed Kit.

'The facts show that Harold married Gertrude in Berwick in 1910. There is an entry in the church record to prove it. Also,' Emily went on, 'Harold had a small notebook in which he wrote down notes about his work; he was keen to learn whatever he could from the skilled artisans in the shop. Interspersed amongst these notes of how best to cut various fabrics and which sewing stitches were most suitable for particular joins, were personal entries; a sort of diary. When he died unexpectedly, it was the only thing she had of his because he kept it at his work and the owner gave it to her. Nobody would have guessed that it contained entries about his life and of intimate feelings and future hopes. She treasured it and kept it all her life.'

'Did you piece together the personal references to make it into a story?'

'Sort of.' Emily hesitated. 'But, sometimes, the reader can sense the meaning from just a very few words and it was clear that his niece was the apple of his eye. He'd write four-word entries like "happy Sunday teaching Kit". It conveyed a warmth and deep-seated affection without the need for extra words.'

'I remember the reference in her letter to accompanying her father – who she believed was her father, that is – to the shop on Sundays when they had a backlog of work. But how did you get hold of the notebook to read?'

'In the same way as you received the fountain pen,' replied Emily. 'It was given to me by Old Kit. Not so much bequeathed as in your case because she gave it to me in person. She was in the care home at the time. The Newmans visited her regularly and so did I. She could be an irascible woman. She wasn't all sweetness and light and there was an underlying sadness in her. However, she was interesting and had all manner of tales to tell. Time spent with her was never dull.'

'Did she have an ulterior motive for giving it to you?'

'No, I don't think so,' said Emily. 'She knew she was near her end. Just a matter of a few weeks before her gods would be coming to collect her. I think she wanted to give it to a woman because a woman would understand the unwritten sentiments expressed in the few words that Harold had written.'

'And you had known her over a long period.'

'Yes. For many years only on a business basis when she came to the office to see my boss, Thomas Newman. But I was a regular visitor in her last few years in the care home.' There was a heavy silence on the line as both parties organised their thoughts. 'I didn't really look at it at first. We were very busy in the practice. And then she died and there was the memorial service to organise followed by retirements and helping Edmund to settle into his new role as partner. It was only when I had some spare time on my hands and you enlisted my help in establishing Old Kit's parentage that I sat down and read it properly. It was then that I appreciated that the notebook had a story to tell other than just notes about tailoring.'

'So, you put two and two together and trusted that you made four.'

'Exactly. I believe there was sufficient in the notebook to guide me to the truth.'

'Did she know that Harold was her uncle and not her father?'

'One of the burning questions,' acknowledged Emily. 'Not from him, I'm inclined to believe. Not whilst he was alive. After his death …' she trailed off. 'When Harold married Gertrude, I told you that it was a marriage that fulfilled a purpose, and one in which some mutual fondness and respect developed. You see, Gertrude Mullins had her own difficulties to overcome. She too was the unwanted runt of her parents' large litter and would have been uneducated and treated almost as a slave by her own family. Her chances of a favourable marriage were slim. Harold was a decent man and offered her a safe and secure home in which she would be treated respectfully. She was in need of a home and he was in need of someone to look after the baby and bring it up as her own. It would have been a symbiotic relationship in which both parties would have benefitted from the union.'

'Something in it for both of them,' commented Kit, 'yes, I can see how that could work.'

'In her letter to you, she alluded to attitudes in the family changing after Harold died. Whether Gertrude spilled the beans and told her four sons that Old Kit was their cousin rather than their sister we can't tell and may never know. And how and when she found out may also remain an unsolved mystery, but an educated guess would be that Reggie would have had pleasure in confronting her with the news as soon as he found out.'

'It would have inflamed his already feisty manner towards her. Something more to add to the injustice he felt as the first-born son not receiving his proper dues.'

'Yes, you can understand how it developed from just a small sore into a festering wound,' said Emily. 'Unfortunately for Reggie, not only did the wound fail to heal, but he got subsumed in his own anger. It turned into a pyrrhic victory. Nobody won.'

'What I can't understand,' said Kit, 'is how my great grandaunt got a passport if she didn't have a birth certificate. How would that be possible?'

'The second burning question,' observed Emily, 'and I've no plausible answer to that. In today's society we are used to having to prove our identification: a passport or driving licence and two utility bills. Go for an appointment anywhere and they are taken away and photocopied before the person with whom you have the appointment deigns to speak to you. But demands for endless documentation were very different before the widespread use of computers and especially in the first half of the twentieth century when the population tended to stay put in its local area.'

'Maybe she got someone to vouch for her date of birth.'

'Maybe,' agreed Emily, 'or paid someone to vouch for her more likely. However, what we can safely assume is that somehow, she procured one.'

Kit was still sitting at the bench long after Emily had rung off. She had switched off the lamp and was sitting in the dark hunched over with her elbows on the wooden surface, resting her chin in her hands. It was peaceful there and she had the opportunity to digest Emily's news. Its accuracy wasn't certain but she didn't doubt for a moment the veracity of the chain of events. It was at the same time both illuminating and upsetting. Suddenly, from seemingly nowhere, tears welled up and coursed down her smooth cheeks. It was the parallels between their early lives that kept popping up. They were emotionally draining. Her great grandaunt had been abandoned by her maternal family only to be saved by her young uncle who she grew to cherish as her real father. Kit knew all about being young without parents. The gnawing hole it made in everyday life. The deep hurt and frustration, and later, she had to admit, the shame she had felt in the company of her school friends when they were collected by their parents and she waited quietly to one side for her grandparents to arrive to take her home. At the time she couldn't appreciate their kindness; it was only with time that she learned the value of their love.

Gradually she took control of her emotions and dabbed her handkerchief on her by now puffy cheeks. Emotions were not scientific she told herself and would bring nothing useful to the party. Emily had turned up trumps, and but for the question of the birth certificate, had found answers to all the questions including how Old Kit had managed to conceive twins. Answers were now beginning to outnumber questions and explain inter-family attitudes. Her brothers were in fact her cousins and Reggie's intuitions were proving to be well founded.

* * *

They drove out of town into the sparse landscape of Northumbria on their way to a country house conversion that had seen it reincarnated as an events venue. Formerly, it had been the seat of a wealthy family over several centuries; bestowed on them by some bigwig of the day in the seventeen-twenties for services rendered. Time and harsh weather had taken its toll on the fabric of the building ever since, and at around the millennium the family had chucked in the towel, sold up and moved to as posh an area of Edinburgh as their sale proceeds allowed. Edmund's mother had spotted the advert in a local paper for the "wedding festival", and accompanied by Emily on the basis that three heads were better than one when making decisions of a costly nature, she had driven her future daughter-in-law to the transformed manor. It was a girls' day out but they were girls with a mission as the wedding was scheduled for early March to coincide with the university Easter vacation and decisions about simply everything had to be made as Kit's free time was limited.

It was a fine day for the time of year. The wind had moderated and the incessant rain fronts had finally blown through. The weak sun had brought out all the prospective brides from miles around to find their ideal wedding dress and to select all the accessories and knick-knacks that become "essential" for the success of a modern wedding. The threesome was full of cheer as they moved about the ground floor of the manor house from one restored grand room to another making their selections and taking samples and business cards for later consideration and possible orders. Once the dress itself had been selected and tried on, a task made complicated by the enormous selection of gowns of all styles and prices hanging obediently from racks around the room, it was already lunchtime and they made their way across a courtyard to the crowded refreshment stalls which were doing a fine trade in grilled local farm pork sausages and home-made turkey and sage hot pasties. They lingered awhile over coffees laced with hazelnut liqueur produced by artisan brewers using local produce; the day was turning chilly and the warming alcohol made them glow.

On the journey back to Berwick, sitting in the back seat and listening to the easy chatter of the two best friends, Kit imagined that the day would have been similarly joyous with her own mother if the car crash in which she had died had not happened. Edmund's mother and Emily had taken on the role of surrogates for which she was truly grateful. Notwithstanding her grandparents' gallant efforts to provide her with a family life during her formative years, Kit would soon become part of the Newman family and would have a sense of normality for the first time since the loss of her parents and twin brother in the traffic accident. A few more weeks, a relocation in the new academic year to Edinburgh University where she would have visiting lecturer status and research facilities, a new home with Edmund and her erstwhile life would be truly behind her. And what made her really smile was her "find" at the fair; a fabulous pair of high heel shoes with an ivory satin finish that perfectly matched the wedding dress. Yes, she had a lot to feel happy about.

* * *

Adam sat impatiently on the plush leather sofa in the consultant's waiting room. He had walked practically the whole length of Harley Street after discovering that he'd alighted at the wrong tube station when he really needed to be at the Regent's Park end of the mile-long street. He sat fidgeting. He was the only patient in the waiting room. Slyly, as if trying to mask his action from someone's attentive eyes, he felt the lump on his head. It was hot and squidgy and had an uneven contour. He sensed it was larger now than a few days ago when he consulted his general practitioner. He'd had to admit to his doctor that his wife had been badgering him for several weeks to do something about the lesion as it was weeping little trails of blood onto the pillowcase most nights. He had scoffed at her suggestion that it might be something serious but his doctor had moved very quickly to arrange today's private appointment with the specialist once he had examined it, and hence Adam was feeling apprehensive.

The consultant dermatologist, a man with an Italian accent and an unpronounceable surname, was sympathetic to his story of procrastination in seeking medical advice. He understood that Adam was a busy man and how easy it was to delay or forget one's own health, but in so doing Adam had done himself no favours. It had taken no more than a brief inspection for the specialist to make the diagnosis as the lesion had all the classic signs of malignancy. Now, it was just a question of establishing how far it had already spread, and when asked about his general health, Adam had to admit that he had not been feeling his usual energetic self recently. It was always hard to deliver bad news, the consultant told his patient, but the prognosis was poor for skin cancers on the scalp and neck. He would arrange for some scans to be done forthwith to provide evidence of any metastasis. He was sorry that he had only bad news to convey. Adam sat rigidly in his chair unable to respond to the situation. He would have liked to have dismissed the information as alarmist twaddle but his instincts told him that it was not so. Eventually, he mumbled something about how long he had left, and when told that it would be dependent in large part on the scan results, but generally a period of about two years, Adam stood up, shook hands with the consultant, and walked out into the cold air in a daze.

One month after his scan and the confirmation that the growth was advanced and inoperable, Adam took to his bed and was nursed with palliative treatment until his death a further month later; the two-year period of grace that his family had hoped and prayed was possible was rendered hopeless by the depth and spread of the melanoma into the temporal lobe and cerebellum. According to the specialist it was the most aggressive form of tumour known. With his wife and twin girls at his bedside and his father, Henry, pacing back and forth downstairs on the squeaky oak flooring in the long hallway, Adam slipped away peacefully. He had been unable to converse for several days and his last movement was a slight rub of his thumb across Clare's hand which gently cradled his.

His wife and children were upset and distressed but it was his father who was most affected by his son's demise. He had poured all his hopes and energies into giving his children, Adam and Annie, a start in life second to none, so that, unlike for Henry himself, they might be accepted into whatever profession they chose to pursue in life without behind-the-back sneering references to their grandfather's humble beginnings. He wanted them to feel that they belonged in the upper middle classes and would never feel the need to justify their background. Adam had made that transition. Annie had not. And now his main hope for the future appeared dashed. It was a wretched time for Henry which was not about to improve.

The first announcement of the death of the sitting member of parliament for the north London constituency of Grove & Islington and chairman of one of the influential select committees, was broadcast by the 24-hours news channels in their eight o'clock evening slots. It was classed as "breaking news" with a flashing strap line beloved by broadcasters to draw their viewers' attention to the importance of the message they were conveying. A more in-depth résumé of Adam's life and background was screened the following morning with an analysis of his achievements and hints at his failings. A by-election would now be required to fill the vacant seat. Later, an oncologist of note was interviewed to explain the virulence and dangers of melanomas and to warn the viewing public of the importance of regular self-checking of seemingly unimportant moles and skin blemishes and the need for urgent action if changes were detected. A parliamentary colleague then spoke at length of Adam's skills in political debate and the intricacies of chairing an all-party committee where party lines had to be respected but not at the expense of the truth.

The first to react pragmatically to the new circumstance was Clare. She would miss her father as they were on the same page in regard to their constant need to ensure that they maintained or acceded their current place in society. For father and daughter, presentation was king and principles, where possible, followed at a distance. They had grown particularly close since she had graduated and joined the political glitterati as his private assistant. It was a safe seat and she was well versed in politics. From the outset, Clare knew that she wanted to be selected as the labour candidate for the constituency. She considered that in the likelihood of her party's selection committee being male-dominated and of pensionable age, her youth and gender might work against her but as the daughter of the deceased member, who had raised the profile of the constituency during his time in office, she should have an enormous advantage over other candidates no matter the experience they might claim. She would set about preparing a top-notch curriculum vitae straightaway; it would be factual, but if needed there would be room for some creativity. What she absolutely didn't want was some so-called help from her grandfather, Henry. In the corridors of politics, he had blotted his copy book too many times and his association with the unions would be a hindrance to her selection. Henry recognised the snub, dressed up in some sickly sentences from Clare about how kind it was of him to offer his help but making it crystal clear that she would consider his participation in any form as interference. Clare guessed she had the guile and tenacity to win through by her own devices and twin sister Avril knew better than to stick her nose in where she wouldn't be welcomed. There was in Clare's estimation, just one Achilles heel. She was young and normally wouldn't have been expected to be married and settled down with a kid or two. But the legacy of the philandering Roaches would not be ignored by the selection committee and Clare would need to show that it would not happen again as she had a steady boyfriend with whom, in the fullness of time, there were expectations of marriage and offspring.

With a tight majority, the government wasted no time in calling the by-election – wrong-footing the challenging parties on purpose by giving them a minimum of time to organise their candidates and troops for the close battle that lay ahead – and with a helpful prior know-what-I-mean nod from a government whip, the selection committee met to make their choice the day following the by-election announcement. Of the four candidates who had put their name forward to represent the party, three were women. Clare viewed the selection list with some apprehension; it appeared skewed towards the male applicant. She wanted to protest that votes for a female candidate could very well be split evenly amongst the three of them thus allowing the man, a former member of parliament who had lost his marginal seat at the previous general election, to take all the votes from those on the selection committee who wished to continue with a man as the constituency representative. But she stayed her hand realising that no good would come of such a complaint as it would be manner from heaven for any misogynists amongst the selection party; women whining again.

At the selection committee she would be sweetness and light and ensure that she told them what they wanted to hear. Yes, she did support the government's line on important issues of the day such as trade barriers, immigration, economic policy, foreign aid for the third world and the minimum wage but she would also like to see policy refined, clarified and modernised with equal opportunities for all in education and waiting times in the health service substantially reduced. On the subject of sport, especially dear to her heart because of her late father's position in the government as sports guru she told the nine-strong committee members sitting shoulder-to-shoulder around a long table at the front of the committee room – milking the situation to obtain every last drop of sympathy for his untimely death – she would certainly uphold his efforts to encourage wider participation by the general public in outdoor sports. She, herself, had knowledge in depth of field hockey having been a regular player since her early teenage years and rising through the ranks to a trial at Bisham Abbey for elite athletes. She could see the panel was impressed and took the opportunity that she had artfully created to adjoin a deprecating one-liner that although she might be regarded as an elite athlete by some, she was not elite enough to play internationally. It brought a few murmurs of hard luck from the panel and established some much-needed rapport. The interview then swung to personal affairs when one of the lady members enquired about relationships. Clare was ready with a reply she had practised at home a number of times. Yes, of course she had future aspirations for a family of her own but right now, and at her still tender age, a steady boyfriend was as far ahead as she could contemplate. And when put on the spot by the other female selector for a little more detail, Clare was able to mention her recent trip to Vienna to see her boyfriend who was in pharmaceuticals. He was there on secondment for an important trial of a new drug and was working with European colleagues. She had met him through hockey; he was a top-level player and currently held a high position in its governing body.

There were still hurdles to jump but she had made a good opening impression amongst the selectors. The open discussion with all four candidates present, which would follow the individual interviews, would be an altogether trickier path to negotiate but Clare was confident that she could see off the other women. She was unlikely to get the better of the experienced male candidate on debating skills alone but she had poked around in his former constituency and found some dissatisfaction amongst his staff with his work rate and together with some general gossip she had overheard while working at Westminster for her father, she felt she had ammunition to use to her advantage.

As tradition dictated, the by-election took place three Thursdays later. In the interim, Clare and a hastily assembled team of young activists walked as many streets of the constituency as possible delivering leaflets, and whenever possible, speaking to residents about her policies and how hard she intended to work to resolve their problems. It was a thrilling time for Clare. Her ambition was on a steep upward curve since her triumph in being selected to fight the inner London seat, and the new opponents from the main parties held no fears for her. She wasn't cocky about her widely predicted win but she was already working on her winner's speech, but two matters soon to arise would turn it into a close-run affair.

On the Sunday prior to the by-election, hints of impropriety surfaced in one of the leading heavyweight broadsheets regarding the financial position of the late Adam Roach. According to the article by a well-known journalist, there were debts to pay but insufficient resources to meet them in full. The following morning, a tabloid of a less restrained nature splashed its front page with the headline "it's a write off"; a reference to the legal position of a debt when it exceeds the value of the estate. The article went on to deliver a blistering assessment of those members of the upper and ruling classes who considered that the law and morals of the land never applied to them.

Although privately aware of the situation, the overt speculation about her late father's affairs came as a jolt to Clare; she kept a low profile for the few remaining days before voting began. There were tense moments at the count and her agent was in barely civil mood. By midnight it was clear that she had won the seat but with a much-reduced majority. At the declaration there were the usual polite words of congratulation from her opponents but little genuine enthusiasm from her own party helpers. But Clare wasn't a person to allow weeds to thrive under her feet, and in a head-on confrontation with her agent, she made it clear to him that the sins of the fathers could not be passed down to the next generation. It was a biblical reference which the agent had better take on board forthwith otherwise he could consider himself a member of the band of unemployed.

The transition from personal assistant to full-blown member of parliament would have been relatively smooth for Clare had it not been for her father's creditors and her Aunt Annie. Despite the untimely revelations about Adam's gambling debts, the party closed in around her to prevent any further embarrassing disclosures by the media. In private, despite protestations that she had no inkling about her father's gambling addiction, she received a lambasting from the chief whip and a warning to work hard, keep her head down and follow the party line. It proved a salutary time for Clare; she was forced to take stock of her situation. She had her parliamentary salary and some savings but no roof over her head as the family house in the grand terrace in Islington, mortgaged to the hilt by her father, had to be sold to pay off the baying bookmakers. And they made it clear that as they were never going to fully recoup what was owed, they would be watching her every move in parliament. They would give her no smooth ride and she could count on the subject of non-payment of debts being brought up time and time again by her constituents. Clare was feisty by nature but it was a daunting time and like her Aunt Annie, she was never going to turn to her grandfather for support. Henry had no place in her future whether or not he had the means to facilitate her career.

It was Aunt Annie's unexpected intervention that set the cat amongst the pigeons. Not having heard directly from her for many years, meeting only in recent times at Old Kit's memorial service, and never having been bosom friends in the first place, Annie's inquiry about accommodation in London came out of the blue. Could she stay with Clare on some odd dates in the future when she was down from the north-east on business?

The marble-floored corridors of Whitehall never buzzed with frenetic activity. Activity there always took place at a measured pace no matter its priority. The group which had sanctioned the enrolment of Annie Williams née Roach, or to be more precise, her brainpower, gathered quietly in the same room as previously.

'In the light of the death of Adam Roach and the developments consequent to that event,' opened the chair in a formal voice, 'I have brought you together again to further discuss the role in which we wish to use her.' She looked around the polished mahogany table at the faces of her four colleagues and noted their respective nods before continuing. 'We had set Annie on a course to discover and trap the network of villains, probably internationals, who are disrupting certain parts of our banking transfer system, and to this end she is already engaged with an IT expert.'

'A hacker,' said Mr. Atwell, in a tone that made his distaste for experts of such dubious standing very evident.

'We now need to decide,' continued the chair, ignoring Mr. Atwell's correct but superfluous remark, 'whether the longstanding involvement of her brother in the world of gambling, of which we have been aware and tracked for some considerable time, compromises her position now that the information is in the public domain courtesy of the press.'

'And how, if at all, the election of his niece to Westminster will affect the situation,' added the younger man with the full head of hair.

'Just so,' said Dame Barbara, hiding her annoyance at his unnecessary interruption. 'I am led to believe from senior colleagues,' she went on, addressing herself in particular to the representative from intelligence, 'that the imperative to root out the gang responsible for corrupting our banking transfer system is of great urgency. Therefore, unless we are certain that Annie's work is compromised by the media attention associated with her brother's demise, we should allow her to press on in that role.' Dame Barbara paused. Her fellow committee members sensed she was about to make a disclosure of importance. 'The suspected insider is Adam Roach,' she announced finally. 'He had been on our radar for some time.'

'He was living way above his means,' commented the man from the intelligence agency, 'and his death is timely, relieving us of the need to remove him from the scene.'

'And all the associated scandal that that would have caused,' added Mr. Atwell.

'Just so,' repeated the chair. 'We would have had to get rid of him shortly. We only allowed him to survive this long so that we could trace the link to the actual gang committing the scam and expose them too.'

'If his death is followed by a blip in the scam, temporary or otherwise, then we will know for sure that he was the person responsible for leaking the information,' Mr. Atwell suggested.

'It makes the position of his daughter, Clare, the new member for Grove & Islington, interesting to say the least,' said the chair. 'She could be approached to do the same as her father.'

'But would she?' asked the younger man with the full head of hair. 'Would she?'

'She might to save her father's reputation,' answered Dame Barbara. 'As things stand, he has died at a young age of a cruel illness and apart from his gambling debts, and he is by no means the only parliamentarian to have huge gambling debts, no public mention has been made of his criminal activities.' She then invited the older man to give them any relevant details of Clare Roach's background.

'To recap,' he began, 'Adam Roach had twin daughters, Clare and Avril. Both went to university. Clare gained a first at Cambridge in politics, philosophy and economics. On graduation, she joined her father at Westminster as his private assistant. Although young in years at twenty-three, by all accounts she has acquitted herself well in that role.' He hesitated. 'She can be quite prickly. She is not well disposed to criticism which might make for an interesting time at Westminster where criticism abounds.' He looked at the others around the table hoping to see some wry smiles but saw none and carried on. 'According to hearsay, she is not on chummy terms with her grandfather, Henry, who I should remind you is also a former member of parliament. Rumour has it that he is simply too rough and ready for her. His, is the face of her distant working-class background which she has been at pains for most of her life to erase.'

'What about friends?' asked the chair.

'There's an interesting connection there. Apart from general politics, which is by far and away her main interest, her only other long-established hobby seems to be field hockey which both she and her twin have played since their early school days. Her circle of acquaintances and friends are mostly hockey generated. It appears that she is keen, or at least was until her father's death, to climb to the top in the political world of hockey. Her trip to Bisham Abbey, essentially a trial to establish whether or not she was good enough to be considered as a future international player, was arranged at her behest – she pulled a few strings – rather than a result of her club requesting the trial based on their knowledge of her ability.'

'Continue on,' urged Dame Barbara.

'Well, reports suggest that she hobnobbed there with anyone and everyone who was influential. The hockey CEO turned up on the second day and she made a successful play for him. Shortly after they were seen together in a London restaurant, and not long after that she turned up in Vienna to share a long weekend with him.'

'Is he important to the story?' asked Mr. Atwell.

'Not him, per se,' replied the older man, 'but his connection is intriguing. His name is Martin Oakeshott and he is the former long-term boyfriend of Georgina Kit Irwin, who in turn is the great grandniece of Kit Audrey Harrison.'

'Not that damned woman again,' groaned the chair in anguish. 'Will we never be shot of her.'

Clare's shopping trip had not been to the posh postcode areas of central London. The outer London suburbs served by the tube were all she could currently afford for a place to live. It was the first time in her life that money wasn't flowing freely and she was feeling the distinct discomfort of having to make ends meet. For Clare, it was a balancing act of finding a rental property she could afford but in an area that had at least a modicum of street-cred. She would have liked to have remained in her own constituency but prices there were beyond her means; Grove & Islington had been on the "up" for many years, and with its fashionable terraces of substantial houses and refurbished smaller, bijou parades occupied by intellectuals and "artistes" from a range of different cultures, was now considered as one of the top addresses and was outside her pay range.

She had considered alternatives. Do as so many elected members from far flung constituencies did: rent a small place, as cheap as possible and as near as possible to her new workplace, and share it with another member of parliament. After all, they did all receive an allowance for just that situation, although in Clare's case she would be using it for her main residence which was not, strictly speaking, permissible. Still, such a minor transgression would surely be defensible, she thought. So, when she received the request from Aunt Annie, Clare took her up. The odd night or two on the sofa was within reason, and hopefully Annie wouldn't find it uncomfortable.

Annie arrived one Monday evening and after the obligatory kiss and exchange of family news they departed to the nearest pub. With each to her own thoughts while Clare was at the bar getting their drinks, a general summing up of the other was taking place behind an inscrutable face. Clare was surprised that Annie had chosen a Campari and soda and that her nails were painted fashionably deep mauve. It didn't fit with the mother earth lifestyle for which her aunt had tossed in a high-end job some years previously. And plain Aunt Annie was not quite as plain as Clare remembered her. Dressed eclectically in a version of a trouser suit, the bold colours and classic cut suited her size. What's more, Annie was in effervescent mood. Apparently, she was back working part-time as a consultant, giving actuarial advice to local authorities. She had been called in by a north London borough and would be in conference with them for a couple of days before heading home and hence her request for some handy nearby accommodation. Clare never questioned why if she was again earning megabucks, she hadn't checked into an hotel and put the cost on expenses. If she had done that then she might have realised that Annie was telling her a pack of carefully rehearsed lies. Instead, she took it verbatim that her aunt was now engaged in meaningful work.

'Your father's sad passing,' said Annie, sipping her second Campari and soda, 'should be a lesson to us all not to neglect our own health.' Clare did not reply but made the right noises of agreement. 'He would have been proud of you. Taking up the challenge to win his seat whilst you were still in a state of bereavement.' Clare nodded and her eyes glistened over and Annie thought but did not say that Clare might be human after all. 'It's a period of adjustment for you now, and for your sister and mother. Of late, I seldom saw Adam. He was plying his trade in the capital and I was doing my own thing in the country. But he was my brother nonetheless. Your grandfather will be upset. Very upset. He put a lot of store by Adam.'

'Henry will get over it,' replied Clare rather crassly.

'I dare say, but people tell me that losing a child is an exceptionally hard loss to bear.' They fell silent for some minutes reflecting on the new order. 'My father, Henry,' continued Annie eventually, 'is not smooth round the edges – a reference to his first-generation gentrification being incomplete – but he was enlightened. He ensured that I had the same high standard of education as my brother. He's not a bad man.'

'If you say so.'

'You can admire traits in someone without actually liking them.'

'I get your point.'

'I hope so because one day you might need his help,' said Annie.

'Meaning?' said Clare with arched eyebrows.

'Meaning that you should never destroy your bridges as they may come in useful one day.'

'Is this a lecture?' asked Clare indignantly. 'I'm no longer a child and people who live in glass houses shouldn't throw stones. I don't need lessons from you.' Clare stood up as if to leave and glowered down at Annie, but the words sunk in and after a few seconds of reflection she retook her seat.

'I'm sorry, Clare, to have upset you,' said Annie. 'My brother's gambling addiction is the subject of much speculation in the corridors of power. Speculation that won't go away until it is answered robustly. We need to talk.'

Aunt Annie occupied the second bedroom that night; the fellow member with whom Clare shared the London flat had been called away unexpectedly to her constituency in Norfolk and wouldn't return for a couple of nights. Annie would have a proper bed to sleep in and Clare wouldn't have to lie that her bad back would prevent her from giving up her own comfortable bed to sleep on the sofa.

They picked up takeaways on their way back to the flat and sitting in the cramped lounge, Annie spreadeagled herself on the two-seater sofa and Clare sat in the only armchair. The time had come for some plain speaking.

'Were you aware of how deep your father had got involved in the world of gambling?' questioned Annie without beating about the bush, as soon as she had finished the last morsel of her pizza and cleared the cardboard box off her knees. 'Or, indeed, of the dubious people he was dealing with?'

'No,' replied Clare truthfully. She was reluctant to expand on her one-word answer but knew instinctively that she needed to do so. She sighed; a deep audible breath of relief. 'I knew something was wrong. There were subtle differences in Adam.' She had been calling him "Adam" ever since she had started working for him at Westminster; "Daddy" hadn't seemed appropriate out in the cold light of the working world. 'He appeared anxious most of the time. It wasn't like him because he was normally a confident person.'

'Something troubling him?'

'Yes. He wasn't talking about the future in the way he normally did. I put it down to us growing older as a family. Avril had already flown the nest and I was ready to leave too. I wondered whether he was feeling a little melancholic.'

'Out of character for him,' pronounced Annie. 'I never knew my brother to be sentimental or mindful of others.' It was a harsh criticism but one they both knew to be true. 'Could the changes you noticed be put down to his medical condition?'

'No, I don't think so. The deterioration in his health was very swift and started after his change in character.'

'Then it must be something to do with his gambling, or more precisely, his debts which he knew he couldn't pay off. Would he have turned to Henry for help?' asked Annie, but the question was rhetorical as Annie felt sure she knew her brother better than Clare knew him.

'I just don't know.'

'They always got on well together,' said Annie. 'They were big buddies.'

'That's true,' confirmed Clare. 'They did get on well.'

'So, it's a pound to a penny that if he was in dire financial straits, he would have asked Henry for help,' Annie conjectured, 'unless, of course, ….,' she trailed off.

'Unless what?'

'Unless he had done something or been involved in something that Henry would have regarded as dishonourable.' Clare looked disbelieving. 'Henry does have scruples you know,' added Annie. 'He may seem like a wide boy to you living on his wits and wheeling and dealing to his own advantage but he still has barriers he won't cross. He draws a line at taking advantage of some types of people and he won't get willingly involved in certain dodgy businesses.'

'Such as?'

'Well, for example, he wouldn't "facilitate" the sale of arms to certain third-world dictatorships, and he wouldn't take advantage of those individuals who couldn't fend for themselves. He kept to the Queensbury rules in boxing.'

'And everything else was fair game?'

'That's about it,' agreed Annie.

'So, what are you hinting at?'

Annie rearranged herself on the sofa to sit upright and took a decision. It was strategic. From her investigation for the

Westminster people, and working with the former hacker, she was pretty certain that her brother was mixed up in the bank transfer fraud. He was the source of the insider information and must have been using the bribe money he received to pay off as much of his debt as possible. But he was on a rollercoaster of betting and losing, and the more he lost the greater was his need to obtain bribe money. If matters had stopped there it would have been shocking and criminal in itself, but if he had had the common sense to open up to Henry about his failings then Henry's principles might just conceivably have stretched to allow him to pay off his son's debt once and for all and to stay quiet and mind his own business. Adam might have got away with it. But Annie had uncovered more and now it was a question of how much she told Clare.

When she had first been plucked by the Westminster people to help them with some spurious algorithms, neither they nor she could have anticipated that her own brother was the source of the insider knowledge. But she had, and now she was in London and due to report her findings to them tomorrow. But, unless she was very much mistaken, there was more to it than that; more to it than Whitehall's Mr. Atwell would be expecting. And Annie was beginning to accept that her brother's death came as a blessing in disguise for if Henry had learnt what Annie had uncovered then he might have felt so ashamed of his late son as to disown him. And that would have broken his heart.

Annie also had other considerations on her mind: her young boys and her husband, Hugh. Would she wish them to be tarnished by association? She had expectations for her boys in the same way that Henry must have dreamed of prospects for Adam and Annie. And she loved dear, simple Hugh; their marriage was one of genuine fondness. She wouldn't want to expose any of them to the scrutiny of the media, but that would be bound to happen if she related what she knew. There was more too. All that silly nonsense spun to her by Mr. Atwell about a gang of eastern Europeans being behind the fraud. He had couched it in non-committal language redolent of the higher echelons of the civil service but at the same time had made it clear how he wished her to believe how matters stood. It hadn't taken Annie's grey cells long to realise that she was being used to identify someone far closer to home than a particular groups of Slavs a thousand miles away. The money involved in the fraud wasn't going abroad to gangs of middlemen who would broker deals with factions all over the world. The money was staying here in the United Kingdom.

The aroma of fresh coffee brought Annie back to the present. Clare had slipped out to the kitchen to get hot drinks and biscuits whilst Annie was so obviously thinking through some process. 'Are you ready now?' she asked when re-seated in the armchair.

'Ready?'

'Yes. Ready to tell me whatever it was that you were working through in your mind,' said Clare. 'I think you were trying to come to a decision.'

'Almost,' replied Annie uncertainly. 'Almost ready but not now. Not right now. I must sleep on it. Too many Campari and sodas for a clear head.' It wasn't true. Annie was wide awake and had made her decision but wanted to see how tomorrow's interview with Mr. Atwell in Whitehall played out before she told Clare. 'You know,' she said, expertly switching to a safer topic, 'another branch of our family wouldn't have made coffee, they would have gone to bed with a cup of tea or cocoa instead.'

'May I remind you, Mrs. Williams,' said Mr. Atwell quietly but sternly the following day, 'that when you agreed to take on this project which we had organised for you, you signed the official secrets act.' Annie made no verbal reply, she simply nodded. She had taken the same lift to the fifth floor where Mr. Atwell was again waiting for her, and as before, they had walked down the corridor together and entered the same room. Seated now at his desk opposite him, she realised that his was the only name she knew, even the letter from human resources outlining a job description and remuneration package was signed with an anonymous title. It was a masterpiece of Whitehall gobbledygook. 'Then,' continued Mr. Atwell, 'will you please report your results.'

This would be the critical moment; there would be no going back. No room for a change of mind or for wistful regrets at making the wrong decision. And Mr. Atwell was no fool; he was of an intellect similar to Annie's. In his early seventies, his ability to cut and thrust with words and concepts might be on the wane but would be made up by his years of experience. Annie had to convince him that she knew much but not quite the complete story for she had, after a restless night in the flat's second bedroom, decided to stick with her original decision. Blood was again proving thicker than water. Annie cleared her throat and started. She had no written notes; it was all in her head. She sat calmly with her hands in her lap. 'You set me the tasks of discovering who was providing the insider knowledge for the bank transfer frauds, and to whom the fraudulent money was being paid. You gave me the names of various persons who you considered as possible candidates for the spilling of such sensitive details. One of them was my brother. With the aid of the computer guru, I have been able to establish that Adam Roach was indeed the culprit.'

'I see,' Mr. Atwell replied, 'and in what way can you substantiate your claim?'

'A computer trail and the oral confirmation from a parliamentary assistant that he attended meetings that would give rise to such information.'

'But other suspects too were in the right place at the right time to learn of any large money transfers.'

'But they didn't leave a computer trail,' stated Annie evenly, 'and none of them were being pressed to repay large debts.' Mr. Atwell pursed his lips and ran the palm of a hand over his bald patch while digesting Annie's statement. 'And the other matter, the recipients of the money. What news of the eastern Europeans?' he inquired.

'We found computer evidence,' replied Annie, describing her work with the reformed computer hacker 'of international attempts at interference in our banking system, but the noses in this particular trough were home grown.' Annie knew that this information would come as no surprise to Mr. Atwell for the story they had told her of some Albanian gang was poppycock. They were well aware that the money was finding its way into domestic coffers and the talk of eastern European gangs was all blather to test Annie's trustworthiness. Mr. Atwell gave Annie a steady gaze. 'And have you been able to identify the receiver of these funds?'

'Not yet,' replied Annie, 'but I am narrowing down the field.' The fact that Mr. Atwell did not quibble with her previous assertion that the funds were going into a domestic pocket was tantamount to accepting that Annie was reporting her true findings. Annie had convinced herself that being economical with the truth by withholding some details was not the same as being untruthful. 'I will report again when I am certain and have proof.' Her statement left little room for manoeuvre and Mr. Atwell was forced to concede the upper hand to Annie. She walked away down Whitehall humming a tune and this time no one followed her. All she had to do now before leaving for home was to explain to Clare the harsh reality that the death of their father and brother respectively came at an opportune time as they would not have to endure the trashing of his name when the media learnt of his true behaviour as the crime would be hushed up by the powers that be. Furthermore, if Annie could find the ways and means of withholding the name of the person who had actually received the millions of pounds of taxpayers' money – Adam's bribe money being peanuts in comparison to the enormous amounts being transferred – then, with some luck, the whole sorry affair could be consigned to history.

Annie's train north, the same journey that Kit was becoming familiar with, left the terminus on time. A young woman, running late and still out of breath from dashing across the concourse, negotiating the ticket barrier and sprinting to the nearest carriage before the doors closed, had walked through the carriages until she found a suitable seat to spend the next ninety minutes to the first stop at Peterborough, where she would alight. She had sat down in relief not giving any thought to the occupant of the adjacent seat. Annie stirred from her thoughts as the latecomer arranged a holdall in the overhead rack and a large hessian shopping bag under her knees. When she inadvertently knocked Annie's arm while opening her daily broadsheet, she realised that she was sitting next to her Aunt Annie. For a moment they stared at one another with a certain disbelief that the other person really was who each thought she was.

'Avril,' exclaimed Annie, 'what are you doing on this train?'

'Going home to Peterborough,' replied Avril, 'had some work to do in London and I'm now on my way home. And you?'

'Ditto.' They had never met often in their lives as Annie and her brother had gone their separate ways. But the last time she had met her niece was recently at Adam's funeral. 'In London on radio channel business?' asked Annie.

'Yes, a bit of that,' agreed Avril, 'and to see my twin sister. She was close to my father and is missing him. She said you were going to stay overnight with her.'

'We had a pleasant evening together,' said Annie cautiously, not knowing how close the sisters were and whether the subject matter she had talked about with Clare had been shared. She need not have worried. The twins' brief meeting had amounted to no more than a courtesy call and apart from the exchange of a few words of general sympathy and a half-hearted hug, the visit served to underline how little they had in common although Avril was genuinely impressed by her sister's effort and resolve in winning the by-election so soon after the loss of her father and Clare was furious to have seen a photo of her twin in the field hockey journal accepting a prize from Martin Oakeshott. 'I had a job interview,' added Annie. 'I hope to return soon to the world of insurance.' There was some general small talk about family members, hopes for the future and the like and soon the train was pulling into Peterborough. Avril waved her aunt goodbye from the platform and wondered when next they would meet.

It had also been an overnight trip to London for Avril; a biannual hockey reunion with chums from her former club. Mid-week, it had been a jolly affair but with due attention paid to everyone's need to go to work the following day. An Italian restaurant with a nearby tube station had been the perfect venue for a lively evening of good food enjoyed in a friendly and warm atmosphere. Avril was not the only "guest". With a sprinkling of boyfriends and someone's lonely husband in tow, Martin was not the sole man present. They numbered eighteen and the restaurant had re-jigged their table layout to accommodate such a large gathering. As well as catching up with current and former members, there was much to learn about a restructuring of their league system and it was to their guest of honour, Martin, that they turned for an authoritative explanation.

'I've met you before,' said Martin to the young woman sitting directly opposite him. 'I'm sure I presented a trophy to you not long ago.'

'You did. It's on my desk at work,' Avril replied smiling. 'But I thought I'd heard that you were working in Vienna.'

'That's right. I'm on secondment there but back here for a few days to sort out in my base laboratory an issue that has just arisen. I believe I've mentioned that I'm in pharmaceuticals.'

'I'm in local radio and I'm sure I'm repeating myself. I gave you my business card,' said Avril. 'Is there anything to interest our listeners in what you are sorting out? They take medicines too,' she quipped.

'Hopefully not the type I'm working on. I'm trying to sort out a hiccup that we have found in a new drug to be launched to treat a tropical disease that's prevalent in sub-tropical Africa.' Avril smiled and nodded in accord.

The following morning, they met by chance when travelling on the underground. Both had stayed overnight with a hockey friend from the reunion. Avril was heading for King's Cross and Martin for Paddington but when Avril reached her stop and Martin had to change lines there too, they decided to enjoy a coffee together. Engrossed in conversation, Avril suddenly realised that she was short of time and left in a hurry to dash across the concourse to her waiting train. Martin finished his coffee and headed off for the circle line. Sitting in an uncrowded train, he turned over in his fingers the business card for Radio East Midlands station on which Avril had scrawled the days and times of her listeners' questions and answers slots plus her mobile number. He would try to tune in one day to listen to her programme. She was so very different from her twin; chalk and cheese. As he left the tube, he wasn't to know that by now Avril's train had already pulled out of the station and that she had encountered her aunt. Had he known of this chance encounter, he might have wondered what odds a betting man would have accepted for that to occur as one woman lived and worked in Cambridgeshire and the other in Tyne and Weir. He was still thinking of that scenario as he changed escalators on his way up from the circle line hidden from daylight in the bowels of the earth, when he spotted a familiar face on the down escalator. At one point she was almost within touching distance as they appeared to slide past one another effortlessly in some kind of choreographed scene from a dance. She was looking straight ahead and didn't see him. He caught his breath. It was a shock and he turned his head involuntarily to follow her disappearing figure as the escalator took her beyond his view. He'd have recognised those blonde curls anywhere. He used to flip them with the ends of his fingers and they would bob up and down like spring coils demonstrating the physics law of momentum.

In a daze and running on automatic pilot, Martin headed for his train on platform eight. He knew the journey well but at this particular moment his mind was disengaged. His company had provided hotel accommodation for his short stay in Reading near the laboratory, but his mind seemed unable to process such practicalities as he felt stunned by the chance sighting of

Kit. Later, sitting on the end of the large double bed in his room, his mind ran over the thirty seconds or so in which his mental world was again turned into disorder. It was a phone call from a colleague that finally broke his reverie, and as he prepared to meet his boss for dinner, he told himself for the thousandth time that Kit was no longer his to pine after. And, it was true, he *had* snapped out of the doldrums. He *had* moved on. After the fiasco with Clare, he had been very wary of women. No dates and no flings. He was thirty and desperately wanted a family, but who would take on the child of a notorious murderer? He hadn't dared to tell Kit the story in all the years they had been together, so was it really likely that he would summon up the nerve to tell that to any other woman? No. Highly unlikely, in fact, probably never. The millstone round his neck was not likely to budge, ever.

On a mental nudge from his boss over dessert, Martin slipped back into business mode and outlined some small changes in the new drug's preparation and storage processes that would render it less prone to denaturing. The European body had found nothing wrong with the medication's concept, formulation and efficacy, he attested, it was simply a matter of logistics; provision of proper storage units and a training schedule for the end-user would solve the snag. The roll out of the drug would be expensive for the company and the shareholders, including their university partners, and they would not take kindly to a botched job. Later, in the hotel bar when he was alone savouring the fulsome flavour of a single malt whisky, Martin's thoughts drifted back to the face on the escalator. A few hours had passed since spotting Kit, and although it was true that such a small incident had temporarily upset his rhythm, it was also true that he was already brushing off the pain that their parting had caused. He was in a much more positive frame of mind and he had met Avril who he liked. As soon as his secondment was over and he was back home permanently, he would start listening to her broadcasts and arrange a trip to her new hockey club in Peterborough.

The news of her father's failings, delivered by Aunt Annie in plain words, came as no great surprise to Clare. She would have been astonished if Annie had told her that he was pure and white like a fresh covering of snow. However, even Clare wasn't prepared for the extent to which her father had strayed from the path of righteousness. To receive money for what was in stock market trading terms generally described as insider dealing, was one thing, but to agree to the proceeds of the fraud being diverted into the coffers of some sleazy porn baron with a penchant for buying football clubs was quite something else, and her hackles rose at the very thought of women being so vilely disabused. But Annie wouldn't tell her who. Wouldn't or couldn't? She didn't know which, but according to Annie, a severe case of politics was causing a nasty migraine in certain Whitehall departments and the condition was now being treated vigorously. Clare guessed that Annie knew who the bastard was, but for some purpose was withholding the information. Maybe the sinner had ties to an Arabian fiefdom or oligarchs of former communist countries and a denouement would serve only to escalate affairs. Better the devil you know than the devil waiting in the wings, thought Clare justifiably. But Clare didn't have time to waste on speculation; she was busy shoring up her own position as member for Grove & Islington in the light of various facts about the previous incumbent that had leaked out into the public domain. But she had made a shrewd guess about a football club connection although the anonymous owner would turn out to be someone far closer to home. And if she had looked carefully at some of the clubs in the premier league and the transfer fees that were spiralling beyond their legitimate means, she would have taken much more interest in the performance of a certain team on the box. But Clare didn't play football, she played hockey.

Radio East Midlands's coverage of light music, national news and local activities was honed to near perfection on the needs of its listeners; a semi-rural population with pockets of urban and suburban residents. Much of the credit for this satisfactory position was due to Avril's hard work and foresight which was recognised by the station's directors. When a senior presenter stepped down to concentrate on retired living, Avril was not only promoted to take over his morning slot but was also invited to become a working director. She was on the same wavelength as her listening public and was keeping the station in the vanguard of broadcasting with her topical spots for audience participation. Although the catchment area was relatively small – Kit had tried to tune in from both London and Berwick to her spots about fraternal twins but without success – news of Avril's abilities had spread to larger and longer established stations and a few enquiries were gradually appearing on her email about whether it was her intention to stay small or go back into circulation in order to go big. It amused Avril that the job market was now using the same terminology as the marriage market when one partner suddenly found him or herself surplus to their former partner's requirements and moved back onto the available list. But Avril had no intention of upgrading to a larger regional station. She loved Radio East Midlands and her thoughts were about becoming its head one day, and in her dreams, buying and owning it rather than using it as a stepping stone to a nationwide broadcaster. Of course, she told herself, only a consortium could raise sufficient cash to own and run a radio station, even a regional one, but it was a happy dream to hold. And she had settled in well to the slower pace of life in the semi-rural surroundings of Peterborough including the hockey club where she had been welcomed with warmth.

The order of the day, it seemed to Avril, was to stay away from the topic of politics and keep a low profile whilst the subject of her father was still receiving attention in the press. And she wasn't going to bandy about her connection with his successor in parliament either. Avril felt sure that Clare cut corners whenever it suited her and that at some time in the future she would be held to account. Avril didn't want to be any part of that scene. Providing a service for her local clientele of news, reliable information and a sounding board on matters that interested them was her objective. And the bereavement and separation listener ringing-in slots, dubbed "know what" after the runaway success of "how to" internet amateur videos, were finding favour. There was no theoretical stuff with professors, clergy and behavioural specialists pontificating with best practice ideas about how to handle such difficult circumstances. It was all practical information from grass roots listeners who had been there, done that and survived.

Avril wondered if Martin would tune in. She'd given him the daily timings on the back of the business card. Of course, he was abroad currently but when he returned home, she wondered if he might find it helpful. Naturally he'd have to be in the right area of the country to receive the broadcast. She didn't know where he lived and so reluctantly dismissed the possibility that he would. There was also the real likelihood that he might not consider it a manly thing to do; seeking help of any kind, even as an anonymous listener, was regarded by many men as unnecessary and sissy. She speculated that if Martin knew that the percentage of men ringing in to pose questions or give advice was almost forty percent, then such qualms might be set aside in favour of more enlightened thinking. Martin needed help of that she felt sure; the look in his eyes the giveaway of an unhappy person.

Neither twin's wish to distance herself from the dishonourable dealings of their father was realised. Little packets of detail seemed to emerge on a daily basis like water from a dripping tap. Although the actual information given was limited, or often reworked by the journalist from a different point of view, or was just plain speculation, the girls grew tired of the constant need to shore up their positions as innocent parties. Unlike Henry, the girls had youth on their side to meet those demands and were able to brush off any mud that came their way before it could stick. But for him, it was altogether a different story.

If Henry had been a cat he would have been described as feral, indeed, there had been whispers behind his back most of his life that you could take the veneer of sophistication out of the raw, untamed union man, but you could never take the union man out of the persona he chose to portray. But whatever snide remarks were made, the thick skin that Henry had developed from an early age protected him from any feelings of inadequacy or the need for introspection. Had it not been for the serendipitous accident with the band leader's mace which took the life of his elder and first-born brother, Henry almost certainly would have stayed true to his northern roots. Reggie's union subsidies would have gone not on his own private education but on that of the family's first-born son. The death had been another blow to Reginald's sorely-tested belief of the importance to the family of their eldest son. History appeared to be repeating itself unkindly in the case of the Roaches until his wife pointed out that their first born had not been blessed with any useful aptitudes whereas Henry was both brainy and as wily as a fox and might one day turn into an effective communicator.

As the years passed, with the aid of union benefits available only to the higher-ranking union bosses, Henry made the transition from working to middle class and although this was successful in his eyes, he never quite escaped his origins and instead of being seen in other's eyes as a gentleman farmer, he came across more like a flashy spiv. But his mother had been correct. He did have brains and he did have guile and the career he forged in the union movement and in politics formed the bedrock of his success. It was on a one-to-one basis that Henry shone when the flavour of the real Henry came to the fore and the irritating and jarring mannerisms that he had adopted in his quest to be accepted as long-standing middle class were least noticeable. In such situations he made useful acquaintances which he nurtured over time and into which he tapped for information when needed, using his lobbying powers in return on their behalf; an exchange of favours which benefited both parties equally and was, in the main, the reason why father and son were often seen to be enjoying the good life in the directors' boxes in football stadia up and down the country.

Adam's death had had a profound effect on his father. Henry had just celebrated his seventy-second birthday, and separated from his wife for more than ten years and estranged from his daughter for even longer, he felt a sudden emptiness in his life. Adam had always been his favourite child, the one he really loved.

For some weeks he was at a loss to fill the void. His emotions were running high and he preferred to be alone. All that he had held dearly for so long had burst like a faulty firework with a few bright sparks and then self-destructed an instant later. Henry sat disillusioned on an outdoor bench in his fine garden just off the sweeping driveway to the authentic Tudor house that he had purchased forty years previously. At the time he had had to scrape together every penny he could by either fair means or foul to afford the status it conferred automatically on its owner. But the efforts of those days had seemed worth it at the time, he reflected. He had played his cards right and escaped the privations of the north-east to join the ruling classes in the gentler south. And he had spent the four decades that had passed since in wheeling and dealing and lining his pockets and bank accounts so that he could ensure that his son had everything a man could need for a successful life. And now it had come to an abrupt end. The hopes of yesteryear had foundered on rocks and all the efforts made, now seemed worthless. And there was no one to whom he could turn for solace. It was the press that eventually roused Henry from his stupor; their nasty innuendos and wild speculations against someone who could no longer fight back riled him. They were unwilling to allow sleeping dogs to lie peacefully and weren't going to stop until forced to do so. It was their very actions and an unexpected visit from his granddaughter, Avril, that stirred Henry back into the living world.

Henry usually had a jaunty persona. Whether it was because of, or in spite of, the battered felt Trilby-style hat that he wore regularly which gave him the air of a second-hand car salesman from the 1960s was anyone's guess, but, to his grandchildren, it defined him. Clare hated the look and what she believed it stood for – it had coarse and unsophisticated overtones – and as a consequence she limited her contact with him to the barest minimum. Avril, on the other hand, embraced her grandfather's rough edges. Fed up with her sister's superficial view of people, she found truth and substance in Henry's character and had started her hockey reunion trip to London with a prior visit to Berkshire to see how he was coping. He hadn't greeted her with great interest, but his housekeeper had brought them coffee and biscuits in the summer house which was warm despite the time of year, and they had entered into one of the most meaningful conversations they had ever had. They talked of Adam, his widow, his achievements in life and his aims which didn't amount to much given his silver spoon start and the number of helping hands Henry had given him along the way. Without putting it into words, they seemed to arrive at the same conclusion that Adam appeared to have few core values and no goals, but had managed to leave them with an ungodly mess to clear up.

Just in case Henry had put his head in the sand since Adam's death, Avril saw it as her duty to explain to him as much as she knew, or could surmise, about his son's waywardness. She wasn't sure how much he already knew. Some information, courtesy of Aunt Annie had percolated down to her via Clare and she set about ensuring that he knew the gravity of the situation. It was a question of being cruel to be kind as the media were not going to give up until the measure of his debts and the depravity of his associations were revealed in all their unpleasantness. Henry's jaw dropped in disbelief as Avril revealed that Adam's gambling debts had been out of control and that the depth of his indebtedness had necessitated the "sale" of privileged information relating to the country's banking transfer system. If rottenness had stopped there, Avril told him, it would have been bad enough and Adam's name would have been mud as soon as the fraud was discovered as it inevitably would have been. But holding nothing back, Avril continued with the further damning news of speculation that the purchaser of this confidential information had ties with the ill-treatment and wholesale repression of women. She spelled it out in no uncertain terms that he should brace himself as news might come out in time that Adam was mixed up with people from a world in which women were regarded as chattel. Modern day slavery, pornography, and deprivation were words which finally made Henry wince and ask how it had all come down to this. That he didn't really question the veracity of what Avril was telling him was an indication that he had not been entirely blind to what was going on. You must understand, Grandfather, rumours have it that he was connected with the lowest of the low and if that is proved to be true, even if only indirectly, then being a relative of his, will be an uncomfortable association for you, Clare, Annie and her family and for me; a relationship that we won't want to acknowledge willingly. Henry looked at her intently. She was right. It wasn't just a mess that Adam had left, it was a black hole which could engulf them all.

She left Henry mulling over the news. It wasn't just Adam's situation that had been discussed. She'd brought him up to speed about Clare and Annie and told him all about her work at the radio station and her future ambitions for it. It wasn't easy, she had made it clear, to deny any association with her father when Clare had such a high-profile job and was so obviously Adam's daughter. She was learning to step gingerly at the radio station and to weigh her words carefully before she spoke. Adam had left them with a toxic mixture and she had to brush off any derogatory comments about her father as if she barely knew him, which wasn't wholly inaccurate.

Eventually, when Henry took stock of reality, he was amazed at how little he knew about his family. All his thoughts for so many years had been centred on his son, but he had a daughter and four grandchildren too and apart from Annie, he knew little about them. And what he knew about Annie was way out of date. That she had accepted the role as family breadwinner and made a partial return at least to the world of insurance so that they could afford to educate a potentially gifted son, was all news to him, as was Avril's goals in broadcasting. And he hadn't even known until Avril told him where they all lived. Henry rebuked himself for his stupidity and lack of moral discernment. At the very least he should have shown some interest in their lives at Old Kit's memorial service, but his focus as always had been on Adam: what he wanted, what he needed, what was best for him. Henry hung his head in shame. Not only had he failed the others – although he had been sufficiently enlightened to pay for Annie's private education – but in giving Adam everything he wanted on a plate, he had reared a weak man without principles. The words of the biblical verse that there are none so blind as those that will not see spun around and around in his head as further admonishment of his faults. The signs were all there but he had been unwilling to see them. He had been following an image of his own creation rather than a person of substance and despite learning from an early age in the primary school when the family was still living in the north, that the bible said "thou shalt not make unto thee any graven images", he had gone ahead and done just that. And where had it got him? Nowhere really. The only family member who seemed concerned about his well-being was Avril; not his ex-wife, not his daughter, and not his other adult twin granddaughter, or indeed his elderly brother and sister-in-law. He'd not heard a peep out of any of them since the funeral, or perhaps more correctly since the bad press about Adam. And what about his friends and acquaintances? They had not stood up to be counted. They, too, seemed to have melted away into the ether as if he was persona non grata. What value "knowing" all those people when subsequent events showed that you knew them not at all? And realising that you were just as dispensable to them as they were to you. Even his union colleagues with whom he had worked and socialised over decades were cold shouldering him. Henry drew breath and then he sniggered; anyone sitting next to him might have offered him a penny for his thoughts. And if they had, they would have seen a new Henry emerging from a chrysalis.

Henry cast his mind back to what Avril had told him about the scam in which Adam was allegedly mixed up. Something about some football club directors or major shareholders or the like being the possible recipients of the fraudulent money. But she'd hinted that they weren't just ordinary criminals. They were depraved men who had grown rich on the back of slave labour and other abhorrent actions, particularly against women.

Football – the pleasure of watching matches from the directors' box, dining in the members' restaurant, casual chats with star players on first name terms, being photographed by the media sitting next to the head coach, and so much more – had played a big part in Henry's life. Never a player himself, he soon spotted the value of acquaintances with footballing backgrounds and had worked hard on promoting their causes by lobbying on their behalf both in parliament and inside the brotherhood of the unions. What he lobbied for was usually immaterial to Henry as it was the perks he collected for so doing that interested him and how he could use those contacts for the benefit of his son. The wide range of backgrounds of football club executives and owners meant that Henry was always busy representing someone's interest and as Henry's help wasn't philanthropic, there were rich pickings to be made which were not simply matchday tickets.

The ownership of a football club was often seen as marking the culmination in an entrepreneur's ascent to the pinnacle of his business life. It was the lure of the footballing greasepaint and all the ballyhoo and glamour that surrounded the "beautiful" game that went to the head of many a captain of industry. It mattered not a jot to Henry that most football clubs turned out to be money pits for their investors, because for Henry it was all about collecting his dues for services rendered. And what he amassed over the years, aside from the relative fripperies of free seats for the matches, was much, much more. Insider knowledge from all spheres: commerce, horse racing tips, land likely to receive planning permission, proposed government grants in the pipeline, intended government legislation, advance warnings of stock market trends, which fine art to buy for future sale and profit, and how to keep offshore bank accounts secret and out of the revenue's view.

But Henry was not without scruples. Unlike some he had met as he threaded his path through life, he had some form of moral compass. Folk, in some situations were fair game, others were not. Wheeling and dealing and laughing all the way to the bank at the expense of the able-bodied and nimble-minded, and taking advantage of corporate bodies was absolutely fine but anything near the margins of debauchery was not. He knew there were people in football who were so distasteful that just to clap eyes on them was to feel oneself soiled by their very gaze. What they did exactly he didn't know but for one's own protection one better know that there were some you messed with and some that you didn't. Henry shuddered. If his memory served him right, he'd sat around the same luncheon table as one or two dubious characters in the past and although he knew never to judge a book by its cover, he recalled some mean looking eyes sheltering behind shaded lenses. He shuddered again at the thought of child pornography, slave labour, political repression and gender crimes; they were subjects that would chill a good human being to his core.

Was it really true that Adam had involved himself with such people? Had his only son been so bereft of moral integrity that he had sold his soul to detritus like that? Henry had to know; he couldn't live a day longer without knowing. And the only way he would even find out would be to discover himself with whom Adam was in cahoots as nobody else would bother. But on that score, he was incorrect as Annie had someone firmly in her sights.

Chapter 7
GUERNSEY

In many walks of life including domestic living, customs and habits are handed down from one generation to the next, often without any explanation as to why that rigmarole should be followed and usually with just a nod to the circumstances of their particular epoch. The brotherhood of union members was no exception to this unwritten rule. Whilst its membership appeared to plead for future changes in the working environment, its executives continued to embrace archaic traditions. Amongst this elite band of union brothers who led their respective flocks from the comfort of executive chairs and tea served in China cups with matching saucers, the art of accruing and maintaining wealth were skills taught as carefully as those taught by any master craftsman to his apprentice. When told that Guernsey was considered the preferred depository of a union official's cornucopia, Henry had asked why when the logical place was surely Jersey – ostensibly the capital of the whole of the Channel Islands group – with its far wider and more varied choice of banking establishments than on the smaller island of Guernsey.

Henry was of a new genre of union official. His lack of sartorial good taste hid an expensively educated mind and if his peers, be they union colleagues or the upper middle classes in general, thought that his favoured spivvy look displayed a lack of self-confidence then they were very much mistaken. As there was just a seed of common sense in the choice of Guernsey, Henry too opted for a bank in St. Peter Port, but he took a sensible precaution. The treasury was not daft. Why keep all your eggs in one basket on an island that the treasury knew from historical fact was the favourite place of the union hierarchy? It only made sense to Henry if it could be used as a bluff. And thus, Henry's fortune was split lopsidedly into ten percent in Guernsey – where if it was discovered by the revenue, or anyone else for that matter, he could hold up his hands genially and claim that it was a fair cop but not get too over-excited at its detection – with the major tranche of ninety percent in Jersey. Personal visits to such places of discretion had been de rigueur during most of the years that Henry had been using their offshore facilities and up and down the busy main streets of Jersey's capital, St. Helier, other men and women with high finance on their minds mingled with local shoppers and holidaymakers. With daily crossings of the twenty-one nautical miles of open sea between the two islands – in the early days by conventional ferry taking two hours and in more recent times by use of the high-speed catamarans just a single hour – access from one island to the other by sea or by air, was straightforward.

As a crown dependency, the two self-governing bailiwicks forming the Channel Islands are not part of the United Kingdom and are subject only to their own laws although in practice they adhere in large part to the rules and regulations operating on the British mainland. However, where financial services were concerned, the islanders had long since spotted the opportunity to offer close neighbours – Brits and Continentals – a more liberal regime than that available within their own country. It was a mutually convenient association where the investor hid parcels of wealth from a stricter and less benevolent regime in force in his or her homeland, and which knocked the sale of tomatoes off their perch as the top grossing commodity of the Channel Islands. And with over a century of this liberalisation under their belts, the islanders involved in banking had perfected their methods in maintaining a safe haven for their clients' deposits by limiting the places to where the tentacles of his or her majesty's treasury could fully extend. Notwithstanding two world wars and numerous political skirmishes, this laissez-faire system endured for more than a century until the offshore tax regime was introduced in 1986. Its main aim was to ensure that United Kingdom tax residents were unable to accumulate income in an offshore fund to avoid paying income tax so that they would only pay tax on the capital gain made from the fund on its eventual disposal. Thus, it became illegal for the holder of an offshore account to fail to declare beneficial ownership in an attempt to evade income tax on the annual interest gained. That, following the act, such accounts would thrive in an atmosphere of secrecy and daring-do by becoming "must have" status symbols would never have occurred to the legislators, but as the proportion of declared accounts increasingly failed to tally with the number in existence, the task of the revenue to determine who held what became overwhelming. And those sufficiently determined to keep their tax bills to a minimum sought advice from private banks to keep it that way.

In past years, Henry had usually taken the Poole to Jersey ferry route; a journey of just under five hours in moderate seas. Sometimes, when the ferry schedules obligingly synchronised, he was able to transfer directly to the Guernsey ferry and be in St. Peter Port by the early afternoon to be in good time for his appointment. His visit there was a carefully choreographed show. The idea of fiscal propriety amongst union leaders was so fanciful that Henry regarded it as pointless to pretend otherwise and hence he approached his chosen banking institution in the high street openly and casually as if he was there to do nothing more exciting that to cash a small cheque. He didn't know the forces at work but guessed that local "investigators" monitored the comings and goings through the banking hall of British residents and reported back to their paymasters on the mainland those they suspected of tax evasion.

It was on his return journey – Guernsey to Jersey to Poole and home to Berkshire – that the real business was done the following day. With the same care and attention as always, he would alight at the terminal in St. Helier and make his way by foot the short distance into the main part of town, passing a variety of guest houses on his way.

His overnight stay on Jersey was low key and the choice of an ad hoc guest house with "rooms available" was in keeping with the low profile he desired. With space in his briefcase for overnight essentials, he would emerge the following morning refreshed from a good night's sleep and continue into the financial quarter without arousing notice. He would pass the domestic banks and one or two international finance houses with their glossy entrances and marble floors, and make his way up a particular side street where he would press the intercom on the facade of an olive green painted, narrow, three-storey building. When the buzzer sounded, he would push open the door and make his way to the first-floor offices of Channel Investments, where, following the satisfactory presentation of his passport to the receptionist, he would be guided into the office of his investment adviser. To any casual observer, or indeed to anyone unfamiliar with the methods adopted by the banks to ensure that their ultra-cautious account holders should feel that their deposits were safe with them, the building, nondescript in every way and without even a number pinned to its wall, gave no hint of what might occur inside. Indeed, with no windows on its frontage, passers-by would see no hint of life behind its rendered walls and would walk right passed without comment. That the building was owned and staffed by employees of the investment bank would have been news to them.

It was valued customers only who were invited to the anonymous building; clients of longstanding, and even more importantly, clients with large balances. Henry scored highly on both counts. While the exact definition of longstanding had not materially changed over the years –

twenty years plus being considered the absolute minimum – the definition of what constituted a large balance had risen meteorically like a rocket rising from the launch pad on Cape Canaveral. This was not just the result of general inflation, but was also fuelled by an increasing affluence amongst the middle classes together with the know-how and time to delve into matters that hitherto had been the sole domain of their betters.

In his initial days as a client, Henry did not meet the criteria for special handling and any business he chose to transact was done in the high street base where secrecy was a far lesser issue. But with the passage of time, the insider tips from his contacts, and a shrewdness worthy of any investment banker, through a strategy of keeping it simple, Henry amassed a small fortune. It was amassed for Adam and with a short liquidity, it was available to him whenever needed. But as the cashless society grew and the readies over the counter were in retreat, so Henry had to adapt his saving habits to conform with modern day trends. He no longer arrived on his annual trip to the island with a briefcase stuffed full of fifty-pound notes – the result from various tip-offs of on-the-nose bets on outsiders which ran in the three o'clock race at Chepstow or the four-thirty at Pontefract or wherever – or high-risk punts on latest technology start-ups or newly discovered mineral deposits in outback Australia were jettisoned in favour of more conservative equities in the increasingly popular tracker funds market. By the time he was upgraded to the anonymous building in the side street, he knew as much about sheltering his investments as the advisor on the other side of the expensive desk.

It was by air that Henry made his first, and what he planned to be his final trip, to the Channel Islands. Flights to the islands had mushroomed in recent years with many local airports on the mainland offering daily services to the two main islands – some with onward connections to Sark – which were far more convenient and comfortable than rolling and yawing for several hours in heavy seas. He had come to a decision as to what to do with his fortune now that Adam was dead. Ordinarily he would not have chosen air travel as passenger numbers were limited on the small aircraft used to ply the routes and remaining inconspicuous amongst such small numbers would have been impossible.

Not only did Henry break the habit of a lifetime by flying there, he also broke his routine of overnighting in Jersey on his way home. With an early morning arrival in St. Helier and a ticket booked on the Guernsey ferry in the late afternoon, he would have ample time in which to conclude his planned business in Jersey before taking the ferry to St. Peter Port where he had reserved a room in the swankiest hotel. Accordingly, Henry made his way quietly to the faceless building in the side street and was duly let in when he spoke into the intercom. He was clutching his briefcase which was bulging with documents but this time was devoid of any overnight essentials. It would be a long meeting as Henry had many affairs to reorganise. He settled back in the comfortable client chair, lit a cigar – a totally illegal privilege afforded to the super rich only – and started briefing the banker on his requirements. Later, they were joined by another man.

Eventually, installed in the exclusive hotel with a sea view over the busy harbour he lingered for some time watching the constant activity as boats arrived and sailed away from Guernsey. He had afternoon tea in his suite followed by a long soak in the magnificent free-standing bath and sat again on the sofa in the bath robe and slippers provided. He was in deeply pensive mood. He had set in place nearly everything necessary and tomorrow morning he would make his final moves. But first, he had a letter to write to his granddaughter, Avril. Ordinarily, Henry didn't have a soft spot, except for his late son, but right now his feelings were in turmoil. He knew he would have to keep his emotions in check in his letter to Avril. He dare not write from the heart; the letter must reflect a man of sound mind. He stepped onto the balcony, lit another cigar and thought carefully about the words he should use.

At reception the following morning, when asked whether he had enjoyed his short stay in the hotel, Henry replied truthfully that it had been a calming experience. He doffed his spivvy hat – the only overnight essential he had crammed into his briefcase before leaving the mainland – at the young receptionist behind the desk and, letter in hand, made his way the short distance into the centre of town where he bought a stamp and slid his precious letter into a post box. He was in good time for his appointment at the Guernsey bank to transact his remaining piece of business, to hand over into the bank's safekeeping his new and final will that he had had drawn up the previous day in Jersey by the solicitor who had joined his meeting with the investment banker. He had also handed in a recent photograph of himself and after reassurances that his account was in order, he took a taxi for the short distance to the airport. His work was nearly done.

The cliff path network along Guernsey's wild south-east coast meanders from La Vallette, near the capital, for almost thirty miles before finishing at Pleinmont in the Les Buttes southernmost region of the island. The maritime heathlands and cliff top grasslands are a favourite of casual walkers as they can enjoy the splendid views out to sea without strenuous effort or the need for heavy backpacks. He found the Route de Petit Bot and strolled the mile or so down to the coastal path swinging his empty briefcase back and forth as if he was a child without a care in the world. The road petered out into a narrow dirt track which took him to the cliff edge. He stood stock still in contemplative thought. It was breezy and he removed his hat lest it should be caught by a gust and fly off with the wind. He folded it neatly and put it in his briefcase; it was an allegory of all that was or had been dear to him and he didn't want to be separated from it. A kestrel hovered overhead low in the sky. He craned his neck to watch the bird gracefully circle around before taking up a new position from which to repeat the hover. He marvelled at its powers to do so without any apparent movement of its wings.

He had kept the tone of the letter to Avril businesslike. Standing there alone on the cliff top, he recalled the words he had used. Nothing about his feelings although he would have liked to have thanked her for visiting him and bothering to find out how he was coping with the loss of Adam. He wanted to tell her that he couldn't live without him and even if he could, he wouldn't have been able to bear the disgrace of Adam's associations with such odious people when it became public knowledge as it undoubtedly would at some future point. He wanted to tell her that he had no option, but he didn't. His heart was broken and could never mend. He had played his final ace and hoped that he would find salvation on the other side. She was his best hope that something useful could be done with his fortune. Henry steadied himself, said the Lord's prayer slowly, and tightly clasping his briefcase, he jumped.

Henry's presence on the island and his leap off the cliff had not gone unnoticed. His arrival at Guernsey's small airport by taxi from the hotel and the few minutes that it had taken him to find the road leading down to the cliff tops coincided with Kit and Edmund emerging from the arrivals hall and getting into a taxi. Kit noticed a man who looked familiar standing some way off from the taxi rank looking about as if searching for something or someone. It wasn't until they arrived in town that she realised that the man she had seen was probably Henry Roach. Edmund was sceptical when she told him but Kit felt fairly certain, but as they were there on important business, she put it to the back of her mind. Such a coincidence would have been amazing.

An elderly couple out walking the coastal path in an easterly direction towards St. Peter Port and enjoying the fine weather also spotted the kestrel. Like Henry, they too were fascinated by its flying skills and followed its progress from one hovering point to another. When it was almost overhead of Henry, they noticed him. He was standing alone near the cliff's edge. There was something in his stance that made the wife anxious. He was bareheaded and clutching something to his chest. Without further thought she yelled out "stop" and they started waving their arms wildly. They were on the far side of the bluff but could see Henry through a gap in the rocky crags. He might not have heard them in the strong breeze and would probably not have seen them so intent was he on his final action. In horror, they cupped their hands over their mouths as they saw him leap into the abyss, his briefcase torn from his grip by the onrush of air as he spun and somersaulted out of control towards the sea lapping on the narrow stony beach.

The alarm was quickly raised but recovery of the body proved a slow process as it had come to rest amongst rocks at the very base of the cliffs. It was painstaking work for the rescuers who had to abseil down from a strong point on the cliff top and then inch their way along to the rock upon which the body was sprawled. The briefcase had come to rest in a rock pool not far from the body and was recovered before it could be swept away by the incoming tide. Identification was straightforward as the passport found on the corpse matched its general age and gender. The death was attributed to suicide when the elderly couple confirmed that they had witnessed the event that morning. All that remained for the police to do was to inform the mainland authorities and make contact with the next of kin. One of the rescuers grumbled that the man could have chosen a less dangerous place from which to recover his body and a police agent was annoyed that a non-islander was using Guernsey's "facilities", otherwise it had been a text book recovery with minimal police action. It was not until the following day that Avril and Kit became involved.

Avril scooped up her post from the doormat as she left home in a dash to be on time at the radio station. It was ten past seven and she liked to be at her desk promptly at seven-thirty to prepare herself for the day ahead. The unopened mail consisted of three letters: a utility bill, an invitation to a building society AGM and the third bore a Guernsey stamp. She dealt swiftly with the first two but paused before slitting open the one from the Channel Islands. She knew nobody there and wondered if it was just a random circular, although the letter felt quite thick.

She was immediately surprised to find some type of document enclosed in a handwritten letter which slipped out and fell onto her metal desktop with a thud. It looked formal and had a post-it note stuck prominently on its upper surface on which was written in the same handwriting as the letter, "photocopy". She didn't know why, but Avril felt a sense of alarm. The clock on the wall showed seven forty-one. She didn't have time to read the letter now; work matters were more pressing and she stuffed it in her handbag to deal with later.

Kit and Edmund had arranged to stay three nights in Guernsey, transforming their "business" trip into a mini break and giving them a short respite from the heavy workloads at home. It would be their last break together before their impending wedding. When they awoke the following morning, Kit got up to make them coffees and noticed that a newspaper had been slid under the door. Edmund had splashed out on a suite – it was a grand hotel in the style of the interwar years with big rooms and high ceilings – and they sat in comfortable armchairs around a low coffee table. It was Edmund who drew her attention to one of the front-page articles in the Guernsey Press & Star. It was about the apparent suicide the previous day of a man named Henry Roach.

'Henry Roach, are you sure?' demanded Kit.

'That's what it says,' confirmed Edmund.

'It's not any old Henry Roach,' said Kit excitedly. 'It's *our* Henry Roach. I knew he looked familiar but I just couldn't place him at that moment.'

'Who looked familiar?'

'The man I saw yesterday at the airport when we arrived. I told you. Don't you remember?'

'Vaguely,' admitted Edmund, now more on the ball and realising that this might have serious implications. 'I wonder how this will impact on our task today,' he added seriously.

'Why should it have any impact other than to reduce the number of Old Kit's relatives?'

'I don't know right now, but I suspect it will,' Edmund said warily, 'and what was he doing in Guernsey? Same as us maybe. And can I remind you that since you discovered that Old Kit's four brothers are in fact her cousins, Henry is her first cousin once removed and not her nephew.'

'True, but I can't see what difference that would make.'

They both reread the article. The incident had occurred less than an hour after their arrival at the airport and so fitted in with Kit's assertion that she had seen Henry as they were getting into the taxi to go to the hotel. The passport in the dead man's jacket pocket had led to a swift identification once the rescuers had retrieved his body. All injuries were consistent with his fall and due to the witnesses, there was nothing to suggest foul play. His body had been taken to the morgue whilst the island police set about notifying the mainland authorities.

'You don't need a passport to travel to the Channel Islands from Great Britain,' Kit said thoughtfully.

'Maybe he wanted to establish his ID,' replied Edmund, 'after all, *we've* brought our passports to do exactly that.'

'You may be right because he was wearing a suit when I saw him. He was not in holiday attire. So, he might have had an appointment with someone and felt he needed to appear formally dressed.'

'The article gives no clue as to why he was on the island,' said Edmund, folding up the paper and laying it on the coffee table. 'If we weren't here ourselves on a sensitive matter then I would be very inclined to contact the Guernsey police for more information.'

'I suppose he was affected by the death of his son,' said Kit, 'he wasn't acting rationally whilst his mind was disturbed.'

'That suggests a spur of the moment action, one that is driven by emotion, but my guess is that it was pre-planned. From what my father has told me, there is no doubt that he cared greatly for his son and his early demise might have triggered a planned irrational response.'

'No parent wishes to witness the death of their child before their own. It's unnatural. It's just not the normal order of events. My grandparents were broken for many years by the death of my mother, their only daughter. It seemed to hit them harder than it hit me.'

'I know,' said Edmund, leaning over and gently stroking her arm, 'I know.' But Kit very much doubted that he could really have understood the heartache involved. Over two decades later, the grief was still visible in her grandparents' eyes. 'We now have to focus on our appointment at Bank Baer at eleven o'clock and I want to run through how I think we should handle it,' added Edmund. 'It's the Guernsey branch of an international private bank. We will need to be on our toes as they will presume that they hold all the cards.'

They shook hands politely with the bank's representative. They had arrived on time but been made to wait in an anteroom for over half an hour. Edmund looked cross and whispered in Kit's ear that if he kept his own clients waiting more than ten minutes then the local outspoken population of Northumbria would give him what for in no uncertain terms. Kit felt uncomfortable, but in the event a folded newspaper on the banker's desk diffused Edmund's annoyance.

'I apologise for keeping you waiting for so long,' said the banker graciously, as soon as they had taken their seats. 'An unexpected problem arose,' he continued, pointing to the paper, 'to which I was obliged to attend.'

'Was that to do with the death of Henry Roach?' asked Kit, the words tumbling out of her mouth before she could gain control. The banker frowned and did not reply. He had not handled the telephone conversation well which had caused the delay. The police had requested an interview with him as they believed he might have some useful information to add to the overall picture of a suicide on the island the previous afternoon. When he had replied that banking regulations prevented him from discussing clients – or possible clients – the police had made it clear that the law overrode banking protocols and his full co-operation would be expected when they met later that afternoon. Before he had time to ask them the nature of their business – a standard phrase used in the banking fraternity even though the intermediary who had arranged the appointment had told him the reason for their visit – Edmund seized the opportunity to take the floor.

'I am led to believe,' Edmund commenced, 'that you have already been apprised that the nature of our business is the demise of Kit Audrey Harrison and to that end I would like to start by establishing our identities. Kit said nothing but looked in awe of Edmund's forthrightness. He handed over their passports, birth certificates, utility bills with addresses, a letter from Kit's university stating that she was employed as a senior lecturer and a photocopy of the page in the Solicitors' Register that showed when he had qualified and where he practised. The banker shuffled the papers giving each a cursory glance before setting them aside, and Edmund continued, 'we are joint-executors of the will and I am a partner in the law practice where the will was drawn up by my father, also a solicitor but now retired.' Edmund retrieved a copy of the will from his satchel and placed it on the growing pile of set aside documents.

'What connection are you claiming with this bank?' asked the banker. He had regained his aplomb and was making it clear that he was now in charge of the interview.

'We believe,' said Edmund boldly, 'that the deceased maintained one or more offshore accounts with this bank and we are here to take charge of any monies in them.'

'And what proof do you have to support this belief?' asked the banker, crossing his arms somewhat defiantly. It was crunch time. Edmund knew all along that it would come down to a simple question like this. He had no valid proof but the banker would not know that. It was time for some embroidery of the few facts he knew.

'The tax returns of the deceased,' Edmund said, clearing his throat for special effect, 'show that in the years prior to the legislation introduced to close the loophole of undeclared offshore accounts by United Kingdom residents, the deceased declared, over a number of successive years, dividends and interest paid into a portfolio that she held in this bank.' That Old Kit used offshore accounts both before and after the legislation was fairly certain according to his father, but it was a guess by Edmund that she had declared the proceeds.

'Are you able to show me proof from the revenue of this assertion?'

'The rule of six applies here,' replied Edmund. 'HMRC generally archive documentation for six years although this has varied over time and can vary considerably if you are self-employed or under investigation.' This was true and both Edmund and the banker knew it. Moreover, both knew that to be under investigation was frequently the kiss of death for any tax payer stupid enough to proclaim his innocence loudly, as few came through the full glare of the revenue unscathed. 'Some would argue that the very fact that you are asking me to provide evidence is, in itself, proof that she has accounts here. You wouldn't bother otherwise.' The banker said nothing and Kit kept mum. It was all getting rather tetchy.

'Is your only evidence anecdotal?' the banker asked finally through tight lips.

'Anecdotal and circumstantial shall we say,' responded Edmund, 'but with the passage of time that is all that could be reasonably expected. And even *this* bank has its time limit on archiving data.' Edmund was about to play his best card as he added, 'especially accounts that have remained inactive over many years.' This last remark drew a slight involuntary twitch of the banker's hands on his desk and Edmund pressed home his advantage. 'The account would have been completely inactive during the last nine years which coincides with the deceased spending her final years living in a care home.' It was another guess but one which was likely to be true.

'I shall need to verify this documentation,' the banker said pointing to the papers he had set aside. 'This will take time and then I will need to discuss the matter further with a colleague. Would you be able to return at the same time tomorrow morning?' Kit understood immediately that this wasn't a request, it was an instruction and before Edmund could start getting testy at the delay, she answered in the affirmative. 'Very well,' said the banker, 'I shall see you again tomorrow morning but before you leave, I require a copy of each of your signatures agreeing to leave your identification in our hands overnight.' He withdrew two copies of a pro forma from a desk drawer and angled them in front of Edmund and Kit. Edmund read the small print carefully before signing but Kit didn't. She used the fountain pen bequeathed to her by Old Kit and with the certain flourish that comes with the ownership of such pens, signed her name.

Outside, and now with time on their hands, they found an outdoor café with a fine view over the harbour. Seated at a table out of the prevailing onshore breeze, they were able to reflect on the truncated meeting.

'Was it satisfactory?' ventured Kit.

'I think so,' replied Edmund. 'The fact that we have not been dismissed out of hand is promising.'

'At least we weren't told to get on our bikes,' agreed Kit. 'Maybe he will be a little more forthcoming tomorrow when he has scrutinised our paperwork. What a good thing you suggested we stay a couple of extra nights.'

'Of course, I took it into account when I made the suggestion,' he said teasing her.

'Oh, what a lying clairvoyant you are,' she said, leaning her head on his shoulder. 'It had never even crossed your tiny mind.'

'That's a bit harsh isn't it, fiancée. I bring you to this lovely island and you tick me off just when I was about to whisk you off your feet with a trip to the Pleinmont Observation Tower.'

They strolled around the five-storey tower hand in hand and climbed the high concrete steps to the viewing platform. It had been built by the Germans in the 1940s as part of their sea defences; its brutal appearance in the landscape had failed to soften with the weathering of age. The panoramic view from the top was stunning and in the cloudless sky it was difficult to discern where sea met sky. They counted the recreational small boats out on the flat sea and the large cargo vessels in the far distance on their routes to various ports worldwide and from their high vantage point watched the Sark ferry slip out of St. Peter Port harbour on its one hour crossing to the small island. When Kit reminded him that it was from cliff tops nearby that Henry had flung himself to his death the previous day, they decided to walk there and inspect the scene in an effort to visualise his last living seconds. They would leave the following afternoon and with gentle persuasion Edmund agreed that if they had sufficient time before their flight home then they should visit the offices of the Guernsey Gazette & Press to learn as much detail of his suicide as possible. Kit felt his death could be significant to the task she had in distributing Old Kit's offshore monies to needy and deserving family members and Edmund would take the opportunity to quiz the reporter, if available, on the likely reason as to why Henry was on the island.

* * *

It was with some apprehension that Avril finally settled down to read the handwritten letter and to inspect the enclosure with the post-it note. She hadn't had a single opportunity to read it at work and at some time during the hectic day had decided that it was best left for home reading. She couldn't guess what it was all about but her instincts were still sounding a warning bell. There was neat, flowery writing in blue ballpoint on the front and back of the first page and some writing in capital letters on the front side of the second sheet. She was sprawled on the couch initially as she started to read but within seconds she was sitting bolt upright. It was from her grandfather and the letter contained disturbing news.

Dear Avril,

You will doubtless be surprised to receive this letter from me, and especially to read its enclosure which is a photocopy of my last will and final testament. The original, drawn up yesterday by a solicitor in the Channel Islands and duly witnessed, has been sent by secure post to the offices of Newman, Wilson & Saddler in Berwick-upon-Tweed. I feel sure that you will remember that this firm has acted over many years as the organisers of your great grandaunt Kit Audrey Harrison's numerous family gatherings, the last of which was her recent memorial service in Newcastle Cathedral. I believe this legal firm to be completely trustworthy and impartial and that you can deal with them with confidence. I have named you as joint-executor with their junior partner, Mr. Edmund Newman.

I imagine that your first thought will be to wonder why I have done this and that your second will be to question the urgency for letting you know. So, I must explain that your father's death has hit me hard and the continuing revelations seeping out into the public domain about his impropriety has hit me even harder. And in the light of those exigences, I feel unable to continue. I am in a cleft stick as I find that I cannot live without him and yet cannot bear to live with the results of his behaviour. People may argue that to act now is to act hastily while my mind is disturbed, but I know my mind like nobody else and it is clear to me that to act now is to relieve a heart irreparably shattered by these recent happenings. And to that end I have put my affairs in order in the hope that you will have the opportunity to redress the balance of your father's actions by using the proceeds of my estate to do good. When you read this letter, Avril, I will be dead by my own hand.

Avril trembled. She felt sick. What she had read so far had winded her like a punch to the solar plexus. Her grandfather had purportedly taken his own life and she was reading the events that led him to this decision as if they were part of some lightweight holiday novel. She took a deep breath and continued.

I have listed my assets on the reverse of this page together with a rough estimate of their worth in order to assist you and Edmund Newman in achieving probate. You will see that the grand total of my estimates amounts to a sizeable figure

– Avril looked fleetingly at the list and agreed that the total was sizeable but not really exceptional bearing in mind twenty-first century property prices in the south of England –

and the distribution of these monies is covered in the will with the largest amount going to your aunt Annie for the education of her children, a relatively small amount to your sister Clare and the residue to you. Make a photocopy of this letter and send it to Mr. Newman when you contact him, but do not mention the second page as this contains information for you alone. The letter ended with a sad postscript: I very much appreciated your recent visit to Berkshire to enquire how I was coping since your father's death. In retrospect I believe it should have been my role to offer support to you and your sister.

Avril turned to the second page. There was very little on it and what was there were instructions. Underneath two short sentences in capital letters there was some sort of annotated map, followed by another short sentence and finally Henry's initials. It didn't make a lot of sense but it was clear that something on the Channel Island of Jersey needed sorting out and as Henry had written that he wished her to "redress the balance", it would be, presumably, with whatever she found there.

'Good morning,' said Avril when her call to Berwick was answered – Henry had jotted down some contact numbers at the end of his list of assets – 'I should like to speak to Mr. Edmund Newman please.'

'Mr. Newman is out of the office today but will be back tomorrow,' replied the helpful-sounding voice at the other end of the landline. 'Can I help you instead? I'm Edmund's assistant.'

'I don't think so,' said Avril hesitating, 'unless you can confirm that he has received a letter, probably yesterday, bearing a Channel Island stamp.'

'As a matter of fact, he has,' replied the male assistant. 'I noticed it because of the amazing coincidence. You see, he has been in Guernsey for a few days and is travelling home today.'

'Oh,' replied Avril, somewhat dumbfounded, 'that really is a coincidence. Would you ask him to ring me tomorrow after midday,' she added, leaving her name and number with the assistant. 'It's a matter of some priority.'

* * *

There had been an overnight shift in the banker's approach to his second meeting with Kit and Edmund. He had clearly reappraised his position. Edmund wondered if it was the result of accepting the authenticity of their documentation. If so, then hitting him hard with what they believed to be the account number should clinch their bona fides as the representatives of the late Kit Audrey Harrison. The frosty introductions of the previous day had been replaced by a welcoming smile and the offer of freshly brewed coffee, and once again Edmund took the initiative.

'The account number,' he started, 'was something that we somehow failed to mention yesterday. An oversight in the welter of information we had to convey.'

'Understandable,' replied the banker, all smiles. 'Maybe Miss Irwin would write it down on this pad using her elegant fountain pen.' He pushed the pad across the desk and Kit wrote down the number in the slow, fluid strokes that such pens dictate. 'May I enquire the source of this number?' he asked, assessing it carefully. 'For instance, was it given to you in person by the deceased who you claim holds an account at this bank?'

'Not in person exactly,' replied Edmund. 'It came into Miss Irwin's possession as a bequest.'

‘I inherited the fountain pen,’ explained Kit hastily, ‘and found the number on a slip of paper that was wedged into an inner tube in the casing when I was cleaning it for future use.’

‘I see,’ said the banker. ‘May I inspect the pen, please?’

‘Certainly.’ She handed it over and the banker appeared to compare it with something in his folder.

‘Thank you,’ he said, returning the pen and addressing Kit directly. ‘May I please now ask about a scar on your finger.’

‘It’s not on my finger, it’s on my left thumb,’ corrected Kit immediately, ‘but why you should want to know about that I’ve no idea.’

‘It’s very simple, Miss Irwin. Your great grandaunt left details about both the pen and the scar on your thumb as a way of proving that you are indeed who you say you are. And I am under strict instructions to help facilitate to the best of my ability your plans as joint-executors of her will.’

Total capitulation was how Edmund described it when they were finally outside walking briskly in the direction of the police station with just forty-five minutes spare to discover as much as they could about Henry’s death before the short taxi ride to the airport.

‘Not exactly total capitulation,’ said Kit, taking the scientist’s logical approach. ‘He had to bow to reality. My pen and my thumb won the day because, as he explained, their client had given her own death a lot of prior thought. She ensured that only the holder of her fountain pen and a person with a barely visible scar on her left thumb could claim to be her successor.’

'Yes, it was a neat trick,' agreed Edmund. 'Who'd have guessed that the pen was part of a set.'

'And had the perspicacity to leave the matching propelling pencil with the bank,' added Kit.

'And to have also put in place a failsafe system in the shape of a tiny scar. Whoa. She was some sort of devious woman.'

'After that, there was nothing he could do but give in gracefully.'

Kit was keeping her feet firmly on the ground. She had just discovered that she had inherited a fortune. The amount was so large that it was impossible to treat it seriously. It made a mockery of her annual salary and savings and the former monthly budget that she and Martin had always tried to maintain. Unlike Edmund, she put it out of her mind as they entered the offices of the Guernsey Gazette & Press.

'I'd like to speak to the reporter who covered yesterday's suicide story, please.'

'Out on another storyline,' said the disinterested clerk, barely bothering to look up from behind the counter which was strewn with paperwork.

'We were just wondering if the reporter knew why the deceased was on the island,' said Edmund, stepping in to prevent Kit from mentioning that she might be a relative of the dead man, as to have done so would have brought into question their own clandestine reason for being there. 'When will the reporter be back?'

'No idea,' replied the clerk unhelpfully.

'Have you got a mobile contact number for him?' persisted Edmund.

'Not supposed to give that out. All enquiries are meant to be channelled through official lines.'

They were getting nowhere fast. Time was running out and it was clear that the clerk was set on being unco-operative. It took a couple of banknotes, slid across the counter by Edmund, to break the impasse and secure the journalist's mobile number.

'We have to deal with the unpaid tax that will arise from Old Kit's undeclared account before we start declaring a relationship with the man who took his own life,' Edmund said in earnest, 'get that out of sequence and our own integrity will be challenged. And unless we play out cards carefully, the amount of tax to be paid will make the national papers.' Edmund was right, Kit concluded, but that wasn't going to stop her from contacting the reporter.

Kit wasn't the only female member of the Roach family exercising her mind. Avril's world had also been turned upside down. As soon as information about her father's death trickled through to the media, the twins came within their unerring spotlight as it made good copy. The tabloids in particular were quick to sensationalise the golden sleaze triangle of politics, suspected financial corruption and a dodgy termination of life. She had alerted Clare and for once they had found some common ground to comfort and support one another. The first salvo of innuendoes would hit Clare the harder. Still learning the ropes of parliamentary dos and don'ts when responding to the press, she would have to curb her tongue and ride it out with a series of no comments.

As Clare really did know nothing about her grandfather's affairs, they decided that it should remain that way – no correspondent could slip her up and to be unaware of what was going on in your grandfather's life was not unusual – with Avril taking charge of dealing with the media and whatever it was that had to be done as joint-executor of his will. As part of the media herself, she already knew how to avoid some elementary pitfalls and would be mindful of how to conduct her business. The call from Edmund came early the following morning and it was apparent from the agitation in his voice that he had been taken totally by surprise. It wasn't something he felt that could easily be discussed over the phone or be handled by an exchange of emails and so a meeting was agreed at a halfway point and two days later they met in a tearoom in York.

'Hallo, Avril,' said Edmund, as she approached his table. She was on time and he liked that; clients who arrived late for appointments were the bane of his working life. 'Will it be tea and Danish pastries or are you going to set the world on fire by asking for coffee in a tearoom?'

'At this time of day, it can only ever be coffee,' she said, smiling. His little quip had eased the formality of their meeting. It could have been awkward for both of them.

'I hope you didn't have to rearrange too much of your work schedule to get here today,' Edmund said. 'I left a couple of clients disgruntled with last minute reshuffled appointments, but this seemed more important. However, I must get back in time for late afternoon meetings.'

'We'd better get on then, no time to waste. How should we proceed?'

'Could you tell me how all this came about, please?' asked Edmund.

'Nothing much to tell,' replied Avril. 'I received a letter in the post. It came from Guernsey according to the postage stamp. The letter was from my grandfather. I vaguely recognised his handwriting. A photocopy of the will was enclosed. The letter instructed me to contact you.' She handed over the letter, carefully omitting the section Henry had advised her to keep secret, which Edmund read attentively.

'From what I gather,' said Edmund, also acting with great care about his presence on the island at the time of Henry's suicide, 'before your grandfather took his own life, he made a new will and it was forwarded to me via the solicitor who drew it up.'

'That is my understanding too.'

'Do you know why he chose to do so on Guernsey when he lived in the Royal County of Berkshire?'

'I don't. No.'

'It doesn't seem to make sense,' Edmund declared. Avril stayed silent waiting for Edmund to suggest why. 'I can only conclude,' he said eventually, 'that it has something to do with his offshore account. It's perfectly legal to hold them but illegal not to declare the earnings. I shall have to contact the revenue to ascertain the situation.'

'Otherwise,' asked Avril, 'is it straightforward?'

'In terms of providing for his close family, that is, his daughter and grandchildren, all is in order and it is likely that the bequests can be paid out in full as soon as his financial assets are liquidated and without the sale of his property, providing that he does not have any unpaid tax outstanding.'

'And there would be if he has failed to declare his offshore account.'

'Exactly. Did he have an accountant?'

'That seems likely but I don't know. In truth, I know little about him. We weren't on bad terms. We simply didn't see much of one another. He was all wrapped up in his son. Adam was his number one and nobody else really counted.'

'He hasn't listed a contact number for an accountant but just looking at his list of assets, I can see that some are fairly complex,' said Edmund.

'You could try contacting his union. Although long retired from his union work, he was a union man through and through. They might be able to shed some light.'

'Then there is the question of a mortgage. Did he still have one or had he paid it off?'

'I think mortgages were generally arranged through brokers who worked mainly for the unions. They could arrange preferential rates for all manner of financial services.'

'Yes, you're right. I think that's my starting point,' agreed Edmund. 'You should realise that if there are no large bills outstanding,' stated Edmund, 'then after paying the bequests, you will be left with the property which I'm assuming is worth a pretty penny.'

'*If* the property isn't mortgaged to the hilt, but *if* it is,' said Avril in her most pragmatic frame of mind, 'then it could be zero.'

'That's true.'

Avril's position wasn't the only thing on Edmund's mind. After he had driven back to Berwick, seen his late afternoon clients and set in motion their requirements, he turned his attention to what they had learned in Guernsey. It was almost midnight before he settled down in his office to ponder his next move with a glass of beer and a pizza from a late-night takeaway. He was dog-tired but important decisions had to be made sooner rather than later.

The gist of their second meeting with the banker was that Young Kit met the security demands that Old Kit had put in place for the control of the account to be passed to her. It would be seamless, the banker had indicated with a knowing look, if you keep your mouth shut. Power over the account was now hers and there was no requirement to inform anyone else. In fact, the banker made it clear, Edmund Newman was present at the meeting only at Miss Irwin's pleasure. Before they left, a full-face photograph of Kit had been taken for their records together with a photocopy of her passport details, and then they were out on the street with their heads spinning at the amount Old Kit had managed to amass.

Casting his mind back as the banker went through page after page of individual investments – gilts, equities, bonds, cash in various currencies, property, sustainable crops – Edmund accepted that it had all been very professionally invested. Doubtless the bank charges for their services were stratospheric but such trivial items were glossed over as inconsequential.

For Edmund, it was a restless night that followed. Just a few short hours in which thoughts of how to proceed tumbled about in his mind. Until now, Kit had been his joint-executor but she was now also his client. He had to remind himself that the offshore account was hers and hers alone. True, Old Kit's intention was to distribute it as Young Kit felt justified, and sure, he didn't doubt that she would do that to the best of her ability, but he had no power to get matters under way. He rather doubted that she could be hurried; she would probably take the long view that important decisions needed to be thought out carefully. She was of course right, but Edmund had to consider his own position as a solicitor. He had to be seen to be honest and to be upholding the rules of his professional body. Instinct told him that he had a duty to inform HMRC about Old Kit's millions in Guernsey before he applied for probate. He had to ensure that any possible tax liability was brought to their attention and was seen to be paid, and it should be done without delay. Any hint of impropriety on his part would be pounced on by the press if word got out about the secret millions and a scandal would ensue. Reputation was everything amongst those who practised law. The question he kept turning over in his mind was how he could get Kit to act swiftly on this point. She had already made it clear that she was "uncomfortable" with the press. She guarded her privacy vigorously and although she would understand the common sense of dealing with the tax issue expeditiously, she wasn't going to allow the media to dictate her every action.

Long distance chats by phone or internet were proving no substitute for real live conversations. Despite having a matter of weeks only to complete her contract with the university, Kit was still stuck in London and Edmund was three hundred and fifty miles away in Berwick. It would be a tricky conversation over the landline trying to urge her into immediate action, but there was no alternative as he didn't have the time to journey down to see her. And the next day the conversation didn't get off to a promising start; she was busy preparing a lecture and he was interrupting her train of thought.

'In our capacity as joint-executors we need to be whiter than white,' started Edmund chattily.

'What does that mean?' questioned Kit with a testy ring to her voice.

'It means, dear fiancée, that we know that Old Kit had one more asset than she owned up to having. Therefore, we cannot proceed with probate until we establish if it represents a tax liability on her estate and if it does, to pay whatever is due. Not to do so would be to commit an offence.'

'So, what is it you are proposing?'

'I must inform the revenue as soon as possible that the executors have discovered an asset that may give rise to unpaid taxes,' replied Edmund. He was trying to keep patient but Kit was being obtuse; she was making him spell out the obvious in simple words.

'What does that mean for me? You know I don't do high finance,' she asked woodenly.

'In simple terms, it means that we can no longer allow the Guernsey offshore account to be kept a secret between the bank and the account holder. We have discovered it and we must declare it. The information needs to be out in the open.'

'And then as its owner, I can expect the whole of Old Kit's extended family to write begging letters to me at best or to challenge her will. Once they find out how much is in the account, they will go bananas.'

'Put that way, yes.' It would have been pointless to argue, thought Edmund, as she was in a negative mood, but he added nonetheless, 'and it won't just be distant family who are reacting. You can bet that the public in general will also be on your heels because the media will have whipped up their interest too.'

'Well, I don't fancy that at all,' said Kit firmly down the line, 'not at all, and as it's now my account, I want to wait and think it out and not be pushed into a knee-jerk reaction that I might regret.'

'You might regret inaction,' Edmund countered. 'Prevarication is a luxury you may not be able to afford.' Edmund bit his lip. Had he gone too far? It seemed that the lady was not for turning as a famous former prime minister had once told parliament. Would Kit see sense?

'There's no need for that sort of remark,' Kit replied crossly. He could hear her lips smacking together as she spat the words into the mouthpiece. 'Martin would never have spoken to me like that.'

'Well, bully for Martin, but let me remind you that he is not your co-executor and he is not your fiancé. This time he had gone too far; the click on the line confirmed that he had been terminated. Edmund put down the handset, folded his arms, hunched his shoulders, stretched out his legs under the desk, and reflected. Were all women emotional? His sister wasn't. His mother didn't appear to be. Or, maybe women were only emotional with their partners. Should he ring her back or should he send an email? Or, should he wait? The intern law graduate knocked on his door to enquire if Edmund was ready for his next client and Edmund nodded.

The handkerchief that Kit had used to blot her cheeks was wringing wet. It made damp patches on her metal desk when she put it down. Lost in thought, she used it to clean an ingrained coffee stain near the base of her monitor and laughed out loud when the brown blob disappeared. Ever the scientist, she wondered if the composition of human tears could be patented to produce more ecologically-friendly cleaners. But it was just a momentary pause in her fractious mood. She'd snapped at Edmund without good cause and when she'd tried to ring him back to apologise, she'd been thwarted as he was already busy with his next client. She'd tried to refocus her mind on the lecture material but without success. She felt tearful again, problems were piling up and she didn't know how to handle them. She stared through the window at the tops of the newly-planted trees in the courtyard below continuously bending and waving as their slender trunks were caught in the power of the strong breeze. They looked so ill-equipped to survive the wind's onslaught. It was how she felt too. She had lost her confidence to ride out the present storm in her life. She felt ill-prepared to tackle the arising difficulties. The contemplation of her wedding should have been a joyous prospect but the spectre of Old Kit was hanging over her like the sword of Damocles. Would she ever be free, she wondered, to pursue the calm and regulated lifestyle that she had enjoyed for so long before that fateful letter from Mr. Newman Sr landed on her doormat and set in train a series of unwelcomed events? And Martin had been part of that carefree life. Dear Martin with whom she had shared more than five years in a way of living without ambition but free of worry. It had all seemed so simple then. She shook her head in wonderment. Edmund had stirred in her the ambition for a normal life, something that she had never really known, but normality appeared riddled with stress, again something that she had never really known as she had been too young at the time of her parents' accident to understand naked emotions or the toll that they could take on a human being's psyche. When the navel gazing eventually stopped and she switched back into a practical frame of mind, she sent Edmund a short text to apologise for her uppity manner on the phone. She was relieved to hear his voice sometime later and to be able to explain in a calm and ordered way that things had suddenly got on top of her, but that in no way did her mini outburst represent any lack of fondness of him. She had simply lost the plot in regard to all the changes that were happening in her life and the demands that Old Kit's will had placed on her shoulders, but with Edmund's support she would pull through. She had wanted to tell him that she dreaded the idea of people baying at her heels for money. Sob stories, true or false, requesting handouts for every conceivable reason, and charities begging for donations to continue saving this ill-treated donkey and that starving body in some African backwater. And how much she hated publicity and attention, but the words just wouldn't come. She pressed "send" with an air of reluctance.

It was an uncomfortable time for Avril too. Her world was also being turned on its head and she was finding it almost impossible to focus her attention entirely on radio station business. It had not gone unnoticed by her colleagues but when the news broke of the suicide in Guernsey of the father of the late member of parliament for Islington & Grove and their respective relationships with Avril as father and grandfather, consensus was that she should take a short break to reset her compass and deal with whatever problems needed sorting out.

Avril knew what she had to do. She had to follow Henry's instructions and go to Guernsey but for what reason she did not know. There were no scheduled flights from the east Midlands region to the Channel Islands. Avril took the train and tube to Heathrow. Wandering around in the terminal concourse searching for domestic departures, a light tap on her shoulder brought a further complication.

'Martin,' she exclaimed,' further words eluding her such was her surprise at seeing him.

'I'm sorry to startle you,' he said laughing, 'I don't usually have this effect on women of bringing them to a state of near speechlessness. How are you, Avril?'

'I'm ….,' she trailed off as if unable to find a suitable word. 'What are you doing here?' she continued finally managing to change the subject.

'I've just finished my posting in Vienna.'

'And you're on your way home.'

'Yes, wherever that may be. And you?'

'I'm catching a flight to the Channel Islands but still can't find domestic departures.'

'That's because you're in the arrivals hall,' said Martin, 'follow me, I know the way.'

Standing together near the barrier separating passengers from those seeing them off might have marked the end of their second chance meeting – in much the same way that a realisation that she was short of time to catch her train had brought an abrupt end to their coffee sipping when they had met unexpectedly on the tube a few weeks earlier – but it didn't. She looked up steadily into his eyes and before he could say some meaningless platitude of farewell, without warning she flung her arms around his neck. He staggered momentarily, overwhelmed by the sudden gesture of emotion and afraid for an instant that he might misinterpret its meaning. He eased her head from his shoulder and looked deeply into her clear eyes and knew beyond doubt that they shared a love for one another. It wasn't passion, or desire, or even the need to be part of a social couple, it was, instead, a true warmth that radiated between them.

'Don't go,' he said, his large feet shuffling closer to her.

'I must,' she replied, 'but I'll be back soon.'

Avril's travels abroad had been mainly hockey-related: mostly jamborees and festivals in Holland and Belgium where field hockey was one of their most popular sports. The aircraft used, even for those short hops across the North Sea, could accommodate well in excess of two hundred passengers. It was therefore a very different experience to be seated in a small plane with less than seventy other passengers and Avril sat back and drank in the coastline views as the engines throbbed in a steady and rhythmic beat. Before long, the outline of the Cherbourg peninsula and then Alderney came into range followed a few minutes later by Herm, Guernsey and Sark. She wasn't familiar with their shapes on the map but instantly recognised the contours of the largest island, Jersey, as they circled overhead in their leisurely descent to its international airport; the iconic St. Aubin's Bay with its near circular profile of a strip of sandy beach having featured in televised repeats of a popular police drama from the seventies.

Following Henry's instructions, Avril made her way into St. Helier and found the route he had mapped out for her to walk. At the faceless building in the side street, she had pressed the intercom button, announced her presence and mounted the stairs to the first floor where a receptionist had, without further ado, guided her into the spacious office of a senior official. When her passport details proved to be in order and an exchange of information further validated her identity – the short sentences in capital letters which Henry had written above and below the annotated map acting as a means of ensuring that no one could impersonate her – the senior official, a high-flying woman in her late thirties, tapped a password into her computer file, swung the monitor round so that Avril could also see displayed on the screen the holding in her late grandfather's account.

'But there isn't much in his account,' she said, astounded.

'It's now your account and not his,' corrected the official, 'and although there may not seem to be much there on first perusal, there is indeed a great deal.'

'Just one item seems to be listed unless I am mistaken,' countered Avril.

'It's the name of an umbrella company,' explained the official. 'You won't have heard of it. Indeed, we pride ourselves that nobody will have heard of it. It doesn't trade in its own right. Its primary purpose is to hold equity stakes in other companies.' She clicked on the item to display its deeper secrets and three headings emerged: FTSE companies, currencies and football clubs. Avril looked intently at the screen but said nothing. 'You will see many familiar company names,' said the official, scrolling down the list of Henry's favourite equities. 'They are all top 100 companies. You have probably heard of all of them.' Avril nodded. 'Currency holdings,' continued the official, 'are, as I am sure you would guess, held in the only legal tenders that command respect throughout the western world: US dollars, Euros, and of course, the ultra-reliable Swiss Franc. Avril nodded again, eager to get on to the third heading. 'Football clubs,' she continued looking up at Avril and with a slight tone of amusement in her voice, 'may not be quite as you expect.'

'No Arsenal? No Liverpool?' said Avril, scanning the document names.

'Correct. The names you see relate to companies providing services to football clubs. Not very glamorous but greatly more profitable. They are not burdened by colossal wage bills or the whims of enigmatic owners who go into football to boost their egos.'

'Smart. My grandfather was able to feel part of the game of football without incurring the debt or worry that the owners bare.'

'Yes. It certainly was a smart move on his part and lucrative too. The share prices of these companies have increased on average tenfold since the inception of the Premier League and the worldwide exposure the sport now has to television audiences.'

'And the bottom line?' asked Avril, suddenly aware that she hadn't a clue how much all these assets represented.

'Currencies and equities are subject to fluctuations,' stated the official, using standard investment jargon. 'The balance as of noon yesterday was just over seventeen million in GB pounds.'

'No, that can't be true,' replied Avril incredulously, the words emitted one by one as if they weren't part of the same sentence. 'He can't have amassed that sort of fortune.'

'According to our records,' replied the official reassuringly, 'I can assure you that it *is* true.'

'How was he able to do that?' demanded Avril. The question was really rhetorical but the official explained that the large balance was due to prudent management over many decades – by the investment house, of course – coupled with few withdrawals and a canny knack on the part of the account holder to know the right time to buy into new companies. He had propitious timing, she had said, but all that Avril could think about was the potential can of worms she would open should she dare to touch the money. That, and the possible purchase price of Radio East Midlands.

On return, Avril was pleased to find Martin waiting for her at Heathrow. They had exchanged texts confirming her arrival time and Martin was there to meet her because he wanted to be with her. They didn't kiss, but walked away from the buzz of the airport holding hands as if it was the most natural thing in the world for them to do so. There was no question now; they were right for one another and both knew it.

'Where are you staying?' asked Avril.

'At one of those travel-type hotel places,' replied Martin. 'I've booked for a week whilst I try to find somewhere to rent. I'm going tomorrow to inspect a couple of places in the Reading area that I can rent for six months whilst I decide that to do on a more permanent basis.'

'Pity you can't join me in Peterborough.'

'Just too far for a daily commute to my lab in Reading,' he said smiling, 'but otherwise I'd have loved to.' He squeezed her hand and they stopped briefly for a hug.

All too soon, Martin was waving her goodbye as the train pulled out of King's Cross northward bound to her home in Peterborough, and more importantly for Avril, a chance to get back to work in her normal positive frame of mind. She hadn't told Martin about the reason for her visit to Jersey but there was a recognition in his bearing that he had already played out that very same scenario. She would tell him when he came up for the weekend and would be glad to share the anxiety she felt, but until then, her job needed full concentration. She reminded herself that she was media with listeners to consider, schedules to organise, programmes to fine tune, and in the spirit of the blitz the show had to go on.

Martin hated the rental properties he viewed although he accepted that there was nothing intrinsically wrong with them, they just happened to be in the Reading area which evoked unwanted memories of his time with Kit. It was a bad idea, he realised all too late, to look for accommodation in the same area. There would always be associations and recollections of his carefree time with Kit. Maybe he should consider commuting to his workplace; many people did long distance journeys daily. Starting afresh with Avril would be wonderful if she felt the same way as he did about her. And if she did, then this time, right at the outset, he would make it clear that he was the son of an infamous murderer. He wouldn't pussyfoot around the subject again. Candour from the outset and bugger the consequences. And who knows, perhaps she would reveal a skeleton in one of her own cupboards.

It was Friday evening when he travelled up to Peterborough. They had been in contact constantly since Martin had waved her goodbye at King's Cross. For different reasons, neither could afford to take any time off work and although Avril had a broadcast slot early on the Saturday morning, she would have the rest of the day free to enjoy some leisure time with Martin.

She was living in a rental flat in the centre of Peterborough which was within walking distance of the radio station. It was small and furnished with a mishmash of sticks of dark brown furniture from different eras. Its only charm was its location; so near to her office that when once she had overslept, she had walked briskly to the radio station with her winter coat over her pyjamas. But it had a comfortable couch and it was there, relaxing arm in arm, they enjoyed the bottle of sparkling wine and the small box of handmade chocolates that Martin had brought.

Avril wasn't experienced with men. She had had a few boyfriends during her late teens but nothing lasting. Since graduating, her mind had been on other matters and she hadn't missed that kind of male company. When they met, her sister Clare would usually throw in a caustic remark about Avril's lack of appeal to the opposite sex. It was a "plain Jane" remark which did nothing to improve the bond between the siblings. Avril took the view that if romance came her way, she would welcome it but she wasn't going to prostitute her wares in the manner that Clare so brazenly did. So, when she'd met Martin in the casual encounters of the hockey world, without any overtones of a boy-meets-girl date, she had been entirely her normal self. And from what she could tell, it seemed that Martin had liked what he had seen. With a glass in one hand and Martin's arm around her shoulder, she was preparing herself to divulge the reason for her trip to Jersey, but Martin got in first. 'I must tell you,' he said in a staccato voice which gave away his level of anxiety, 'that I had an affair with your twin.' Avril said nothing. 'Well, it wasn't actually a *real* affair,' he added hastily in a more normal speaking voice. 'I had only suggested casually that if she visited me in Vienna, I would show her the sights. I never thought she would take me up on the offer, but she did.'

'That's my sister,' replied Avril, without rancour. 'Follows up all the offers if she thinks there is something to gain.'

'I feel so embarrassed by the whole episode,' said Martin, shifting position on the couch. 'I was glad when she left. She was in a huff. I hadn't been the Lothario she had expected or required.'

'That's my sister,' repeated Avril, squeezing Martin's hand for reassurance. 'Clare is what she is. And in some perverse way there is a certain honesty in that.'

'Do you get along?'

'Our only real bond is our date of birth. We're two entirely different people with different values.' Martin did not reply verbally, but gently pulled her closer to him. His large feet were as still as the grave as he said, 'I've something else to tell you too. Something upsetting. Something so awful that I have never told a living soul.' She looked at him; his face looked drawn. She waited. She could feel his body tensing and finally he said, 'my father was a notorious murderer.'

'But you're not,' said Avril eventually, breaking the heavy silence.

'Not what?'

'Not a murderer. You're not a murderer.'

'No,' responded Martin with some indignation in his voice. 'I'm definitely not a murderer.'

'Well,' said Avril evenly, 'that's all right then. But I think you'd better explain all.' So, Martin launched into his childhood history and left nothing out: his parent's background, the circumstances that had provoked his father's grievous actions, what he could remember of his toddler days with his mother before her mental illness intervened, his days in care going from fostering pillar to post, his visits to see his mother in the institution in the west country, his father's suicide in prison, his time with Kit and his inability to reveal his background to her, and most of all, the endless shame he felt.

'I do remember some fairly recent press coverage about a prisoner's suicide in jail when he had only a further short period to serve,' said Avril matter-of-factly. 'To the ordinary man in the street it didn't seem logical, but I guess your father harboured an element of fear that the press wouldn't allow him to forget what he had done. According to the court, the multiple stabbings of the victim had constituted a frenzied attack and the media loves to get its teeth into such gory crime. It sells tabloid papers by the thousands.'

'You don't understand,' said Martin shaking his head. 'He was my father. I barely knew him, but I am of his flesh and blood. I can't look at his crime dispassionately. He was out of control and I may have inherited the characteristic to lose control in a similar scenario. God forbid.'

'But at the same time,' interjected Avril, 'you feel hurt and wounded when the media keep sensationalising his weakness just to sell copy. You want to run to his support.'

'He was my father, after all,' said Martin quite simply.

'He couldn't have been all bad. He stood by your mother when she became pregnant. He didn't shirk that responsibility and from what you say, it sounds as if he tried hard to make a good life for the three of you.' They both sat quietly; each deep in his own thoughts. 'I doubt very much that the characteristics for violence is passed down the line genetically,' said Avril after much thought. 'From what I've learned from our listeners about disruptive behaviour, violence gets handed down by example. A parent hitting a child can breed future problems. The child can think that it's acceptable to use brutal force to get one's own way. Following another long pause, she said finally, 'I think you're burdening yourself unnecessarily with the sins of the father. You're presuming your own guilt without any evidence that you would act in that way if pushed. In fact, after a tough childhood with no one to turn to for advice or support, you have every reason to be proud that you have come through the system unscathed.'

'I'm not sure about unscathed,' said Martin sighing deeply, 'but it is a great relief to tell you about my background. To share my worries with you.'

'And to see another way of looking at it, I hope.'

'Yes. Sharing it with you is one of the best things I've ever done.' Then he asked hesitantly, 'Does it make any difference to how you feel about me?' Avril answered his question by snuggling closer to him; words would have been superfluous.

'But it still leaves me with many hills to climb.'

'Such as?'

'Nobody at work knows my background. I am always deliberately evasive when asked about my upbringing. It's a technique that I have employed for as long as I can remember. Basically, I give nothing away,' Martin murmured. 'How would they feel about me if they knew the truth?'

'They might be a bit pissed off that you had led them a merry dance because you hadn't had the courage to tell them, but other than that, they would probably think it was all pretty exciting.'

'I could hardly put it on my CV, could I though? When not working, the job applicant likes to play hockey, goes to Bristol once a month to visit his mother in a safe mental facility, and his father is an infamous killer locked up at her Majesty's pleasure.'

'So, did you invent more humdrum parents?' asked Avril, after some thought.

'No. I sidestepped the issue.'

'I'm surprised you were able to do that with those big feet.'

They talked long into the night despite Avril's early Saturday morning slot. She would manage somehow, she had told him, to be bright-eyed and bushy-tailed for the programme, but right now, talking was what Martin needed. Releasing the pent-up emotion of all the preceding years from his system was the way forward for both of them. They had agreed that it was a subject to be treated with great care, for as Martin had pointed out, what mother in the world would wish her young son or daughter to receive their hockey prize from a man whose father had stabbed and killed another person in a display of crazed ferocity, and what organisation, if any, would pick him to be their figurehead. Avril conceded that the way ahead was trickier than she had realised, but as far as she was concerned, it made not one iota of difference to a growing feeling of fondness she felt for him. If they tackled the future together, then with common sense and mutual support, they would conquer their problems. And by the way, she had added as she leaped out of bed at half past five the following morning, she had her own dark skeletons to tell him about. He had sleepily replied that they were made for one another and should do something about it sooner rather than later.

He waited outside the radio station, one of the few remaining old buildings near the town's centre to survive the council's millennium policy to demolish and rebuild in their desire to upgrade Peterborough's image. She had said twelve noon but the minutes ticked by and he started wondering if she had had second thoughts. Suddenly, she emerged on the pavement through the heavy swing door and was by his side.

'Sorry,' she said immediately, 'a local news item of importance just broke and I didn't even have time to text you that I'd be late leaving. Decent pub up the road, shall we go there?' He nodded, and from an upstairs window, they were seen to go off arm-in-arm chatting animatedly.

The pub was not the right place for Avril to make her own confession. Without transport, choices for a suitable spot were limited. They ended up walking along the embankment of the river Nene which was within easy walking distance of the town centre. Normally busy with street entertainers and al fresco snack stalls, the crowds had thinned out as the fans of the local football team had headed to the stadium for the Saturday afternoon's home match. They strolled hand-in-hand for almost an hour, barely talking, increasingly enjoying the landscape as they left the built-up area. They were comfortable with one another without any need to express their feelings overtly.

At a fork in the river, they followed the path leading to Overton Lake. It was dry but cool and the steely-coloured sky made a fine backdrop for blackbirds and crows as they continuously soared and dived in their search for food. 'I was in Jersey at my grandfather's request,' started Avril, even before they had found somewhere to sit out of the wind.

'Jersey, not Guernsey, right?' questioned Martin.

'St. Helier on Jersey to be precise,' confirmed Avril. 'He died on Guernsey, but he had sent me a letter just before his death to go to Jersey.' Martin wiped his fingers across his mouth, there was something familiar about this scenario. 'He had committed suicide,' Avril added.

'I know. I heard it on the national news. Father of member of parliament who recently succumbed to cancer, took his own life.'

'Yes,' replied Avril grimly. 'It's a depressing saga. It's the stuff of pleas for help to a magazine's agony aunt column.' They found a large rock with a flat surface on which to sit and cosied up to one another before Avril continued. 'My grandfather wrote me a letter just before his death explaining that he couldn't go on without his son, Adam. The light in his life had been extinguished and he had no appetite to continue even for the sakes of his daughter and four grandchildren. He simply wanted out.' Avril looked up into Martin's eyes. They were pale and attentive and she pressed on. 'He enclosed a copy of his new and final will and asked me to get in touch with the solicitor who used to arrange the extended family gatherings of my great grandaunt Kit Audrey Harrison as he had named me as a co-executor.'

'Astonishing,' said Martin, shaking his head in disbelief. 'I need to pinch myself to see if this is real or a dream.'

'Why?'

'It's déjà vu, but please continue and I'll explain later.'

'Henry's accompanying letter contained contact names and addresses and a list of his assets. I was to send a photocopy of this letter to the solicitor to help expedite probate.'

'And did you?'

'Yes. But there was a second page to the letter which he wished me to retain and to keep secret.'

'Telling you to go to Jersey.'

'Exactly,' said Avril. 'It wasn't until I got there that I learned why.'

'Because he had a secret offshore account with a balance of millions, I'll bet.'

'How did you guess?'

'I told you. It's déjà vu.'

They grew chilly sitting on the stone. It was time to get moving and warm up. They headed back into Peterborough with Avril explaining how she had followed her grandfather's map and arrived at the ultra-discreet offices of the bank in Jersey and what Henry had asked her to do with the undeclared money. By the time they had got back to her flat, she had told him about how much there was in the account and that she had to find a way of redressing the balance of her father's terrible associations. It was still a shock to her and she didn't know what to do. Should she tell her aunt and sister? Did they have a right to know? Would it be a burden to them as indeed it was already feeling for her? She was grateful to have him as her sounding board.

It might have been the scenario for two people to be driven together by circumstance, making the most of the cards they had been dealt and feeling an obligation to offer support and succour to the other. That it wasn't, was due entirely to the sense of belonging to one another and a growing realisation that they had found a partner for life. Martin reminded her that, effectively, they had known one another for no more than the blink of an eye and that besides his family baggage he came with an ultimately failed long-term relationship with one of Avril's distant cousins. And Avril had responded that it made no difference as she too had "baggage" of a distressing nature and little real experience of the opposite sex. But secrets had been shared and true feelings could be allowed to surface, in Martin's case for the first time since his childhood. They would weather whatever problems came their way together and find solutions in partnership.

In general, Sunday afternoons were less frenetic at Radio East Midlands than other afternoons of the week. Unless an important local story was about to spill, news coverage gave way to mellow music interspersed with sports results of local teams and personalities. They were afternoons to catch up with paperwork and to hear the latest office gossip. A relaxed period which gently meandered along with a minimum of human intervention; a pleasant preamble to the lively planning and scheduling committees that would swing back into action early Monday mornings.

Her new status at the radio station did not preclude Avril from working what some would consider as unsocial hours. No matter what day of the week, she loved being part of it but was rather surprised on this particular Sunday afternoon to find herself the main topic of gossip. The junior female staff, all two of them, were enjoying some friendly banter about complexions. According to them, it was not always necessary to partake in vigorous outdoor pursuits to have a radiant facial skin tone. Knowing nods between the two suggested that some indoor exercise could result in the same effect. They both agreed that Avril had a particularly radiant look that Sunday afternoon and asked her if, ladened with innuendo, she had done anything exciting with the tall man waiting for her at the door the previous day. When Avril told them of her walk with Martin around Overton Lake in bracing weather, it did nothing to silence their suggestive sniggers. But asked if she would be seeing him again soon, Avril replied quite truthfully and without any hint of amusement, that she would be seeing him the Saturday after next when she would be marrying him.

Chapter 8

PARALLELS

Edmund awoke in a start. He had been dreaming about railway lines. The up line and the down line, adjacent to one another, side by side. They were parallel despite going in opposite directions. He sat up in bed hugging his steepled knees and with the duvet pulled tight around his chest, he contemplated the uncanny parallels of his real-life situation with those in his dreams, all sparked off it seemed by the death of Old Kit. And just when he thought he'd got a handle on how to carry out and bring her idiosyncratic whims to a suitable conclusion, another of her great grandnieces had popped up out of the blue to involve him in yet more family turmoil.

Edmund tried to work his way through the sequence of these new events in order to understand them better. He had received in the post the last will of Henry Roach drawn up by a solicitor in Jersey. He had been made co-executor with Henry's granddaughter, Avril. Shortly after, she had contacted him with some helpful information about her grandfather's assets. And just yesterday he had received a text from Avril telling him that she would be getting married at the end of the following week and enquiring whether he would need a copy of her marriage certificate to substantiate her identity. Her new surname would be Oakeshott and she intended to use it from day one of her marriage. "Oakeshott" had rang a bell with Edmund. Martin Oakeshott was Kit's former partner and although the name was not uncommon, he had had the uneasy feeling that Avril's husband-to-be, would turn out to be Martin. In order to assuage or confront his anxiety, Edmund had taken the calculated risk, when replying to her text about the marriage certificate, to congratulate her on her forthcoming wedding and enquire if the newly-weds would be leaving the church under an archway of hockey sticks. Her reply indicated that she would deal with the documentation promptly and although the ceremony would be, at their choice, low-key, she very much feared that at some stage they would be forced under an archway of hockey sticks as her new husband was a big wig in the sport and hockey's publicity machine was unlikely to let such a golden opportunity pass without comment.

In his dressing gown, now sitting at the tiny kitchen table with just a mug of coffee to inspire him, Edmund drew two straight lines down the length of a single sheet of paper. Column one was for items. Columns two and three represented the up and down lines respectively. As item number one in column number one, he wrote "relationship with Kit Audrey Harrison" and in columns two and three on the same line, he wrote "young Kit is her great grandniece" and "Avril is her great grandniece". Edmund felt a little more settled. He had got something down on paper and he would do the same for all the other apparent "coincidences" that he had identified. He worked steadily and within minutes had seven entries in the "items" column. When he filled in the up and down lines, representing his relationship with Kit and Avril's with Martin, the full extent of the "coincidences" was revealed.

He had met Kit as a result of the death of one of his father's longstanding clients. She had been named co-executor of the will together with his father. He had met Martin too because, at the time of their meeting at the memorial service of Kit's great grandaunt, he was Kit's long-term partner. Avril had also been at the same ceremony as she too was a great grandniece. When Avril's father and grandfather had both died suddenly, he had received a will in the post making him joint-executor with Avril of her grandfather's estate. These coincidences were confusing in their own right, thought Edmund, but when considered in the knowledge that both couples were getting married on the same day, it all began to feel quite surreal.

Then there were the Channel Islands. He and Kit had been in Guernsey recently for the first time in their lives, on the very day that Avril's grandfather had taken his own life no more than a mile away from their hotel. They were there about an offshore account and the very day after they returned home, he had received Henry's final will, drawn up in and posted from, Jersey. It was a pound to a penny, Edmund surmised, that Jersey too was the location of an offshore account with a fortune. Kit had the wish of her great grandaunt to uphold by dispersing the fortune to those family members who merited financial assistance.

Edmund wondered if Avril would have a similar stricture to fulfil; a redressing of some kind of balance. It was a distinct possibility.

The excitement in the Newman household was palpable. The wedding of their only male child – son, heir, solicitor par excellence when not in lippy mode – was imminent. Parents, sister and brother-in-law, toddler niece and nephew, Emily, and even the partners in Newman, Wilson and Saddler including the young intern, were all swept up in the forthcoming event.

Time had been allocated by the firm to allow Edmund to take his bride away on a short honeymoon. Father Thomas would set aside a couple of weeks of the leisurely lifestyle he had adopted since retiring in an effort to ease the strain at the now extremely busy practice. Kit was nominally in charge, but it was Edmund's mother and Emily who were ensuring that the carefully planned wedding arrangements were being followed.

Kit had been tearful when he met her at the station. She was stepping into a new life and leaving behind the order of a world she knew well. There was uncertainty written across her face, and Edmund had the awkward task of telling her about Martin's marriage to Avril on the same day as their own. It was a job he couldn't shirk and one which had to be done and dusted before the wedding even if it put a damper on the run-up to the special day. He managed an enigmatic smile at the thought of the twists and turns that the old woman's wishes were still conjuring up from the grave and wondered too if Martin would have any regrets that the woman he was about to marry was not Kit.

★ ★ ★

In Whitehall, seemingly long forgotten events were about to erupt triggered by the "Where is he now?" journalist's short article in a daily tabloid. Dame Barbara removed her half-eye spectacles and swore volubly. She was alone at her desk and chucked a handful of paperclips with venom at the clock on the wall. It relieved her mood fleetingly like a piston opening to discharge noxious gases. Kit Audrey Harrison was alive and kicking even though her ashes had been scattered over some rose beds somewhere up north and it annoyed Dame Barbara greatly. The fly in her ointment would not rest peacefully.

Dame Barbara could never claim that her life had been a struggle. Far from it. She had been fortunate enough to have had most of the good things in life including a happy childhood in a stable, caring household. Born in 1955 to middle class parents whose goal was to work their entire lives in steady but unspectacular white-collar jobs in the civil service, she was in her twenties before she seriously questioned how they had been able to afford to pay private school fees. The independent bursary line had eventually worn thin and when she forced the issue with her parents, she learnt things which she wished she hadn't. Her father and mother were not her birth parents. She was adopted.

At first there was a level of disbelief, followed by a loss of confidence which soon gave way to overt anger. Just why had she not been told these so very personal facts she had demanded of her mother and father. Surely, they must have realised how important this information would be to her. What right had they to withhold it? Aghast at her outburst and hurt by her lack of appreciation of all the time and effort and love and tenderness that they had given her, both parties went their separate ways. Dame Barbara married well and her putative parents hunkered down to a life without their ungrateful daughter.

The civil service offered a steady upward path to those who observed their rules and who had a degree in a non-contentious subject such as geography. It helped too that Dame Barbara's husband had been educated at a public school and was in line to become the CEO of a utility company. And after a fifteen-year period of promotions and faultless behaviour, she was promoted to head of a section attached to MI6. Her title – awarded ostensibly for services rendered discreetly to a charity for the homeless – followed swiftly and thus Dame Barbara joined the cosy ranks of the elite.

At a point in time that she judged judicious, she began the process of tracing her birth parents. Her enquiries were cloaked in discretion and would have been non-attributable had they come to light. She knew the ropes and how to get things done and wasn't shy in using her position to achieve her ends. She had concocted a story to legitimise her enquiries and by a slow but productive path she had eventually discovered her origins. At the outset of her search, she had appreciated that the outcome might not be to her liking. However, there was a latent anger still within her which would not be appeased until she was certain of her background. No documentation was requested and none given. Oral messages were left on a private landline from which Dame Barbara compiled a compendium of the essential facts and hid them in a file marked "utility bills". Apart from her date of birth and the names of the couple who had adopted her, she knew almost nothing of her background. When she learnt that her birth mother's name was Kit Audrey Harrison it meant little to her until she initiated a private search and discovered that she was a woman of some renown. That she had collected a great deal of baggage along the way would become apparent to her illegitimate daughter the deeper she delved.

Hunting down her father proved a greater challenge. Despite Dame Barbara's knowledge of ways and means and the funds to implement the necessary searches, little was discovered about him. The hunt could have been called off at that point with a measure of success but Dame Barbara turned out to be a chip off the old block and wouldn't accept a fifty percent degree of failure. She arranged a meeting with Old Kit under a false pretext and got more than she was bargaining for; the blunt instrument of a head-on challenge was not the right tool for a woman as worldly wise as Kit Audrey Harrison. Where perhaps, with sensitive handling, it could have been a tender reunion of mother and daughter, with an explanation of the circumstances that had led to the adoption, it turned out to be an acrimonious meeting of two strong-willed individuals who weren't prepared to budge an inch; a shouting match with neither listening to what the other was saying. That Dame Barbara would learn more about her background was entirely due to the wisdom of Edmund's father, Thomas. He was the only soul in whom Old Kit had confided about the offspring born to her in her mid-forties out of wedlock and he had kept the secret safe for many years, but learning of the confrontation between the two women, he had advised Old Kit that she owed her daughter some sort of explanation as to why she had not brought her up herself and a polite, informative letter fully covering the circumstances at her birth would go a long way to resolving the hiatus. Old Kit was not convinced but as Thomas had proved a peacemaker on so many previous occasions, she agreed to do as he suggested.

Her letter, heavily redacted by Thomas for both legal reasons and to convey a spirit of friendship, took the form of a printed missive with an indecipherable handwritten signature:

Dear Barbara,

Our meeting several days ago was unsatisfactory from both our points of view. I doubt that either party is content with the unhappy scenario that unfolded. Had there been time for preparation of mind and matter, then we might have been able to discuss the subject in a conciliate manner. Forewarned is forearmed as the proverb tells us.

After deep reflection, I have decided that I do indeed owe you a full account of the factors that led to your adoption so that you may realise that your birth and subsequent adoption were not just the act of a careless mother wishing to be shot of an unwanted baby. Rigorous searches were made to find a couple who could be trusted to love and nurture you until you grew into a woman and could make your own decisions.

You were born in the winter of 1955. I was forty-three at the time and in charge of rallying a textile business from the vicissitudes of the war years. My husband had died on a battlefield in Holland and I had recently learnt that he had left a later will rescinding all others in which he left the business to my twin sons. It was a disappointing situation in which to find myself not just because of all the work and effort put in over more than a decade but because my sons had never shown any business acumen or disposition for hard work. In their hands, the writing was on the wall regarding the survival of the firm and thus I allowed myself the occasional luxury of clocking off before midnight.

I had mortgaged my house in order to provide working capital for the firm to climb out of its torpor – a result of lack of foresight and man management skills by my late husband before he threw in the towel and signed up for the war – and it was very much in my interest to succeed. But when I learnt of my impending demotion to factotum which included losing ownership of the house, I decided to channel my energies and financial resources in other directions. My late father, a man of little formal education but a great deal of common sense and wisdom had instilled in me that in life, when one door closed, another would open and it was just a question of grabbing the opportunity when it arose. Instead of continuing to burn the midnight oil running the tailoring business, I accepted offers to all manner of recreational activities that I had formerly declined: dinner parties, cultural soirees, overseas trips, weekends away in the country with walking groups, cocktail hours, theatre trips and I learnt to drive and service a car. It was at a dinner party for the governors of a local school which I had endowed with a bursary that I first met the man who fathered you. He was there on his own as his wife had been taken unwell that same morning with some minor ailment. We sat next to one another and enjoyed each other's company. Quite by chance, we met a few weeks later in the High Street in Berwick and decided to have lunch together.

As in so many of these situations, one thing led to another and before long we were engaged in a wanton affair. As prominent citizens each in our own right, you will doubtless think that we both should have known better and maybe you'd be right, but the pull on the heart strings was immense. It wasn't a casual affair or one of trivial importance to either of us. We were actually in love. Over a period of months, we snatched furtive time together whenever possible. It seemed all too little then, but in hindsight we lived those moments to the full without worrying about the possibility of breaking up his steady marriage and family life. We acted like truculent teenagers enjoying what we wanted without regard for the welfare of others, almost oblivious to the scandals that discovery would have caused. And that would have happened if I had not become pregnant. It was a seminal moment; it brought us back to our right-minded senses. Suddenly, we were aware of the trouble we would cause and we both agreed that it was unthinkable that our existing family and working lives should be thrown overboard with no regard for the individuals involved – he had a devoted wife and teenage family – or for the efforts each had put into our promising careers. We metaphorically paused, looked one another in the eye, and with honesty, agreed that we had reached the end of the line.

It would be another thirteen years before abortion would be legalised in the United Kingdom. We never entertained the idea of some back street individual carrying out a risky procedure to abort the foetus. There was a stigma in those days relating to sexual proclivity. Adultery, a term little used in modern day parlance because of the changes in our outlook and in the law itself over the past half-century, was a legal and moral offence. It was not just a blot on one's character, it was regarded as a disgrace and had to be borne with stoicism not just by the adulterers themselves but by their close families too. Divorce, children born out of wedlock, extra-marital affairs, homosexuality went on apace behind closed doors, but the moment it became public knowledge, those involved were regarded as beyond the pale. To be ostracised by your friends and neighbours wasn't pleasant and broke the spirit of many well-balanced people. It wasn't the environment in which to bring up a child. I very much doubt that you would have thrived in such an atmosphere or thanked us for such an unkind start in life. With your adopted parents who loved and cherished you from day one, your early years were a happy mixture of stability and learning. They looked after you as if you were their own. You were the centre of their world and your needs and desires were paramount. Do you remember those ballet lessons when you were very young? And the expensive tennis coaching in your early teens? Apparently, they were a source of great fun at the time and stood you in good stead in adulthood as a basis for your love of cultural activities, and just as importantly, the tennis skills opened many doors one of which led to a managerial position in the civil service and another to a marriage with an up-and-coming businessman. It was only then, mid-1980s, that we, your birth parents, stopped funding your lifestyle. Did you ever seriously ask yourself who paid for your expensive private education? Who paid for the extra-mural activities and coaching lessons? Who paid for the ballet pumps and tennis racquets? At some stage you did but by then you were approaching your thirties and about to marry. So, let me make it clear to you that every inch of the way until your marriage, we paid all of those expenses. And we did so willingly because the steady jobs of your adopted parents did not pay sufficiently to afford such frills. Without our careers, which I will remind you may have been in jeopardy had we kept you, these luxuries that you enjoyed throughout your childhood and youth may not have been possible.

It was therefore galling to be told when you cornered me, that we had done nothing for you. Your carping made my blood boil. Standing on the moral high ground and looking down on the lesser mortals around you. You will therefore not be surprised if I tell you candidly that I do not wish to meet you again. The name of your father will die with me. Be grateful for what you have, for what you now know, and look after your adopted parents in their old age with the same love and affection that they showered on you.

Barbara put down the letter with a quivering hand. She was furious. How dare her birth mother write to her in such a manner. Barbara tutted and drew her thin lips covered generously in a bright shade of red lipstick into a downward curve. She tutted again at the perceived injustice being done to her. How dare that woman say what she had. And if she thought Barbara wasn't up to the challenge of discovering the identity of her real father, then she was very much mistaken because she was going to track down the school where *that woman* had been a governor in 1955 and pinpoint amongst the other governors, the one who was her natural father. She had a right to know and he might just turn out to be a parent with some love in his heart for her. And Barbara was true to her word – or what she had promised herself she would do when she learnt of her true worldly beginnings – that she would search for her real parents until they were found.

Energised by indignation, she was able to discreetly set in motion the machinery of a small government department attached to the Home Office of which she was a rising star. It specialised in tracking and tracing citizens and aliens for other departments such as the tax office, benefits department and law enforcement agencies, and reporting back on the subject's whereabouts, associations, and actions. It had been a simple process, and one that had an air of being totally routine, for her to request a list of school governors at a particular school in Northumbria in the 1950s. And as all the governors bar three were female, it had been even simpler to hone in on the man who must have fathered her. At last, she was able to raise a sardonic smile when she thought of her adoption. *That woman* would, and could not deny her the information she sought. But it would come with an unexpected twist and at a price that Barbara would find unacceptable.

Frederick Newman, Edmund's grandfather, had been a governor of Salehill school, a forerunner of grammar schools, for more than a decade before he met Kit Audrey, as she was known then. It was the school he had attended from age eleven to eighteen before receiving specialised private tuition to pass his legal examinations. He had mainly happy memories of his days there, and once qualified and set up in the practice in Berwick, he had been persuaded to return in the important capacity of school governor, working as a team member with the other governors, and contributing in particular his legal expertise. Unusually for those times, the composition of the board of governors was predominantly female, a situation that had arisen as a direct result of the war years and which was maintained throughout the fifties as it had been found to work so well; the down-to-earth and multitasking skills of the women having an emollient effect on the more decisive cut-and-thrust approach of the men. The harmonious results of their periodic deliberations in setting the ethos and values of the school had made it one of the most popular and successful educational establishments in the north-east.

Kit Audrey had gravitated into the role of governor by a process of osmotic repute. In her late thirties, many considered that she had already achieved a great deal in her life with a science degree from a top university, a hand in the development of nylon, the co-founding of Northern Tailoring Limited which brought consumer innovations to high streets throughout the northern counties of England, and the championing of higher education for the working classes, all whilst bringing up a family of four, suffering the loss of a child in infancy and the death of her husband while fighting in the war. Besides dispensing their wisdom and support to the school staff, the governors as a group, coming from different walks of life but with the same interest in serving their community, became a friendly circle who with their spouses socialised from time to time with restaurant meals and the odd theatre trip and it was not uncommon to see two or three of them enjoying a cup of coffee together in a local café when they met by chance whilst out shopping. It was from this base of a shared rapport and in a cordial and relaxed atmosphere that Kit Audrey made the simple mistake of telling Barbara in her letter that she had met her father whilst they were serving as governors at the same school. Without that slip the name of her birth father would undoubtedly have been taken to the grave by Kit Audrey, as was her intention. But Barbara was to learn from the searches she set in motion in the late 1990s that all three male governors serving in the 1950s were long since dead and buried. Two had been in their late sixties at the time of Barbara's conception and had died of natural causes in their eighties. The other, the only one who could reasonably have been her father, had died prematurely at the height of his business career of the long-term effects of a tropical disease that he had picked up whilst serving in the Far East during the second world war. Despite modern medicines, it had whittled away at his core for more than thirty years until his body finally succumbed at the early age of fifty-six. His death had made the newspapers as he was a captain of industry and a Downing Street adviser.

Barbara pondered whether this should be the end of the line. Was there anything worthwhile to gain from digging deeper? Would discovering that she had half-brothers and sisters through her father's offspring really mean much to her? Was it really worth taking the risk and jeopardising her own family unity just because she had become obsessed with tracking down her own background? After all, she would have half-siblings with

Kit Audrey's children, assuming that she had carried other children. There could be no harm, she mused, in a simple search of Kit Audrey's history now that she had reliable dates and places about her mother's life. It would be a search she could do herself without it being linked to a government department, and an afternoon at Somerset House was all that was needed to uncover that her mother had given birth to four children: two pairs of twins.

The information didn't register until later that same evening after her youngsters were in bed and her husband fed. They were watching a news discussion programme; an item about experimental work on wheat genes to radically increase the crop's yield. And then it hit. She gasped audibly. Her husband raised his eyebrows and gave her a quizzical look, and she had replied that it was just something to do with work; a piece of information finally fitting into a jigsaw. Her mother had had two sets of twins. The question Barbara asked herself was whether she was one part of a twosome too. Did she have a twin sister or a twin brother? And that, Barbara knew, was something she *did* have to know.

The British Medical Library is situated in the Bloomsbury area of central London on the corner of Tavistock Square, and within easy walking distance of Russell Square tube station. Barbara took the Piccadilly line from near her home in South Ealing and arrived early the next Saturday morning. In that era the library was open seven days a week with free admission. It was cool and quiet in the main reading room. Once she had found the section relating to twin births, and selected an assortment of the most promising journals, she chose a reading desk close to a large window and settled down to discover the answers to the questions she felt needed posing. She didn't have the luxury of Young Kit, some twenty-five years or so later, being able to search the internet and ask questions of, or get explanations from geneticists worldwide at the tap of a computer key. She just had to wade through the volumes in the hope that she would find sufficient passages in layman's language that she could understand so that she could make an informed judgement. After two hours she gave up. The subject matter had become too complicated to understand after the initial introductions. But she felt satisfied that she had understood two main points iterated in all the books: it was the female line that gave rise to double births and any subsequent births by a mother whose first-born were twins, were also likely to be multiple births.

The concept of having a genetic soulmate in life simultaneously entranced and appalled Barbara. It did seem highly likely that somewhere out in the world at large, she had a twin and it could not be discounted that that twin was identical. Lost in her thoughts as she weighed up the situation and considered her next step, if any, she missed her stop on the Piccadilly Line and found herself at the western terminus of Hatton Cross, as it was before the Heathrow extension was built; a long way from home. She cursed her lack of attention. She had promised to be home by a certain hour so that her husband could meet up with some of his friends to watch an international rugby match at Twickenham. He wouldn't be pleased, she knew, but her lapse might well fuel her demand for a regular nanny. They were both working full-time in demanding jobs and sorting out childcare on an ad hoc basis was proving taxing. She arrived home just in time to placate his annoyance and recount a no-blame version of events although the look on his face betrayed real belief. Sitting at the kitchen table watching her youngsters playing on the floor, Barbara knew that she wouldn't rest easy until she had done everything possible to determine the truth. Austere by nature, or perhaps by upbringing, the idea of kith and kin in the shape of a twin pulled remorselessly on her heart strings.

From a large, rectangular office window on the third floor of a stone building in Birmingham, the renter of the spacious office with a small, separate waiting room and a private cloakroom, looked down from his eyrie at the traffic circulating in the city centre. It was mid-morning and people were still scurrying about the streets as if late for an appointment or in a dash to attend to more things than time really permitted. He looked at his watch. His next client was due in five minutes. He had just finished rereading the brief she had given him and reviewed his findings. Everything had to be as near perfect as possible. He could class all his clients as upper crust. He advertised an elite service and charged accordingly. And, additionally, they paid through the nose for his one hundred percent discretion.

He hadn't met her previously but knew that the woman with the upright stature and aged around the mid-thirty mark who was crossing the road on a diagonal bearing which would take her to the entrance to his building, was his next client. She looked very familiar, a fact which made him smile and gave him a sense of satisfaction that he had done his job well. When she entered, he quickly sensed that she wasn't a woman for wasting time and when seated by his desk, he got to the point straightaway by showing her a photograph of someone she couldn't fail to recognise.

'Where does she live?' asked Barbara immediately.

'In the north-east, Mrs. Brown,' replied the investigator, using the nom-de-plume by which Barbara had chosen to be addressed as an extra layer of security.

'And you are certain that she is my twin?' The investigator inclined his head but said nothing. Barbara realised that it was a stupid question to ask. The photograph said it all. She was, in effect, staring at herself. 'How did you trace her?'

'I have my ways,' replied the investigator. Many clients asked this very same question but he had learnt over the years how to politely dodge telling them the actual mechanics of his work. 'My tentacles spread far and wide,' he said smiling.

'Was she aware of the snap being taken?' Barbara asked quite reasonably.

'Yes. But not in the context of this search.'

'So, she has no idea of my existence.'

'None that could be attributable to my enquiries.' He shrugged his shoulders. 'Who knows what she knows and what she doesn't.' He passed his detailed report across the desk to Barbara. 'Would you like to read through it now and ask questions? Or, would you prefer to read it at home and ring me to clarify any queries?'

'I should like to go through it here,' replied Barbara rather imperiously, 'line by line.' She would neither be leaving nor paying until satisfied that she had the full story.

Her identical twin had been born exactly one hour and fifty-three minutes after Barbara came into the world on a Thursday in late November at a quarter past midnight, and hence the twins did not share the same date of birth. In the original plan – twins were expected – both babies would be adopted by a couple found and vetted by the adoption agency and approved by the natural parents. Within days, both would have been whisked away to start their lives quietly in a large bungalow on the outskirts of Tunbridge Wells. But fate intervened when Barbara's sibling contracted jaundice which failed to resolve in the normal time period of ten days. Left with a conundrum, and in the uncertainty of how best to resolve the situation – time being of the essence to fit in with the carefully prepared arrangements of the couple in Kent – it was decided that they should take the first-born, as planned, and the unwell sibling would follow as soon as well enough to do so. But when three weeks had passed and a further problem with the baby's head had arisen, probably a result of the difficult birth, the maternal emotions of the natural mother, Kit Audrey, came into play. As the days passed it became equally clear that the second child's medical problems would take months and not weeks to resolve and that, against her will, her natural mother had started to bond with the child and hence releasing the baby to the couple in Kent would no longer be an option.

It was at this point that Frederick Newman stepped in and provided a solution. Unknown at the time to Kit Audrey – it would be several years before she would embark on a professional relationship and platonic friendship with his son, Thomas – he was a pillar of his community and a man of integrity. He was also a patron of the charitable agency given the responsibility for arranging the adoption of the identical twins. When the unexpected medical difficulties arose and it became apparent that the original plan to home both babies with the couple in Kent would not work out, it was Frederick who suggested an alternative. For the best reasons, both parties were proving difficult to satisfy – the Kent couple had planned the twins' arrival into their life in minute detail so that the girls would be brought up in their early years entirely as their own and the thorny question of adoption delayed to a stage in their lives when the twins were old enough to understand its implications, and where their natural mother was concerned, nobody could have prevented the unscheduled bonding that took place between natural mother and sick infant– thus Frederick's suggestion provided a route around both problems.

As a patron of the charity and not a trustee, he had no legal responsibilities and was not involved in the day to day running of the organisation. His position was purely honorary; a distinguished person of the community acting as a figurehead. But in such a capacity, unfettered by petty rules and regulations, he had more freedom than the trustees to provide wise counsel, and his suggestion that as there could now be no question of reuniting the girls at a later date – to do so in later childhood or adulthood could be regarded as cruel – it might be better, once the baby was released from medical care, to separate them geographically too so that there would be no reasonable chance of them meeting casually in the future. Through his professional work he knew of a couple who had lost their only child in a train accident several years previously. They had applied for adoption but been turned down by various agencies on the grounds of being too old. However, he was prepared to vouch for their upright characters and as they lived in Kelso and were financially sound, he suggested that they might be the perfect pair to take on the ailing twin at short notice. It mattered very little, in his opinion, that they were in their early forties, if they were able to provide the child with a happy environment in which to live and grow, and with Frederick keeping an alert eye on events, the child who they named as Emily, blossomed.

Chapter 9

WEDDINGS

To the casual observer there were no parallels between the two weddings taking place on Saturday the twentieth of September, one in Berwick-upon-Tweed, the other in Peterborough. It wasn't just the geographical distance between the two venues, or indeed the amount of planning that had gone into the programme of each happy couple's day, or even the honeymoon arrangements that had been carefully or hurriedly thought out by the prospective bridegrooms that made them appear so dissimilar. None of those really applied. It was the sheer size and premeditation that appeared so contrasting. Where one had a guest list exceeding three figures and had been in "the planning stage" for several months, the other's quick turnaround of less than a fortnight with invitees well under a dozen, were in stark contrast to one another.

For Avril and Martin, it could have felt like a whirlwind plucking them up unexpectedly as singletons and spitting them out a few days later as a married couple, but so certain were they of their future partnership together that they were completely unfazed by the hectic hours leading up to their union. The juniors at the radio station had been temporarily taken aback by Avril's engagement but were soon full of enthusiasm for the occasion, and one of the main presenters had stepped in to fill Avril's weekend slots so that the Sunday could be their honeymoon day. The short list of invitees, hastily pencilled on the reverse of a shopping list, numbered nine: Martin's boss at work, Martin's second in command on the hockey association's main committee and a university friend with whom he had learned the basics of field hockey, Avril's boss, Avril's mother, Avril's Aunt Annie and her husband Hugh, and the two excitable juniors at the radio station. They had jointly decided that Clare's appearance at the wedding would be, at the very least, inappropriate, but a telephone conversation with positive vibes between the twin sisters went a long way to smoothing the creases in the fragile material that bonded them together. Clare would be busy that weekend anyhow on constituency work.

Apart from notifying their guests, there hadn't been much to arrange. A lunch at a pub in Peterborough in a private room above the saloon bar would follow the civil marriage in the city's Register Office. Martin would wear a work suit with a crisp, white shirt and a silver-coloured tie. Avril had gone to the shops and purchased a skirt suit in a fashionable grey-blue which she would wear with a white round-necked blouse and a white orchid corsage on her left shoulder. She contemplated high heels for the first time in many years but found them so uncomfortable when trying on, that a new pair of flatties were chosen instead. Their honeymoon would be a day at home in their new rental property in Bedford sorting out their few sticks of furniture and preparing for new travel arrangements on the Monday when they would both be back to their normal working schedules, Avril by car and Martin by long distance commute. Unbeknown to either, and on the grounds that Avril was media, and media management at that, Radio East Midlands had organised a newspaper photographer to record the happy event. The resulting image, with all the professional traits of a skilful cameraman well versed in his art, captured a scene that would sell plenty of copy.

There was, however, no time for relaxation in Berwick. Planned in detail – it had been a tour de force – by Edmund's mother with the help of Emily, and to a minor part by Kit herself. There were schedules to be met, bullet point items to be ticked off when completed, guest seating arrangements to be organised, and speeches to be practised.

As a well-known figure in his own right in the Berwick area, Edmund had many friends and acquaintances from his school days, his transition through the law practice from student to junior partner, and his early steps into the local political arena. When his father's colleagues and associates and his mother's equestrian chums were factored in, the resulting guest list generated some lively discussion to whittle it down to an acceptable number. The lopsided list, dictated by Kit's lack of close relatives save her grandparents – who would remain in Cornwall for health reasons – and by her various work and social friends who would find the long journey up to the Scottish borders difficult to fit into a weekend with ease, required a large reception venue and thus the wedding breakfast, in all its traditional glories, was held at a country park in the vicinity with the lavish facilities necessary for such occasions. Dressed in a full-length, off-white, organza dress with three-quarter length sleeves and embroidered bodice, Kit would look the picture of splendour, and with the men in top hats and tails, tradition would be upheld.

As the big day approached, doubts overtook Kit. The inner and controlled calm that had become part of her personality – a trait which may have grown in response to the horrors of her parents' death – was no longer her rock and guiding star. It was absent. It wasn't there. She couldn't turn to it for comfort and guidance when needed. It was as if part of her had died.

'Penny for your thoughts,' asked Edmund cheerfully, as they rearranged his cottage to accommodate all her worldly possessions. She had arrived "home" three days previously; the final links with her job and life in the south severed.

'Just deciding what I need to take with me for the overnight stay at your parents' house,' Kit replied without much spark.

'Not much stuff, I guess,' said Edmund, stumped for a meaningful reply. He had sensed his bride-to-be's melancholy. 'Cold feet?'

'No. Definitely not.'

'Just a momentary waiver perhaps?'

'Not even that,' responded Kit much more positively. 'Not even that.' And it was true. There seemed to be no turning back now as she had sensed changes in her body, wishful thinking or not. She would do a pregnancy test in the morning and the day would turn out doubly special if it proved positive. And if the theory she had researched of multiple births stood up to practise, then it could be twins.

In a bright and happy mood after the church service, Kit and Edmund greeted their long line of guests at the country park where many weeks before the accoutrements of modern weddings had been chosen.

'I feel a bit like royalty standing here,' Edmund whispered into Kit's ear, as he shook hands with each guest in turn and told his wife how he came to know them: work, rambling, school/university, politics, drinking mates whilst living in Newcastle. 'I don't know whether to bow or curtsy,' Kit giggled, champagne glass in hand, and her curls bounced familiarly on her slender shoulders. She giggled again and decided that the next drink should be a glass of sparkling water.

It turned out to be a grand day for the Newmans in all respects but one. The schedule went like clockwork. The arch directors – Edmund's mother and Emily – were able to sit back and enjoy the fruits of their planning. Even the speeches were short, succinct and came with a smattering of genuine humour. Soon the couple were leaving for their honeymoon in a bright yellow electric powered car that would have done Noddy proud. Three nights in a boutique hotel across the Scottish border and days out rambling the splendid countryside; the interregnum before the start of their real life together.

'Not drinking tonight?' asked Edmund, as the snack they had ordered was delivered to their room.

'Too much booze already,' replied Kit yawning. The pregnancy test, sitting securely in her handbag, had shown negative and it was with a tinge of disappointment that she hadn't had the opportunity to tell him that his heirs had been present at his wedding. It was a shame; one box had been left unticked. She threw herself on the bed and was instantly asleep.

Aunt Annie gazed thoughtfully at the photograph in the local newspaper's mid-week edition. The happy couple in the foreground were, as expected, beaming. Standing behind them, poised seemingly to throw confetti, were faces she recognised from her grandaunt's get togethers of yesteryear. In particular, the face of a woman she had seen regularly at those gatherings and who she had also *seemed* to have encountered in more recent times in Whitehall.

Since her initial trip to Whitehall, Annie had known that Emily and the lady she later found out was named Dame Barbara, were identical twins. It hadn't taken an enormous leap of imagination to tie one to the other, such was their likeness. When on being shown out of the building after her initial interview, Annie had crossed the road and looked back to survey the building's cold, grey facade, she had seen a woman staring down at her from a second-floor window; a woman with a face identical to a woman Annie knew in Berwick. And, at the time, it had been all that Annie could do to mask her amazement. True, the hairstyles were different and they didn't appear to share the same dress sense, and from what Annie could recall of Emily – not much really as she usually took a back seat – did not have the same haughty air of the southerner.

Thought processes whirred in Annie's brain. How much did Emily know of the existence of Dame Barbara and vice versa? The newspaper story was of a wedding in Berwick held on the same day as Avril's in Peterborough. Avril had already sent her aunt an electronic version of the wedding photograph to appear shortly in her local rag in which Annie and husband Hugh were clearly discernible. References were made in the accompanying prose to the bride's recent sad history of the deaths of her father and grandfather within weeks of one another and that she was the twin sister of the now member of parliament for Islington & Grove. If Dame Barbara, by some remote chance, came across it, she would know instantly that she was not a singleton. But in that regard, Dame Barbara was way ahead of Annie.

The wedding photograph of the grand affair in Berwick that had made the local paper was displayed prominently on its front page. References were made to the groom's work as a partner in a long-established legal practice serving the community and to the bride's distant relationship with the well-known philanthropist, Kit Audrey Harrison.

It was mostly the newspaper reference to the new Mrs. Newman's distant relative that set the cat amongst the pigeons as far as Dame Barbara was concerned, although the mention of that same relative by the Peterborough correspondent recording Avril's marriage did nothing to improve matters.

Up until his death, Dame Barbara's section had been closely monitoring the activities of Adam Roach in respect of the money transfer irregularities. As a result, Annie and Henry, too, had come under the umbrella of their attention as sister and father of the suspected fraudster. On a slip of her concentration, Dame Barbara had forgotten to terminate the surveillance after Adam's demise, and thus junior members of her team, still collating information which might be pertinent to the fraud, were to realise via the medium of the newspaper images of the weddings, the personal detail that Dame Barbara had an identical twin sister. Nothing was said, but when Dame Barbara chose to study the appropriate files, she was livid to find a picture of Emily staring back at her.

She might have weathered that uncomfortable storm such was Dame Barbara's hold on her own temper and her ability as a senior civil servant to compartmentalise information in such a way that very few eyes other than her own would ever see it and even fewer people would understand its significance, but the last straw was an article in a national daily that very morning by the "Where is he now?" journalist referencing Avril's marriage. It questioned whether her new husband, Martin, could be the elusive little boy in the infamous Oakeshott stabbings in the 1980s, under the snappy subtitle 'East Midlands radio presenter, sister of new parliamentary member for a London constituency, marries field hockey supremo'. Dame Barbara winced. Her days of cloak and dagger games was up. Nobody in a senior position in Whitehall would accept the baggage she was now carrying. Guilt by association, or in her case, compromised by her newly-found relatives, her previously pristine record would now bear indelible blots. It was the end of the line, and she know it. A short, hand-written missive announcing her intention for a phased retirement over eighteen months so that she could spend more time with her growing family was all that was needed to set in train the gradual severance of her current associations with officialdom in the discreet way so beloved by Whitehall. And it would have been a sad moment had Dame Barbara not spotted the doors of future opportunities opening.

On the Monday morning following the wedding, the radio station's juniors were full of it. They were bursting to discuss the wedding with Avril. She had only been out of the office for a single day, apart from the wedding day itself, but they were pumped up with questions to ask her about her new husband now that they had found out that he was a senior research chemist and the head of field hockey in England. They were also wowed by Avril's understated glamour on her wedding day. Apparently, Avril's twin sister, Clare, considered her frumpy, but the juniors agreed that on her special day, Avril had looked anything other than a "plain Jane". True, they giggled, she was wearing flat shoes, but with ankles like hers, who would want to draw attention to their feet.

As had been anticipated, this particular Monday afternoon's 'question and answer session' was proving particularly popular. Avril was well received by her listeners and many rang in with their best wishes for her future happiness. The subject matter of the session was ostensibly recurring mental health issues, or as the station advertised it "mental somersaults", a comparison with the rise and fall of an acrobat propelling himself upwards with great effort only to be remorselessly pushed down every time by gravity. And the opportunity to introduce a voice close to home came more suddenly than they could have foreseen.

The newly-weds had also seen the "Where is he now" article and after much thought and with hearts in their mouths, they had decided to pre-empt any further upsetting speculation by laying the facts out on the table for everyone to see and to judge. "Coming clean" as they called it, had been a hard decision for two essentially private individuals but without being pressed by Avril, Martin had taken the lead in bringing his childhood troubles to a final full stop by saying that the days of hiding away were over. So, when the first caller asked an ambiguous question, Avril pounced.

'Frank from Kettering asks the intriguing question,' said Avril, repeating for her listeners the essence of his question, 'whether mental somersaults are an inevitable part of normal existence? And that even the most stable people on the planet are subject to mental highs and lows. Is that correct, Frank?'

'Yes. Basically, are we just making too much of the ups and downs we all feel when dealing with life's normal problems?'

'Turning minor difficulties into massive mountains to climb,' added Avril. 'Don't you think that all depends on the type of problem encountered, Frank?' responded Avril.

'Possibly, but we all have to learn to deal with obstacles.'

'Thank you, Frank,' said Avril crisply into her mic. 'Betty, from Wisbech. 'Was the previous caller being a little harsh?'

'No, I don't think so,' responded Betty in a clear and unhurried voice. 'He was being a realist. As a member of the older generation,' she went on, 'I can tell you that there was very little help available to us in my youth other than the support of your own family. There were no helplines to contact, no sympathetic ears to listen to our tales of woe, and no one willing to dry our tears when we were down. Now there seems to be counselling for just about everything.'

'Thank you, Betty, for your thoughts,' said Avril, taking the opportunity to cut in as Betty paused momentarily to draw breath. She had to allow opinions and ideas from all quarters to be aired. 'Daryl, from Market Harborough,' she continued, 'I believe you work in the school sector. Is that right?'

'Yes, Avril,' boomed back Daryl's deep voice. 'I'm a physical education teacher at a secondary school.'

'How long have you been doing that?' asked Avril.

'For over ten years and I love my job,' replied Daryl. 'I wanted to say that the kids at my school respond very well to physical challenges. Some come into the gym looking very morose, really down in the dumps. But if I set each student the challenge of surpassing their own personal best in, say sit ups, and they achieve it, then they'll leave the session in a much more positive mood.'

'So, what you're saying, Daryl, if I understand you correctly,' interjected Avril, 'is that if you can somehow engage them in a task which can have a positive outcome, then the resulting feel-good factor will adjust their attitude to their worries.'

'Correct. Exercise classes should be available routinely on the health service as a first step in trying to combat depression.'

'Our next caller is Alison from Stamford,' said Avril. 'Do you agree with Daryl's take on mental somersaults, Alison?'

'I don't. No. I think that view is far too simplistic when in fact mental health issues are extremely complex.'

'In what way?'

'Some patients, both young and old, have a stable family to help them over their down periods. And that's all they really need. You're lucky if you've got that. A helping hand to give you a clear vision of the way ahead. But for so many, that situation simply doesn't exist.'

'Are you involved professionally in such matters?' Avril enquired.

'Yes, I work in social care.'

'Go on,' urged Avril.

'I see on a daily basis the problems encountered by children, orphans or those without family backup, and adults of all ages who drop out of life and take to living rough because of pressures they can't handle in what the majority of us regard as normal life. And it's a similar experience for ex-prisoners too. Often abandoned by their families, they come out of prison with nowhere to go and with a yoke of shame around their shoulders.' Avril held her breath. Now was the perfect moment, she knew, for her husband to offload his past publicly. There would never be a better time to do so. Her monitor pinged as a new caller was added to the list. Avril gulped. Martin from Bedford was on the line and would be the next caller but one.

'Hallo, Ron from Peterborough. Sorry to have kept you waiting. What contribution would you like to make on this subject?' asked Avril smoothly.

'I think it's a bandwagon effect,' replied Ron in a forceful tone.

'Sorry, Ron, but what exactly do you mean by that?'

'I mean that all these so-called mental issues don't really exist. Just people jumping on the bandwagon of mental health because it's the trendy thing to do.'

'Have you been affected personally or are you just speculating?'

'People don't seem to have any shame these days,' continued Ron in the same vein and without answering Avril's question, 'and no backbone either.'

'Thank you, Ron,' said Avril, cutting him off as quickly as she could. 'I don't think your thoughts would be shared by the majority of our listeners. In fact, our next caller, Martin from Bedford, wants to talk about the concept of shame. Go ahead, Martin from Bedford.'

'Hi, there,' said Martin hesitantly, followed by an uncomfortably long lull. Avril didn't know whether or not to step in, but Martin eventually found his voice. 'Referring back to your previous callers, Daryl and Alison I believe, I can speak from experience about how difficult life can be without a steadying figure in your background.'

'Do please tell us your story, Martin,' instructed Avril, relieved that he had got over the first and most difficult hurdle.

'At about the age of three, I was taken into care,' Martin started in a firm tone. 'My father was in prison and my young mother had been sectioned and was unable to care for me.' A lump came into Avril's throat; it was a heart-rending beginning to anyone's life. None of her dedicated listeners could fail to be moved by this intro. 'I spent my childhood in either care homes or being fostered out in the community,' Martin continued. 'Some care home staff were well-meaning; others didn't give a toss. And it was the same for fostering. You could be lucky or unlucky with whom you were placed. I was never lucky enough to find anyone I could turn to with trust. I had only myself to rely on.'

'We can feel your pain, Martin. Do please continue at your own pace.'

'I spent a lot of time alone. I didn't have any school friends because that would have involved telling them about my parents.'

'And I imagine that you didn't want to do that lest they abused you,' said Avril.

'Nobody's going to want to be friends with a boy whose father is a murderer and whose mother is detained in a mental home. It didn't take me long to work that out,' Martin said with great feeling. 'I kept myself to myself and learnt very quickly how to deflect such questions.'

'How did you get out of the cycle of unhappiness?' Avril asked a little too tenderly. Raised eyebrows were exchanged between the technical staff and production manager. Was this any old Martin, or could he conceivably be Avril's Martin? It wasn't clear yet but would become so shortly.

'At what age were you required to leave the care home?'

'Care orders cease at age eighteen, but if you can find a job which provides accommodation and food, then you can go when you're seventeen.'

'Is that what you did?' asked Avril, despite the warning frown on her producer's face. Her cheeks were flushed. She knew she was close to her time limit but also that her listeners would be riveted by the broadcast.

'Sort of,' replied Martin. 'I got into the habit of using my time alone for studying and to earn cash doing casual jobs. I won a bursary to a sixth form college and then a scholarship to university. I hoped to escape my past.'

'And was life better there?'

'Yes, much better, but I still couldn't rid myself of the shame I felt about my father being a notorious killer and my mother confined in a secure mental institution.' Martin paused before taking what he knew would be the final denouement. 'It wasn't until I met you, Avril,' he continued, 'that I was able to unburden myself of the horrors of my childhood and see life from a different perspective.'

'Well, that's good to know,' said Avril in as cheery a voice as she could muster. 'I'll see you later at home, husband.' When Martin's line clicked off, Avril signed off promptly too with a well-rehearsed ending for her loyal listeners. 'As for the sins of the fathers, the Bible tells us that "you shall not bow yourself down to them, nor serve them". Mental health for the majority of us is all about finding someone with whom to share our darkest secrets because as the old adage goes, "a problem shared is a problem halved".'

They didn't have a switchboard at Radio East Midlands. Switchboards had already become obsolete by the time the station ranked as a substantial player in local broadcasting.

But if they had, the correspondent's favourite expression regarding such devices, of being overwhelmed by incoming calls, would have been pertinent. Instead, the juniors were overrun by listeners wishing to congratulate Avril and Martin for their courage in coming out. Martin sounded like a great bloke and they wished her many years of happy marriage.

The producer too was satisfied; the station's audience figures had reached a previously unimaginable number. All was well in the good ship, Radio East Midlands. The frowns were gone except for the "Where is he now" journalist who knew his potential big story had just hit the buffers, and who could do nothing more than file a short paragraph stating that the former young boy, now thirty and recently married, visited his ailing mother regularly every month.

Chapter 10

REFLECTIONS

Martin had chosen, prompted by a few sly hints from management following his "coming out", to concentrate his future attention on the development of new anti-viral drugs. According to his boss, it would keep him mostly in the laboratory away from commercial pressures and the tiresome need from time to time to represent the pharmaceutical company at product launches and functions. Martin took the "suggestion" with good grace, he loved working in the lab at the cutting edge of science and it was no skin off his nose if the company didn't wish him to represent them. As one of the company's chief scientists, he was king in his own particular patch and was left alone to get on with his work, and as was his modus operandi, he worked methodically and diligently ensuring that he kept up to date with the scientific literature and always researching more fully subject areas that impinged directly on his own field whether by attending symposia or arranging meetings.

The reports on the outbreak of a severe acute respiratory syndrome in China in 2002, later named SARS for convenience, took his full attention. SARS was a strain of coronavirus. It had originally affected people in the food industry but had spread to healthcare workers as sufferers sought treatment for their condition. It was a single-stranded RNA virus which infected the epithelial cells within the lungs. Victims died unless they received prompt medical treatment. Back then, the scientific world held its breath fearing a pandemic but China and its neighbouring countries acted with great urgency and brought it under control within twelve months.

The greater his knowledge of the limited efficacy of the current crop of anti-viral agents, the more Martin realised his need to work with specialists in other disciplines, especially those trying to develop new vaccines. It would only be through a combination of different scientific skills that effective medications to combat future strains of viruses that modern medicine could succeed. Over the following years, Martin built up professional relationships with virologists, epidemiologists, geneticists, and various public health agencies around the world. Before the first outbreak of Covid-19 in December 2019 was officially acknowledged by the Chinese authorities, Martin was already hearing whispers on the scientific grapevine of an impending crisis.

For only the second time in his life, he was in the right place at the right time, he told Avril one evening; the first of course having been their chance meeting in a railway terminus which eventually led to marriage. So, your time has come, had been her response and they had smiled and hugged one another with deep affection. Before long, as evidence and data emerged from China, and it became clear that a new coronavirus, closely related to SARS, was about to rear its ugly head, the company recognised that Martin was supremely well-placed to represent their interests and in the welter of media attention that the oncoming pandemic would arouse, he was asked, amid much bonhomie, to be their spokesperson. The company wouldn't call it humble pie, but they had both smiled at the realisation that it had taken the prospect of a global crisis for his company to eat their entrenched views about Martin's background. Martin's large feet were in free dance.

Just before their tenth wedding anniversary they had revisited Jersey. It was a promise they had kept to walk the same streets and see the same sights as they had done shortly after their marriage when they had gone there together to dispose of Avril's inheritance and fulfil the desire of her grandfather to redress the balance.

Much had changed for them in the preceding decade. The process of Martin's "coming out" had been far from straightforward. Initially, it had been all smiles and congratulations on throwing off the shackles of his past, but they were to learn that prejudices run deep and it wasn't long before the burden of his past began to affect Avril too. There were crimes of daring-do, or of the underdog having his day that appealed to the general public but the crime of frenzied murder was not one of them. Cold shouldered by many, including disappointingly some work colleagues and hockey mates, Avril and Martin had

had to keep a low profile until his background lost its news worthiness and became a dead topic.

It was on their only day of honeymoon when they were busy re-arranging furniture in the hastily rented flat that the subject of what to do with the seventeen million in Jersey was decided. Both agreed that its dispersal should be as swift and as discreet as possible; it was an encumbrance that neither wanted. By the following morning, when both left their new but temporary home to go to work for the first time as a married person, what to do with the legacy had been sorted.

Avril had been given an email address for the bank in St. Helier and when she made contact, the banker rang her back on a secure landline. She outlined her wishes and after some discussion as to how best to achieve her goals, the banker promised to prepare the necessary documentation for her to sign in person at the bank. It would be a pleasure to see her again, she had commented, but she should ensure that she treated her visit there with the same degree of caution and security as on the previous occasion. And it would be necessary to take her marriage certificate.

There had been an intense conversation about the pros and cons of declaring the legacy to the Inland Revenue. Avril had been an advocate for making a full and honest declaration at the earliest possible moment but Martin had counselled caution. They had no way of knowing, he had argued, just how much tax would be owing on such a large sum of money that they presumed had been accumulating over many years. If the entire balance or a large proportion of it was wiped out by the tax owed, then how would Avril redress the balance as Henry had instructed? He must have known, Martin had argued logically, that a large amount of tax was owing otherwise he would simply have left his entire estate to a charity of his choice or similar. Hidden implicitly in his letter to Avril, although not set in words, Martin argued further, was her grandfather's desire to avoid unnecessary contact with the authorities. Paying taxes would achieve nothing for good causes, and to the treasury, seventeen million would constitute less than a drop in the ocean. If she was to fulfil the role Henry had set out for her, then some way would have to be found to donate the money anonymously and close the account in Jersey leaving no trace of either Avril or her grandfather.

It had been left to the skill of the banker, generously rewarded via a variety of management handling fees, to make the dispersals Avril had stipulated. The bulk of the inheritance, ten million pounds, would go to a charity set up to provide funding for further education for children leaving care. It would be aimed at those teenagers whose academic abilities were insufficient to win bursaries or who were best suited to gaining qualifications for trade skills. It would pay the college fees, accommodation and living expenses for up to three years and provide the child with a dedicated mentor to help them to springboard into mainstream living. The second tranche of legacy money, five million, would be used to buy a substantial stake in Radio East Midlands. Directors who played an active role in the running of the station were expected to invest in the business to show their commitment to the cause. Avril had not been in a financial position to do so at that time, other than to have made a nominal deposit to show willing, but with the banker's sleight of hand, the beneficial owner of the money, Avril, was masked by hiding it in a newly-created private limited company of which Martin and Avril were the sole directors and shareholders. When the heat was off and memories had faded, Avril would point out to the powers that be, that she was in fact a major shareholder in the station. She was going to take a leave of absence and wouldn't be actively engaged in broadcasting in the foreseeable future while she and Martin started and raised a family, but she would definitely be back as it was her goal to fill much more of its broadcasting time with information about good causes.

There remained just three further disposals: one million would be invested prudently and dedicated to the care of Martin's mother – she was still only sixty and Martin had never given up hope that one day she would be released into his care – a further million – at Martin's insistence – would be used to buy a fine family home in a quiet suburb of Bedford where Martin could offer their children the safety and stability that he had never known, and a much smaller sum would be set aside for Aunt Annie, without her knowledge, should she ever be in need. She was after all Henry's next-of-kin and although Annie had vowed never to accept a penny piece from him following a hiatus in their relationship when Annie decamped from a well-paid job in London to self-sufficiency in Wales, unexpected events could change attitudes.

For some time to come Martin would be the sole breadwinner. Despite the preconceptions of some of his colleagues towards his infamous background, Martin still loved his job. He adopted a low profile, worked hard and expected nothing in return other than his salary, but like his wife, he had the distinct impression that eventually his day would come, and in the late autumn of 2019 it did.

The intervening years had been remarkable by their very lack of any meaningful hiatus to interrupt their happiness. With three children in five years – one set of twin boys followed by an exuberant girl – their family was a showcase to the world of family unity. As the children grew and the demands on her time slowly decreased, Avril's voluntary work with the charity she had set up increased. She was approached on a number of occasions to join the management committee but her heart was still with the radio station which she re-joined in 2018. Just within its signal range, Avril had kept tabs over the years on its choice of programmes and presenters. She felt it had lost its way and in so doing lost its audience. The time was ripe for her to declare her vested interest in the station and to guide it back onto a schedule of local news and interest. Personnel had moved on since her unmarried days working at the station and Avril felt no pressure to explain how she had previously managed to accumulate five million pounds to buy a stake in the business. Within months she had taken over the reins and was reshaping it in her own image. Her cheeks glowed as she slowly achieved the goals she had planned in her head over the preceding years. You will get nowhere in life without strategy, she had told her children over and over again, because strategy is king.

* * *

Life had moved on too in the north of England. Kit's curls still bounced on her shoulders but were now flecked with strands of white hairs and Edmund had put on weight despite his continued love of rambling. There had been tense times in the early years of marriage; an inability to produce offspring being the chief cause. And several years passed in a rollercoaster of unfulfilled expectation. There was no denying their mutual affection, but the lack of progeny after five years grew into a barrier of red-hot coals between them, and Edmund finally cracked.

The events leading up to his affair happened well after the dispersion of Old Kit's estate. That sum, once tax had been paid – an amount which rocketed sky high due to compound interest being charged on multiple penalties and used by the Treasury as a form of slapped wrists – was now less than one million pounds. At the time, Edmund had whistled through his lips on learning that ninety per cent of his deceased client's fortune had gone in tax owed. Compound interest, he had declared to his wife, was an evil thing, but Kit had no regrets. It seemed to her that less money to divvy up would make her task simpler. After due diligence, and a consultation in bed with her joint-executor, Kit's mind was made up. Kit had made a huge effort to check the current circumstances of every member on the family tree, and the only persons remotely worthy of a monetary windfall were the wives of the loathsome twins. They were making a real success of business and had come a long way in the world of catering since their initial step in 1982 with the fast-food stall on the construction site in Gateshead. According to Edmund's discreet enquiries, the brothers, still alive, were no longer receiving state benefits which Kit assumed was thanks to the financial support from their wives. The women, now partially retired and pushing the seventy-barrier, had been joined by their three children who mostly ran and managed the small chain of fast-food restaurants in the Tyneside area that the wives had opened before the start of the new millennium. But the wives' business acumen, work ethic and ensuring that the gruesome twosome was no longer on the state's payroll was not the reason why Kit had chosen them. Further subtle enquiries by Edmund had ascertained that out of their profits one year, they had made a generous donation to a charity for the welfare of children leaving the care system, a charity set up in recent times to help these young people, often orphans or abandoned babies, adjust to normal life. A voice on the end of a phone line; someone with whom they could touch base, get a listening ear and sometimes advice and support. It transpired that the wives had volunteered as confidantes and one day a week they took pride in carrying out this Samaritan role.

It was a few weeks after Old Kit's legacy had been paid anonymously into the bank account of each wife that Edmund learned a little more about the founders of the charity to which the wives had previously made a sizeable donation. He had asked an accountant friend to check out its credentials as a matter of general practice, and was flabbergasted to learn that its founders were listed as Martin and Avril Oakeshott who resided in Bedford, and that it had been funded with working capital to the tune of ten million pounds by an unnamed source. He pursed his lips, sat back in his executive chair and crossed his arms over his chest in quiet contemplation of the dynamics of the situation.

With Avril, he had been co-executor of her grandfather's will, and together they had liquidated the assets he had listed in his letter to her and dispersed the monies according to his stated wishes. But Kit had seen Henry in Guernsey on the very day of his suicide. They had been there because of Old Kit's offshore accounts and Edmund became more certain that, like his great aunt, Henry too had taken advantage of the Channel Islands' secretive banking methods. Was the ten million a gift from some generous person who had no association whatsoever with Old Kit's extended family or did it represent the amount that Henry had accumulated in an offshore account? If it did then it wasn't just one false will he had had to deal with, thought Edmund, it was two. Whatever the answer, it led directly to Edmund's affair with Clare.

There was no value, Edmund realised in hindsight, in setting out to prove, as he had done, that the new charity's working capital had been donated by Avril or that it represented the proceeds of tax evasion. It would have marked an enormously generous act on her part and who would really have cared if all the money went to the charity because taxes had been dodged? Nobody. But at the time, with his marriage in a rocky state, Edmund was like a dog with a bone and couldn't leave the subject alone.

Despite his busy job, he had just taken his first steps into the melee of local politics. Politics had been on his mind for some time and when the opportunity arose to put himself forward for election as a local councillor, he took it. A visit to Westminster followed on the pretext of meeting influential people in and around parliament and Edmund ensured that Clare would be amongst them. In spite of some fairly salacious newsprint, Avril's twin had risen from the backbenches to junior minister for sport. She was still unmarried but according to gossip was not starved of lustful encounters, so when she met Edmund –late thirties but still debonair – who she remembered from her great grandaunt's memorial service at Newcastle Cathedral, there could only be one outcome.

Some might have described Clare's climb up the greasy political pole as meteoric, but it had not been due to her intimate associations. She had got where she was as a result of her sheer ability although she had never tired of relating the story of her field hockey trial with the elite players at Bisham Abbey in order to promote her chances of securing the junior ministerial job in sport. Since her father's demise, she had shared the Islington family home for a few months with her mother until circumstances dictated its disposal to pay outstanding debts. Her mother had returned to her roots on the Isle of Wight and Clare had rented an apartment in a less salubrious area of London. Visitors to her accommodation were numerous and included Edmund on occasions when he could dream up reasons for business meetings in the capital. It was true that he had corporate clients in The City but he was captivated by Clare's attitude to casual sex. It was a nice side dish to the information he was seeking, and it lasted longer than the scant gen that he had been able to wheedle out of her. Apparently, her father's meagre estate had been completely wiped out by his debts, and her grandfather chose to leave her a very modest sum. Avril, of course, had come up trumps, she'd told him, and bought a house for over a million somewhere out in the sticks near Bedford. It was news to Edmund. She might have bought an expensive house but it was not funded by the residue of her grandfather's estate which he had left her as the residue had turned out to be less than the five thousand pounds that Clare had received. That, and an oblique reference to her Aunt Annie being involved in "affairs of state", had been all that Edmund had prised from Clare's lips and when one early morning on leaving the flat to catch his train back north and Clare had asked for her key back, he knew the affair was over. As he left, she had just said, "Gossip, just far too much gossip. Sorry mate but my job's worth more than your casual leg over". There was a sense of relief that his selfish escapade with Clare was over, and he thanked his lucky stars that Kit appeared to be none the wiser. Beside learning that Avril's million-pound house had almost certainly been bought on the back of Henry's undeclared earnings in a Channel Island bank, and that her aunt had mysterious connections with Whitehall, it had taught him how much he cared for Kit. They would find a way to have children, and in the meantime, he would grow up and support her more demonstrably.

After five years without success the time arrived eventually to consider fertility treatment. Kit was dead against it but with persuasion and much coaxing finally agreed to give it a try. It seemed to be the only avenue left to them; all other channels had been explored. They started with hope but as the months ticked by their positive approach faded. When a second procedure also ended in failure, they decided to abandon all hope and get on with life childless. It was a decision which they took jointly and although they knew their future would be tinged with regrets, it brought them closer together. Kit gave up university lecturing to become a secondary school teacher in a local comprehensive. She brought basic physics, taught in a playful and relevant way, to many children who had no aspirations of academic achievement. That they attended regularly and enjoyed the lessons was all the reward she needed.

One surprising day, after seven years of marriage, Kit realised that she was pregnant. She kept it to herself for as long as she could not daring to believe in the pregnancy test result, but the arrival a few months later of twin girls was proof enough. Edmund was over the moon even though there would be no Mr. Newman Jr to follow in his footsteps. Kit pointed out that in modern times of gender equality, a Miss Newman in the practice would not only be a refreshing change but would also obviate the need for a silly suffix after her name. Only a man could have dreamed up such nonsense, she had told him.

The arrival of the girls brought contentment to the wider Newman family, and in particular to Edmund. With busy days at the office with his legal duties and council work some evenings, his weekends were exclusively for his family. And now that Kit wore sensible shoes most of the time, they could deposit a twin securely into each's backpack and set out regularly at weekends on favourite rambles. Life was hectic and thoughts of Old Kit and her long association with the Newman family no longer drifted into his mind in odd moments. But, in that regard, there was a surprise in store when Emily came to babysit one evening. She'd had a visit from a woman named Dame Barbara who'd told her that they were identical twin sisters. Kit and Edmund were looking forward to an adult evening out; a rare treat without the infants. A grown-up dinner for two in an award-winning restaurant in the countryside, but Emily's news on arrival delayed their departure.

'What did you say?' asked Edmund incredulously.

'I have a twin sister. She's identical,' replied Emily almost matter-of-factly. Edmund appeared stumped for words but Kit had had the perspicacity to get as much detail as she could and over dinner they talked over the news. 'Emily is not just any old identical twin. It would seem from the story that she was told by this Dame Barbara character that the pair are the illegitimate children of Old Kit,' said Edmund, after the waiter had taken their order. 'It's incredible,' he gasped.

'The connection with Old Kit, if it turns out to be true,' agreed Kit, 'is difficult to accept but ever since your father's letter landed on my doormat ten years ago asking me to travel north about some distant family affair, I have never ceased being amazed at all the twists and turns one woman could generate.'

'Who is this Dame Barbara woman? Where has she popped up from and can she be trusted?'

'We'll find out more when we get home. I hope we won't learn anything upsetting,' responded Kit thoughtfully.

It was the following morning before they learned the facts. Kit had persuaded Emily to stay overnight as she had done on several previous occasions; they had a big house with guest bedrooms and everything Emily would need for an unscheduled stay, and after feeding, cleaning and playing with the infants they had time to chat

'You may remember,' Emily started, addressing herself to Kit, 'that when you asked me to research the ancestry of Old Kit herself to explain how she came to conceive two pairs of twins, I told you that one day when I was visiting her in the care home, she had given me an old book which she herself had been given by her late father. It was a notebook cum diary.'

'I do remember,' replied Kit, 'and you said it contained notes and tips about his daily life and his glowing love of Old Kit.'

'Of course, we now know what he knew. Old Kit was not his daughter, she was his niece. A fact that we believe she never knew.'

'Go on,' urged Kit, her breakfast completely forgotten.

'I thought at the time while I was helping you with the research that that was it. The notebook contained nothing more than these types of comments. It was not until I sat down and read it properly one very wet and cold weekend that I realised that there was more to it than first met the eye.'

'What did you find?' asked Edmund.

'Old Kit herself, my mother actually,' Emily said looking at them both intently, 'had penned some comments. She had taken over where her uncle had left off.'

'What were they about?' inquired Kit.

'About the business. The first one must have been written during wartime because it made reference to a lack of skilled staff and how difficult it was to obtain cloth. It was followed by several references to technical problems and difficulties with cash flow. Then the tenor of the comments changed and I had the impression that several years had passed since the previous entry.'

'No dates noted?' said Kit, totally absorbed in the story.

'None,' responded Emily, 'strange really because the entries started to read like a diary. They had an emotional content.'

'In what way?' questioned Edmund.

'They were personal references. Difficulties she had encountered with people. Family upsets. That sort of thing. The comments were guarded but you could feel the pain. Sometimes initials were written followed by an exclamation mark. I assumed that the initials referred to a family member who was giving her grief. I looked at the invitation lists for Old Kit's get togethers to try to put a name to the initials.'

'And did you succeed?' asked Edmund.

'Sometimes. Yes. I took JBH to be a reference to her twin sons, John and Bernard Harrison. But other initials I failed to identify.' A cry from an infant took Kit to the playpen while Edmund went into the kitchen to prepare fresh coffees whilst all the time trying to work out, if the story was true, the exact relationship between Emily and Kit. 'It was through this old notebook,' resumed Emily, when they were all back at the breakfast table, 'that I had the sense that Old Kit had had an affair which resulted in pregnancy.'

'A woman's intuition?' asked Kit.

'Yes. The nuances in her few, disjointed words spelled out much more than she might have realised. She had chosen her words carefully and together with several other entries around the same time, told the story of a love affair.'

'A love affair that went wrong,' declared Edmund.

'No. I didn't get that impression but it is plausible. It seemed to me that it was more about a love affair that resulted in unplanned twins, and gave rise to a concern of how to do her best for them.' Emily paused. 'There were repeated references to "the Kent couple" and "hospital visits" and, later, with what I felt was an air of finality, to "separation and settlement of the girls". After that, entries of that sort, expressing latent passion and feelings dried up and there was a reversion to the former, brisker approach.'

'Terse,' said Edmund, finding the exact word to sum up Emily's descriptive thoughts. 'But how did you make the leap from these short diary entries to being convinced that Old Kit was your mother?'

'She was in the care home for several years,' said Emily looking Edmund directly in the eye, 'and as you know, your mother and I visited her regularly. Sometimes I went on my own. She could be good company with all her tales to tell. She became gentler as she became frailer.

A sense that her time was running out. She would often hold my hand, and occasionally stroke my arm or cheek. She'd say something endearing sometimes. I thought they were just fun remarks like a tradesman calling you "love". It wasn't until I had a knock on the door recently and was confronted by my own face when I opened it, that Old Kit's words and actions slotted into place like a key turning a mortice lock.' It was spellbinding stuff that had Edmund and Kit on the edges of their seats unable to move until they knew the full story. 'But she said she was Dame Barbara. I opened the door fully and she just stormed in uninvited,' added Emily raising her arms.

'Oh,' screeched Kit involuntarily, before clamping a hand firmly over her mouth. She looked as if she might throw up such was her concern of the conduct of the meeting.

'She sat down on the sofa, opened her handbag and took out a newspaper clipping of a photograph taken outside Newcastle Cathedral and pointed with a well-manicured finger at a person captured in the picture. Her question was superfluous. Of course, it was me. And the photo was genuine as it had been taken at a memorial service. And that was another thing she didn't need to tell me. The woman being remembered at the service was our mother. Suddenly, all the bagatelle balls were resting in the correct holes and apart from the detail, I could work out the full story.'

'So, what had happened?' demanded Kit, 'for this woman to appear on your doorstep.'

'Apparently, she always read the obituaries in The Times. Upon her demise, Old Kit's life and times were reported because of her association with Northern Tailoring and with the introduction of nylon. It was 2010 then of course, and Dame Barbara was a high-ranking civil servant. She was fifty-four. And wouldn't be expected to retire until age sixty. Her branch of the civil service didn't encourage interest being taken in their elite employees. They preferred them to remain unknown to the outside world. So, as far as they were concerned, any association with Old Kit would be unwelcome.'

'The grey brigade,' commented Edmund.

'Something like that,' agreed Emily. 'But covertly, she made some enquiries. She hired a private detective and soon found out about me. Where I lived, what I did, etcetera. She did nothing more for several years but when she reached retirement, she felt free to do as she pleased. Hence, one fine day, she arrived at my front door.'

'Wanting to achieve what?' asked Kit rather bluntly.

'Wanting to …,' Emily's voice trailed off, unable to find the right words to express her thoughts. 'Wishing to tie up loose ends,' she added eventually. 'But she didn't have to explain that to me because I felt the same need as she did. The need to embrace my twin sister. To hold her for a few seconds in my arms. To cherish her close presence by my side and to discover just a very few facts about her life and upbringing.

It was bedtime before Edmund and Kit had a chance to chew over Emily's startling news. When she left that early morning and the day nanny had arrived, it had been a mad scramble to get to their demanding jobs on time. There had been no moment to ponder on her words although

Edmund had worked out that Emily and Kit shared no more than a distant cousin relationship since it had been established that Old Kit was her supposed father's niece and not his daughter.

'Just when I thought we had seen the back of Old Kit forever,' said Edmund, as they snuggled together under the duvet after a tiring day, 'up she springs again like a child's jack-in-the-box toy.'

'It's exasperating in so many ways,' agreed Kit, 'but it's also wonderful for Emily that she has a close blood relative. Just imagine how lonely life could feel without a single close family member.'

'I can't,' said Edmund truthfully. 'I would be the loneliest person in the world without you and the kids.'

'So, Emily's twin,' started Kit speaking softly, 'had a happy childhood in Kent, went to Oxford University as an English scholar, married a man nine years older than herself who was becoming a bigwig in industry, has two children in their early twenties, rose to a high level in the civil service before she retired, and was given a gong for her troubles.'

'The synopsis of a life. All points covered in roughly fifty words.'

'Yes. But apparently she felt the need to pursue a channel of enquiry that could bring disorder to her well-ordered life.'

'Wouldn't you have done the same?' whispered Edmund.

'Probably. Undoubtedly, actually. Who could resist such a search? Not me, anyhow. With close relatives thin on the ground, resistance would have been near impossible. Goodnight,' said Kit, kissing his cheek and turning over onto her favourite side. But sleep didn't come to either of them. It was Edmund who gave in first; sitting up and accepting that sleep wouldn't come while information was buzzing about in his head.

'I've known Emily all my life,' he said, after Kit too had given up the notion of immediate sleep. 'But I never knew her background other than as my father's trusty secretary and my mother's best friend. To learn now of her adoption by a couple in their mid-forties living in Kelso, her schooling in a well-known boarding school in Edinburgh, followed by a secretarial course and three years working for Rangers Football Club, is all news to me.'

'What did you expect?' asked Kit. 'That she just materialised one day in your father's office and had no life before that.'

'Of course not. I suppose that I just took her presence for granted. She spent a lot of time with us including Christmases. We were like her family and she was treated as such.'

'But you never enquired about her past.'

'I grew up in her presence,' replied Edmund. 'I didn't enquire about my parents' past so I had no reason to ask about hers. I knew the basics, of course. She was an only child, purportedly conceived when her parents were already middle-aged. She was well-educated, came from a happy home and had no close relatives once her parents died. That seemed to be all the knowledge necessary. Her engaging personality said the rest.'

'She never married?' Kit asked. 'Did she have boyfriends?'

'I believe so. It's not the sort of thing a young boy asks of an older woman. My sister would probably know. I suspect that she did have boyfriends but simply rarely mentioned them in my presence.'

'I am surprised,' said Kit, all of a sudden galvanised as if a neural pathway in her brain had become unblocked, 'at what she wears on the third finger of her left hand.'

'Her late mother's wedding ring. Why should that surprise you?'

'Whether you believe it to be the ring of her adopted or birth mother is irrelevant because,' stated Kit, 'unless I am very much mistaken, that's a man's ring.'

⋆ ⋆ ⋆

The subject of who raped Grace had always been on Kit's mind, although for many years it had been very much on the back burner. But it was a loose end that Kit's training as a scientist told her was in need of tying up. Like a DIY-er painting an entire room but leaving the skirting boards for an indeterminate date in the future; an incomplete job could never give rise to true satisfaction. The subject of Grace would niggle away at Kit forever unless she made a concerted effort to solve the mystery, and it was the death of her grandparents which was the spark.

Her grandfather died at the good age of eighty-one. Heart issues had dogged him for many years and the end when it came, according to her grandmother, was not without kindness. On Edmund's insistence, her grandmother moved north to live with them in a menage á trois plus noisy twins. Kit had loaded her grandma's personal stuff into a hired van and driven the six hundred odd miles north to Berwick with a sad, but relieved old woman. They both knew it was the right time for role reversals and Kit would care for her with the same willingness that her grandma had done for her. Young at heart but old in body, Grandma Roach settled in as a valued member of the household and most days she could not be separated from her magic iPad. For all the world, it seemed that she had made a successful and happy transition from her former quiet life with her aged husband to a multi-generational home with a lifestyle very unlike the type she had formerly led, but within less than twelve months she had lost the will to carry on. When a particularly virulent flu struck that winter, she had neither the capacity nor, it seemed, the desire to overcome it. She slipped away peacefully leaving a gigantic hole in Kit's heart.

One evening, when the twins were sleeping soundly, Kit produced her well-thumbed ancestry chart from 2010 to remind Edmund of Old Kit's descendants. 'Why are you showing me this?' asked Edmund, perplexed.

'I was rummaging through Grandma's things, sorting out what to keep, what to give to charity and what to just dump,' Kit started, 'and then I came across this letter to my great grandfather, Peter,' she added, handing it to Edmund.

'The paper's frail and the longhand is difficult to decipher,' commented Edmund, passing it back to his wife before he could cause any damage. 'What's it about?'

'It's about Grace and who raped her.'

'Oh, my goodness. Not Old Kit again.'

'Yes, a loose end that I've been trying to tie off for ages to produce a "*quod erat demonstrantum*" finale to the family saga.'

'Go on then, spill the beans.'

'The letter is from Old Kit to her favourite brother – we now know that Peter was actually her cousin but Old Kit doesn't appear to know that – outlining what she believed happened to Grace.'

'Which was?'

'You can see from the chart that Grace and Sybil were Old Kit's first-born twins. Apparently, Grace was affected by the death of her one-year-old twin from natural causes and never fully gained her independence. She was cosseted and protected from the real world by her mother as she could fall prey to anyone with a mind to take advantage of her.' Kit removed her spectacles and held the letter up close. 'It's difficult to read,' she said, 'not only is the longhand squiggly but also because it has been written with a fountain pen and the ink has faded.'

'Surely not the fountain pen that she bequeathed to you,' interjected Edmund. 'Now that would be uncanny.'

'Same sort of nib thickness so it probably is one and the same.'

'I really shouldn't be surprised,' said Edmund, shaking his head. 'What did the letter say?'

'There was a lot of emotional and heartfelt stuff but the bones of what she wrote was that Grace had been out at a church young people's club and returned home somewhat dishevelled and in a state of anxiety, and that Old Kit feared that she had been sexually assaulted. Her fear was realised when four months later Grace was pronounced pregnant.'

'She had not been chaperoned?' asked Edmund.

'Presumably not. I guess most parents would consider a few hours at a local church hall with other young people as being a good idea, and in Grace's case, as being somewhere safe to go where they wouldn't have to worry about her.'

'A safe haven,' said Edmund, mulling over how he would protect his girls from predatory boys when they were of that age. 'I seem to recall,' Edmund continued, 'that in Old Kit's long letter to you, she hinted that she knew the culprit.'

'That's right, but how I don't know. She did hire a private investigator who might have come up with the names of some of the young men present that evening. Maybe she knew some of them and had reason to dislike one in particular. But it all came to nought as she had no proof.'

'So, how are you able to identify the culprit all these years later when Old Kit herself couldn't?'

'This letter,' replied Kit, placing it gingerly on the table out of harm's way, 'makes reference to a St. Margaret's church. According to my Google search, there is a St. Margaret's in the area of Berwick where Old Kit lived at the time.' Kit paused to fidget with her spectacles before continuing with some appalling news. 'Since the millennium,' she continued, 'there has been a plethora in the news of so-called "historical" crimes perpetrated by people of supposedly high standing against juveniles and people with limited mental capacity.'

'I know. It's shocking. A culture of abuse.'

'When I followed up my initial search, I found that St. Margaret's was one of the institutions that had been flagged for inappropriate behaviour, and there are legal cases pending against both clerical and non-clerical staff who ran and maintained it during the fifties and sixties even though they are all dead.'

'The victims would be very elderly now.'

'Or dead, just like Grace,' said Kit, 'and the offenders too.'

'So, no retribution possible now,' said Edmund, 'only the public slurring of their names.'

'That might be considered by the victims' descendants as something better than nothing.'

'Grace's direct descendants are Marion and June. I somehow doubt that that couple of deadbeats would give a toss,' said Edmund. It was plain speaking and Kit was hard pressed to disagree. 'They are condemned as a group,' summed up Kit, 'and not as individuals.'

'It would seem so,' agreed Edmund, 'I can try delving into any cases that come to court, but I doubt it would be worthwhile.'

'Then we will have to accept that we can't pin the rape to any particular person,' concluded Kit. 'Chances are it would have been the vicar or a lay person such as the verger. She would have known them from Sunday school and trusted them.'

'And all she got for her trust was abuse. A culture of abuse that would have ensnared other young adults who were similarly wet behind the ears.'

'It beggars belief that people in authority or famous for one reason or another can find pleasure in taking advantage of those in lesser situations. There are some shit people around,' said Kit with feeling.

'But we must move on,' said Edmund, giving her a light kiss on the cheek. 'The past is the past and you in particular have done your best to set Old Kit's world to right.'

★ ★ ★

The Official Secrets Act, 1987, was always regarded by Dame Barbara – since her recent retirement she had let her hair down and was now usually going under the name of Babs except when dealing with petty officials in the planning department of her local council or when she needed an appointment pronto with the chiropodist – as a blunt instrument with which more harm was done than good. But the long arm of its influence still applied to her. She had been a Crown servant, and by virtue of her former position as head of a small investigative unit, it would be an offence for her to disclose without lawful authority any official information about national security or intelligence.

She had been irked for some time by these restraints which would accompany her to the grave. From her previous position, she had knowledge of information she felt should be in the public domain: cover-ups, scandals, frauds, debauchery and treason. Under her watch, it was information which had been strictly controlled and kept under lock and key and she intended that most of it would remain that way. But the discoveries of her newly found identical twin sister, her birth mother, and her relationship to Annie Williams and Annie's brother, the shamefully self-serving Adam, had caused her some serious thought. The cover-up of Adam Roach's traitorous conduct in selling information to the highest bidder to feed his gambling habit – an Albanian gang set on establishing a foothold in western Europe – which would severely disrupt the nation's banking transfer market to a tune of multi millions of pounds was, in Babs's opinion, intolerable. The failings of the late Adam Roach should have been exposed in all their gory detail as a warning to others that even in death, reputations can and should be trashed according to the enormity of the crime. It had been a clear-cut thought until revelations of kinship had clouded matters. Adam Roach was Babs's first cousin twice removed. Did she ought to think carefully before drip feeding titbits of information anonymously to the media? Where would it all end? Would she risk sacrificing the good name of her husband and own children on an altar of ridiculously puritanical standards? It was food for thought which made Babs dither. And what too of her real mother's association with Whitehall? Kit Audrey Harrison's fortune was not based solely on nylon and tailoring. She'd been on the payroll of Westminster too as a government adviser to the Labour administration in the sixties. She spread her left-wing views with scant regard for the status quo, and stuck her nose into Whitehall affairs with criticisms of how they operated and what they chose to monitor as if they were her juniors, her lap dogs. Babs tut-tutted. For one as staunchly conservative with both a small "c" and a capital "C" as Babs, that wretched woman had been nothing less than a discordant and tiresome interloper and Babs was joyous when the electorate eventually booted out their policies of egalitarianism. Babs tut-tutted again. Unelected advisers acting like God. But they got their comeuppance in the end.

Over the course of the next few months, and not without serious regard for her newly discovered family members, she had released little packets of classified information which made their way onto the correspondents' floors of several national newspapers. And so well versed was Babs in the dark art of anonymity, that this leakage of restricted data could not be traced back to her, or indeed, to any other person or organisation. She had carefully mixed the compelling with the relatively anodyne and ensured that no one journalist received all the pieces of each puzzle. They would have to work together to learn the full story of Adam Roach's abuse of his position as a member of parliament, his use of money obtained fraudulently to pay off his gambling debts and his association with some despicable eastern European low-life.

Babs had been doubly careful to shield Emily from any association with the information she had leaked. She liked her, and although they had agreed to meet on only one more occasion somewhere on neutral ground to flesh out their upbringings, their journeys through life thus far and their aspirations for the future, she meant her no harm. One more meeting, they had both agreed, would suffice. They were not seeking to become best friends, close chums, co-habitants, to exchange daily texts or go shopping arm-in-arm in the high street, or anything of that nature. They had made contact. They had the knowledge and comfort of the other's presence, and they would leave it at that and get on with their respective and separate lives. But where Adam's living close relatives were concerned, Babs calculated, no undeserved notoriety would come to his widow, his sister Annie or his daughters Clare and Avril when the media got stuck into discovering and exposing with forensic detail every fault of the erstwhile parliamentarian. Feature articles, Babs knew, could be a messy business.

The story broke not weeks later, but months. It had been a painstaking affair slotting the puzzle pieces together to expose the full story and which had demanded a collaborative effort between previously rival correspondents. Editors had been wary of the veracity of the evidence and of making false or misleading allegations which could result in litigation, and had initially declined to go to print. But the journalists' persistence had prevailed and when it was finally published in a national Sunday paper, it was done amid a full panoply of whistles and bells in a fanfare which could not be missed.

Gambling addiction and its resulting debts was not the newsworthy item of the feature; addiction was known to be rife in all strands of society and rarely made headlines on its own. The key component of the story was the involvement of eastern European plutocrats in one of the leading London football clubs, Stanmore Rovers. The exposure of this controlling family clique which had grown mega rich on: slave labour, the trafficking of asylum seekers, the menacing with intent to do bodily harm to any person standing in their way and various financial scams targeted at some of the most vulnerable in our ageing society were the reasons why it was front page news. But it didn't stop there. The family's patriarch, an untrustworthy-looking individual with a gnarly skin and deep wrinkles had been seen on camera on numerous occasions as he hosted guests in the chairman's viewing box. With a top chef in attendance on match days, over several seasons he had entertained the stars of the screen, the tennis courts, the Grand Prix circuits, those with political influence and the grandees of industry, to the best of everything. The guests had been a carefully selected bunch. Only those who could wield influence had been invited to enjoy a day out mingling with the football stars and eating with the directors and managerial team.

As the TV cameras had panned around the grandstands before kick-off and dwelled more than momentarily on the director's splendid box with its commanding view over the pitch, on at least one occasion Clare's face had been seen in sharp focus. Neither Kit nor Avril had any interest in football whereas both husbands were aficionados. But no bells had rung when Clare's image had appeared so clearly through the large viewing panels. She was a politician after all and with a shrug of the shoulders Martin and Edmund had accepted that that was what politicians did to up their profile. It was only when the titbits that Babs's had leaked had led via the media to the denouement of the patriarch's bad habits that bells were heard not to be ringing, but to be tolling for all those associated with him, in no matter how minor a way. For the patriarch himself, the authorities found a way to withdraw his legal right to remain in the United Kingdom.

The media had a field day like no other, reporting in lurid detail the inadequacies of Adam Roach. Resting oblivious in his grave, the full force of their words fell on the shoulders of his daughters. Clare tried to put a brave face on things and stick it out but the game was up when her agent told her that the constituency party committee were baying for her blood. He advised her to step down straightaway. It was unfair, she told him, as she had been totally unaware of her father's misdeeds and for once her agent agreed with her. But the resignation came as no surprise to the press as they had left her with no alternative. In the style befitting a sophisticated democracy, she thanked her parliamentary and constituency staff effusively and with fingers crossed on a hand held discreetly behind her back, she hoped that memories would be short and that she would be fighting a by-election soon.

It didn't turn out to be an easy time for Avril either. She might have expected some compassion from her media colleagues but none was forthcoming. She was the twin sister of Clare and the daughter of Adam and that's what counted, and a majority shareholding in a local radio station was no protection against their implied allegations. Unfortunately for Avril, through her late grandfather, Henry, they found a trail to the Channel Islands which led in turn to questions raised about the funding of various projects including the charity. It was another period when the Oakeshott family had to hunker down until the dust settled as there was no denying that the source of the charity's start-up funds had been them. But a "no comment" response was all the press got to their repeated enquiries about the source of the ten million and gradually their persistence waned. It had all gone, after all, to a good cause.

At that point, the fall-out from the leaked information should have been over. Babs had achieved what she wanted. The authorities had waved an irrevocable goodbye to the eastern Europeans and in a hasty but necessary realigning of their top echelon, Stanmore Rovers had welcomed new management with a trusted track record. Those who had been seen to be enjoying the former owner's hospitality wisely kept in the shadows; serious lessons would have to be learnt for another day. What Babs had not anticipated – it having never occurred to her in her wildest thoughts – was the image of her husband standing at the plate glass window, one hand deep in trouser pocket, the other holding a glass of wine, while he surveyed the players warming up on the pitch. When she calmed down, she had to remind herself that he was a captain of industry and his presence there was unlikely to have any other than an innocent significance. It was not, however, a subject that she could casually bring up over the breakfast table – oh, by the way darling, what were you doing with that despot from the eastern Adriatic? – and it was lucky for her that her Whitehall training over so many years had kicked in and stopped her from jumping headlong to the wrong conclusion because her husband had something to tell her. In the interests of everyone, to close various unsatisfactory chapters, he had accepted caretaker chairmanship of Stanmore Rovers, so that the hiatus in orthodox management and the concomitant despicable behaviour by the patriarch and his acolytes could be glossed over once and for all. Babs smiled. It was the perfect answer to her unspoken question and although she hated football with a passion, she would be accompanying him with good grace to the best seats in the stadium whenever he so wished.

⋆ ⋆ ⋆

Although she had set her mind, by her very nature, Annie's re-entry into the world of actuarial science had not been without bumps. There were no smooth steeping stones for a personality as complex as hers. It was not the science per se that was the problem. It was the ever so boring world of insurance premiums that got to her. What was to like about a job which required her to calculate how much Mr. X in Leamington Spa should pay for his house insurance or how much Mrs. Y would have to cough up for driving her Nissan Micra to and from the supermarket, or even, how much young Mr. Z would need to pay into his pension fund for the next forty years to ensure that he had sufficient in his old age to pay his gas bill? Nothing, as far as Annie was concerned. Some generic algorithm would suffice, it didn't need her brilliant mind and superhuman intervention to weigh up the complexities of each situation to produce the best possible outcome for both insurer and insured. It was not surprising therefore, that when the opportunity arose to diversify, she took it.

It had all started with a phone call from her niece, Avril. They had kept in touch over the years but mostly just at Christmas; a scribbled account inside the Xmas card of the fortunes of each family during the preceding year or a folded A4 sheet of computer print annotating a selection of holiday/landmark images in their lives. But this phone call was altogether different. It was about something specific, and it interested Annie immediately. Since she had been cut loose by the Whitehall department – without any form of recognition of her achievement in trapping the individual responsible for leaking the details which led to the banking transfer fraud – she had been in a state of stalemate. There was no question now, as breadwinner and woman of mature years, of chucking in the actuarial towel and pissing off with family in tow back to some rural setting with pigs and chickens. What was so exciting about the phone call was: calculus, algebra, advanced statistics, and joy of joys, the chance to outwit some current modelling software.

According to Avril, when Martin was headed off metaphorically by his company down a professional side street some unenlightened years ago when the news of his parentage broke, he had elected to pool his skills with scientists from other disciplines in an attempt to produce a vaccine to eliminate Dengue Fever, a debilitating tropical disease. The group was successful and their vaccine was licensed in late 2018 when production commenced, and by mid-2019 it had been widely distributed in equatorial countries. So, it was all smiles from his company, Avril had continued, as the marketing of a new therapeutic, even if it was for a little-known tropical condition, would prove to be a steady money earner.

Annie had waited patiently at her end of the telephone line to learn her connection with this unfolding story, and as Avril pressed on, she listened intently. Evidently, rumours had begun to spread amongst the scientific community back in mid-2019 of a new virulent form of coronavirus which was thought to have arisen in a relative backwater of China. The group had set to work immediately by studying all known data about this type of organism, giving special attention to SARS, as almost from the start it had become obvious that it would be of global importance. In fact, Avril had gone on to say, they had been working in increasingly stringent conditions as the severity of its effects became clear. The family had seen little of Martin in the flesh during the last fortnight as rules for the safety of laboratory personnel had tightened and Martin, amongst others when not at work, was having to stay in the local university's halls of residence. Annie had hung on exasperated. She wondered if Avril would ever get to the point; for a media person she was being overly verbose. Finally, she did. It appeared that Martin wasn't satisfied with the set of modelling algorithms used by the group to predict vaccine efficacy. He questioned whether the group's stats guru, a university-based mathematician was up to the job. Avril had previously mentioned her Aunt Annie's brilliance in this area and Martin now wondered if Annie would help as they were at a challenging point when there were no real statistical past trends to indicate the future. It was all of Annie's dreams come true. The chance to be part of, what was for her, a meaningful project and she could do it all from home on her laptop.

Within hours she was in contact with Martin via video link and within days she had found flaws in the modelling software in current use. Working flat out – husband Hugh taking care of the household – and savouring every moment of it, she had produced a model based on actuarial science rather than machine learning. She had pointed out to Martin that there could be no value in machine learning unless the original tenets of the problem were based on correct assumptions which was not the case with the software they were using. And never had Annie beamed so stunningly as the moment when Martin, displayed on her monitor sitting at his bench, thanked her warmly for her input which he believed would make future predictions far more trustworthy. He hoped she would stay at their beck and call as there would come a time, he could foresee, when explanations of modelling theories to a non-scientific audience would be required and she would be the person to do it. It was a moment of triumph, or as Annie recognised more precisely, a moment of triumph for integral calculus.

Chapter 11

HANDS, FACE, SPACE

2020

Entry and exit routines to the pharmaceutical laboratory had always been strictly controlled but were now even more rigid. All personnel including the administrative staff had to go through a series of time-consuming steps before being allowed access to their own particular work space. Unnecessary contact and face-to-face exposure in the actual laboratories had to be carefully avoided by the scientists working at their benches and thus they appeared at times to dance around one another like automatons in some pre-planned rigmarole to avoid touching. Such procedures slowed their progress to produce a vaccine to combat the coronavirus which had now spread to all parts of the globe. Despite the scientists and technicians' familiarity with the wearing of gowns, masks, gloves, foot coverings, hair nets and eye protection, the use of ultra-protective equipment now mandated by government, was cumbersome and made tasks requiring any form of dexterity tiring.

While safety was considered paramount, it was also made clear to the researchers that a race was on to be the first to produce an approved vaccine. Funded mostly by big business, but with hefty contributions from the tax payer, no one was left in any doubt that association with the first laboratory to produce and market an effective vaccine worldwide would result in a lifetime of individual and national fame and a succession of glittering rewards for both would follow. It was a time of hectic endeavour while the world held its breath for a solution to a virus which appeared to hold all the aces, but even in a pandemic, nationalism was prepared to raise its ugly face.

Martin had not seen his family in the flesh for weeks. Like other senior colleagues his only interaction with them was via his personal laptop and although he looked forward eagerly to the daily conversations when he could share in his children's new experiences, he found the stilted nature of the cyber-meetings with his wife unsatisfactory as they seemed only to enhance their physical separation. Since their marriage some ten years previously, they had only been separated on a handful of occasions and they were both finding it tough to be apart.

With the help of outside university institutions, the research exploratory stage of vaccine development had come to an end with the identification of some natural antigens that had the potential to prevent the disease, and with the concept of a possible vaccine, they had just commenced the pre-clinical stage involving tissue cultures and animal testing in a laboratory setting to determine if it could produce immunity. It was gruelling work in the clumsy protective gear and as Martin walked away from his bench, tired and sweaty, after completing yet another long shift, all he could think of was a long, cold drink. He would have enjoyed it surrounded by his family in his own home in the leafy suburb of Bedford where they now lived in a splendid house, but following government guidelines for the strict lockdown, temporary accommodation had been arranged for the pharmaceutical company's key personnel in one of Reading University's halls of residence.

To escape his single room, basic by modern standards with limited kitchen and washing facilities and with communal recreational provisions off limit, Martin made full use of his permitted one daily exercise period by walking the streets and parks of Reading. It was late spring and his large feet pounded the pavements and tracks in a variety of five-mile circuits. One evening, without intention, he found himself in the quiet street where he had lived with Kit for almost five years. Startled, and somewhat bemused at how he had got there, he stood looking at the small dwelling in which they had spent much of their early adulthood in a carefree atmosphere. Could they really have passed those years together skirting around their family backgrounds such that neither had any real inkling of each other's upbringing? It didn't seem possible now that two articulate people living happily cheek by jowl for so many years could appear to care so little for the other's family history, and on reflection, Martin realised that neither he nor Kit wished to share their life with the other, warts and all. They would just share when they wished but hide when they didn't. Hands stuffed in pockets, Martin sighed deeply as he made his way back to his room to restart the whole process of work, rest and a little play. It all seemed so incomprehensible now, he thought, it mattered then but it didn't matter now.

* * *

The dry cough had been worrying Edmund's mother for several days. She had told Emily, and together, they had decided that if it was still present the following morning then she should tell Edmund.

'Hallo, my dear,' said Edmund's mother. There was something in her voice that made him uneasy. It was not her normal cheery and upbeat tone.

'Hallo, mother,' her son replied rather warily, 'to what do I owe this early morning call?'

'It's your father. He has a dry cough. And he's looking pasty,' she added.

'I see. Anything else?'

'He hasn't mentioned a loss of taste or smell, but he's definitely not his normal self.'

'Have you taken his temperature?'

'Not yet. I don't want to alarm him.'

'Well, do it straightaway and ring me back.'

'Bad news?' asked Kit who had been earwigging the conversation.

'Could be. My father's symptoms are worrying.'

It was late March. The first Covid-19 attributed death had occurred the previous week. A familiar pattern was beginning to emerge on the television news, with learned medics supported by scientists explaining the current state and reporting the number of daily new cases and deaths in the United Kingdom. It was, for the whole nation, a time of adaptation as new rules for the conduct of life came into force.

By the time Thomas Newman was admitted to hospital the number of reported daily deaths had risen to almost thirty. It had not been easy to get medical attention. His surgery had been reluctant to allow him to attend in person at the practice for fear of cross-contamination and no doctor had been available for a home visit. When Thomas reported a loss of taste and smell, Edmund took matters into his own hands and drove him to A & E. He was admitted to a ward where all the staff were kitted up in strange garb as if they were extras on a Sci-Fi film set and to which neither Edmund nor his mother were allowed admittance.

The following days turned into a nightmare for the Newman family as the health of their figurehead member, who until recently they had regarded as a robust eighty-year-old, became more perilous. At some point, when it was clear that oxygen therapy alone was insufficient, the doctors advised mechanical ventilation. But Thomas was too ill to give a competent reply himself and it was left to Edmund to give consent for his father to be intubated. With all the concerns about the dangers and lasting effects of such a serious procedure, Edmund's shoulders had to remain broad to take the right decision for his father while supporting his family. It was the hardest decision of his life but with the agreement of his mother and sister, Edmund refused to give consent.

One week later, while in a coma, Thomas Newman died without his family at his bedside. They had been unable to hold his hand while he slipped away. He had been unable to register their words of love as he lay prostrate on the hospital bed. They had not even had a glimpse of him through a glass pane in a ward door. Instead, they had stood outside the hospital entrance clutching one another, totally bereft. Only his wife had known of his recent diagnosis of motor neurone disease. The tell-tale signs had been there but his children had not noticed. Through her tears, she assured them that they had made the right decision. Thomas would have considered it as a kind way out, she'd told them; it was the choice he would have made himself.

There was no funeral. It was early April and funerals were banned; churches were closed and congregations of any sort were forbidden. Despite the rules, Emily moved in with Edmund's mother, to give best friend support. Edmund returned home to Kit and his daughters. His sister returned home to her own family. They all felt destitute. They felt like the living dead.

Everyday life started to kick in a few weeks later. There were still the usual mundane things to be done: grocery shopping, ironing, bills to be paid, the wheelie bins to put out, going to work, petrol to get, the children to amuse. All around them life never stopped even for an instant to mark their grief, it carried on as normally as covid restrictions allowed as if nothing had happened. Busy at work, Edmund had little time to dwell on the loss of the much-loved Mr. Newman Sr.

The office was empty apart from the practice manager and Edmund, the other partners and junior staff preferring to work from home via laptops. Video calls and zoom conferences were now the order of the day. Life was virtual and for that Edmund was grateful. The gaping hole that the death of his father left in his life gnawed away at his being and the responsibility of becoming leader of the family pack weighed heavily. At lunchtime breaks, he would sit at his desk eating the sandwiches Kit had prepared for him that morning while watching on his monitor the latest information about the pandemic on a twenty-four hours news channel. It had become standard practice by the media to interview experts from the different disciplines involved: virology, epidemiology, immunology, pharmacology and mathematical modelling. The programme presenter would pose their viewers' questions and expect answers in terms understandable to the man in the street. Edmund recognised Martin the moment he appeared on screen; he still looked the tall gangly man he had first met at Old Kit's memorial service. He replied calmly to the interviewer, answering questions without flannelling and to the point. He had a nice steady manner and gave the impression of knowing his subject inside out. Viewers would have felt reassured. Edmund wondered if Kit too had seen Martin on the box giving his expert opinion. Had she been watching at that precise moment? It was unlikely, he considered, but possible. And should he tell her if she hadn't? In normal times the thought of not doing so wouldn't have crossed his mind as, after ten years of marriage, his wife was well-adjusted to life without Martin. But these were not normal times and the recent death of her father-in-law had unsettled her. She had grown to love him as if he was the real father she had barely known and of whom she had no more than sketchy memories. Edmund rubbed his hands and looked up to the ceiling for inspiration. It was a tricky one.

* * *

With Martin confined to the halls of residence for some indeterminate period when off duty, working from home would be Avril's only possibility. And she would have to increase her workload as the radio station was about to lose several members of staff due to the pandemic restrictions. It would be a daunting workload with home schooling to do too.

Just before the lockdown came into force, she made the round trip to the radio station's offices in Peterborough to collect the professional grade equipment she would need to maintain some live shows and with help from the sound engineers, set it up in an upstairs bedroom which she had chosen to use as her studio. They lived in a salubrious street of detached houses set back from the road and separated one from another by wide gardens; extraneous outside noise would not be an issue except in a leaf-blowing season. The children, banned from playing with the equipment, stood quietly outside the closed studio door as Avril went live on air for the first time.

'Good morning to all you Radio East Midlands listeners,' said Avril confidently into the microphone which, with the children's help, they had mounted on a boom arm with a shock stabiliser. The "studio" had a professional air about it with a counter top – formed from a suitable length of unused MDF found in the storeroom having been left over from some previous project – on which sat juxtaposed Avril's laptop, mixing desk, microphone and a microphone processor to amplify her voice. The room had been re-arranged so that the single divan bed was on its side up against a wall with the few sticks of furniture shunted into a corner. The studio had ample working space to swing around on the executive chair and although it was not soundproofed like a real studio, the sound engineer had given the nod that the quality was extremely satisfactory. 'It's nice to be back with you live,' Avril continued brightly. 'We will do our best to bring you all your favourite slots.' Avril smiled to herself; it was great to be back broadcasting again and feeling the pressure of the headphones on her head. But with ears pressed to the keyhole, all the children could hear was the muffled sound of indistinct words.

'In order to comply with the new regulations announced by the government, I am speaking to all you lovely listeners,' said Avril, explaining the new set up, 'from a bedroom in my family house just outside of Bedford. I trust you are hearing me loud and clear. Our sound engineers have worked hard to bring you both quality and reliability. We are operating with a skeleton staff of studio managers and producers who are doing their best to make the shows run seamlessly. Most shows are live but some are pre-recorded.' Avril moved the sliders on the mixing desk as she prepared to answer her first caller. After the opening jingle, she said 'there is no particular theme this week while we are all adjusting to the prevailing circumstances. I have Edgar on the line from Peterborough city centre. Go ahead, Edgar.'

'Hi, Avril. I just wanted to say how pleased I am that you have found a way to keep the station operating,' said Edgar, 'and to ask if that tall man with the gangly physique who is becoming a regular on television answering questions about vaccine development is your husband?'

'He is, Edgar, and I'm very proud of the work he is doing. He's using his skills as a research chemist who has recently brought to market a remedy to counter a tropical disease which annually affects tens of thousands of people living in equatorial regions of our planet. Thank you for your call, Edgar. Now, it's Amanda from Stamford. What would you like to say, Amanda?'

'I'd like to say a simple hallo to my daughter in Peterborough. She's living in a high rise with her baby son and has no one to help and no outdoor space. I think it would give her a boost to get a mention on the airwaves.'

'You want to give her a metaphorical hug,' responded Avril laughing. 'What's her name?'

'Alice.'

'Well then, Alice. Consider yourself hugged by your mum and most of our listeners too,' said Avril. 'We're happy to pass on messages and lift moral so don't hesitate to ring in if you want to do the same as Amanda. Next up is Brian from St. Neots. Hallo, Brian.'

'My wife is in hospital with the virus,' said Brian, falteringly, the emotion of his situation hanging heavily in his voice. Avril didn't interrupt the short silence which followed. Eventually, Brian continued. 'She's now off the ventilator, thank goodness. She's holding her own thanks to the wonderful staff. I have only seen her on an iPad which a nurse held up to show her face. I was able to talk to her although she couldn't respond. So, I want to express my gratitude to all the hospital staff for keeping her alive.'

'That's a distressing story, Brian,' commented Avril, 'that you've been worried about your wife for so long, but it sounds as if it might have a happy ending.'

'Fingers crossed,' replied Brian, a little more cheerfully. 'I just want to thank all the NHS staff.'

'I'm sure our listeners will join you in that, and wish to thank the key workers in so many other settings too.'

Avril was drained at the end of the phone-in slot. It had been allowed to overrun. There was a perceived need out in the community to share the anxieties that lockdown was causing. The ripple effect was reaching everyone; it seemed that everyone needed some form of comforting. She had Martin for that and as usual, looked forward to his evening video call. Just the two of them exchanging their true thoughts. She was awakened from her moment of reverie by knocks on the door. She should hurry up and come downstairs as Daddy was on the television, the children cried out.

'What are your views, Dr Oakeshott,' asked the news channel's health correspondent, 'on today's escalating Covid-19 hospital admittances and the death toll?'

'I'm afraid to say that they are expected,' replied Martin honestly. He couldn't be evasive on such an important issue. 'The modelling, you see, is indicating an exponential rise in both admittances and deaths. Daily deaths are doubling every seven days.'

'You paint a bleak picture,' said the correspondent.

'But we have it in our power to mitigate these statistics. Masks and social distancing are paramount in controlling the spread of the virus.'

Avril watched with pride as her husband responded patiently to the questions. He had come a long way from the man she had first met; the man who used to live in fear of people discovering his background.

'When will Daddy be coming home?' the twins asked in unison after their father's spot in the limelight concluded.

'I wish I knew,' said Avril sighing deeply, 'but I just don't know.'

In Berwick, Kit was getting used to seeing Martin giving expert opinion about the latest covid data. At first it had come as a shock; his presence without permission in their lounge a sort of intrusion into the Newman domain. He looked well, she thought, and content too. But this particular news briefing had come with a sad twist when the health correspondent had concluded the interview by offering Martin his condolences on the loss of his mother. For just a fleeting moment Martin had lost his outward poise, betraying his inner emotion. It had not been a covid-related death as the correspondent seemed to imply. According to the staff, she had just gone downhill and given up. Covid restrictions precluded visitors in the secure home and Martin's work trapped him in the laboratory or the halls of residence. She wouldn't have been able to understand why he wasn't visiting her; the monthly visits he had made without fail for almost two decades. She might have pined for him. He would never know for certain but he felt a strange warmth that his trips to Bristol over the years might not have been in vain. Martin nodded his acknowledgement of the correspondent's words and moved on swiftly.

It was now several weeks since the demise of Thomas, and sufficient water had had time to pass under that harrowing bridge. It was also time for the Newmans to move on. Edmund's mother and Emily had steeled themselves to sort out and dispose of his personal belongings. It was not a task either relished, but it was one that had to be done. Clothes were sorted out for the charity shop or placed in black bin bags ready to be taken to the dump. They kept one or two of his favourite knickknacks but a beloved tie-hanger contraption which was the curse of his wife when putting his clothes away in the wardrobe got short shrift. It was the only moment a modest smile curved their lips. There were documents too, neatly bound together with elastic bands or a length of soft string, requiring attention or disposal and the women agreed that they should be left to Edmund.

The documents turned out to represent a fascinating mixture of his father's life. A biopic of what he had valued during his years on earth; mementos of special passages in his life that he had found himself unable to throw away. One dark evening, with the kids in bed, Kit spread out the various parcels of documents on the kitchen table. They started with a little wad of cheque stubs dated in the late nineteen-fifties – probably representing the first cheques he had ever issued as a young adult – and several return tickets by rail to Newcastle at a cost of one shilling and ninepence each in 1955 to see home matches at Newcastle United.

'I didn't know your father liked football,' said Kit.

'He was a dyed-in-the-wool Newcastle United supporter. When he was a young man, late nineteen-fifties early sixties, football was a game for the masses. Played by hundreds and thousands throughout the land and watched by millions on the terraces. Crowds at St. James's Park would have been sixty or seventy thousand on a regular basis for home matches. And unless I'm very much mistaken,' Edmund went on, holding up an originally manilla-coloured large envelope now grey with age and dust, we will find inside this stringed parcel, some match programmes of that era.'

'Matches that had a particular meaning for him.'

'Yes. A match falling on his birthday, or the very first match he went to after the second world war, probably with my grandfather. The programme would have had sentimental value.'

'Nice. The continuity, I mean. Nice. I never really experienced that sort of continuity.'

'We must get Emily to look after the girls the next Saturday afternoon they're playing at home. We'll hop on the train, be there in fifty minutes and buy two seats in a posh part of the ground.'

'Build some continuity from scratch,' said Kit smiling. 'I'd like that.'

An hour later, they were still unwrapping and marvelling at the keepsakes Thomas had hoarded over the years. Items which hadn't seen the light of day for eons, and which Thomas had probably forgotten were still there, all stored away in the eaves, but still ready at a moment's notice to be discovered by some enquiring mind.

They had found school certificates and letters informing Thomas that he had been admitted to the Law Society, all grouped together as a unit. In another parcel, there were old building society passbooks of accounts long closed or defunct. Yet another had cigarette cards separated neatly into groups and with elastic bands – now all perished – around their chubby middles.

'They would have been considered as "collectibles" in those days just after the war when cigarette smoking was rife and toys were hard to obtain,' Edmund informed Kit. 'There would have been all manner of themes: national flags, football heroes, boxers, famous actresses, military uniforms. They would have been swapped in the playground on countless occasions to get all the cards in a particular series.'

'This little bundle shows exotic birds,' said Kit. 'The cards are in good condition and fairly clean. Would there be a market for them now? They must be around seventy years old.'

'I'll check it out with a Google search,' replied Edmund. 'It would be amusing if they were worth something at an auction house or on eBay.'

'You never know,' summed up Kit. 'So, now just one large bundle to go. To reveal its hidden secrets.'

'I think its full of photos. Should be interesting.'

It took them a further hour to sift through the glossy images of people and things from a different era and proved far more interesting that either could have imagined.

Sepia prints from the early nineteen-hundreds, small and printed on thick, stiff paper to much larger images printed in the fifties on flexible paper with white crinkly borders; from holiday snaps on Holy Island to family groups posed in formal tiers on special anniversaries, the range was enormous.

Edmund recognised some of his relatives but had to admit when questioned by Kit that many faces were unknown. They pieced together photographs of the shop front which had metamorphosed over the decades to become today's legal chambers of Newman, Wilson & Saddler in a prominent location along Berwick high street, and where Edmund now spent the majority of his working life. And there were sufficient snaps of the high street to show the changes that had occurred to Carter & Roach, formerly grocers but currently purveyors of outdoor clothing.

'Where I bought my first set of outdoor clothing,' squealed Kit in delight.

'And your first waterproof pair of walking boots,' Edmund reminded her.

'The boots that have done fifty thousand miles by now and still don't need servicing.'

'More importantly, Carter & Roach are a link with your past.'

'Continuity?'

'Exactly,' agreed Edmund. 'You do have some. When he came back from the second world war, your great grandfather, Peter, worked there. He married the owner's daughter and "Carter, grocer" became "Carter & Roach, grocers".'

'The quintessentially northern corner shop,' observed Kit. 'We must gather together all the snaps of the high street we can find and I will put them in a photobook for posterity. A twenty-first century version of the standard photo album but which will allow us to annotate with our knowledge of the persons involved.'

'That's a great idea,' agreed Edmund, but pointing at the remaining pile in the middle of the table added, 'we still haven't finished with the photos.'

A glass of wine later, the snaps had been divided into: sports-related, house and garden, Edmund and his sister growing up, and miscellany.

'I think this parcel has remained undisturbed for more than twenty years,' remarked Edmund. 'No photos from this millennium.' They started on the house and garden pile followed by the growing-up group with Edmund pointing out the various houses in which they had lived, the red plastic car he had used in the garden to get from the back door to the sandpit, his sister's scooter and the swing strung to a stout branch in the apple tree. 'We fought like savages to be the first on the swing,' said Edmund, 'and pleaded with my father for another one but he refused. Told us to learn to work together.'

'To interdigitate.'

'To what?'

'To interdigitate like micro-electrodes on a substrate,' said Kit. 'Have you forgotten your basic physics?'

'Share space in harmony? Yes, that's what he meant and that's what we learnt to do.'

There was now just one pile left: miscellany. 'Maybe this one should be in the sports group,' said Edmund, showing his wife a close-up of his father receiving a scroll bound with a red ribbon from an older man in a suit. Father must have won something or passed some exam and he's being presented with his certificate. Edmund fell silent, deep in thought. 'I think the man presenting the prize might have been a former chairman of Newcastle United. Obviously, he was much younger then but his face is familiar and he's missing part of the little finger of his left hand. He came from a humble background and legend had it,' continued Edmund, 'that on his first working day down the mines he was involved in an accident with a piece of heavy machinery which resulted in the partial loss of the digit. He vowed never to go down the pit again. He escaped the lowly expectations of his family by jumping on a train to Newcastle, got a job as a navvy, worked hard, bettered himself, and became a successful businessman.'

'Another rags to riches story.'

'Exactly. When the football club was at a low point, he injected money and became the owner for several years. He was very popular with the fans as he was a decent man and a true Geordie. He used the legal services of Newman, Wilson & Saddler on a number of occasions, mostly in my grandfather's time. He died some years ago, cancer I believe.'

'Let me have a closer look,' said Kit, grasping the photo and taking off her spectacles to give it a really close inspection.

'You won't know him,' said Edmund, surprised.

'You're right. I won't know him, but I reckon I've seen that ring before.'

'The one on the ring finger of the injured hand?' said Edmund, whipping the snap from Kit's grasp. 'It doesn't really look remarkable as signet rings go. A plain band, presumably gold, with an oval shield on which he presumably had his initials engraved.'

'It's a man's ring,' stated Kit. 'The band is thick. It's in proportion to the size of a man's hand. Even tall women usually have significantly smaller hands than men.'

'So?'

'It wouldn't look dainty on a woman's finger. It would look awkward. That's why it stood out on Emily's finger. She said it was her real mother's ring, Old Kit's wedding ring. But it isn't. I think it's her real father's ring.' Edmund said nothing but Kit knew he echoed her thoughts. 'It takes a woman to spot something like that,' Kit went on, 'Old Kit would have had the shield part cut out and the jeweller would have simply re-joined the two ends together.'

'If you're right, and I'm not saying you are,' said Edmund hesitantly, 'then to be absolutely certain, we would need to discover the whereabouts of the missing portion.'

'You're right there but I can't offer any explanation as to where it might be.'

'But I can,' said Edmund beaming. '*I can.* It was in my father's desk at the office. When he retired, I moved into his office. It was more convenient for our clients being on the ground floor. The room was redecorated, the flooring changed, and I bought a new desk, one which could cope more effectively with twenty-first century wires and cables. When I cleared out his old desk, I found lots of odds and ends in crevices amongst the fluff and dust of ages past, and the little golden shield was one of them. I remember thinking it must have some value because it looked like gold when I rubbed off the surface grime.'

'What did you do with it?'

'Can't really remember,' replied Edmund, rubbing the stubble on his chin. 'Might be anywhere now, but I wouldn't have thrown it away.'

'That's not particularly helpful,' said Kit, frustrated. Edmund was not the tidiest of persons, and it didn't help when she had to nag the children to be more orderly.'

'But I do recall the initials. Three of them intermingled in a flowery font. J, L and C. James Lewis Carlisle. And he, my dear wife, was a former football club chairman.'

'And Emily, my dear husband,' retorted Kit, 'is wearing his ring.' They shared a quiet moment working out the scenario of how the ring ended up in Emily's possession, until eventually Edmund put their thoughts into words. 'My father must have somehow had a hand in it,' he pronounced. 'Part of the ring was found in his desk drawer. How else could it have got there?'

'We must presume,' Kit responded speaking slowly, 'that the shield part was cut out of the ring a long time ago. Probably shortly after they decided to bring their affair to an amicable close. I assume he gave it to her as a mark of their love for one another. He wouldn't have been able to give her anything else without causing tongues to wag.'

'True.'

'And as we have already concluded,' said Kit, 'they regarded secrecy about their affair and the birth of their twins as being in everyone's best interest. Would she have confided in your father?'

'Possibly. But why would she give him the engraved portion? It makes no sense.'

'And I bet when Emily started wearing the ring on the pretext that it was her birth mother's wedding ring, that your mother will have come to the same conclusion as I did. It wasn't Old Kit's wedding ring from her marriage to her first and only husband, it was, instead, her lover's ring.'

'If you're so convinced that my mother shares your opinion, then why hasn't my mother mentioned it to me?'

'Because, quite simply, Emily is her best friend and she doesn't want to do anything to upset her.'

'Square one, again,' said Edmund. 'We're in Hampton Court maze.'

'Does it matter?' enquired Kit gently. Do we have to solve the conundrum? And is it to anyone's advantage if we do?'

'Probably not. I just don't want the memory of my late father to be mired in any scandal. And if I don't know the answer then I can't defend him.'

'There are lots of questions in physics without answers,' remarked Kit reflectively, 'which I may go to my grave without ever knowing a satisfactory solution.'

* * *

Avril, too, had had some sorting out to do but until now it had remained a long way down her list of jobs to do. How she found time to do anything was amazing bearing in mind the absence of all her usual helpers – gardener, cleaner, personal assistant at work – due to covid restrictions. Her desperate pleas to the gardener had fallen on the stoniest ground possible: his wife. She would, apparently, not permit him to set foot in a single client's garden for fear of an airborne contaminated droplet falling onto his overalls and being transported back to their washing machine to be spread to her. It was an impasse that resulted in the usually well-tended lawns and borders looking in a sorry state, a look which was echoed indoors where the lure of extra pocket money to include general dusting and the sweeping of tiled floors did not chime well with the kids.

At a particularly low point in the nation's fortunes, when the upward spikes in hospital admissions and deaths were reported ad nauseam, the children asleep, and Avril unable to settle to any normal task, she removed the small bundle of her grandfather's personal possessions from the back of a cupboard where it had lain undisturbed for several years. Although Avril herself had collected up her grandfather's effects – there being no one else prepared to do so – in the passage of time since, she had completely forgotten its contents. With no bag or carrier to hand at the time, she had wrapped the effects in one of her grandfather's woollen jumpers, using the sleeves to secure it with a knot. Now, with a damp cloth, she wiped off several cobwebs and as much dust as possible before untying the knot and emptied the effects into her lap. The first thing to catch her eye was his watch; the gold casing still shiny after so many years. It was Swiss made and automatic according to the gold print on its face and within moments of being turned this way and that, it started ticking. It brought a smile to Avril's lips. She decided that it must be quite valuable but she would keep it. It wasn't a watch suitable for a girl but she could pass it on to one of Aunt Annie's boys. There was a photograph of her grandmother –Henry had been estranged for many years – in a silver frame peeking out from behind an oval mount which made her look, curiously, Victorian. She hadn't studied the picture before and viewed it for several minutes trying to conjure up memories of the lady who always came with a big bag of presents for her and Clare at Christmas time. There was a lapel badge with the logo of his union and an old season ticket for entry to Stanmore Rovers when they were in a lower league. Cradled in a silk handkerchief with Adam's monogram, she found a small picture of her father, Adam, drawn on a square of thick card with chamfered edges. It was a pencil drawing in the cameo-style. Henry would have held it in the palm of his hand and gazed at it whenever he was feeling low in spirit.

The last item was in an envelope. It contained a British passport: old style, navy blue, non-flexible, sharp corners, with two areas of its front cut away for recording passport number and name. The six-digit number had been printed by rubber stamp, but the passport holder's name had been written in black biro. Baroness Kit Audrey Harrison of Berwick.

Avril turned on the television just in time to see the prime minister, flanked by the chief NHS officer on his right and Martin to his left, hand over to Martin for a fuller explanation of the daily covid data. Martin didn't look well and Avril stared at the screen, alarmed. Even to her non-scientific brain his explanation of how the vaccine under development would work against the coronavirus seemed an over-simplification. Martin paused as if stumped as to what to say next. Eventually, he said, 'next slide please.'

This book is printed on paper from sustainable sources managed under the Forest Stewardship Council (FSC) scheme.

It has been printed in the UK to reduce transportation miles and their impact upon the environment.

For every new title that Matador publishes, we plant a tree to offset CO_2, partnering with the More Trees scheme.

MORE TREES
LET'S PLANT A BILLION TREES

For more about how Matador offsets its environmental impact, see www.troubador.co.uk/about/